ANCIENT DECEPTIONS

ANCIENT DECEPTIONS

THE ANCIENT SECRETS NOVELS, BOOK 4

J.M. PENCE

QUAIL HILL PUBLISHING

Quail Hill Publishing

Eagle, ID 83616

Quail Hill Publishing E-book: November 2021

Quail Hill Publishing Print Book, 2nd edition: February 2026

ANCIENT DECEPTIONS

"There are two equal and opposite errors into which our race can fall about the devils. One is to disbelieve in their existence. The other is to believe, and to feel an excessive and unhealthy interest in them."

—C. S. Lewis

CHAPTER 1

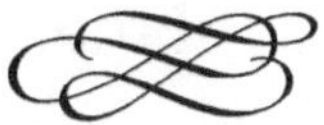

St. Petersburg, Russia

Michael Rempart rested his arms on the railing of St. Petersburg's Trinity Bridge as he gazed at the Neva River far below him. The wide, choppy waters ran cold and gray, while an icy mist shrouded the area in a damp haze.

A tall man with coal black hair, dark brown eyes, and forty-three years of age, he was an archeologist. Early in his professional life, he took risks that had led to a couple of incredible discoveries, a Spanish galleon filled with gold doubloons being the most famous. His perilous adventures, along with movie-star good looks, soon earned him a show on television presenting archeological discoveries to an awestruck public. But all that was in the past, and he looked back at that period as his "young-and-foolish years."

Also, as much as he hated everything about it, he had the ability of an alchemist, an innate skill passed through the male line of his family from at least the time of Elizabeth I. Theirs wasn't simple alchemy, the kind where crazed sorcerers tried to change chunks of worthless metals into gold, but alchemy on a higher plane, alchemy that could change a man from a being who ages and dies to one that's as incorruptible as gold. In other words, one who is immortal.

Michael particularly hated what he had watched the quest for immortality do—the death of his brother, and the soul-crushing destruction of his father.

He continued across the bridge.

At its end, a brief walk brought him to the Peter and Paul Fortress. The Tsar known as "Peter the Great" had built it in the early 1700s to protect the city he had founded, a city barely visible at the moment through the fog. Many called St. Petersburg the "Venice of the North" because of its canals. It was a beautiful place, but at the same time, sadness hung over it, as if it had seen too much death and chaos.

Despite, or perhaps because of its brooding sadness, Michael's melancholy soul had always felt a kinship with the city. Its location, far to the north, meant that most of the year was cold, with a long, dark winter. A popular local joke was, "This year's summer was warm and sunny, but I was at work that day." The happiest time was around the summer solstice, June 21st, when the sun skimmed the horizon. Called the White Nights, it was a time of festivities with people staying up all night, partying, drinking, and acting with wild abandon—a few days of light and joy in a long, dark year.

Michael related to that. Only in his case, he felt as if the darkness had lasted many years.

On the far side of the fortress stood the Cathedral of Saint Peter and Paul. For centuries its multi-tiered bell tower, crowned with an angel atop a massive copper-sheeted needle, was the tallest structure in St. Petersburg, making it visible throughout much of the city. Usually a long line of people waited to enter the cathedral, but it was now only ten minutes before closing time and the guards no longer checked passes.

Michael hurried past them into the main body of the church. It was lush and bright with intricate murals, marble, and extravagant quantities of gold leaf. He didn't know what had brought him there. Intuition, perhaps. But the feeling had been powerful, and he had learned to follow such instincts.

Within the cathedral, nearly all the Romanov rulers from Peter the Great to Tsar Nicholas II and his family lay entombed. At one time the Romanovs were the wealthiest family on earth, and Michael felt the irony that a family with such riches and power had faced so much tragedy, beginning with

Peter himself. His son, Alexei, was the first prisoner in that very fortress whose prison grew to be one of the most feared in all of Russia. In it, Alexei had died from being tortured before he could be executed for conspiring against his father.

Michael walked toward the altar. Ahead of him, a woman stopped in front of an ornate iron fence near Catherine the Great's marble sarcophagus. She took off her fur hat and shook her head, causing her long brown hair to fall freely around her shoulders. Then she bowed her head in prayer.

Michael's heartbeat quickened. Something about her was familiar, and he found himself nearing the iron fence to better see her profile. He blinked, unbelieving. She looked like Irina Petrescu, the woman he had come to St. Petersburg to find. But so far, every lead had failed.

"Irina," he whispered.

She couldn't have heard him, yet she glanced his way and just as quickly averted her head and hurried off. Was it her? Her face was similar, so similar. And she was as beautiful as ever, maybe even more so, a woman at age thirty-eight as opposed to a youthful twenty-one when he'd last seen her.

He went after her, not letting himself lose sight of the tall, brown-haired woman despite the crowd that suddenly pushed toward the exit as the guards informed them the cathedral was about to close.

The woman didn't turn toward the exit, however. She continued to the left side of the cathedral, and he saw her turn into the room set up with seven caskets as a memorial to Nicholas II, his wife Alexandra, and their five children, all tragically imprisoned and then shot to death by the Bolsheviks during the Russian Revolution.

Michael hurried after her.

Once he reached the chamber, he found a group lingering there to pay respects to the family that the citizens of the time had turned against. Michael pushed his way past them, hoping to enter the room, only to find his way blocked by a thick velvet rope stretched across the wide entrance.

Michael leaned against the rope to see the inside of the chamber. No one was in it.

He spun around to search the crowd for the woman he'd followed, with no luck.

He had seen her walk into the room and had kept his eyes firmly fixed on the entrance until he could reach it. He hadn't seen her leave, but she wasn't there now.

He was about to duck under the rope as she must have done, and then to look for an exit door hidden within the paneled walls, when a guard approached him bellowing orders. Michael didn't know the language, but from the guard's expression, he didn't need to.

He took one more quick look, then returned to the spot where she had prayed. A beautiful icon of the Virgin Mary was there with a plaque indicating it had been donated by Princess Milica Petrović-Njegoš of Montenegro, a name that meant nothing to him. He then left the cathedral, searching for Irina as he went.

His mind whirred with what had just happened. Seventeen years had passed since he last saw her, and perhaps his imagination was playing tricks on him again. It wouldn't be the first time.

Two prior times, there in St. Petersburg, he had spotted a woman who absolutely resembled Irina, and those times, too, she had disappeared. But he hadn't been as close to her as he'd been in the cathedral, and he hadn't felt as certain about who he had seen.

This time, if he truly had found Irina Petrescu, how had she managed to leave the cathedral without him noticing? Or had she, again, simply vanished from his life?

CHAPTER 2

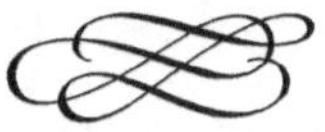

Transcarpathia, Ukraine

Dr. Yakiv Koval, a professor of archeology at the University of Kyiv, was kneeling on the rocky soil, trowel in hand, sure that this time, finally, he was going to find something important, something that would bring him the fame he deserved.

Koval was a burly man due to his enjoyment of food and vodka, but was also muscular from working on digs. His dark brown hair was long, thick and refused to remain in place, but tended to fall wildly about his head. Between his build, his hair, and the loose, oversized clothes he wore, he resembled a big brown bear. Still, he preferred to believe his lack of female companionship was due to his being selective rather than unappealing to the fairer sex.

His knees hurt from his heavy weight pressing against sharp stones, his head ached, and he felt cold. The air in these mountains already held an icy sting. Winter was fast approaching.

"Look, sir! You must see this!"

Koval looked up to see Feder Melnyk standing at the edge of the deep pit where Koval worked. The twenty-two-year-old graduate student in archeology excitedly waved a paper over his head. "We just got back the ERT analysis. It gives an eighty percent chance that the cavities beneath the surface are man-made. They may be tunnels."

Koval grunted as he climbed out of the pit, feeling every bit of his fifty years. He took hold of the electrical resistivity tomography report and read it for himself. He had learned to never trust the conclusions of his students or anyone else.

Koval was in charge of the dig on the southern slope of the Carpathian Mountains in an area known as Transcarpathia, a region currently owned by Ukraine. With him were two younger professors, five archeology students, and an ever-changing number of volunteers.

The possibility that there were tunnels under the site was the reason Koval was there. The Knights Templar were known for putting secret tunnels under their chapels and fortresses. Finding tunnels gave added credence to the local belief that the Templars, in the thirteenth century, had been the first to build on this land. Documents showed that a Byzantine monastery once existed there, but by the 1500s it, too, had been abandoned. Koval's team dug in hopes of discovering the Templar chapel. So far, they'd found a few pieces of pottery and tools, but they were no more than three hundred years old and not of archeological interest.

To find a Templar chapel or fortress in that location would be a major discovery because this would be the first proof that the Templars had traveled this far east. A supposed Templar ruin existed in Serednie, Transcarpathia, but Koval didn't believe for a moment it was legitimate.

As soon as he finished reading through the ERT analysis, he hurried down the mountainside to the campsite, which consisted of a single large tent set up to provide shelter for their equipment and a place for folding tables and chairs on which to work.

Inside that tent, professors Veronika Masur and Dmytro Tischenko were cataloging the bowls and water jugs found the day before. "Veronika, Dmytro, the report came in!"

The professors rushed to his side as Koval placed the analysis on a table. "It says the tunnels are so straight they do not appear to be natural, and are so deep, they were likely formed several centuries before the Orthodox monastery was built."

The professors made high-fives all around. The students, three men and two women, huddled at the entrance to the tent along with volunteers from the Ukrainian cities of Lviv and Kyiv. Koval wasn't surprised to see them. He expected Feder had told his fellow students about the report before bringing it to him. Since there was no cell service at the campsite, the student "in charge" had to travel from the dig into the town of Potchiv and back at least once during the day to transmit and receive messages. That week was Feder's turn.

The town was twenty-minutes away by foot from the dig site. From the town, the land gradually rose toward the mountains. The camp had been set up on the last bit of flat ground. To reach the dig site, the team had to travel up a steep mountainside to an unnaturally flat, shelf-like area. There, they were digging into what they called "the pit" to hopefully find the Templar ruins.

Beyond the dig, the mountain again rose steeply, providing a secure wall so that any fortress or chapel built there could not be attacked from behind.

The archeologists understood why knights would have chosen such a spot. On it, they had a secure rear plus a view that stretched for miles of the valley before them.

Despite ancient lava flows that had enriched the soil, the valley was lightly populated, and the surrounding mountains were even emptier. That the tiny village of Potchiv had internet service, poor though it was, was nothing short of miraculous.

Koval waved his arm at the students and volunteers. "Come in, come in! Join our celebration! With this news, the Templars being here is all but certain, and our discovery will become known to the world!" But then a calculating grin crossed his face. "The real question is, of course, why has their presence been hidden for nearly eight hundred years? Were they hiding something special here?"

As the students and volunteers drew closer, Dr. Veronika Masur rolled her eyes at Koval's words. "Oh, yes," she said, "what better place for the Templars to hide pieces of the True Cross, or maybe even the Holy Grail, than out in these god-forsaken mountains? Yakiv, do you ever stop trying to think of ways to get attention for yourself? You sound like a press release and we don't even know, for sure, that we're standing over tunnels, let alone who built them."

Koval loved the way Veronika was always willing to spar with him, and the idea flashed that perhaps it was her way of hiding the attraction she felt for him. She was his height and quite strong, as was necessary on a dig team. She kept her blond hair short—very practical—and wore no make-up. Her face, though, was a bit soft, her cheeks flabby and the end of her nose bulbous. Her body was more hefty than shapely. At least her hips were wide if they were to ever want children. But he was getting ahead of himself. Besides, she was the only woman around. Or the only available woman. He had seen too many of his fellow professors stupidly get themselves into trouble paying attention to female students. And Yakiv Koval wasn't a stupid man.

He forced his mind back to the dig. "If we can get newspapers, especially international ones, to pay some attention to us, we'll get all kinds of funding for this dig," he explained. "And we might even be able to travel all over Europe giving talks about our discovery. Think of it, Veronika. Paris! London! Why not promote what we're doing here? If we don't promote what we *may* find, and show nothing but these pottery pieces, not only will the University cut off our funding, but might even call us home in disgrace. Surely, you don't want that."

She shook her head and then smiled. He felt a little wakening deep in his groin at how she looked when she smiled at him. "You're a glib bastard, Yakiv."

At that, the students snickered, and she looked down, apparently having forgotten they were there. Yakiv hadn't. He looked at them and shrugged. "You wouldn't mind being part of the team that found a Templar chapel in the Ukraine, would you?"

They shook their heads.

"Good. Now, get your tools. Waste no more time on anything you might find before we reach the chapel. From this report, we have to go down another twenty or more feet to get to its roof. If we're very lucky, the chapel roof hasn't caved in and we can enter it. From there, we'll dig into the floor, to the tunnels. But we need to move quickly. Winter will soon be upon us, and even though the mountains protect this area from the truly cold northern blasts, it will be difficult to reach the chapel before snow storms stop everything. But I can feel in my bones that what we find here will be incredible!"

CHAPTER 3

I*daho Falls, Idaho*

Bethany Gooding dug through to the bottom of the wooden toy box that her father had built for his five daughters some years ago. She was the last of the girls still living at home, and the toy box was now hers alone. At age twenty-one, she no longer kept toys in it, of course, but it was a fine chest to store books, papers, family photos, and...

She grasped a small locking steel box. She took it over to her bed, found the key in the nightstand, and unlocked it. Three thousand dollars lay inside, money that she'd managed to save while working at the Brigham Young University-Idaho library and living at home.

Home was a wooden, clapboard-sided building with two stories and an attic that had been used as an oversized bedroom when all ten children lived there. But now, her three oldest sisters and two oldest brothers were married and lived nearby. Another brother had moved to Salt Lake City, one was doing mission work in Indiana, and her youngest brother was still home. And then there was her sister, Rachel. No one knew where she was.

Bethany was tired of listening to her parents constantly preach to her about how she was living her life all wrong. They warned that if she kept on the way she was, like Rachel, she would be lost to the family.

They always used the word "lost," but Bethany wasn't certain if Rachel was really lost, had been shunned by the community, or if—God-forbid—she was dead.

A couple of years earlier, Rachel Gooding had left her large Mormon family and their farm in eastern Idaho near the Utah border and, to everyone's amazement, had traveled to Oxford University—"The" Oxford University, in England. She had received a full fellowship to work on a doctorate in the field of archeology. Their entire small community had been shocked, worried, and inordinately proud that one of their own was so intelligent as to be lured far from home. It was a wonderful opportunity for her, and her parents weren't about to stand in her way.

While Rachel was away, however, something changed her.

Bethany was four years younger than Rachel, and Rachel was the sister she had always looked up to. She found Rachel's life far more exciting than that of their older sisters who seemed content to live on their farms, raise children, and spend hours every Sunday at church, then cooking and eating with the family. Growing food on the farm, preserving what their families needed, selling some, and finding new recipes seemed to occupy their every waking hour. Bethany found that beyond dull and wanted much, much more in her life.

Rachel had broken away. Bethany hoped to do the same.

The university was close enough to the family farm that she could return home every night to sleep. But she was so desperate to go off on her own, to find excitement, she even considered serving as a missionary. After all, Latter-day Saints (the term the community used for themselves since they were told not to use "Mormon") encouraged young women to serve in a mission for eighteen months to spread word of their faith. Young men were expected to go on a mission if at all possible, but young women weren't pushed to do so. Bethany went as far as an interview but was told she "needed to ponder on the church's basic tenets" for a while and try again later.

But then, last summer, after Rachel's first year at Oxford ended, she came home for a visit. With her was her roommate, a Welsh woman named

Ceinwen Davies. The family had been surprised that Rachel's roommate was already in her thirties and quite worldly. After only a few days on the farm, the two women drove to Salmon, Idaho, the town closest to the area where, some years earlier, Rachel had gone on a class field trip and she, her fellow Boise State students and teachers, all ended up lost in the mountains.

None of the family understood why Rachel wanted to return there. And even more baffling, after Rachel and Ceinwen came back to the farm, they immediately left to go to, of all places, Japan.

Bethany remembered hearing her parents wonder where they had gone so wrong in raising Rachel that she preferred running all over the world instead of coming home, getting married, and living a proper life.

And, as if Rachel going away wasn't bad enough, her parents got a call from Ceinwen telling them Rachel had met a "wonderful" man in Japan, fell in love, and was staying there with him. She added that Rachel expected that her parents wouldn't approve, and had asked Ceinwen to let them know she was all right.

Bethany's parents had accepted the story, but she hadn't. She and Rachel had been close, and she couldn't believe Rachel wouldn't phone or at least text her to talk about the man she'd fallen in love with. Something had to be wrong.

Bethany contacted Oxford University to see if they had any information on Rachel's whereabouts, but they refused to divulge anything.

Then, something miraculous happened. Oxford sent all of Rachel's belongings from her dorm room back home. Even though her father had ordered them burned, their mother had—and this was the miracle—defied him and stacked the boxes in the cellar where she kept her preserves. As encouraged by the church, her mother kept at least a year's worth of food in storage.

One night, Bethany waited until everyone was asleep and went down to the cellar to go through Rachel's boxes. She was frankly shocked at how little she found of a personal nature. It was as if Rachel had done nothing but study and write reports while in England. No wonder she got an A or A+ in every class. Bethany was both impressed and appalled.

But then she discovered her mother had also stored Rachel's belongings from her time at Boise State. Bethany doubted they would be of interest, but took a look anyway.

Bethany's parents had convinced her that Rachel had been in no real danger when she was lost in the Idaho wilderness. They also had sworn everyone was fine and she shouldn't worry. But the newspaper articles Rachel had kept told a vastly different story.

The newspapers also wrote about Dr. Michael Rempart, an archeologist who apparently once had had his own TV show. Bethany couldn't imagine anyone watching such a thing, but she did remember Rachel saying the archeologist who had helped rescue her and the other students was the reason she wanted to study archeology.

Bethany returned to her room, turned on her laptop, and began searching for Michael Rempart. She learned he had recently spent a lot of time in Asia and had a couple of strange cases coming out of China and Mongolia. She wondered if he was somehow involved in Rachel's sudden urge to visit Japan. It was the only thing that made sense to her.

Despite hours of searching, she could come up with no location, phone number, or even an email address for Dr. Michael Rempart. But she wasn't about to give up. She had to know more.

CHAPTER 4

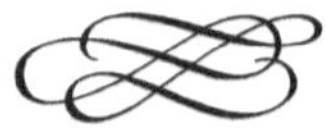

S t. Petersburg, 1900

"Stana, it arrived!" Militsa jumped out of her chair as her sister entered the drawing room. Bursting with excitement, she handed Stana the plaque she had received that morning. It announced that Princess Milica Petrović-Njegoš, her formal name, had been awarded a diploma as a "Doctor of Hermeticism" for her study of the occult and alchemy from the Advanced School of Hermetic Sciences in Paris.

"It's wonderful!" Stana, whose actual name was Princess Anastasia Petrović-Njegoš, gave her sister a hug. "Now those swine can no longer poke fun at you, at us, for saying what we know is true."

They were in the blue salon of Militsa's mansion on the Gulf of Finland near Peterhof, the palace built by Peter the Great in the style of the French palace at Versailles. Militsa went over to the divan covered in a sky-blue satin, and Stana perched on the edge of a settee embroidered in yellow, green, and deep blue silk. The small table before them held sweet wine and a variety of cakes.

The elite of St. Petersburg often called the sisters the "Black Princesses," or worse—the Black Crows, the Black Peril, and even the Montenegrin Spiders because they had been born in Montenegro ("Black Mountain"), and were the daughters of the king who, despite being a king, was impoverished. After being invited to St. Petersburg by Tsar Alexander III, they moved to the city. Both soon married Russian Grand Dukes, and equally soon, ignored their spouses.

"I have invited Papus here," Militsa said, referring to the head of the school that gave her the diploma. "And I told him he must bring Monsieur Philippe with him. The man is taking Europe by storm and I know Alexandra will adore him. He might even know how to help her produce a son." In the first six years of marriage, the Tsarina Alexandra had given Tsar Nicholas II four daughters. But it was her "job" to provide a son, the next Tsar, and since she hadn't, the country considered her a great failure.

"And if this Monsieur Philippe can't help her, perhaps you can," Stana said.

Militsa shook her head. "I prefer to use these men as go-betweens. If they fail, it will be their heads that are lost, not mine."

Stana laughed at that. When Nicholas II inher-

ited the throne after Alexander III's death, the sisters managed to ingratiate themselves with Alexandra, the new Tsar's wife. Like them, she was an outsider and felt alone and isolated. Alexandra was German, and a granddaughter of England's Queen Victoria. She felt disliked by both Russian society and the people she reigned over, a situation Militsa had used to her advantage.

"I'd also like Monsieur Philippe to hold a séance for Nicholas," Militsa continued, "to call up his father and get the late Tsar to give the poor boy some confidence. He's as unprepared for the role of Tsar as... as you, Stana. Or my poor, silly husband."

"A séance like that doesn't sound very interesting," Stana said with a pout.

"There, you're wrong. At one séance in Paris, he called forth the spirit of King Louis XVI, and a head dripping blood from its guillotined neck suddenly appeared near the ceiling of the darkened room. And then it vanished into thin air!"

"Oh! It gives me goose-bumps just to think of it," Stana cried, then howled with laughter.

Militsa joined her. "I've also been told Monsieur Philippe possesses rare healing powers. They say he can perform hypnosis and knows the occult well." Militsa nodded knowingly at her sister. "Not only that, I've been told he has particularly great effects on women at his séances. A male friend of mine, a fellow student, went to one and said nearly all the women at some point in the evening would whisper something in Philippe's ear. He would then say he would give her some of his time and if she truly believed, she would be healed of whatever caused her to seek him out."

Stana rolled her eyes. "Ridiculous!"

"Don't be a skeptic," Militsa told her. "After all, he supposedly has 'psychic fluids and astral forces.'"

The two chuckled. "I have an idea of the kind of fluid he would give them," Stana said. "And there's nothing psychic about it! But if he's charming and handsome enough, I may have to ask him to 'cure' my migraines."

"If he's as interesting as they say, he can cure me of anything." Militsa gave her sister a sly grin. "And if we're lucky, Alexandra will feel the same."

CHAPTER 5

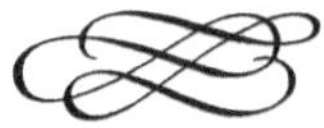

Michael headed for the Pushka Inn, a boutique hotel on the Moika River a few blocks from what had once been the Winter Palace of the Romanov Tsars, and which now housed the world-renowned Hermitage museum. The afternoon's strange occurrence at St. Peter and Paul's Cathedral had proven what he'd begun to suspect after his first few days in St. Petersburg: that what seemed to be real was bogus; and what seemed to be impossible was not.

Michael was quite sure all this difficulty in finding Irina had to do with his father, William Claude Rempart. Michael and his father had never gotten along and had never been close. Even as a small child, Michael had feared the man. After Michael's mother's death, he felt completely alone in the world, despite the wealth and riches of the Rempart family.

But all the money in the world couldn't buy William Claude the one thing he wanted—immortality. Only alchemy could grant him that. Michael's father had devoted most of his life to finding a way to become immortal, yet so far, he had failed. The quest had driven him into the world of the demonic, and in turn, it rendered him all but mad.

William Claude's last hope was to control the philosopher's stone, the prime agent needed for alchemical transformations, that was believed to be the most powerful ever created.

It was so powerful it had taken down an ancient Chinese Empire because within it dwelled three demons. The master of the stone controlled, to an extent, those demons, although no one could ever completely control a demon.

More than anything, William Claude wanted that stone, which was known as "the red pearl." And Michael possessed it. The two had a vicious encounter over it, and afterward William Claude's home, a mansion on Cape Cod, caught fire. Michael had believed his father died a horrible death in the fire, but he then learned no body had been found.

Because of that, he had his assistant, Li Jianjun, a whiz at Internet searching and hacking, scour the world for William Claude.

Eventually, Jianjun picked up evidence that William Claude was in St. Petersburg, Russia. He hired a private investigator to follow the leads, and the investigator had been successful. Jianjun had sent Michael a picture of his father seated at an outdoor café in front of the Kazan Cathedral on Nevsky Prospect. But Jianjun hadn't realized that Michael knew the person sitting with William Claude in the photo—Irina Petrescu. She was the woman Michael had spent a good part of his life in love with and searching for, until he'd been told she was dead.

Seeing her alive in that photo had made Michael's world tilt, and he had immediately left for St. Petersburg.

But now, Michael began to wonder if his father had wanted to draw Michael to the city by adding the image of someone who resembled Irina to the photo. His father had significant powers derived from alchemy and knew a number of dangerous men—men who could assist him anywhere in the world. Such men could even have threatened Jianjun's private investigator and forced him to modify the photo. Jianjun did say the investigator had left St. Petersburg shortly after sending the photo.

Michael suspected his father had assumed he would bring the red pearl with him to St. Petersburg, since the one time he'd left it out of reach hadn't turned out well. Michael could easily imagine his father sending out men to search Michael's room and possessions to look for the red pearl whenever Michael was out trying to locate Irina.

Or, if that didn't work, William Claude likely hoped that he could get close enough to his son to read Michael's mind.

The man not only was an excellent mind reader, but once inside a person's head, he had the power to "encourage" certain behaviors.

Michael remembered the last time he saw his father at Wintersgate. There, he would get severe headaches from William Claude's attacks on his thoughts—-trying to discover the red pearl's hiding place—until he learned how to block them from his mind.

He wondered if William Claude had realized he couldn't get through to Michael's thoughts even though they were both in St. Petersburg, and for that reason he caused Michael to see someone who might be Irina. A distraction, a way to assure Michael would lose focus.

He stopped at an outdoor café, took a seat, and ordered an espresso. Scarcely paying attention to the waiter or anything else around him, so lost was he in his own thoughts.

Just what, he wondered, was William Claude up to?

He should know Michael would never give him the pearl.

The waiter handed him the coffee. He added two packets of sugar, drank it down, and then took out his cell phone and called Jianjun, who was home in Vancouver, Canada. Jianjun was still attempting to locate Irina or William Claude. A week earlier, his private investigator had found them both in St. Petersburg, but now that Michael was there, both were gone—and so was the P. I. "Are you having any luck?" Michael asked.

"Nothing, boss," Jianjun said. "I can't come up with even a trace. I've run out of options."

"I saw another Irina today," Michael said.

"Could it have really been her?"

Michael hated Jianjun's question. Three times now he thought he'd seen her. One time, as a car sped by, its passenger had made a point of staring at him. He was almost certain it was her.

Another time, he saw her step into an elevator. She faced him just as the doors shut.

And then, today at the Cathedral.

"Who knows? I watched her turn into a room, but when I got there, she was gone. It made me question if she was ever real, if she was alive, or if she had died the way my father had once told me. It could be I'm seeing some projection—that my father is somehow tapping into my hopes. I wouldn't put anything past him and his abilities."

"I'm sorry, Michael," Jianjun whispered.

"William Claude knew the hope of finding her could easily get me to travel halfway around the world. And he was right." Michael drew in his breath. "He would know the only reason I'd leave my home, leave Ceinwen, would be to see and confront Irina. To ask her to explain certain things that simply never made sense to me, yet have preyed on me all these years."

Michael had tried not to think about Ceinwen, the woman he'd only recently begun living with, because he knew he'd hurt her.

His last argument with her, always in the back of his mind, flashed before him once more.

"It's been nearly seventeen years since you last saw her, Michael!" Ceinwen Davies had said to him when he told her he was going to St. Petersburg. "She's no longer the sweet young girl you once knew. People change in that much time. You've changed."

Michael gazed at her, his heart heavy. Ceinwen was a Welsh woman he had met in Japan a year earlier and had fallen hard for. In all the years since losing Irina, he'd never felt as deeply about another woman as he did about Ceinwen. By trade, she was a hard-nosed, cynical, realistic journalist. But Michael had decided she must be every bit as crazy as he was because despite everything they had gone through in Japan, and all the insane, unbelievable things she had witnessed there, she wanted to stay with him and had even agreed to move with him to a house he rented in Idaho. He had to admit that he didn't understand her, and each morning was surprised to find her still in his bed. If she had any sense, she would have left long ago and run back to Wales. Amazingly, she hadn't.

But on that day, he had turned his back on her and continued to pack. "I know all that," he told her. "But I have questions about things I've never told you."

"And why would you believe any answers she might give you?" Ceinwen demanded. "What is she doing in St. Petersburg with Claude? The man is a danger to you. That alone tells me you can't trust her! Or is it that... you still love her, Michael?"

He stopped what he was doing then and placed his hands on her shoulders. "No. Believe me, Ceinwen, that ended years ago when she walked away from me. It's you that I... I care about."

He should have told her then that he'd fallen in love with her, but for whatever reason, the words wouldn't come. She waited... one beat... two... then she folded her arms.

"Go then," she said. "Clearly, I can't stop you."

She even drove him to the airport.

"On the other hand," Jianjun said, bringing Michael back to their conversation, "what if your father doesn't know my private eye caught him and

Irina together? What if he doesn't know you're in St. Petersburg? He could have moved on and now is somewhere else in the world."

"There's little he doesn't know," Michael said.

"But if he staged the whole thing with Irina," Jianjun said, "why would he lure you to St. Petersburg and then not face you? It doesn't make sense!"

Michael had pondered that question many times. "He may have thought I'd bring the red pearl with me, not trusting it out of my sight. He might have spent time trying to find it and couldn't."

"I wish I knew," Jianjun said.

"So do I. Anyway, I'll stay here searching for two or three more days, and if neither I nor the three private eyes I've hired can find Irina, I'm coming home. I'm tired of playing games."

"That sounds good."

"Besides, I've got a lot of fence-mending to do with Ceinwen. I was worried about leaving her alone and told her to go back to Wales and stay there until I returned. She didn't like that at all."

"Oh! Not good, boss! Did she go?"

"I hope so, but I'm not sure. Once, on the phone, I asked if she was in Wales or still in Idaho. She said, 'Why do you want to know? Are you afraid I'll disappear like your old girlfriend did?'"

"Ouch!" Jianjun said.

"No kidding. We talked once more when I told

her your private eye had disappeared and the ones I hired were having no luck. She said not to bother to call her with updates, but only to tell her when I was coming home—if ever. Then she hung up and hasn't answered my calls since."

"Well, you've always known she has a temper."

"Yes, but it's been a while since she's directed it at me."

"Did you leave her a message?"

"No."

There was a long pause, then Jianjun said, "I'm sure you two will work it out once you're home."

"I hope so." Michael vowed to do whatever it took to get her back. But first he had business here he needed to finish. And it was about more than Irina, although she was a big part of it. Being here now made him feel... hope... that he was close to finding answers to questions that had plagued him for years.

"I'll be glad when you're home, boss," Jianjun said.

"Me, too."

He hung up and then walked across the massive plaza on the south side of the Winter Palace. The square was the site of what was known as "Bloody Sunday" when, in 1905, a group of workers, their wives, and children went to the Winter Palace to petition the Tsar. But instead of meeting, the Tsar had his soldiers fire on them, killing hundreds—some say thousands. That was often considered the spark that lit the Russian Revolution. From that same square, the Bolsheviks stormed the Winter Palace to take over the government in October 1917.

From the Plaza, Michael soon reached the Moika River. A tourist boat with a bunch of revelers sailed by, and people waved at him, including men holding up open bottles of vodka in gestures of good cheer. He couldn't help but smile and wave back.

As he watched the boat turn down a canal leading to the much larger Neva River and disappear from sight, Michael again had the nagging idea that when William Claude realized the red pearl wasn't in St. Petersburg, and that he couldn't penetrate Michael's thoughts, he might have gone to Idaho, to Michael's home, to try to find it.

But surely he would realize that Michael wouldn't leave it in his house.

And always, when he thought of home, he thought of Ceinwen. He hated the way he had brought danger into her life—although when she talked about her work as a journalist, she was no stranger to it.

Once again, he hoped she was safely back in Wales, although William Claude had to know Michael would never endanger her by telling her where he had hidden the pearl. She should be safe from him.

And yet, the more he thought about her, the more worried he became. William Claude had once threatened to hurt or even kill her if Michael didn't give him the red pearl. That hadn't turned out well for him, but was he insane enough to try again?

With that thought, Michael phoned Ceinwen. Yes, she had a temper, but she wasn't one to hold a grudge. This time, he hoped, she would answer his call.

She didn't.

He reached his hotel. In his room, he stood at the window with its view of the Moika and the buildings across the street. The city was lovely, but its sad history weighed heavily upon him. What, he asked himself, was he still doing here?

He phoned again and when Ceinwen still didn't answer, he left a message. "I'm sorry about the way I've been acting. I'm tired and angry with myself. Nothing has turned out the way I expected, and..." He wanted to say something about his feelings for her, but the words wouldn't come. Finally, he simply said, "I'll be home soon, and I hope to see you. Let me know where you are and how you're doing. Call me, Ceinwen. Please."

He hung up, feeling disappointed in his inability to be open with her. Years earlier, he had given up on love, on ever finding anyone who could deal with him, his strange ways, and his even stranger family and lonely, troubled upbringing. But then Ceinwen had burst into his life. She would "brook no nonsense" from him, in her words. And he found himself completely captivated by her.

But he never told her any of that. It wasn't the kind of idealistic, love-on-a-pedestal emotion he had once felt with Irina. He guessed there was always something magical and forever-lasting about one's first love. But with Ceinwen, he felt the closeness, a oneness, as if he was attuned to her the way he had never been with anyone else, and he was sure she felt the same about him. It was ironic, but every word she had said to him during their argument before he left for St. Petersburg—that he and Irina had both changed and that she might be a tool of his father—he had worried about as well. He shook his head. This was getting him nowhere.

A couple of hours later, he tried her number again. And did the same two hours after that. By then it was night, and he decided not to wait there for three more days. He was going back to Idaho immediately, and somehow hoped to get her to an-swer his calls. To let him know she was safe.

CHAPTER 6

Bethany Gooding started out before dawn the next morning to make the long drive to Salmon, Idaho. She had no idea what she was going to find there, or if anyone in the town remembered the strange events of some three years earlier, but she knew she had to try.

Her thick blond hair was pulled back in a high ponytail, and she wore black, ripped skinny jeans, a snug pink T-shirt, and sandals with heels. She told her parents she was going to the University, and probably wouldn't be home until late. Her mother frowned, as usual, at her clothes. But Bethany had won that fight a few years earlier.

The two-lane highway was little traveled, and went from the flat, relatively fertile land around the Snake River where the Gooding farm was located, to climb high into the mountains as it skirted the edges of the Bitterroot range between Idaho and Montana. She hadn't realized until she was near Salmon and drove past the Sacajawea Cultural and

Interpretive Center that the woman who had helped Lewis and Clark find their way to the Pacific Ocean was a Lemhi Shoshone and born in that area.

The town of Salmon was small and old. The highway went right through the main street and most of the buildings showed their age. The brick ones seemed to be in the best shape, the wooden ones the worst, and none looked new. Off the main street she did see a number of attractive, older homes.

She was headed for the Lemhi County Sheriff's office. She had learned that Sheriff Jake Sullivan had been a part of the group that had been lost in the wilderness while searching for Rachel and her classmates.

She entered the office to find an older woman sitting at a desk. "Hello," she called out cheerfully. "Can I help you?"

"I'm looking for Sheriff Jake Sullivan," Bethany said.

The woman took off her glasses. "Oh, I'm sorry. Jake's out of town at the moment. But Deputy Mallick is filling in. I'm sure he can help you."

"Oh, no, that's all right."

"You hold on, there, dearie." The woman got up and knocked on the door then stuck her head in.

"Dez, some little gal is looking for Jake. You should talk to her."

"Really?"

The woman faced Bethany, leaving the door open. "You can go in now."

She stepped into the office. The man seated at the desk slowly looked up, but when he saw her, his blue eyes widened and he jumped to his feet. He was tall and kind of lanky. He wore a gray shirt with a silver and gold badge and an embroidered Sheriff's Department patch on one sleeve and an American flag patch on the other. "Can I help you, miss?"

"Well, I'm not sure. I was hoping to speak to Sheriff Sullivan," she said.

"I'm afraid he's kinda taken off for a few days."

"A few days?"

"I'm Deputy Mallick. In charge... for now," he said a bit shyly. "Why don't you tell me what this is about?"

She looked him over. She liked his looks, his curly light brown hair, and eyes the color of the expensive blue china her mother kept on a high shelf in the dining room glass cabinet—the ones she was saving for a special occasion that never seemed to come. But he did seem young to be in charge of a sheriff's station.

Bethany wasn't sure where to start. "Well..."

"Is something wrong?" Mallick asked. "Some crime committed, or something?"

The man sounded almost hopeful that something had happened. Maybe sitting in this dark office wasn't exactly the most exciting way to spend one's day. "No, at least, I hope not. I wanted to ask Sheriff Sullivan about something that happened near here about three years ago."

Mallick's pleasant expression became a scowl. "The disappearance?"

"Yes. That's it. Were you here then?"

He sat back down, leaving her standing. His scowl deepened. "I take it you're a journalist or a magazine writer or something like that."

She was stunned. "Not at all."

He folded his arms, his eyes cold. "Then why are you here asking about those days?"

"Because my sister was involved."

His brow furrowed, and he looked at her closely. "Your sister?"

"Rachel Gooding. Did you know her?"

He put his hand to his chin and rubbed it a moment. "Yes, I knew Rachel. In fact, I saw her just last summer."

"That's great!" She stepped closer to his desk. "And I guess you also know Michael Rempart. I need to learn about him, about all that happened."

Mallick looked troubled. "People died. Students, even a professor—Michael Rempart's brother —who led the field trip."

"I understand that," Bethany said.

Mallick nodded, then stood. "This might be a long conversation. Would you like to go next door and have some coffee while we talk?"

Bethany was surprised that the deputy opened doors for her and even paid for her coffee. The boys she was meeting these days, even those at Brigham Young, wouldn't have done that, or would have asked if it was "all right" before presuming to be gentlemen. She couldn't help but smile at the man.

He smiled back.

She sat while he got their orders, including almond croissants for them both. She was grateful to eat something after her long drive. As they shared a small table, she explained that she was looking for her sister. She knew Rachel had gone to Japan, but after that she had disappeared. Michael Rempart seemed somehow involved, but she knew nothing about him or what had happened in the past. She wondered if the past had played a part in Rachel's disappearance.

Mallick appeared stunned that Bethany knew so little about what had happened in the wilderness north of the Salmon River. She wanted to hear all about it, and after checking with the office secretary that nothing was going on, the two finished their coffee and then walked through the small city park down to a tributary of the Salmon that flowed through the town. As they walked, she learned his name was Desmond, but everyone called him Dez. He was twenty-eight, had never found the right girl to marry, loved his job, and was a believer but not a churchgoer. She told him a little about herself, her large family, and her job at the BYU library.

When they found a pretty and secluded spot by the water, they sat and Mallick told her what he remembered about the disappearance and deaths that happened in the area. Bethany was horrified at how long and deadly the episode had been.

He didn't have a lot to say about Michael Rempart, other than that the guy seemed strange. "But then, last year, some odd things started up again in Salmon," he said. "Deaths of ranchers. Ones that looked like they might have been done by animals, but when studied closely, were not. Some were unaccounted for, but others were done by men. We even lost a deputy."

"I'm so sorry," Bethany said. She had never come face-to-face with sudden, tragic death and couldn't help but wonder how this man, after losing a colleague, could still put on his uniform and come back to work each day. She doubted she could ever be so brave and found herself regarding him with new respect.

"Now that I think of it, Jake mentioned that the girls—your sister and Ceinwen—thought Rempart should come here to Salmon to help with whatever was troubling us. They tried tracking him down, and finally located his assistant. I'm afraid I can't remember his name, but I can find it back in the office. Seems to me, Rempart was in Japan."

"I was wondering about that," Bethany said. "That would explain why my sister suddenly went there."

"But then," Mallick said, looking at her sadly, "a few weeks or so later, Rempart, Ceinwen, and the assistant came back here. Rachel wasn't with them. Jake asked but ... God, what was it? I think they said she was ill. Some kind of virus or something, and they left her in Japan but she was well taken care of."

Bethany gawked at him as her anger flared. "She was sick? And they just left her there? Why would they do that?"

"Hey, it's all right." He took her hands. "I'm sure they wouldn't have left her if they thought it would hurt her. They all seemed to really care about her. Even the strange Michael Rempart, I think, has a real affection for your sister. She's a nice person."

Bethany couldn't help but search his face for a sign he was lying. But all she saw was compassion, and maybe a little something more. Or was that wishful thinking? She realized they still held hands and eased hers away. "Thank you. Is there anything else you can think of?"

She could see him hesitate, and that scared her. "What is it?"

"Nothing," he whispered. "Nothing I can explain, anyway."

She thought for a moment. "Since we're talking about things we can't explain, I'll confess something to you about Rachel. She was always smart and bookish and did well in school. But she was no genius. She was just Rachel. But after she came back from having been lost, she was a different person. She learned things quickly, too quickly. I watched her read, and she'd go through book after book in no time. It was as if she could barely turn the pages fast enough. And she'd remember everything she'd read. It was freaky. I didn't get it and tried to ignore it. I told myself Rachel had learned the power of concentration. But it also scared me, and worried me. Maybe that's another reason I'm desperate to find her. I don't know that she's still my sister."

He studied her. "And you're thinking that's why she hasn't come home?"

She nodded.

"One more thing." He held her gaze. "If you decide to investigate more about your sister's disappearance, don't trust anybody or anything."

Any*thing*? An odd word to use. But instead of questioning it, she froze at his intensity, then simply nodded.

"And now, let's go back to the station," he said. "I'll find those phone numbers for you. Are you sure you want to drive back to Idaho Falls tonight? It's a long trip, and it gets dark early this time of year."

"I'll be fine. I still live at home, and my folks would have fits if I stayed out all night."

He smiled. "Got it."

At the office, he was able to find a phone numbers for Michael as well as his assistant who he now gave a name—Li Jianjun. He wrote out the information she needed, then they exchanged phone numbers in case he thought of anything more, or she had more questions. Finally, there was nothing left but for him to walk her to her car.

"Drive safe," he said. "And don't hesitate to let me know if there's anything else I can do for you."

She opened her car door but before getting in

faced him once more. "Thank you for all your help today. I really appreciate it."

He hooked his thumbs in his pockets. "Say, if you ever want to come up this way just to see the sights, maybe go up to the main part of the Salmon River and see it—it looks like a picture postcard—just let me know."

"I'd like that." She was beginning to feel foolish the way she kept smiling at him but she couldn't help it.

He smiled back, but then his expression changed as he added, "Promise you'll be careful."

A sudden feeling of dread struck her. "I will. I promise."

She quickly got into the car. He stood back a bit, but she noticed that he continued to watch her as she drove out of town.

CHAPTER 7

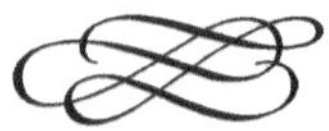

Andriy Plaviuk crept from the inn and hurried down the moonlit road heading away from the dig site. When he reached a footpath scarcely visible from the road, he turned onto it.

He trudged along as quickly as he dared, his flashlight showing the way. Night in these lonely mountains scared him. But night was the only time she allowed him to see her.

After a quarter mile he reached an old cottage. He paused to catch his breath, his heart pounding.

He could scarcely believe how friendly she always acted toward him. No one else even liked him. Throughout school and at the university, he was either ignored or treated like a pariah which always put him on the defensive and ready to verbally attack anyone who gave him a look he didn't like. Which was fairly often.

Everything about him was awkward, clumsy, and weak. He knew that and told himself he didn't care, although at times he thought he disliked himself even more than the other kids did. His only friends were people online that he'd never met. One of them suggested he look into becoming an archeologist where he could spend months at a time away from other people except the few with him at a dig site.

He tried it, only to discover he didn't like the people on the digs either. He would have changed majors, but then he met Stana.

She was a history major working on a Ph.D. One day she told him about the dissertation she was researching about a fortress built in the Carpathian Mountains by the Knights Templar. She had a lot of evidence about it, including its location.

Andriy was fascinated, although perhaps more by her than her dissertation. She was beautiful, with long, curly black hair that formed a thick, sexy mass. It fell half-way down her back and it was all he could do not to bury his face in it. But he never even dared to stand close to her, let alone touch her.

So he concentrated on her work. After looking over her evidence, he found it intriguing enough to bring to his faculty adviser, Dr. Yakiv Koval, and asked if it might be worth his time to write it up as a project. Koval grew so excited by the research, he not only agreed it would be a good topic for Andriy to pursue, but also got approval from the University for an actual dig.

To Andriy's complete joy and astonishment, when he told Stana about the dig, she wanted to join him—in secret, of course—at the site!

She found a small cottage to rent near the dig and told him she planned to keep a diary and take pictures of everything done there. She also swore him to secrecy and told him she expected to make a book out of it one day—a book in which he'd play a major role.

Andriy was ecstatic. At the end of the visit she would tell him when his next visit would be allowed. Once in the cottage, he would sit quietly having a glass of cognac with her as she talked about Russian history, especially the time of the last Tsar. Then she would show him the door.

Everything was perfect until he learned that Professor Koval had selected Wasyl Boiko to be the leader of the students at the dig site instead of him.

Andriy couldn't wait to tell Stana. He was furious at the slight but Stana told him he shouldn't let it bother him. "There's a much more serious issue to deal with," she told him. "Last night, I went to the dig site and saw some very strange people there. They were frightening."

"Frightening? That's hard to imagine," Andriy said. "Probably some locals thinking we keep expensive equipment there. I guess we do, but it's all specialized. The most useful thing for anyone around here would be a shovel. I'm sure they weren't anyone to fear."

"No. They weren't locals. They were dangerous."

"I'll check the area out, if you'd like. I suspect they've already gone."

She put her hands on his chest. She'd never done that before, and when she looked up at him with her dark brown eyes, his insides flip-flopped. "No. Please don't do that. I'm much too afraid for you, Andriy. What would I do if you were harmed? I beg you, suggest that Wasyl go instead."

That this gorgeous woman feared for his safety made him puff up his chest. "I can handle this. No need to involve Wasyl. Besides, I can't stand the guy!" Andriy said.

She then eased her hands to his shoulders, looking up at him. "Well, that stupid professor put him in charge of the students instead of you," she said. "And I think he needs to do something to earn his title. Am I not right?"

With her so close he could scarcely think beyond wondering if he dared put his hands on her waist, or leave them hanging by his side. "Yes." He didn't touch her. "You are."

"Of course, I am." She stroked the side of his face and it took every ounce of muscle control to stop the quiver running down his spine. "Now, promise me you won't go."

"Okay, but I'm not afraid. I'm only agreeing because you asked."

"Good. I know you're brave, my dear, brave, Andriy. And now I don't have to worry about you." She gave him a quick hug then stepped back from him. "Now, listen carefully. I'd like you to tell Wasyl that they perform a strange ceremony late at night, and he might want to see it. Tell him you went once, but you're too scared to go again. That will definitely interest him."

"They do? Really?" he asked.

"Of course not, silly!" She scoffed. "I'm just giving you words to intrigue Wasyl. Will you do it, or not?"

Of course he would. He'd do anything for her. "Yes," he whispered.

"You make me proud," she said, then gave him a quick peck on the lips.

He couldn't believe she'd done that and was all but walking on air as she led him to the door and sent him on his way.

* * *

Ceinwen Davies woke with a start, her heart beating fast. She looked at the clock. Seven a.m.

That wouldn't be a bad time to wake up if she had been able to fall asleep before four in the morning.

She was afraid to sleep. Her dreams were growing increasingly horrific with ugly, demonic images assailing her, and the strange bite mark she'd received on her neck, the bite from a ghoulish creature—the bite that refused to heal—grew hot and burning as she slept.

When Michael was with her, he would lightly rest his fingertips against her neck and the pain would subside. Then, he would hold her until she felt no more fear. But he wasn't here.

She ached from missing him. Normally, if a man she was seeing suddenly announced he wanted to spend time with an old girlfriend—which, frankly, had never happened to her before—she would have packed her bag and left with a "good riddance."

But Michael meant so much more than that to her, and she had had enough experience with his father, Claude, to know that the man—or more accurately, the monster—was capable of anything. For that reason, it was fear and frustration that ruled her emotions rather than anger when she thought about Michael going off alone to St. Petersburg to find Irina. She was sure Claude was behind it and knew in her heart that going there was dancing to the devil's tune.

She got out of bed and walked into the kitchen of the home they were renting on Lake Pend Oreille in northern Idaho. Their cozy A-framed home had wooden beams, a massive fireplace, a deck over-looking the lake, and top of the line kitchen appliances that made her want to cook old Welsh favorites. For over a month they had lived there together, and she had never been so happy. She was in love. Michael might be difficult, but she knew his heart and believed he loved her even though he didn't know how to accept it, say it, or even to believe it. Maybe someday ...

But her happiness vanished when Michael learned that his father had gone to Russia after the fire at the family estate. Such news meant his own life could be in danger, as well as hers.

Ceinwen had always believed alchemy was a ruse--a hoax for the greedy. Not until she met the Remparts—Michael and Claude—and saw the power behind alchemy, did she understand that it was far more than making gold. It was also a portal to other planes of existence. It opened the door to worlds beyond where most people lived. She had learned from Michael that the Chinese had a name for it, the island of P'eng Lai, a place where people called the blessed *hsein* lived. They were those who used alchemy to achieve such a degree of longevity they were considered immortal.

Most cultures didn't name it or find it in any way blessed. For most, immortal beings were angels or demons—and those who returned to this world, this dimension, were far more often demonic.

William Claude not only knew how to conjure up and make use of such demons, but Ceinwen knew a powerful demon lived inside him and the two were so firmly aligned she had no idea if Claude controlled the demon or the demon controlled Claude. But she had witnessed its power firsthand.

She shuddered at the thought. With Michael's father she had seen visions of Hell, and could only pray that meant Heaven also existed. Prayer, too, was something her experiences with demons had taught her.

She prayed Michael would safely return home. She had received his message of apology. He had said he was coming home "soon." Just what did that mean? For an archaeologist, it could mean a decade.

And he had said nothing about Irina. Had they met? What was so unexpected about the visit? Why was he angry? And why was she so angry at him for going? How did she fit into his life now that the "love of his life" was in it once more? Not until he told her exactly what was going on, would she answer his questions.

Jealousy? Hurt feelings? Hell, yes—on both counts.

At times she wished Michael would use his ability with alchemy to level the playing field against his father. She had seen him do it when he had no other choice, such as when he used it to stop William Claude from killing her. But she also knew he hated alchemy and each encounter with it cost him dearly.

She had learned, from both Rempart men, that the ability to be an adept at alchemy stemmed from a genetic as well as a spiritual level. Very few men could do it. For the Remparts, it was believed to be an inherited characteristic that passed through the male line. The first known alchemist in that line was a man named Edward Kelley who supposedly had created gold for Elizabeth I. He was close friends with an older, wealthy man named John Dee. The two also collaborated to write a famous book on angels. The angels supposedly spoke to Kelley in a language he called Enochian, and he would translate the words for Dee, who wrote them down.

Ceinwen had been especially amused when she learned that the silver-tongued Kelley even talked Dee into swapping wives when he saw that Mrs. Dee was far younger and more attractive than his own wife. Mrs. Dee soon became pregnant with

Kelley's child. Amazingly, that didn't end the men's friendship, and before long, the two were summoned to the court of the Emperor of Bohemia to create gold for him, just as they had done for Elizabeth I of England.

When Kelley wasn't able to perform the transmutation, Dee abruptly and wisely left for home. But another wealthy patron, Vilém Rozmberk believed in Kelley's ability, and gave him money to continue with his alchemy. Rozmberk even gave the hand of his daughter to the already-wed Kelley. But Rozmberk couldn't save Kelley from the wrath of the Bohemian Emperor. When Kelly continued unable to produce gold, he was thrown into prison where he died.

His widow had kept the name Rozmberk and, with their son, left for France. Through the centuries, after more travels, the name eventually became Rempart.

Male children of the line did show alchemical abilities, however, proving that Kelley wasn't a complete charlatan. If nothing else, the gold they produced over the centuries massively grew the Rempart family fortune. The family itself did not flourish, however, and Michael was now the last of the line.

Ceinwen found that surprising because she had witnessed first-hand the ability of the Rempart men to charm and seduce. Even Michael's father, years older than her, had managed to win her over for a time before she discovered his true nature.

Now, the man or monster was the main cause of her fear of falling asleep.

"Claude," as he had urged her to call him, kept appearing in her dreams as charming as he had been when she first met him at Wintersgate. But once she had warmed to him, he tried to seduce her. And once, as she slept, he had come to her and turned into a demon. The demon had been both horrible yet bizarrely seductive, like some twisted sexual fantasy. It reeked of evil, but held her enthralled and devoid of free will. The thought of the demon's intimate caresses in her dream—or what she hoped was only a dream—still made her all but physically ill.

She never told Michael about the dream. It was her terrifying, terrible secret.

A chill suddenly went through her, the kind her grandmother would have said was "someone walking over your grave." It usually meant something bad was about to happen.

Feelings and intuition had become a new part of her life. People claimed her maternal grandmother had had "the gift." Of course, her mother never said that. Glynis Davies didn't believe in such nonsense, and convinced Ceinwen and her brothers not to believe in it either. Ceinwen had even made a name for herself as a journalist by debunking stories that stemmed from supposedly supernatural events.

But then she entered Michael Rempart's world and all of her practical, worldly beliefs turned to ash.

She not only came to believe that there existed more planes, or dimensions, than the one most people saw, but she had walked in them, loved in them, and nearly died in them. More than once.

She rubbed the goosebumps on her arms. Was this feeling about Michael? Was he in some kind of danger? Or was she?

Her gaze drifted over the home she and Michael had shared. He wanted her to leave it while he was away. It was too isolated, he'd said, and he didn't know what would happen if he encountered his father again while searching for Irina. In the past, William Claude had used Ceinwen to get Michael to do his bidding, and Michael didn't want to give him that opportunity ever again.

If she came to be in danger while there, alone, he couldn't protect her.

She had told him she understood his fears, but she never actually promised that she'd leave the house. Afterward, she had decided not to. But now, for some reason, she felt a chill. Did it have to do with Claude... or with Michael? And could it mean she had lost Michael, and that Irina had won?

It was madness, she told herself and went into the bathroom to take her morning shower. In fact, she would call Michael back later that morning. She was well over the snit that had caused her to stop talking to him. Just hearing his voice should drive these strange foreboding thoughts away.

As she stepped out of the shower, she saw a shadow in the bedroom. She grabbed a towel to cover herself.

"There's no need for that, Ceinwen," a familiar voice said. She gasped and ran to the bathroom door to shut and lock it. But his hand reached it before she did. He pushed the door wide and stepped into the room. "It's too late for modesty. Not after all we've been to each other, all we've done together."

Claude Rempart stood before her.

CHAPTER 8

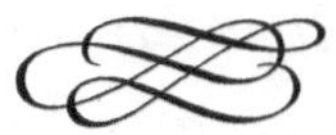

S t. Petersburg, 1905

"I have met the most wonderful person, Militsa," Stana said, bustling into the elegantly appointed morning room as her sister was having tea. The room's walls, furniture, and drapery had been designed to look like something out of the French court before the revolution. Even the everyday tea set was gilded in gold. "You must let me introduce you so you can bring him under your spell. He will work wonders for us both. He claims to be a man of God, but he's much, much more. His name is Grigori, and he's from Tobolsk province in Siberia."

"A man of God?" Militsa scoffed. "Surely, you jest." She waved to a servant to bring tea and pastries for her sister, along with a decanter of cognac, her sister's favorite drink.

"Not at all. We need to introduce him to the Tsar. He will impress our Nicholas, I'm sure, and perhaps Alexandra as well. First, though, we'll need to prepare them to receive him. He's a bit 'different.'

Once he's inside the court, he will be able to give us all kinds of information about the intrigue, envy, and temptations there. He's but a poor man from a small Siberian town and will need our guidance. His manners are atrocious, he smells bad, and some say you can find all kinds of mysterious things hidden within his beard. Nevertheless, you must connect yourself to him."

"That's hardly a recommendation!" Militsa said, patting her hair to make sure every strand was in place. She waited until Stana was served and the maid left the room. "Our last 'find,' Monsieur Philippe, ended up being a pompous fool. Are you sure we should trust this man?"

Stana sipped the tea. "You'll understand when you meet him. He wears a simple robe, his speech is somewhat incoherent as he talks far too much about God, and he isn't always able to come up with quite the right words to use. He bows rather constantly, with sharp, awkward movements, and he waves his hands as if to punctuate his words. But none of that matters when you meet him. It's because of his eyes. They're sunken and stare at you with surprising impudence for a man so lowly. It's almost as if he can see right through you ... as if he's—pardon the expression—undressing you with his eyes. Believe me, something about his eyes is quite mesmerizing."

"Oh? Mesmerizing?"

Stana shifted the chair a bit closer to her sister, knowing that the walls have ears when servants are near. "There is talk he's a hypnotist and a healer. I've heard he often has women stay at his home to grow closer to God by listening to his words and following them. He has a wife and children and it's said they're the reason he won't allow men to stay at his house. If you ask me, he doesn't want any competition! He's often seen walking with the women through the village and will hug and kiss them quite openly."

Militsa laughed. "So you're saying it's not only his eyes that fascinate them?"

"It's said they are all quite devoted—some irrationally so. One tried to kill herself with jealousy when time came for her to leave his home. And there's talk he's a Khlyst."

"Oh! Now that is interesting!" Militsa's eyes brightened. Militsa and Stana knew little about the Khlysty sect except that while nominally Christian, they renounced all holy books, the priesthood, marriage, baptism, confession, and just about every teaching of the church. Instead, they called their church a ship, the sect's leader "Christ," and they would choose a virgin as their "Mother of God." The sisters found the most fascinating thing about them to be their sacred rite, usually held in a cellar and always in secret. The rite was said to consist of an

intense whirling dance with rapid spinning and singing, sometimes with self-mutilation or flagellation, and ending with everyone falling to the ground and engaging in group sex.

"I wonder if that's the secret of his attraction," Stana mused.

"We must have him teach us all about the Khlysts, minus the mutilation and whipping, of course," Militsa said. "You say he's now in St. Petersburg?"

"Yes. He went on a pilgrimage and it brought him to us."

"Does he have a name besides Grigori?"

"His family's name is Rasputin."

"Ah—a common enough name in Siberia," Militsa said.

"So it is."

"I do believe he'll be a very nice plaything for us." Militsa said, already thinking of how she could make good use of such a man.

CHAPTER 9

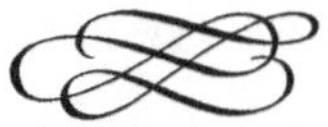

Ceinwen sat in the great room facing Claude. The light rumble of her phone's vibration told her a call was coming in, even though Claude had shut off its ringer. She could only hope the call was from Michael and he would somehow guess something was wrong when she still didn't answer.

Claude was a tall, angular man with high cheekbones and dark, heavy-lidded eyes. His thick mane of pure white hair was worn straight back off his face, and reached to the high collar of his black silk, elegant jacket that buttoned to the neck.

He had "allowed" her to get dressed while he sat on the bed and watched. It only added another item to the mental list she kept of reasons to get even with him. And she would. Somehow.

Very soon after the prior phone call, the phone vibrated again. Claude saw the name on it, smiled, then lifted it so she could see. She felt her heartbeat quicken. Why would Jianjun be phoning her unless something had happened to Michael?

Claude's smile worried her most of all. That man knew things no human should.

Claude then took out her phone's SIM card, put it in his pocket, and powered off the phone.

"I think things are working out well," he said with yet another skeletal smile.

"If you're here," she said, "why did you cause Michael to go to Russia?"

He shrugged. "Better to have him in my playground than his own. But the foolish boy didn't take the red pearl with him. I thought for sure he wouldn't let it out of his sight. He's been known to cart it all over the Old Silk Road, so why wouldn't he bring it to St. Petersburg? Yet he didn't. We searched. His little girlfriend, Irina, was good at that."

Ceinwen felt the color drain from her face.

"Did he tell you much about her?" Claude asked with a broad grin. "Those two picked up right where they left off years ago. Rutting like goats. He still loves her, you know. Amazing, isn't it, after all those years?"

"You're sick!" She spat out the words. "And I don't believe you!"

"Actually, I did you a favor by not letting you take Michael's call. If you had, you would have heard him say he's taking Irina back here to live with him, and that he wants you out. The only reason he's not here with her already is because it took a while to get permission for her to enter the U.S. on a non-tourist visa. He wants her to be able to stay in this country. With him, of course. Maybe as his wife, finally. Also, she has a daughter, an *older* daughter. Hmm, makes one wonder who the father is, doesn't it? But that aside, they're both on their way here. I suspect that's why, when he couldn't reach you, he asked his little Chinese pal to phone. Michael hates the thought, I'm sure, of seeing your tears—or fury—when he shows up here with your replacement."

"You're despicable."

"Me? Or Michael?" Claude chuckled. "He surely dropped you fast enough when someone more interesting, and definitely prettier, showed up. Didn't he?"

She hated his words. A part of her was sure he was lying, but another part...

Everything he said made sense. She reminded herself that even the devil could quote scripture. Although William Claude wasn't the devil, he was possessed by a demon. A demon she had seen, and felt. It was his alter-ego, and it was a lot bigger, stronger, and more powerful than the frail old man who stood before her. The last thing she wanted was to ever see that demon again.

"Leave me alone, you old fool," she said. "I'm

tired of your nonsense. And I'm hungry! I'm going to make myself something to eat."

"No. You will sit and wait." His voice was suddenly louder, deeper, and Ceinwen couldn't stop the shudder rolling through her. He continued. "I don't trust you, and you'll be much easier for Claude to control if you're weak with hunger." Then he laughed, and it wasn't William Claude whose laughter she heard, but that of the demon.

Yakiv Koval stood in front of the tent at the campsite, hands on hips, and glared at the ancient jitney as it pulled to a stop. It was just arriving with the students and volunteers coming to help at the dig. He and the other two professors had driven over, as usual, in his Renault. The car was a bit cramped, but Koval didn't like facing, first thing in the morning, a bunch of raucous students or the zealous wanna-be archeologists who tended to fill the volunteer ranks.

But now, he was angry. The jitney was over a half-hour late.

"Where were you?" he yelled at the driver, who also happened to be the innkeeper.

"I was on time!" the man yelled back. "One of your students never showed up. We waited and waited and finally gave up. So don't blame me. You need to run a tighter ship!"

At this point, Doctors Veronika Masur and Dmytro Tischenko came out of the tent where they were documenting the team's progress. A sudden suspicion struck Koval that lately, the two were always together. It hadn't been that way at first. Veronika had been stand-offish, in fact. She still was around him. Why not around Dmytro? Besides, he was only in his late twenties. Had the female professor suddenly turned into what the Americans called "a cougar"?

He eyed Dmytro. The guy had "loser" written all over him. Medium height, with small eyes, a pointed nose, stringy dark blond hair, and a pudgy face and body, as if he'd never lost his baby fat. And his clothes were no better than those the students wore. Koval stood a bit taller and sucked in his stomach.

Come to think of it, Veronika wasn't all that great either. She was too muscular for his taste. Her blond hair was shorter than Dmytro's, and why didn't she bother with at least a little makeup? Koval wondered how he had ever found her attractive.

He turned his back on both of them, glad to have finally worked out his feelings toward the pair. If those two professors, clearly far beneath him, found each other tantalizing, it only showed how inferior to him they were.

On the other hand, he couldn't do anything but stare at Galyna Ivanova's lovely young body as she got off the jitney. What a beauty! Svelte but buxom, long blonde hair, pale blue eyes. It made him feel young just to look at her. He went over to her now. "Who's missing?" he asked the whole group, but his eyes clung to Galyna's. She smiled up at him. Yes, the girl knew how to respect wisdom. "Wasyl," she said.

Koval frowned. Wasyl Boiko was his best student. The kid was usually the first off the bus and the last one to get on it at the end of the day. He was going to be an excellent archeologist. Koval was even thinking about offering him a teaching assistant position. The fact that he was also a nice-looking young man and attracted the attention of equally alluring young women who might want to join Koval's future teams, was also a plus.

"Who saw Wasyl last?" Koval bellowed at the group.

"He didn't sleep in his room," Andriy Plaviuk said. Wafer thin, with light brown hair, plain eyes, and overly red lips, he was no one Koval ever bothered to pay attention to. In fact, no one else did, either.

The three male students shared a room, as did the two female students, although Koval suspected the sexes didn't stay as separated as they should have. He didn't mind young people having their fun, but the news about Wasyl's wanton ways infuriated him. "He didn't? Don't you think you should have started with that information? It's important." He glowered at all the students. "If he wasn't in his room, where was he?"

Andriy shrugged and then his eyes darted toward Olena Lysenko before returning to Koval. "I thought he was busy."

"Don't look at me!" Olena cried. To Koval, she was just "all right" with curly, long blonde hair, and a decent but rather flat-chested figure. Her main problem was Galyna—she simply couldn't compare. "I have no idea where he goes or what he does. He's nothing to me!"

Oh, ho! Koval thought. She sounded like a woman scorned. "Okay, so he's been missing since overnight. He might have hitched a ride to a larger town for some fun, and things got out-of-hand. He might be somewhere sleeping it off or is having trouble getting back to Potchiv. If he's still missing this afternoon when we get back to town, we'll contact the police. Probably, we'll find him in his room nursing a hangover."

"That's not the kind of boy Wasyl is," Veronika

said, her expression stern. "He's taking all this quite seriously."

Koval raked his eyes over her, still miffed about her possible interest in Dmytro. "How would you know? He's a grown man. I imagine that if the right woman came along, one who looked beautiful to him, he might have said fuck the dig, he had better things to fuck with." With that, Koval laughed at Veronika's shocked expression.

Her face tight, she marched away.

Koval faced the students and volunteers who all looked uncomfortable. "Go back to the spots you worked yesterday. There's a lot to do. We're running low on money, winter is coming, and we've got to show progress or the dig will be dropped, and it's too important. If we're right about this dig, we might change everything historians thought they knew about Templar history. Now, go!"

He watched them disburse. His fellow professor, Dmytro, didn't go to the northwest corner of the dig as he should have, but instead took a step toward the tent Veronika had escaped to. "Dmytro," he called, stopping him. "I want you to work with Feder and Andriy today. Be friendly with them. Those boys might know a lot more about Wasyl than they're saying. For all we know, they've found the local whorehouse and are spending time there. If so, it's something we've got

to stop." Then he grinned. "Or, check out for ourselves, eh?"

Dmytro didn't smile back, but just nodded and
headed for the area with the two students.

Three of the volunteers remained there
gawking at Koval. "Go!" His voice boomed. They
hurried after Dmytro.

"Idiots!" He muttered as he entered the tent
and went to the table where Veronika worked. "I'm
sorry for what I said out there. I was trying to sound
unworried, and it came out all wrong."

She looked up at him. He did like her brown
eyes, he decided. "I'm worried, too," she admitted.
"I hope you're right when you say Wasyl will be in
the hotel when we go back to town."

"You have such a good heart, Veronika," Koval
said. "It's what makes you one of the most popular
professors at the university. Now, let's get out of this
tent. The day is a bit warm for once. You should be
outside joining the rest of the dig. We can work on
analyzing these pieces when it's cold and rainy. But
not today. Come." He held out his hand to her.

To his surprise and pleasure, she took it as she
stood, but then let go of it immediately as she
grabbed her backpack filled with her instruments
and supplies and proceeded out of the tent.

The actual dig site was about a five-minute walk
up the steep hillside. The trail they took had long

existed, but with the dig team's daily use, it had become packed solid and free of brush. After a while, as they climbed, he took her hand again. He noticed her lips tighten, but she didn't pull it away.

They had just reached the top of the hill, to the flat shelf where the dig was located, when they heard a scream. Galyna and Feder were on the mountain behind the dig, and Koval could see them running down. When they saw the two professors, they hurried to them.

"It's horrible," Galyna cried. "Too awful!"

Koval opened his arms to catch her and to his delight she went to him, clutching him tight and burying her head against his shoulder as she burst into tears. "What is it? What's going on?" he asked as he gently stroked her back.

Feder stopped before reaching the teachers, but the young man was the color of ash. "It's Wasyl." He stopped and swallowed but appeared woozy. "He's on the mountain, in the brush beyond the dig. He's dead."

"What?" Veronika cried. She grabbed the boy's arm as if to stop him from keeling over. "What happened? What did you see?"

"Maybe an animal," Feder whispered.

Galyna tried to back away from Koval, but he held her tight as the other students, volunteers, and

Dmytro now climbed out of the pit where they'd been digging and circled them.

"How did you find him?" Koval asked, his gaze occasionally jumping from Galyna to Feder.

"Uh..." Feder swallowed and looked at Galyna. "She had to take a ... a bathroom break and didn't want to go alone, so I went along to keep watch. I mean, to watch that she had privacy. But as we went back into the brush, we found him."

A likely story, Koval thought, pulling Galyna closer. "Will you be able to show us?" He searched her eyes.

"Let her stay here with the others." Veronika's voice was sharp. "She's clearly too upset to go any-where. Feder can show us."

"Come on," Olena took Galyna's hand and led her away from Koval.

"Yes," Koval said, running his fingers through his hair, shoving the dusty strands off his face. "Let's see what's going on. The rest of you, go down to the camp."

He, Veronika and Feder walked around the dig to the brush beyond. As Feder led them up the mountainside, a lot farther than would have been necessary for the "bathroom privacy" that he had claimed, Koval's suspicions grew about his students' intent. He'd have to watch to see if Galyna was truly interested in Feder or if she was more of an "any port in a storm" type of woman. If so, he could provide a fine port for someone as pretty as her.

He sighed, wondering what Wasyl had gotten himself into. Why, he wondered, was the boy all the way out here? And alone? It made no sense to him.

Finally they reached a spot where Feder stopped and pointed.

Koval and Veronika looked at each other. They saw nothing from where they stood, but then slowly continued on in the direction Feder pointed. It took another five or six steps before they saw a man's outdoor hiking shoe. Just a shoe.

A bad feeling crept through Koval. Veronika placed a shaky hand on his shoulder, staying behind him. He continued forward.

"Oh ... God!" He backed away, then took a deep breath before he stepped forward again.

Veronika followed and then gasped. He was surprised that she didn't turn and run. If he weren't in charge of all this and compelled to show a brave face, he would have.

The boy had been stripped naked and lay on his back. Horrible gashes, as if done by an animal with massive claws, had been raked over his chest, arms, legs, and face. Worse still, the center of his body, from his rib cage down had been ripped open and everything was gone—skin, stomach, intestines, manhood, everything.

Koval's stomach suddenly flipped. He backed away and threw up.

Veronika walked to his side and waited until he was finished emptying his stomach. "That was no animal attack," she said.

"Of course it was," Koval said, embarrassed that she had seen him lose it while she was able to stand there, strong, and talk about the horror they had just seen.

"An animal couldn't undress him. And I doubt we have any that could have eaten so much of him and not left blood and viscera all around. It was too clean, too ... precise. I almost wonder if he wasn't tortured before being killed."

"Stop!" Koval placed a hand on a tree to help him remain erect. "You're upset. You don't know what you're saying. We can't let anyone know what you've just implied. The boy was attacked by wolves, probably a pack of them. Nothing more."

"We'll have to call in the authorities. They'll know what they're seeing."

Koval nodded. "We also have to think of ... of how to explain this to the university."

"And to the boy's parents," Veronika added firmly.

"Yes, of course."

They found Feder and went down to the camp where everyone gathered around them.

Koval spoke. "For some reason, Wasyl was up on the mountain, perhaps alone, last night. Apparently he was attacked by an animal—a wolf, we think. Maybe a pack of them. I want all of you to return to town immediately. You'll have to walk, of course. There will be no work here until the authorities are through investigating the place. But also—listen carefully—I need you to say as little as possible about what happened here. It was an unfortunate occurrence by a student who foolishly came here alone at night. Wasyl was unlucky, that's all. And we will not make speculations or speak ill of the dead. Do you understand?"

They nodded.

"Feder and Galyna will remain here with us for now," Koval said, then faced Dmytro. "You'll need to walk back with the students and volunteers. Veronika and I will talk to Feder and Galyna in depth, then I'll drive them back to town. I'm afraid my car doesn't have room for five."

"Oh?" Dmytro looked surprised and annoyed by the request. "As you wish."

Everyone picked up the backpacks and satchels that they used to carry their water, lunches, and equipment, and headed back to Potchiv.

Koval took Galyna's arm and led her out of the other's hearing. "Did you say anything to Olena or anyone else about what you saw?"

"Only her. I told her it was horrible."

"But did you say, precisely, what you saw?"

"I said he was … mangled, and his insides had been eaten."

"Did you say he was naked?"

"No. I wasn't sure … I scarcely looked beyond the hole that had been his … his …"

"I know, but I need you to make sure. Think! *Did you tell her he was naked?*"

"No. I'm sure I didn't."

He nodded and then he, Veronika, Feder and Galyna went into the tent. He put four chairs facing each other, and they all sat. "This is going to be very, very difficult," he said. "You know that the police will be all over this. The problem is simple. In an animal attack, the clothes would be shredded, but not gone. It's hard to imagine a wolf running off with a pair of men's trousers. So, there will be questions. Lots of questions. And we will have to abandon the site while everything is sorted out."

"But if it wasn't an animal," Feder said meekly, "what was it?"

"I suspect Wasyl ran into thieves. They probably stole everything from him—starting with his cell phone, and then his clothes. They must have knocked him out, then wolves or other animals saw him and went in for the kill."

"Who would do such a thing?" Veronika asked. "The town is tiny and everyone knows everyone else."

"That's the problem," Koval acknowledged. "It's the reason any investigation could go on forever and would ruin our futures. That's why we've got to come up with a story."

"A story?" Veronika's voice dripped with skepticism as she, Feder, and Galyna eyed each other.

Koval pressed his pudgy fingers together. "It must be one the police will believe but also won't spread, and the best I can think involves the two of you." His eyes went to Feder and Galyna, then continued, "But first, tell me this—were you two together last night? I'm not judging, I just want to know. And if so, where?"

Galyna looked at Feder, then admitted, "We were in my room."

"And Olena?"

"She went into the boys' room and slept in Feder's bed," Galyna said. "Or maybe with Andriy. I don't know for sure."

"Okay, but we know Wasyl wasn't there," Koval said. "So here's what we say happened. The three of you went out together and got a bit drunk last night, and decided to have some real fun. You know where I keep my car keys and that I'm a sound sleeper, so you stole the keys and drove up to the dig site. There, with more vodka, you decided to have sex—all three of you. You went up to the dig and continued past it, climbing a bit up the mountain, and there, you all stripped. But then you heard wolves. Wasyl went to see what was going on. You heard him scream and then all went silent. You two got scared, grabbed all the clothes, and ran back to the car. You and Feder waited for Wasyl, but after a while, you thought he might have gotten lost or hurt or was hiding from the wolves and afraid to move, so you drove back to the hotel, thinking you'd find him in daylight. You two did go looking the next morning—but when you found him, you saw that he was dead."

"I can't tell a story like that," Feder said, his usually reddish cheeks now flaming. He was quite blond and hours in the sun gave him more sunburn than tan. "It's not true. Not in the slightest."

Koval's eyes burned with anger. "Why not? Would you rather be part of an investigation? Do you want a lot of interest in what you guys were doing out here as the investigation drags on and on? Do you think having newspapers in the country write about the lurid investigation of a murder in the Carpathian mountains involving a group of students will do anything to help your career prospects? No! The best thing we can do is give the police the kind of story they'll believe. And—here's the important part—it is also the kind that they'll know is best to keep quiet about. If word got out of 'sexcapades' that led to a death, reporters will descend on the town. That's the last thing local police want. So we give them this simple story of young people wanting some fun, and then tragedy struck. Yes, it has some 'raw' elements, true, but mostly it's just sad, and not anything they'd want the news to get hold of."

"He does have a point," Veronika said, her arms folded over her ample bosom as she rocked on the back two legs of her chair. "Much as I hate to admit it."

Galyna squeezed her hands together. "I don't know if I can do it," she whispered. "When I think of Wasyl's body. I mean ... what *did* happen to him out there? Forget about our story. What is true? Don't we need to know that?" Her voice became tinged with hysteria. "If not animals, *who or what killed him?*"

"It won't work," Feder said. "Anyone can see no animal killed Wasyl."

Koval's lips tightened as his gaze jumped between the two students. "All I can say is let's hope the police realize that if they have no answers, heads may roll for such incompetence."

"Who cares about the police?" Veronika shouted. "I want to know how dangerous this place is. I've heard tales about-–"

"If it wasn't an animal," Koval interrupted, "then, some person lured Wasyl out there. I never heard of him being with any woman from the team, so maybe he went there with someone from town. A man, perhaps. A local man who wanted to keep his interest in Wasyl out of the public eye. That could be the reason for them to have gone up onto the mountain. Or maybe it was one of the volunteers. There have been more than one I noticed eying Wasyl. He was quite handsome. Some might say beautiful. And if so, who knows what really happened to him?"

As the other three grasped what Koval was suggesting, they didn't know where to look, what to do, as their eyes darted about, all speechless at the way this had turned.

"Another possibility," Koval said, "is that we're on to something with this dig and someone is trying to stop us by scaring us into leaving. With a find as important as ours might be, the death of one student is nothing. If we were to leave, someone else could come and claim the find for themselves."

"But if that's true, and we don't leave," Feder said, "what's stopping whoever did this from coming back? Maybe killing someone else?"

Koval grimaced. "I suppose we could request one or two armed soldiers to protect us. After all, such a find would add to the glory of the Ukraine, and bring tourists and their money here."

"Good luck with that!" Veronika said. "I can't believe other archeologists would kill Wasyl. That's crazy talk!"

"Give yourself a few more years in this field," Koval snorted. "Then, you'll believe that and a lot worse. Besides, he, or she, probably hired some killer who got carried away. And that's just one theory of many."

Veronika looked heavenward and shook her head.

They all remained quiet as the shock of Koval's suggestions sank in.

"So," Koval said after a while, "I'll ask the three of you, do you want to stay with me, or leave? But if you leave, you must not ever speak of this. If you do, I'll make it my life's work that you'll never work as an archeologist in this lifetime, do you understand?"

"And if we stay with you and tell your story about the three of us students being together last night, then what?" Galyna asked. Koval was un-nerved to see just how hard her eyes had become.

He swallowed hard. "Your futures will be just fine."

She nodded. "I can do it. You?" She faced Feder.

He nodded, but said nothing.

"Veronika?" Koval asked.

Her lips formed a straight line. "Let's get this over with."

CHAPTER 10

Li Jianjun left Vancouver, British Columbia at one in the morning to drive to the airport in Spokane, Washington. In his mid-thirties, he was a Canadian citizen although he had been born in Beijing, China. His family had moved first to Hong Kong, and then Canada. For a while, Jianjun worked for Microsoft in Seattle, but then realized his ability to research and hack into Internet sites was far more profitable than his job. His most interesting work was with Michael Rempart who had also become his best friend.

The early morning hours, Jianjun discovered, were the best time to go through the border crossing. Few people were there, and the guard had little interest in why he wanted to enter the US.

He said it was for a sister's wedding, which was more believable than the real reason—to give a friend a ride home. It was kind of ridiculous for him to drive 670 miles in order to save Michael from taking Uber or a bus or whatever he would use to travel the ninety or so miles from Spokane to his home near Sandpoint. But right now, Jianjun was happy for any excuse to leave Vancouver.

The city no longer felt like home. He and his wife, Linda, were finally getting a divorce. While Michael was being tormented by his failure in St. Petersburg, Russia, Jianjun felt as if he'd gone through hell in Canada. He had a lot to tell his boss when they met in Spokane.

Last year, when Jianjun had gotten shot and nearly died during one of his "adventures" with Michael, it had been Kira Holt, not his wife, who stayed with him in Salmon, Idaho, and nursed him back to health.

To be fair, when he finally got around to telling Linda of his injuries, she had volunteered to come and take care of him. But he told her to stay away.

It wasn't hard for her to guess why.

He and Kira had stayed together in Salmon for nearly three months, but once he was fully recovered, Kira abruptly said goodbye. Not only goodbye, but she told him he was to go back home and not contact her again, ever. To hear her words, he would have thought she hated him, except that she was crying when she said them, and the look on her face told him how she really felt. But then she ran from him, got into her car, and headed to the airport.

He could only guess it was because of his marriage. He had told her he wanted to end the marriage, but Kira understood the whole "Chinese traditional arranged marriage" situation and understood how difficult it would be for him. He'd probably be drummed out of the family, disowned, and to him, family had been everything.

He told her he didn't care, that he loved her. But, it seemed, she did care.

Or she left for some other reason—like he was a nobody and she was a brilliant doctor of psychiatry. Or he was boring. Or a lousy lover. Or anything else he could think of to trash himself.

Whatever the reason, she was gone and, as she had ordered, he returned to Vancouver.

But no sooner had he reached "home" than he knew it was wrong for him to stay there. He was living a lie, and it was wrong for him to do that to Linda and to himself, traditional marriage or not.

Finally, watching Michael go off to St. Petersburg to find the woman he had once wanted to marry in hopes of coming to terms with that whole situation and to find a way to move on with his life, convinced Jianjun he needed to do the same. Life was simply too short to spend it with someone he didn't love—and frankly didn't even like—just because his Chinese parents had arranged the marriage for him.

Somehow he gathered the courage to ask Linda for a divorce and, even worse, to tell his parents what he had done. He then moved into a tiny apartment.

As he knew would happen, everyone rushed to Linda's defense, and he became the scum of the earth. Worse than scum, in fact.

They both found lawyers and Jianjun offered to give Linda the house. But, since she was employed, and he wasn't, he didn't have to pay alimony. Linda tried to explain to her attorney that he got a terrific amount of money from the archeologist, Michael Rempart, when he did work for the man. But Jianjun convinced both attorneys and even the judge that Michael had retired from archeology and Jianjun might no longer have any job at all.

Linda's attorneys had tried to contact Rempart to prove that Jianjun was lying, but they hadn't yet found an address for him, let alone gotten him to answer their calls. And Jianjun wasn't about to help them out. Also, the place Rempart had called home, Wintersgate on Cape Cod, had suffered significant fire damage and there were no plans to restore it. Plus, his mailing address was a "virtual mail" service.

Although Jianjun had claimed Michael could

be anywhere in the world, Linda refused to let her attorneys give up the search. She called Jianjun an embarrassment to his parents and all his ancestors going back seven generations. He was tempted to ask what she knew about the eighth generation, that they wouldn't be embarrassed, but he decided that might set her off again.

And his parents had stopped speaking to him.

While all that was going on, he realized the need to figure out what to do with the rest of his life. What if Michael really was giving up archeology? What was Jianjun to do then? He was tempted to contact Kira, but his feelings about everything, including her and the way she had suddenly abandoned him, were too raw. The last thing he wanted was for her to feel as if he were pressuring her to take him back, as in "Hey, Kira, I've divorced my wife so I can be with you. And here I am!"

What if she still didn't want him? He didn't think he could handle any more rejection at the moment. He would wait to talk to Kira when he was feeling strong enough to accept her thumbs down of him without feeling suicidal—if that day ever came.

So, now, he sat in the airport terminal waiting for Michael's plane to arrive. The guy had faced a ridiculously long flight with stops at Amsterdam and Seattle, and Jianjun knew he was anxious to get home and hoped Ceinwen was either there waiting for him or was on her way back to Idaho from Wales.

Jianjun had gotten himself a room at a nice resort right on the lake in Sandpoint just in case she hadn't gone to Wales after all. He kind of suspected she would wait for Michael's return and he wouldn't want to be in the way of the two lovebirds on their first night back together.

But he had a lot to discuss with his boss when Michael was in the mood to talk about mundane things, like Jianjun's upcoming divorce and if they were ever again going to set up an interesting dig.

***

Ceinwen stared at her useless phone on the counter. She wondered if Michael was still trying to reach her or if he had given up on her, on them ... and if Claude's words about Michael and Irina were true.

Whatever was true, right now, she was on her own.

It wasn't the first time she'd had to face life with only herself to rely on.

"I'd like some coffee," she said. "You?"

"How very thoughtful of you, my dear," Claude replied.

She used the French press she'd gotten for

Michael, and soon put a cup on the coffee table in front of Claude, then sat in an easy chair with her own cup.

He took the coffee to his lips and loudly sipped. "It doesn't taste as if you've poisoned it," he said.

"Of course not," she murmured, then rubbed her stomach.

"Hungry?" he asked.

"Yes." She glared at him.

"I'm only hungry for you," he said with a smirk.

"That's a bad line even for a monster. I'm going to eat something." She marched toward the kitchen.

"No! Turnaround, Ceinwen," he ordered.

She did and was shocked to find him right behind her. She hadn't seen or heard him get up or cross the room. She backed away but soon bumped into the kitchen counter and had to stop.

He grinned and moved closer. With each step Claude faded and a tall gray-green demon took his place. The thing placed its claw-like hands on the counter on each side of her, trapping her between its long arms.

"Keep away from me, Claude! You're repulsive!" She tried to break free, but it was like pushing against a cement wall. With each shove of her arms, it moved closer until its scaly body pressed hard against hers. When she saw that its eyes glistened at her struggles, that it enjoyed showing its power over her, she stopped fighting.

With horror she watched a long snake-like tongue slowly ease from its mouth toward her, finally reaching the wound on her neck, the skin still raw like some malevolent stigmata that refused to heal. It licked the wound up, down, then side to side. Heat and pain wracked through her. She fought the feeling until she couldn't bear it any longer and cried out, begging him to stop.

"I can make the pain go away." The voice sounded in her head, its tone so soothing, so calming, it all but curled around her body. The tongue left her wound and slipped under the neckline of her shirt.

It felt warm, seductive, and the thought filled her ... *Why not enjoy this?* He wanted her; Michael didn't. And with that she knew Claude was in her head, toying with her mind. Repulsed, she pushed at him. But once again her struggles seemed to excite the beast, causing its yellow eyes to redden as its snaky tongue slid along her neck, to her ear, then to her mouth.

She let herself appear to succumb as she remembered that on the counter behind her was a wooden block that held a variety of knives. Her lips parted, and she arched her back, her groin thrust forward. The demon eased back to peer down at all she seemed to be offering.

As it eased the pressure that held her in place, she was able to twist just enough to grab the longest knife behind her and in one quick move slashed it right through the demon's tongue.

The knife went through it as if it were no more than air which, perhaps, it was.

She held the knife, unbelieving.

The demon vanished as Claude laughed so loud and so hard at her expression his old man self returned. "You're such a fiery one, my dear. No wonder my son was captivated by you. Oh, but we are going to have fun as we wait for him to return home. It makes me hope his plane is delayed. Although, of course, if you tell me where the red pearl is, I may just leave immediately."

"You know Michael would never tell me where he hid it."

"And I also know you might be smart enough to figure it out on your own."

She scowled. "Maybe if I cared about it. But I don't. You're wasting time here."

"I have nothing but time. And I can't think of anyone I'd rather spend it with. Especially as I try to help you remember all you know about Michael's possible hiding places."

"I told you, I know nothing about it!"

"I have ways to make sure you're telling the truth. Trust me, you don't want me to use them."

"Go to hell, you old fool!" She swung the knife at him. He might look old and frail, but he grabbed her arm in midair stopping her strike.

"Actually, my dear, I may already be there." He waggled his eyebrows and then, with his free hand, easily pried the knife from her fingers and tossed it away. Then he captured her arms. "Come to think of it, I am hungry. I noticed some bacon and eggs in the refrigerator. Cook me breakfast. I want a lot of energy for all that is to come."

She spit at him.

He slapped her hard and shoved her toward the cooktop. "Get to work."

She took a large cast-iron frying pan from a cabinet, added a generous amount of vegetable oil, and put several slices of bacon in it, then took out a smaller pan for the eggs.

"And toast," he called from the sofa where he lounged. "With jam. I'm sure you and Michael must have some."

"Lemon curd," she replied.

"Delicious."

She waited until the pan with the bacon was quite hot then, when he wasn't looking, took some of the lukewarm coffee left in her cup and splashed it onto the bacon grease causing it to loudly pop as the grease splattered. She managed to jump out of the way, but cried out, clutched her left hand against her breasts.

"Are you all right, my dear?"

She put two fingers of her "burned" hand in her mouth, sucking on them, all the while blinking as if to hold back tears.

"Let me see what you've done to yourself, foolish child," he said as he strolled toward her.

She looked up at him, feigning fear, her fingers still up to her mouth.

"Let me do that for you," he murmured, as he gripped her left hand and arm.

At that moment, she grabbed the pan with the bacon, not even caring that the handle was hot, and swung it so that the grease flew from the pan onto his chest and neck. He howled with pain, dropped her hand, stepped back and looked down to see what she'd done to him. She then gripped the hot frying pan handle with both hands and used it like a baseball bat against his head.

She heard a sickening, wet thwack just before he fell.

She didn't stop to look at him, didn't stop for anything but to grab her phone and handbag as she ran out the door. Michael's car was on the driveway and she pulled out her key fob, hitting the remote start so it was running as she got in.

But before she pulled the driver's door shut, pain from her burned hands causing her eyes to water, she heard an earth-shattering roar come from the house.

The demon!

CHAPTER 11

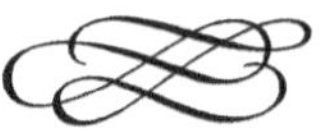

Professor Dmytro Tischenko had been sickened by everything Koval, Galyna, and Feder told the local authorities the day before about the students' activities on the night Wasyl died. He didn't believe any of it.

But he decided it was best to keep such thoughts to himself.

After all, he was here for only one reason: to advance his career. As such, he was on constant lookout for something unique, something special that would gain him notice. He'd grown up as the fourth of six children, which put him in the middle. He wasn't the oldest or the first to do anything. By the time the fourth child did whatever, it was old hat. And he wasn't the "baby" who was cooed at and gushed over.

He had grown up just outside of Lviv, often said to be Ukraine's most interesting city, not especially high praise in his opinion. He hated his home and hated Ukraine with its constant state of not enough food and seemingly endless wars.

He had worked hard to get into the University of Kyiv. He wanted to become an archeologist simply because it got him out of cities and, if he was lucky, out of the country. At the same time, he sometimes regretted not returning to Lviv and marrying Tatiana who he'd lusted after since they were both fourteen. But that would lead to a life of boredom, and he wanted much more. At this dig, he might find it.

Dmytro's thoughts turned to two nights earlier. His hot, stuffy bedroom had caused him to wake up early and open the window. As the sun brightened the sky, a bicycle rider neared the inn. He recognized Wasyl. The boy turned to the side of the inn where bike racks were located. A short while later, he'd heard a door in the hallway open and shut. It could have been Wasyl's room.

After breakfast, Dmytro had stepped out of the inn and looked at the bikes on the rack. Only two were there, one old and rusty, and the other appeared ridable.

That night, Dmytro woke up around midnight and decided to check on the bicycles. The newest one was gone. Dmytro planned to ask Wasyl the next morning what he was up to but never got the chance. The next day Wasyl was found dead.

Dmytro thought about saying something to the police, but he could see that leading to lots of questions like, "Why were you so interested in Wasyl's movements?" "Did you ever follow him?" "What else did you watch him do?"

On the day Wasyl's body was discovered, Dmytro had checked the bike rack when he got back to the inn. The newest bike was still missing. But then, the next morning, it was back. Who would have put it there? And why didn't the police ask about it?

He could only assume Koval had found the bike and returned it to avoid the police questioning his "three students at an orgy" story.

Dmytro pushed a rock under the back tire—a rock that a rider would have to kick out of the way before riding the bike. Each day after that, Dmytro checked the bike. The rock was still there.

The police continued to question everyone about what had happened. Most people, Dmytro included, said they had no idea. Dmytro's only uncomfortable moment came when the police talked about Wasyl and Galyna. Their questions made him think they were considering the possibility that it wasn't quite the consensual three-some they'd been told, but aspects of jealousy could have come into play. They suggested that Feder might have had strong feelings for Galyna, and saw Wasyl as a threat.

Dmytro was tempted to tell them it would have been more likely that Wasyl was in love with Feder than with Galyna, but that might have led them down another rabbit hole, asking more and more questions for which Dmytro had no answers.

Dmytro doubted Wasyl's nighttime bike rides had anything to do with having a sexual encounter of any kind. Wasyl had to be finding something fascinating at the dig site. He couldn't think of anywhere else the boy might have gone on a bicycle in the middle of the night.

Dmytro decided he should check out the site for himself. He had waited until he was pretty sure the other professors and students were asleep and rolled the bicycle out to the street. He took a deep breath as he faced the darkness. All he had to do was get on and ride up to the dig.

He peddled only a few feet when he heard a shrill cry and then a black cat darted across the road in front of him. His heart all but stopped and his legs began to quiver so badly, he had to get off the bike before he fell. He knew he couldn't go on, and as he pushed the bicycle back to the rack, he felt every bit the weak-willed, spineless failure everyone important in his life had always said he was.

CHAPTER 12

After learning so much about Rachel's past from the handsome Deputy Mallick, Bethany was determined to find Michael Rempart and find out what he knew. Back in her bedroom, she scoured the internet for information. She wished she knew more about in-depth searches and spent time going to sites that gave suggestions on what to do when typical search terms didn't yield needed results.

For several days her task seemed hopeless until, while tracking anyone with the unusual Rempart name, she found a small article saying a fire had badly damaged the Rempart estate in Cape Cod. That's it, she thought. It was such an uncommon name, and she'd seen a news mention somewhere of Michael sailing off of Cape Cod in his youth. It had to have been his home or to be somehow connected to him. There, she should be able to track him down.

She announced to her parents that she was

going to Boston to see some of its historical sites. She should have realized that would make them immediately suspicious since she had never shown any interest whatsoever in history. In college, she had majored in English because she enjoyed reading novels, only to learn it wasn't the smartest career move. But since she was twenty-one years old and had saved money for the trip, her parents couldn't stop her.

She rented a car at the Boston airport and drove to Wintersgate. "Unbelievable," she said as she got out of the car and stared at the estate. On a bluff overlooking the water, the place was massive, dark, and foreboding, but more than anything the damage from the fire held her gaze. The bottom of the home looked relatively untouched, but the upper floors and the turret, a sort of tower-like structure, were charred black. It made her think of one of her favorite English novels. She imagined Thornfield Hall might have looked like that after Mr. Rochester's crazy wife torched it.

She looked around and noticed movement in the garage, a separate building from the house.

Bethany approached, then called out, "Hello!"

An older woman came to the opening. "Oh my, child! You scared me! How did you get in here?" The woman patted her short, gray hair and then smoothed her dress as she approached.

"The gate was open, so I just drove in," Bethany said. "I'm looking for Michael Rempart and I was hoping someone here could tell me how to reach him." Bethany took an envelope from her handbag. "I have a letter for him. It tells who I am and why I really must see him. It may be a matter of life or death."

The woman straightened her back and huffed a few times as if to show her irritation at being disturbed for a mere life or death matter. "Well, as you can see, Michael Rempart isn't here. No one is. The place needs repair and so far no one has stepped up to do it."

Bethany was relieved that the woman didn't deny knowing Rempart. That had been her main fear when making this trip. "Are you a relative?" Bethany asked.

"Of course not! I was the housekeeper when there was a house to keep. Now, I'm overseeing the property."

"I see. I'm Bethany Gooding." She smiled. "And you are?"

The woman's lips tightened. "Patience Hewson."

"Can you give me Mr. Rempart's address, or some means of reaching him?"

"By 'Mister' Rempart, I'm assuming you mean Master Michael. If so, I have no idea," Patience said haughtily. "If you ask me, he was the one who caused all our problems here."

Bethany was taken aback at the forceful statement, but she had to ask, "What other Rempart lived here? Perhaps that person can tell me where Michael is?"

"His father is out of the country."

"Do you know how I can contact him?"

"You cannot."

Bethany didn't understand why not, but decided not to push it. "Will he return soon?"

"You certainly are persistent." Patience rolled her eyes. "I doubt he will ever return here."

"Michael's father won't return?"

"Mr. William Claude Rempart is very set in his ways and hates change. His house is forever changed, so he's gone from it. And soon, I leave as well. I'm going to join him to resume my position as his housekeeper." The woman heaved a sigh. "He needs me. What can I do but go?"

"What if I gave you the letter?" Bethany asked. "Would you be willing to ask Mr. William Rempart if he would send it on to his son? It has to do with my sister, Rachel Gooding, who I believe Mr. Michael Rempart liked very much. It's very important."

Patience once more pursed her lips but took the letter, folded it, and put it in her pocket. "I'll personally hand it to Mr. Rempart and ask that he send it on to Michael."

"Promise?" Bethany asked.

She tilted her head back and looked down her nose. "I do not need to promise. I said I would do it, didn't I?"

Michael sat in the passenger seat of Jianjun's car, exhausted after over thirty sleepless hours on planes and in airports. They were on an empty stretch of highway after passing through Coeur d'Alene, Idaho, when Michael noticed a black car on the opposite side of the road heading toward them. It looked familiar, and he leaned forward, watching closely as it passed by. "That's my car! Ceinwen's driving. Damn! What's going on?"

Michael tried reaching her on his cell phone, but she wasn't answering. "Why is she in such a rush? I left a message saying about what time I'd be home. Where could she be going?"

"Maybe she didn't get the message," Jianjun said.

Michael frowned. "Or maybe she did. Turn around. I need to talk to her, to find out what's happening."

"Here?" Jianjun looked around. The highway

was narrow with ditches on both sides of the asphalt.

"Hurry!" Michael said.

Jianjun waited until he reached a straight area with a clear view of traffic on both sides, then made a U-turn and stepped on the gas, going as fast as he dared. But Ceinwen had also been speeding.

When they again reached Coeur d'Alene, the traffic became heavy enough that everyone had to slow down. Jianjun, however, having driven in some of the biggest, most congested cities in the world, managed to squeeze his way into openings that more rational drivers wouldn't have dared, and so moved through traffic with a lot more speed than Michael would have thought possible.

"Remind me to take you with me if I ever go to St. Petersburg again," Michael said, impressed, even as he searched the traffic for Ceinwen.

They were almost out of Coeur d'Alene, and giving up hope when Michael saw a black BMW break from the pack.

"That might be her," he said.

Jianjun maneuvered and sped up. He didn't dare go too fast, knowing this area would be patrolled. Clearly, Ceinwen thought the same because she'd slowed down to the speed-limit. "Where's she going?" Jianjun muttered.

"I wonder if she's heading for the airport,"

Michael said. "She may finally be listening to me when I told her to go back to Wales. If that's where she's headed, I won't stop her."

"Are you sure about that? Maybe if you two talk—"

"No. She stopped answering my calls, never called back. And now she's leaving just as I'm heading home. It's a pretty clear message."

Jianjun said nothing more.

"But keep following," Michael added after a while.

Jianjun did. There was no reason for Ceinwen to recognize his car, and he stayed far enough behind that she couldn't see the driver or passenger in the Lexus behind her.

She turned into the Spokane Airport parking lot, and Jianjun followed. He was able to find parking not far from her.

They watched as she went to the Delta counter and bought a ticket.

The ticket agent seemed to be giving her directions and telling her to hurry. She did.

"She's most likely going to Cardiff," Jianjun said a short while later. "Back to Wales."

"How do you know?"

"I'm watching her credit cards. She just bought a ticket from Delta Air. The price matches a one-way ticket to Cardiff. The first leg," Jianjun continued, "is to Minneapolis, and the plane leaves in twenty minutes."

Michael's face froze. "She must have just decided to leave, knowing what time I'd be back. That could be why she was speeding."

"I don't know." Jianjun shook his head. "That doesn't sound like Ceinwen to me. If she has a problem with you, I see her as someone who'd stick around and have it out."

Michael grimaced. "I guess this is the one time she decided to take the easy way out. I'd like to watch the boards and make sure that plane actually leaves the airport. And who knows? Maybe she'll change her mind again and not get on it."

Jianjun's eyes were sad as he listened to Michael. The plane being delayed gave Michael temporary hope that Ceinwen might leave it. But then the plane took off.

Michael and Jianjun went out to the parking lot. "Want to take your own car, boss?" Jianjun asked.

"No. I'll give her a week or two. She might come back. If not, I'll come pick it up. How about if I drive your car? Driving will help me think about something besides how badly I've screwed up everything."

Jianjun handed over his keys.

CHAPTER 13

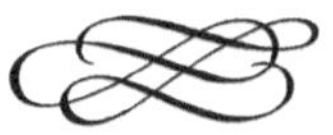

S t. Petersburg, 1916

Word quickly spread through St. Petersburg of Rasputin's death on the night of December 17, 1916, and of how his assassins, members of the aristocracy, had invited him to their home where they killed him. There, they had first tried to poison him, but he did not die. They shot and beat him, but he did not die. Finally, they put a bullet to his head and were so afraid he would again rise up against them that they tossed his body into the icy Neva River.

The next day, his frozen corpse was found.

The authorities decided to burn the body so that no "cult of Rasputin" would ever rise up.

Militsa sat in her room, all the drapes drawn, tears streaming from her eyes over the death of the one she loved above all others.

"What will we do without him, Militsa?" Stana cried as soon as she was allowed into her sister's bedroom.

"They were all so jealous of him, the small, petty

men. Jealous of his influence with the Tsar and Tsarina, with you and me, and even with God. So they killed him!"

Stana sat at her sister's feet, her head on Militsa's lap and sobbed.

"Did you know," Militsa began, her voice bitter, "he told Alexandra that his life was in danger? And now members of our own class have brutally killed the only man who could save us. Soon, they'll arrest Nicholas."

"I can't believe a mere mortal could have killed our dear Grigori," Stana murmured.

Militsa hardly listened. "Grigori once said he was a vessel similar to Pandora's box in that within him were all the vices, crimes, and everything bad that existed in Russia and its people. But once that vessel was broken, all that evil would spread across the land. He warned Alexandra that if he were to be killed, all would be lost and she and her family would not survive. He said, 'When I die, Russia will perish.' And so it shall."

"There's nothing we can do," Stana said, desolate. "The people are rejoicing. They're dancing in the streets that he's gone, calling his chief assassin 'the hero of all Russia.' They hated Rasputin just as they hate Alexandra and swear she was his mistress. No one seems to believe that she actually does love her Nicky. And that their Romanov relatives did the *killing makes it all the harder to bear. Pressure is being put on Nicholas to stop all investigations and admit that the murder wasn't a crime but something to be celebrated."*

"They will pay!" Militsa's eyes were red and wild. "They may have burned his corpse, but with my power, our friend and his followers will continue on. For now, we must go to Alexandra. She must be devastated. We can cry together and perhaps our tears will bring him back to us. His killers, all of Russia, will rue the day they decided to murder our beloved one."

CHAPTER 14

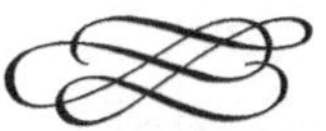

The weeks passed slowly and throughout them, Bethany heard nothing from either Michael Rempart or his father. She guessed the haughty housekeeper she'd given her heartfelt letter to hadn't given it to the father, or the father hadn't passed it on to his son, or Michael Rempart was an ass who hadn't thought she was important enough to answer.

Well, she wasn't one to give up. She still couldn't locate Rachel, and her parents were growing increasingly irritated at her for not "settling down" with some fellow or deciding what to do as a career. Instead she continued to work part-time at the University library, a job she kept by continuing to take a single class each semester to maintain her student status.

She knew her parents worried that she'd "pull a Rachel" and run off somewhere. And they were right. She would love to do that.

She wanted to see the world. She did hope to

find a husband, live on a nice farm, and have a gazil-
lion kids of her own ... someday. But now, she had
places to go, things to do, and a world full of new,
interesting people to meet.

At times, her thoughts turned to Deputy
Mallick. They seemed to have had some sort of im-
mediate connection. Or so she'd thought at the time.
But he hadn't called her and she realized it would
be unfair of her to return to Salmon and encourage
anything to develop between them while she was
feeling a lust for adventure far from Idaho.

For all those reasons, she concentrated on
finding Rachel and Michael Rempart. She believed
they were her key to the kind of excitement she
craved. She had phoned and texted the numbers
Deputy Mallick had given her for both Rempart
and Jianjun. Jianjun texted apologies that he had no
information at all and Rempart never responded.
What was with that guy?

That meant she had to learn new ways to find
people on the Internet. She began by signing up on
sites that were supposed to act like a personal, online private investigator. For only $29.95 (the ads
claimed) she was supposed to be able to have access
to all kinds of databases to track people down.

She did get access, but the sites told her next to
nothing. She joined some groups on Facebook that
were supposed to help search for missing people.

Most were a bust, but one day she saw a comment that opened a whole new world to her. The person mentioned a site on the dark web. She didn't even know what a dark web was and began searching for it.

When she finally found a supposed link she struggled with what to do. The link might get her what she wanted or let in a virus that would completely wipe out her computer.

Holding her breath, she clicked on it and was sent to a browser she'd never heard of. She downloaded it and ended up in a world beyond Google.

She started poking around doing her own odd searches and finding that a lot of sites were chat rooms. Somewhere, she thought, must be a site where hackers talked to each other. She set out to find it.

It took days as she bounced from one weird spot to another. Many of the places wouldn't allow her access, and in others, the comments she received back in response to her serious questions made her angry or made her blush. Whichever, she'd log out and go elsewhere.

Until one day.

She had found a site where people were looking for ways to get even with others who owed them money and refused to pay up. Accessing credit cards, destroying credit ratings, taking over title to homes, photoshopping pictures of a spouse or significant other in bed with someone else, and other fun things to wreak vengeance on hated foes filled the site. She asked what the best way was to start searching for someone who didn't want to be found.

Variations on "I want to be found. Send me your picture." happened more than once, some X-rated. But it seemed like a decent spot otherwise, so she decided to stay and not log out just because some people were rude.

One night she received a message from someone called NEPTUNE. "Stubborn, aren't you? I'm surprised you're still here after some of the responses you're probably getting. If you're serious, I'll help you. I don't waste my time on people here just wanting to hook up. There are other rooms for that."

She quickly wrote a response, using the name she always gave in these chat rooms.

RACHEL: I'm serious. I'd appreciate help.

NEPTUNE: You're also seriously young or naïve if Rachel is your real name. Never use your real name anywhere on the web, and especially not here. Not unless you want some real weirdos tracking you down. And I don't mean only online.

RACHEL: Thanks for the warning. Rachel isn't my real name. I might not even be female.

NEPTUNE: You're female. I can tell that from

the words you use. And sweet. Like your name. Anyway, here's what you've got to do. I suggest you print this out because it'll only be here ten seconds and then I'm taking it down and leaving. Understand?

RACHEL: Yes. But why would you leave?

NEPTUNE: Because I've too much to do to spend time with newbies. Good luck, kid.

She saw a page of information flash before her and hit screen save and then print, not sure why he told her to print it rather than to save it. And then, as he said, ten seconds later as her printer whirred, her screen went blank and the instructions were gone.

The printed sheet had the instructions on it. Out of curiosity, she opened up the screen copy she'd made. It was blank.

But when she followed the instructions she'd printed, like magic, she was in a hacker's paradise, filled with all kinds of instructions and suggestions, all incredibly complex but ultimately doable.

She began spending more and more of her time there. Sometimes the entire night would pass before she'd realize she'd hardly eaten, slept, or showered and it was time to go to work. But she was learning more than she ever had in her life, and it was exciting.

And then, she began chatting with someone

called Aiden and he introduced her to something even more exciting than hacking. He called it "remote viewing."

Aiden told her he was twenty-two and had been studying remote viewing for about a year.

When he first began to talk about it, it struck her as ridiculous. It was supposedly a way, for example, that one person could look at a picture and another person miles away could "view" the same picture in his or her mind and draw it. In a few cases—and she'd read all she could about remote viewing on the internet since having met Aiden—the drawings were close, but never exact.

Aiden suggested that if she concentrated hard and learned to do it, they could view each other in their minds, and it would be as if they were together. She liked that and, nutty as it seemed, threw herself wholeheartedly into learning the technique.

***

"Each day is better than the day before." That was Ceinwen Davies' mantra, and she repeated it each morning and each night as time passed slowly in her "new life." A life she hated.

She was the first to admit she was a mess when she'd reached her hometown of Cardiff. When she got off the plane after her mad dash away from the demonic Claude, she'd gone straight to the home of Rhys Evans, an old boyfriend. In an email earlier in the year, her mother had mentioned that she'd run into Rhys and he'd asked about Ceinwen. Her mother added —and Ceinwen could all but hear her South Wales accent in the letter—that "he had a look about him that told me he still thought lovingly of you."

Ceinwen decided to see how perceptive her mother was. Rhys had been home when she arrived, and gawked at her as if he'd seen a ghost. Once he got over his shock, he invited her in.

She gave him a cock-and-bull story that she needed a place to hide because she'd broken up with a man who had begun stalking her and she was scared. He ate it up, glad she'd come to him, and said she was welcome to hide out there as long as necessary. She took that to mean he didn't have a current girlfriend.

She went to Rhys because, while everything inside her told her to go back to Wales, she feared for her family if Claude decided to go after them. She didn't even let them know she was in Wales and never re-established her cell phone number be-cause she feared Claude could use it to track her. She'd been lucky once with him, and doubted he'd ever let down his defenses around her again.

Throughout all this, she had tried hard to forget about Michael.

She wondered what he must have thought when he saw the state of their home. She might not be a great cook but she didn't usually throw bacon grease all over the kitchen floor, or leave dirty dishes and cups all over the great room. Or blood on the floor.

When she struck Claude with the frying pan, it sounded as if she'd cracked his skull. She was surprised when she heard the demon bellow, that he had been able to wake so quickly. She wondered if Claude, the human Claude, would ever wake up.

She also wondered if Michael had walked into their home and found his father dead on the floor. Or, if he had brought Irina and her daughter home with him? And was the girl, as Claude had implied, Michael's daughter? Was a pregnancy the reason Irina had fled from him so many years ago? Such reactions weren't unheard of.

Thoughts like that kept swirling through her head. She didn't know what to think, what to say, or what to do.

Now, after living with Rhys for nearly a month she was surprised at what a comfortable routine they had fallen into. It began to bother her, in fact. The longer she stayed there, the stronger his feelings for her grew. They used to be quite close, to the point where she would often spend time in his apartment, or he would stay with her, acting as "friends with benefits." At the time, he'd made it clear he hoped she would regard him as more than a mere friend. He was acting as if he'd like to go back to that arrangement, and she had to admit, he was an attractive man. It was also nice to be with a man who wasn't afraid to let her know how he felt about her.

The more she reflected on how nice it was, the more she knew it was time to move on. But it was difficult to tell him she was going to walk away from him once more.

She was reflecting on what to do as she returned to the apartment from grocery shopping. She found the door jamb broken, and she pushed the door open.

Rhys looked like hamburger on the carpet, half-naked, bloodied, with gashes all over his body as if he'd been attacked by ... by what? The gashes weren't like those from a knife. They were too close, and in threes. More like from claws—perhaps demonic claws. She touched his neck and, amazingly, felt a pulse.

As she called an ambulance, he opened his eyes. They were dazed with pain and shock. "I didn't tell him," he whispered.

Beside his hand was a folded piece of paper.

She opened it and read, *Michael has abandoned you. But I haven't.*

Her body went cold with fear and guilt over Rhys.

When the paramedics and police came, she told them she had found him that way, and had no idea who had attacked him. She didn't show them the note. After she answered some of their questions, she asked to be allowed to go to the hospital. The police investigator told her to go to the station after, where he would have a lot more questions.

She started for the hospital, but doubled back to the apartment to pack her bags with the few clothes and necessities she'd bought while there in Cardiff. And then left Wales.

Now, she felt truly alone.

CHAPTER 15

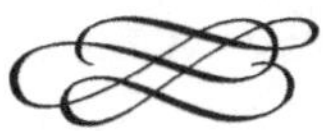

"Miss Petrescu," the supervisor, a short pompous man, raised his chin and frowned as he approached Irina at her easel, "your presence is required at the guard station. You are done for the evening."

Irina was shocked at the man's words. She looked up at the clock—8 p.m. She had another four hours to work. "But my shift isn't over. I don't want to leave."

His mouth puckered with irritation. "Your pay won't be docked."

She was stunned. An hour's pay for an hour's work was the policy. "It won't? You're sure?"

"So I've been told. I suggest you hurry." He sauntered away.

Confused, she changed out of her smock, washed the paint off her hands from the Valentin Serov oil she was restoring, and took the elevator to the main floor with the employee exit. Standing by the door was William Claude's manservant-butler-hitman, who she only knew as Stedman.

"I take it you're the one I should thank for getting me four hours pay without work," she said as she approached him.

"Mr. Rempart made the call, I'm only a delivery boy," Stedman said in his usual snide, haughty manner.

She knew better than to argue. "Where is he?"

"He's in the car." Stedman held open the door as she exited the museum. He walked wordlessly beside her to the Mercedes, its engine still running to keep it warm.

Stedman opened the back door and Irina got in.

William Claude was there waiting. "Such a menial job, Irina. And you call that wages! Aren't you embarrassed?"

"At least I do honest work."

He barked a laugh. "If that's what you want to think, so be it. Drive, Stedman. Nowhere special, but I enjoy seeing the nightlife of this city, so many people desperately seeking happiness at the bottom of a liquor bottle."

"What do you want, Claude?" Irina asked, fatigue filling her voice. "Or did you call me out here just to complain about my job and Russian drinking habits?"

"I'm here to tell you we're going to take a little trip back to the US."

She lifted one eyebrow. "I don't think so."

"Oh, but you do. You want to see Michael again, don't you?"

She felt as if her heart had stopped. "No. Not at all."

"Well, you should," Claude says. "He wants to see you. In fact, he came to St. Petersburg looking for you."

"He did what?" She was appalled. Michael was the last person she ever wanted to meet again.

"He knows you're here, and came. But he couldn't find you. And so, now, we're going to find him."

She turned in the seat so she could face Claude as directly as possible. He looked mostly straight ahead, letting her see only his profile except for an occasional glance in her direction. "All right, Claude. What is this really about? I know you aren't interested in Michael and me suddenly getting to know each other again."

He let her question hang in the air. "I wonder how much of the real Irina is still inside you. The woman I used to know, the one interested in alchemy and immortality? Does she still exist at all?"

"No!"

He snorted. "Well, that's too bad, because *that* Irina would have been thrilled to know that Michael possesses a philosopher's stone powerful enough to achieve everything we'd ever talked about."

Her eyes narrowed. "I don't believe it. There's no such thing."

"Oh, but there is. I've seen it. But my son thinks it's his duty to hide it from the world. When he came to Petersburg to find you, I thought for sure he'd bring it with him, but the idiot didn't. I can't imagine leaving anything so valuable out of my sight, but he did. I even went to Idaho, a backwater place he goes to in hopes of staying hidden from most of the world, or from me—I've never quite de-termined which. But I couldn't find the stone there without him. He's completely focused on not letting me find it. But around you, I know that focus will vanish. And then, my dear, I'll find it ... for us."

"Hah!" she said, glaring at him. "So you expect to use me so you can steal something from your son? Good luck with that, old man!"

"So *we* can take what should have been ours all along, Irina."

"You're crazy! I would never go anywhere with you!" she shouted. "Stedman, stop this car!"

"Drive!" Claude argued, then grabbed her arm, jerking her toward him. "You don't have a choice,

Irina! You know my power. You don't want to feel my anger. Not directed toward you, or that bastard child of yours."

"Why, you!" She swung her free arm at him, but he twisted toward her and grabbed it in mid-air. As they struggled, a tall truck turned onto their street, its high headlamps filling the Mercedes with light. As it did, she saw that the left side of his face —his jaw and neck—looked as if they'd been badly scalded, the skin shiny and puckered.

She gasped.

He pushed her from him. "You're going to regret this, Irina. Believe me, you'll regret it. Stedman, stop the car so the bitch can get out. I'm sick of her."

As soon as the car stopped, Irina jumped out of it and ran.

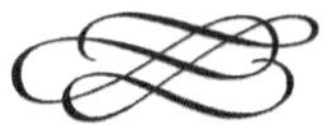

CHAPTER 16

*F*our months later ...

The Ukrainian officials had closed their investigation on Wasyl Boiko's death three weeks after it began because they lacked evidence that anything other than the alleged wolf attack had killed him. Law enforcement in the area had little money to perform investigations to begin with, and even less experience in strange deaths. It was easier to agree he'd been attacked by wolves as witnessed by two other students, and to let it go at that. No autopsy had been performed. Several of the police said they'd never seen a wolf attack look the way Wasyl's body did, but the higher-ups decided it was prudent to ignore such observations.

Since the snows had already begun, as soon as the dig team was allowed to leave, they did.

Now, in mid-March, with the danger of heavy

snows having passed and a hint of spring in the air, the same three professors and four new volunteers had returned to the town of Potchiv to begin where they had left off late last fall. The students would be arriving the next day. The professors expected that the number of volunteers would increase significantly because there was a buzz going around about some possibly significant findings at the site. The news of a student dying there had been kept fairly quiet.

Dmytro Tischenko sat with Yakiv Koval and Veronika Masur in the inn's dining room where breakfast was served each morning. To call the inn "rustic" would have been kind. The decrepit wooden building was a single story with a small sitting room, large dining room, and kitchen in the front. Following these rooms was a hallway with eight rooms off it, four on each side. The best thing about it was the large front porch.

The professors had just begun to eat when two of the volunteers came running into the inn in a complete panic.

"Professor Koval!" a male volunteer shouted. Dmytro couldn't remember the man's name or that of his female companion, but he would never forget their faces that morning. "We saw something up at the dig site."

Koval stood. "At the site? What were you doing up there? It's scarcely light out."

"We thought it would be a beautiful spot to take pictures of the sun as it first began to rise over the mountains and post them to our social media sites. To show the beauty of nature before it's changed by a team of archeologists."

Koval frowned, guessing that a word like "ruined" was more likely for these two to post. He sniffed. "So what was this thing that you saw marring your view of the beauty of nature?"

The man looked at his companion, and she grabbed his arm. They were an older couple, probably in their sixties, and had the leathery, stringy kind of skin Dmytro often saw on people who ate too strict of a diet and spent too much time in the harsh sun. She spoke. "It was a bunch of people or ... or monsters. They wore robes with hoods, and they stood in a circle and chanted."

Koval looked at them, faced the others who had all stopped eating to listen, and rolled his eyes. "Monsters wearing hoodies? How droll."

"When they noticed us standing at the top of the pit—they were inside it—they looked ready to spring at us, much the way a dog looks before it attacks. They were murderous and their eyes seemed yellow and a weird shape. Petro grabbed my hand, and we ran down the hill and back here so fast my feet barely touched the ground. I tell you, if those people, or whatever they are, stay here—the dig will be dangerous. You've got to be sure they're gone!"

"Why don't you both sit down and have a little coffee and some food. The altitude here can affect travelers at times. Maybe you're just hungry?" Koval suggested a little too sweetly.

The man backed away, but the woman was out-raged. "You think we would lie about something like that? Come on, Petro. We're leaving!" She faced the other volunteers. "You would, too, if you saw what we just did." With that, she grabbed Petro's hand and pulled him from the dining room.

Koval folded his arms. When the two were gone he stood up and addressed the other volunteers. "I think those two were here to do mischief. They all but admitted they think we're destroying the beauty of nature. I suspect they're environment fanatics. These things happen. Don't worry, everything will be fine!"

But something about the woman's words caused them to keep playing over and over in Dmytro's mind. All winter he had thought about Wasyl's death and the student's strange late-night rides which he suspected had been to the dig site. He almost went up there alone one night, but then had chickened out. Sometimes he despised himself. He should have gone. And he would now, no matter what! The volunteers had made it back safely, so why shouldn't he?

The professors and volunteers spent the rest of the day putting up the tent and then filling it with their equipment, folding chairs, and tables.

Dmytro called it an early night, saying he needed to be well rested to face students the next day. But in fact he planned to see for himself that very night if anything weird was going on at the dig as the volunteers had claimed.

He had asked the innkeeper to store Wasyl's bicycle over winter, and he had. Now, he took the bike and made it ready for a late night ride.

Around midnight, Dmytro got on the bike. He refused to think about anything beyond its mountain-terrain tires and good-size headlight. Once he reached the campsite, he left the bike by the tent and forced himself to walk up to the shelf-like area of the dig site. The volunteers claimed they saw the frightening people inside the pit that the archaeologists and students had dug.

The moon was nearly full and the stars bright so Dmytro didn't need his flashlight as he climbed up the trail to the dig. Just beyond the spot where the team was working, the mountain began to rise. Dmytro realized the only way to see down into the pit from a safe distance would be to hike up the mountain and then look down. Probably a good spot would be around the location where Wasyl's body had been found. Dmytro carried two knives with him, and patted the pockets they were in. Being there alone was scary, but also the most exciting thing he'd done in months. Maybe ever.

He found a shrub that was tall and dense. Lying flat on the ground and scooting under it as far as possible, he had a clear view of the pit and at the same time felt safely hidden.

There, he lay still and waited.

Around one a.m., lights from torches brightened the pit as a mystical procession rose from it. The men carried fire-lit torches and wore white robes, much like Templar robes, but instead of large red crosses over their chests, they had black pentagrams. The robes had deep hoods that left their faces completely shadowed. Dmytro practically stopped breathing as he counted nine of them—eight formed a circle and one in the center. The central person led the others in chants, almost Gregorian sounding, but eerier and more echoing. The sound wasn't human, which he attributed to the shape of the pit they stood in. Strangely, though, he found the chant to be beautiful.

Dmytro watched, struggling to keep his eyes open. But the men didn't move, and as the melodic, repetitive sound washed over him, he lost his struggles and fell asleep.

He awoke at dawn, with the dig looking the way it had when the team left it the day before. Nothing had been disturbed. No sign existed of the procession or the ceremony he had carefully watched.

It made no sense to him. Who were those men? And why were they here?

They hadn't done any damage that he could tell. But something about their shapes, now in the light of the morning, had seemed off to him—not quite human. But he was sure he was overreacting. After all, if they weren't human, what were they? Or—and the possibility was real—had he dreamed the whole thing?

He hurried back to the inn and as he undressed, he noticed a perfumy but pleasant smell which he supposed was from some flora he had lain on. Then, when he took his shower, he found a strange cut on his right side, just below his rib cage. It had apparently bled, but was scabbed over now. And even stranger were two painful little spots, like puncture wounds, on his scrotum, one over each testicle. Those wounds, too, appeared to have bled.

He guessed he must have rolled onto some sharp rocks as he slept on the mountain although it was difficult to imagine he had slept that deeply, although he had been pretty tired. He thought no more about it.

CHAPTER 17

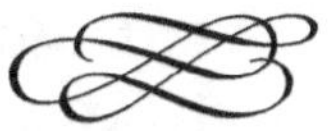

Bethany most loved the hours from midnight until about three in the morning. That was when most people seemed to be on the dark web. She enjoyed the chat rooms and particularly her friend, Aiden.

She had told him about her search for Michael Rempart and he had tried to help her, but without success, in learning exactly where Michael was located. She feared her quest was hopeless until Aiden found an expert in remote viewing. He introduced her, online, to a sweet old man. For the next week, each night, Aiden would connect her to the old man who called himself Merlin and he would walk the two of them through ways to do remote viewing. Then, one night, Merlin contacted her on his own, explaining that she had much more ability than Aiden and he feared Aiden was holding her back. He then commanded that she go outside and find a place under the stars that was quiet and where she would be alone. There, her mind connected with his.

It was scary, unbelievable, and exciting. She was shocked to "see" that where Merlin was located, the sun was still shining, and she saw a massive body of water. He told her that was absolutely correct. He described the oak tree she sat under, and seeing a darkened farmhouse in the distance.

After that, Bethany spent no time with Aiden. She enjoyed talking with Merlin far too much, and being in his world, which seemed infinitely more fascinating than her own.

So, each night, just before one a.m., she would sneak out to the field, sit under the oak tree, shut her eyes, and wait.

Not only did her thoughts and Merlin's meld, but she felt as if she were seeing the world through his eyes, as if she had been bodily transported through space, except that she could not touch, taste, or feel anything, including Merlin—she couldn't even see him. Also, Merlin had once tried to take her hand, but it simply had not worked.

That night, she went out to the field at the appointed time, sat under the oak, and waited. Nearly an hour went by. Disappointed, she refused to leave. And then she heard the familiar, "Hello, Bethany."

Hearing his voice thrilled her. "You're late. I was worried you'd forgotten about me."

"Never. But now that we've learned to connect so well, I think it's time you finally tell me what led you to remote viewing to begin with. Aiden hinted that it has to do with your family, but he wouldn't say what. Do you trust me enough to tell me about it?"

"I think so."

"Do you also believe I may be able to help you?" he asked.

"I don't know anyone else who could help."

"That's what I need to hear. Now, what is the trouble?"

"My sister has walked away from our family." Bethany paused. "I don't know if she's all right, living, dead, or if she wants to come home but can't. Rachel was my idol, and I wanted to be just like her. I feel smothered by the small town where I live, by everything here. But because Rachel left and won't come back, my parents have forbidden me to leave home. I know it's because they're worried and overprotective. But it means my life will remain dull. I may as well be dead!"

"No, no! Don't say that. I can help you," he said.

"I still feel weird talking to someone like you. I don't even know your real name."

"The original Merlin was a wise and great sorcerer. Think of it as my real name, and my location as Camelot. Surely, you know about Merlin and King Arthur's Camelot. So now, I'm not a stranger to you any longer."

"I can do that," she said. His words warmed her, and she wished she could somehow meet, or at least see him.

"Good. Excellent! Now, let us determine who can best help you find out about your sister. Perhaps you want to look at where she was last seen, and why she was there?"

"She wanted to become an archeologist and studied at Oxford. All I know is she and her room-mate, a Welsh woman named Ceinwen Davies, went to Japan to meet an archeologist Rachel knew and liked, Michael Rempart. There, she fell in love with a man named Seiji Nakamura."

"Ah! That is an excellent bit of information," Merlin cried.

"Perhaps we should look for Seiji Nakamura," Bethany suggested.

"I suspect many men have that name in Japan. Also, with the language and cultural differences, remote viewing would be difficult if not im-possible."

"Can we try to find my sister remotely?"

"Same problem, especially since she's probably fighting against any thoughts of her family. She may have set up a block against all of you, whether she realized it or not."

"What can we do?"

"I suggest you search for Michael Rempart. He seems to be the key, much more than her roommate. Why was he in Japan? Why did Rachel go there? He should be able to answer those questions for you. Buried in his mind are memories of your sister—not only of what happened to her and where she might be right now, but simply of her as a person, as the sweet person you love. Use Rempart's thoughts of Rachel as your beacon, and slowly, resolutely, search the country—the whole world if need be—and you should find him."

"That's a wonderful idea." It was as if Merlin had read her own thoughts on how to proceed.

"I'll join you in your search, my mind with yours will be even more powerful than yours alone. We can do this, Bethany. Now, starting tonight. Concentrate."

She did as he said and found it frustrating when nothing came to mind. But Merlin encouraged her, night after night, and even taught her tricks to force her mind to focus on picking up thoughts of Rachel and to ignore all distractions.

Finally, Andriy thought, he was back at the dig site, back at the inn in Potchiv. It was his first day back.

He'd dreamt of being here for weeks, scarcely able to contain his excitement. And most of all, his desire to see Stana again.

Every rational part of Andriy told him that after Wasyl's death he should have nothing more to do with Stana. It was as if she knew what would happen to his classmate.

Andriy had done as she had asked, and told Wasyl about some bizarre people performing an interesting ceremony at the dig site at night. He remembered how, the next day, Wasyl had told him he'd seen something, and said he would go back that night to check out just what it was. But the next day, they found Wasyl's body.

Andriy hadn't heard exactly what had been done to Wasyl, but he'd had the impression it was pretty horrible.

The police had been immediately called in, questioning and watching everyone.

Andriy had hoped Wasyl hadn't told anyone it was his suggestion that got the guy to go up to the dig site in the first place.

He was afraid to go back to Stana's cottage while the police were there. He didn't want them to question Stana, and he'd promised her he'd keep presence there a secret.

And then, Koval sent everyone home.

Andriy should have left immediately, but instead, he snuck back to the cottage.

To his horror, it looked like a shack on the verge of collapse. He didn't know how Stana had managed to make it look so bad, but told himself she must have done it so no one would think anyone had been living there.

Over the long, frigid winter, back at the university, he had tried to find Stana. He was shocked when he couldn't. The history department claimed to have no record of her—or, none that they would give him. He assumed they were just worrying about privacy concerns. Of course, she was a graduate student there!

Once the snow began to melt, he could hardly wait to go back to the dig. Something told him she'd go back to the cottage, and he ached to see her again. He'd never experienced anything like the way she made him feel, had never known anyone like her before.

His first night there, as soon as the inn grew quiet, he snuck out and went to the cottage.

His biggest fear was that she hadn't returned, and the building would remain the ugly ruin he'd last seen.

To his relief, he'd been worrying for nothing.

The cabin looked beautiful to his eyes before

his joy caused them to fill with tears. "She's there," he told himself, over and over as he ran to the door, knocked and quickly threw it open.

Stana sat on the bed.

"I knew you'd come back to me," she said.

His legs shook so badly he could scarcely approach her. "I've missed you so much," he said through his tears.

"Why the tears?" she asked, with a smile.

"I thought I'd lost you," he whispered through his sniffles. "I had no idea where you'd gone, or how you'd made the cabin look so old. And I looked for you at the University but couldn't find you. I was so scared I'd never see you again."

"Come here, my heart," she said, holding out her hands.

He ran his sleeve over his eyes and nose. "I guess it's not manly to cry, but I'm so happy."

"Sit beside me," she murmured.

As soon as he sat, she wrapped her arms around his neck and pulled him close. His arms went around her, he'd never held a woman that way.

She then got up on her knees and pushed him so that he was lying on his back. She slowly unbuttoned his shirt and opened it wide so her hands could stroke his bare chest. Sliding one leg over him, she sat on his groin then bent forward to kiss his mouth, his cheek, his jaw. He seemed completely unsure of what to do, even where to put his hands. She touched her lips to his for only a brief moment and then trailed kisses up his neck. He felt a sudden sharp pain followed immediately by an over-whelming warmth. After a while she lifted her head and he could see blood on her lips and teeth ... his blood.

"I hope you don't mind," she whispered, as she began to unfasten his trousers. "I like the taste of you."

He was breathless, scared, yet exhilarated. He would do anything, give her anything she wanted. Somehow, he found the ability to whisper, "Good."

CHAPTER 18

With the students back, life on the dig team fell into place as it had prior to the winter hiatus. It was as if nothing had interrupted their work, and Wasyl's death had never happened.

And each night, Dmytro rode the bike up to the dig site.

Throughout the day, he would look for any sign of what he had witnessed at night, but he saw nothing. Each night, he vowed to stay awake. But he didn't. Each morning, heading back to the inn, he vowed no more midnight journeys. But when night rolled around again, the dig lured him like a junkie craving a fix. He always went. And once there, he always fell asleep.

"Dmytro, wake up!"

Dmytro opened his eyes at the sound of Koval's voice. He suddenly realized it was daylight, and he was sitting on the ground, a trowel in hand and a bucket half-filled with dirt to be removed from the pit in front of him. He abruptly sat up straight, blinking from the sun, and wincing from the ache in his neck. "Yakiv, sorry. I haven't been sleeping well." He took the trowel and jabbed it into the dirt. The archeologists wanted to get down into the tunnels quickly, but since they couldn't take a chance destroying anything important, the professors and the four students were now proceeding much slower.

"What's causing problems with your sleep?" Koval asked, squatting down beside Dmytro. "You aren't looking very healthy these days. Your face is pale and you seem to be losing weight."

Dmytro wanted to tell him, but did he dare? He didn't want Koval to suspect he was having a mental breakdown and kick him off the team. Especially not now, when it seemed that there really were tunnels below the dig site—and when he believed that something extraordinary was happening around him.

"Would you think I'm letting my imagination run away with me," he cautiously began, "if I were to say I feel as if there's something strange about this location?"

"What do you mean?"

"Have you ever walked into an old graveyard and suddenly the hair on the back of your neck stood on end, as if ... I don't know ... maybe the place was haunted?"

"If you mean the dig, you're letting the volunteers get to you." All but two volunteers had now gone back home saying if they arrived early or stayed late, they would hear strange noises or see the glow of firelight. "They're just a bunch of weak-willed people who jump at anything that seems strange. If you ask me, they're finding this hard work and are using their 'nerves' as an excuse to leave. There's nothing scary about this place."

"You're lucky it doesn't bother you," Dmytro said, his face dejected, but then attempted cheerfulness. "Although I'm sure it's nothing."

"Well, I have been to places that have given me quite a chill, so I can understand what you're feeling," Koval confessed. "You're new to this. You'll come to realize that whenever you unearth the dead, it feels eerie."

"Could be," Dmytro agreed. "Or maybe it's because of what happened to Wasyl. Perhaps I'm just being foolish but it keeps me awake at night. And thinking about it, I don't feel like eating."

"It might not be foolish," Koval said as his gaze drifted over the hilltop with its deep pit, the brush, trees and the steep, granite mountain beyond it that rose high and imposing. "There are times, I also get a strange feeling up here."

"Yakiv," Dmytro looked at him squarely, "if there's anything at all that you know about Wasyl's death that goes against the story told to the police, that in any way indicates that something other than a wolf attack killed him, then I think we need to be very careful. Sometimes ... when I think about Wasyl, as much as I love the site and our work here ... it scares me."

Koval bit his bottom lip. "I, too, worry. But I can't give up this site, so I don't know what else to do."

"Actually, I have an idea," Dmytro said. When Koval didn't object, he continued. "One of my old classmates, Oleg Gubenko, who's now working in the archeology department at St. Petersburg University, wrote to me a little while back saying I'd been on his mind ever since he heard of our dig. He then mentioned that he'd met Professor Michael Rempart when Rempart was in Petersburg recently. He had stopped off at Staraya Ladoga to see the preserved artifacts there—the early church, the first Kremlin, and all. My friend said he could immediately tell the man was not a usual tourist by the way he was looking at the artifacts and the questions he was asking the poor docent. So he introduced himself. They ended up spending the day together. He took Rempart to the back areas where archeologists are still working and even drove him back to Petersburg where they went to dinner. Rempart gave Oleg his card and told him to feel free to contact him if he heard about any interesting digs in the area. Ivan thought of our dig and Rempart's comment and so sent me his address in the U.S. You've heard of Rempart, haven't you?"

"Of course," Koval said. "If even half of what the newspapers and journals have printed about him is true, he's been involved in all kinds of strange phenomena. It's crazy that the man hasn't bothered to write any research papers to tell the scientific world about his findings. He's losing a golden opportunity for promotion and more money."

"I think he's just the person we need here," Dmytro said.

Koval smiled, rubbing his hands together. "I don't know that we need him, but to connect his name to our project would be invaluable. Excellent, Dmytro! Let's write to him and I'll see what I can do about getting some money to bring him here. If we're able to involve Rempart in our project, and the site has anything at all to do with the Templars, we'll get more attention on our findings than we'll know what to do with."

Banff, Canada

. . .

Dear Dr. Rempart,

I am quite certain you have never heard of me. I'm an archeologist with the University of Kyiv, and I'm currently leading a team of professors, students, and volunteers in the Transcarpathian region of Ukraine. One of my fellow professors here, Dr. Dmytro Tischenko, is a good friend of the lead archeologist at Staraya Ladoga, Dr. Oleg Gubenko, who kindly gave us your address. I hope you do not mind.

We believe we may have discovered a chapel built more than eight centuries ago by the Knights Templar. If true, this would be the farthest east of any Templar edifice. For what reason did they travel to a place so far from their usual locations? That is the question my team and I hope to answer.

But we are having difficulties. More than difficulties. That is such a bland word for what is happening all around us. It is the reason I am writing to you. We are aware of the unique findings you have unearthed and believe you may be exactly the person we need here.

Our volunteers have now all left us because of what they claim are mysterious happenings—noises and lights—around the dig site. We are taking all possible precautions to assure there is no danger to the team members. I won't lie. One of our students was killed last year by some wolves, but he foolishly went into the forest alone at night.

Now, our team consists of three professors and four students.

I'll admit that the Carpathian mountains might be a dangerous place for you to come to despite the care we are taking. They are remote and isolated. But I understand such dangers haven't worried you in the past. I can offer you a small, private cottage, food, transportation to and from the dig, and help you obtain the necessary travel visas to work with us. I'm sorry to say we do not have the funds available to pay your travel expenses. But I hope that to be part of a team verifying such an important piece of Templar history may be compensation enough for you.

I have included photos of the dig, some interesting findings, and electrical resistivity tomography readings that show the near certainty of structures and tunnels to be unearthed.

I anxiously await your response.
Fraternally yours,
Yakiv Koval, Doctor of Archeology
University of Kyiv

As Michael read the letter and studied the photographs and readings more than once, a frown lined his forehead. He sat in an easy chair beside a floor-to-ceiling, rock-faced fireplace that warmed the mountain chalet in the Canadian Rockies. Outside, snow blanketed the land.

Without Ceinwen, he had no desire to stay in the home they had shared in Idaho. When he faced the fact that she wasn't returning and wouldn't answer his calls, he headed north on Highway 93. Just outside of Banff he was able to find a completely secluded rental. He spent the winter there. A few times, like now, Jianjun flew into Banff to visit him and, Michael suspected, check on how he was doing.

"Jianjun, look at this letter." He handed the sheet to his friend.

Jianjun was stretched out on the sofa, also enjoying the fire with his computer on his lap, and a bowl of guacamole and a bag of Doritos on the nearby coffee table. He hated his small apartment in Vancouver and visited his friend every chance he got. He put down the computer and took the papers Michael offered.

He carefully read them over and then sat up. "The letter is dated weeks ago."

"I guess there isn't a fast route from the mountains of Transcarpathia to a foreign address." To keep his location private, Michael used a virtual mailbox service that scanned his mail. He used its address on all his correspondence. But the graphs sent with the letter didn't scan well, so Michael had set up a Banff post office box to receive the actual correspondence.

Jianjun scooped up some guacamole with a chip and ate it before asking, "Do you think this letter is legitimate?"

"It reads as if it is. The only problem is I don't remember ever meeting the man who gave out my address. But I do meet a lot of people and one of them certainly may have been the lead archeologist at Staraya Ladoga. I've never been there although I do want to see it someday. What do you think? Is this request worth looking into?"

"What do I think?" Jianjun asked with surprise. "Why would my thoughts about this matter?"

"Because I don't know if I can trust my instincts any longer," Michael admitted with a scowl. "It interests me, but at the same time, the possibility of finding a site built by the Knights Templar in a location no one ever expected they went to, ranks high on my bullshit meter. It's the kind of find that would generate all kinds of newspaper articles since the public knows the Templar name—thank you, Hollywood—even though few people these days have any idea if the Templars were good, bad, holy, or evil."

"That's true," Jianjun said. "Can't say I know either, come to think of it. But there is something about this letter that makes it ring true. It could simply be a much cleverer letter than most because this Yakiv Koval isn't bothering to make outrageous claims and trying hard to persuade. He just says what's going on, that it may be dangerous, and he needs help." He ate a couple more chips before adding, "If you ask me, and you did, I say it would be good for you to get back to doing the kind of work you enjoy. And it'll be good for me to get out in the field, too, and make things work for you. After all, we're both failures in romance, so I guess a weird dig is better than sitting around feeling lonely."

"That's for damn sure," Michael said with a frown. He had thought Jianjun and his girlfriend, Kira, had worked things out, and was stunned to learn she'd walked out on him. The guy had been crushed. At least Michael knew he was to blame for Ceinwen leaving. "Maybe it is worth looking into. Therapy, right?"

"Could be. But there is one thing that bothers me," Jianjun added.

"The location." Michael stated it as a fact. He knew what Jianjun was thinking. He had the same thought.

"You got it." Jianjun's lips tightened, but Michael could see the worry on his face. "I know the distance from Ukraine to St. Petersburg is far, but they're in a common sphere of influence. And border wars are happening."

Michael nodded. "I had the same thought. On the other hand, a lot of interesting archeological sites are in eastern Europe and the Balkans. I can't shy away from them just because my father might be in St. Petersburg."

Jianjun didn't look happy even as he agreed.

"I'll contact the fellow who gave my name to people at this dig," Michael said. "I'd like you to find out all you can about this Yakiv Koval and if his dig team seems legitimate. If it all checks out, I might just pay Ukraine a visit."

<hr>

"You just missed a call from the United States, Dr. Gubenko," the secretary at Staraya Ladoga said as Oleg Gubenko walked by carrying a fresh cup of coffee. "A Dr. Michael Rempart."

She handed him a slip of paper with the phone number.

"Oh? He's a big deal. Are you sure it was him?" Gubenko said, studying the phone number as if it might offer a clue. "I wonder why he would be calling here."

"Whatever the reason, I had the impression he doesn't know any Russian," she said with a smile.

"I hope my English isn't as bad as I fear," he said with a shake of the head as he went into his office and shut the door. He was about to pick up the phone to return the call when he heard a tapping at the window, as if someone were throwing pebbles at it.

He turned to look. The tapping stopped.

"Oleg! Over here!"

The voice came from outside. What, he wondered, was going on?

"Oleg!"

He put down the message and went to the window. He was curious about the phone call, but first he had to find out what was going on in the museum's garden.

Everything about the building was old fashioned, but to Gubenko, it only added to its charm. He lifted the heavy window sash all the way up and then stuck his head out and looked around. "Hello?" he shouted. "Who's calling me? Is anyone out there?"

When he heard nothing, he decided it must have been a prankster. As he withdrew from the window, just as his head was under the window pane, the old wood that made up the sash split apart, and the glass, without any wood to hold it in place, dropped downward. Guillotine-like, it sliced through the man's neck, severing his spinal cord before it lodged in his thick neck muscles.

Nearly decapitated, Gubenko couldn't move, couldn't cry out, couldn't do anything but look at the faces of two dark-haired women dressed as if they were Russian nobility in tsarist times. They stood in the garden and smiled up at him as he died.

CHAPTER 19

Bethany counted the minutes. At 12:58 a.m., precisely, she snuck from her bedroom, a small blanket under her arm, and hurried to the oak tree closest to the barn. There, she spread out the blanket, shut her eyes, and waited for Merlin's greeting. Joy filled her when it came. Together, as they did every night, they concentrated on finding Michael Rempart.

That night, somehow, miraculously, she found him. Her mind connected with his memories of Rachel Gooding. At first, the memories were happy ones: Rachel's joy at being rescued, and later, of being in Japan. But as quickly as Bethany felt those feelings, she was suddenly overcome with sorrow. The sadness terrified her. She gasped, and nearly fainted from the strength and agony of those thoughts. They scared her. Was Rachel dead? What did Michael Rempart know about her sister?

At that, her mind shut down, and she found herself back in her own reality. She couldn't bring back Rempart, not even Merlin, and eventually returned to the house, to her bed, feeling like the worst kind of failure.

The next night, she again sat under the oak, but she was frightened, wondering if she dared to pursue this. Did she really want to know what had happened to Rachel?

She shut her eyes, remaining absolutely still until Merlin joined her.

"You did it!" he cried. "You found Michael."

"But then I lost him and couldn't get him back. I don't think I want to do this anymore."

"Nonsense. You've come too far to give up. Michael has a strong, sharp mind, and his thoughts of Rachel are indeed powerful. But you, we, can now be prepared for that onslaught. You'll find him again tonight, now that we have a good idea of how to do it. But you must go cautiously into Michael's mind—don't let him know you're there. Not yet, anyway. Perhaps in time, you will. Then the two of you will join, just as you and I do. And you'll learn not only who he is, but where he is."

Something about his words made her shudder. She was also surprised at the familiar way he referred to the famous archeologist. It was almost as if he knew the man personally. She wondered if there had been some connection between the two of them, but before she could ask, he immediately launched into advice on how she must approach the brain of a scientist as intelligent as Rempart.

He pointed out that if she got knocked out of Michael's head because it was too much for her "pea-sized brain" she would be useless to her sister, and since something was going on with her sister that made Michael sad, Bethany must find out what it was and try to help. His words were uncharacteristically harsh, but she ignored his insults and listened to his advice on how to carefully ease into Rempart's thoughts to search his mind.

It took another week of slow, methodical work before she was able to overcome her fears and connect with Rempart once more.

This time, strangely, she couldn't penetrate his thoughts on Rachel—or his thoughts on anything. But she was able to see what he was seeing. It was remote viewing in its most traditional sense. If, for instance, someone had asked her to draw a picture of the object in Rempart's hand at that moment—a small hand shovel—she could have done it easily.

The problem came in trying to figure out where he was. It was easy enough to determine that he was at an archeologist dig site. That was child's play, since she knew his profession. But where was the site? It had to have been on the other side of the world since it was midnight in Idaho but the archaeologist was in sunshine, just as Merlin was. And he was surrounded by foreigners. The language wasn't one she was familiar with.

Merlin asked her to write down the words she heard—as many as she could, and then repeat them to him. She did that. It took many tries before he got enough words that he was able to identify the language as a Ukrainian dialect commonly spoken in and around the Zakarpatska Oblast, commonly known as Transcarpathia in the West. Using that, Merlin did some investigating and learned of an archeological dig near that area in the mountains.

Eventually, working together when she happened to be viewing Michael as he arrived in a town, Merlin came up with the place he believed Rempart could be found—a town called Potchiv.

CHAPTER 20

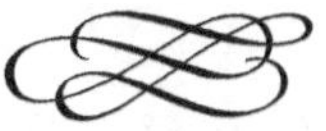

Spring crept slowly into the Carpathian mountains, as if cold winter refused to give up its grip over the barren land. It was May. Michael had been there for ten days and was slowly beginning to feel better about himself and his place in the world.

As Koval's letter had stated, the site would be the farthest east of any European chapel built by the Knights Templar. Aside from their time with the Crusades in the Holy Land, almost all the fortresses, chapels, and monasteries they had built were in Western Europe.

Transcarpathia was far to the east of that. Romania was to the south and going clockwise, there was Hungary, Slovakia, a tiny portion of Poland, and finally Ukraine.

The land had been fought over for centuries and a common joke was that its people in the twentieth century had been forced to learn six different national anthems as the land had been owned by

Hungary, Romania, the Soviet Union, Czecho-slovakia, and the independent Ukraine—plus the anthem for Transcarpathia itself.

Even as Michael's mind raced with thoughts of this strange land and the stranger dig he had joined, he was glad he had come. Dr. Yakiv Koval had checked out well, as had the University of Kyiv's sponsorship of this dig. The only disturbing circum-stance had been that the man who had given Michael's name to the dig team had been killed in some sort of accident.

Before coming here, he had verified the local belief that a chapel had been erected on the site by knights sent by the Pope to help fight the Mongol invaders. Over the centuries, between landslides, avalanches, and the natural settling of the earth, it was buried.

The story about the Templars made sense as Genghis Khan's warriors had swarmed the area in the mid-1200s A.D. killing, looting, and completely destroying towns along the way. Many people had fled into the mountains as the Golden Horde, as the invaders were called, approached. The King of Hungary had ruled Transcarpathia during that pe-riod, and many battles were fought between Mongol warriors and the Hungarian cavalry and infantry. The Hungarians lost most of the battles. Various groups of heavily armed knights, which perhaps included the Templars, joined the fight, but the Mongols continued to push westward into Europe and reached Vienna in 1241.

To build a fortress with tunnels in that part of the world at such a time made good sense.

Michael got into bed. He realized how much Koval wanted him there when he was given a private cottage, fully furnished. The others, including Koval, had small rooms at the local inn. It seemed the team must have paid someone to give up their home for a while. Michael hoped his assistance was worth the expense.

The cottage was rustic, but it had a separate bedroom, comfortable furniture, a wood stove for heat, and even a small kitchen area. The only problem was that, the day after Michael's arrival, the internet service at the inn had almost entirely stopped working.

Daily transmissions from the dig to the university had now become "every few days." When the service came on, out-box messages would be sent and those queued up awaiting receipt would come in.

So far, there was no big news. The team had found nothing to do with the Templars, but that could all change as soon as they reached the chapel. They were quite close. If they found any typical Templar signatures at that level, once the news broke it would get quite a bit of coverage in the archaeological community.

Speculation on what the Templars might have been doing there and what they might have hidden in the tunnels was a fun topic for the dig's archaeologists each evening, their imaginations fueled by beer, local white wines, and a local vodka-type drink called *horilka*.

Michael enjoyed those evenings filled with shop talk. He turned on to his side, hoping for the peacefulness of sleep that refused to come. He still had his demons, personal demons riddled with guilt and remorse about Ceinwen, not to mention the real ones that he kept trapped in the philosopher's stone that his father wanted to control.

His father ... at times while here, Michael had gotten a few almost crippling headaches, the type he used to get when his father's demons were trying to get into his head, to read his thoughts, and in that way learn the location of the red pearl. He had hoped his father had given up on that, but maybe not. All he could do was try to block the onslaught, but when his head hurt badly, he wasn't sure that he succeeded.

William Claude lay down with a hot compress over his forehead. He was certain his son, yet again, didn't have the red pearl with him, and almost never thought about it.

Michael successfully blocked his father from his thoughts, but William Claude wasn't one to give up. He always found a way to succeed, even if it meant using a foolish girl from Utah, or Idaho, or wherever in the world the silly child was from.

Whatever, she'd served her purpose.

It had been dumb luck that caused her to give her pathetic little letter to Patience that day in Cape Cod, explaining how she needed to speak to Michael about her lost sister in Japan. He guessed the girl couldn't accept that her sister was dead. Dead to her, in any case.

And she had told Michael exactly how to contact her.

That allowed William Claude to zero in on her. When he discovered her lurking around the dark web trying to find Michael, the gates opened up for him.

For her, they would become the Gates of Hell, but he'd have plenty of time for that later on.

He gained her trust by posing as a peer, a lovesick young would-be suitor, in fact. But that soon became boring, and he "introduced" her to himself as Merlin, a sorcerer. He would meld his mind with Bethany Gooding's and see what she saw, feel what she felt. And in that same way, he easily pushed her to do everything he wanted.

He couldn't force her, unfortunately. The girl still had free will—and quite a stubborn will, he found, as she constantly defied her parents, hid from them what she was doing, and even considered pursuing a ridiculous interest in Salmon's Deputy Sheriff.

Claude shuddered at the thought. He used the force of his will to make sure Bethany thought about Michael, and only Michael. That would be the best way to find out as much as possible about his son. The girl wanted adventure, so it would be easy to fill her with a burning desire to travel to Transcarpathia.

Under his influence she would pay no attention to how much it cost, the danger involved, or her parents' disapproval.

Maybe once Michael came face-to-face with Bethany and the two talked about Rachel, he would let down his guard enough that Claude could find a way to delve inside those thoughts about the location of the red pearl.

Or, maybe this was all just a waste of time.

As William Claude looked at his ever-aging body, time wasn't something he had much of.

CHAPTER 21

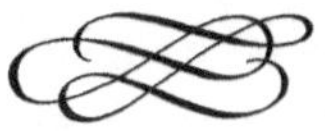

*S*t. Petersburg, 1918

As soon as Militsa's driver stopped on the driveway of Stana's house, Militsa got out of the back seat of her automobile and told her driver to wait. She hurried to the front door and pounded loudly using the large brass knocker. A crying maid opened the door and pointed the way to the parlor.

Militsa stopped at the doorway and looked with dismay at the pile of suitcases and boxes. Stana was kneeling on the floor filling yet another box. "What are you doing?" Militsa said as she approached. "You can't take any of that."

"What do you mean, I can't? I have to. I need it."

"We don't have room for it. I'm afraid we've waited too long already! We've got to run, and be able to move fast. Friends and family of the Tsar living near the Winter Palace and Alexander Palace are being arrested. And ... and we're hearing they *may kill Nicholas, Alexandra, and even their children."*

Stana stood and stared at her sister. "No, they wouldn't. Not even Lenin would do such a thing."

"Who knows what might happen to them in Siberia? If he does give such an order, it will be followed."

"I can't believe soldiers would kill their Tsar. And definitely not the children! Those lovely girls, and the Tsarevich is only thirteen years old. Why harm him? No. I can't believe any of them are in danger. Or that we are!" Stana began to cry.

Militsa grabbed her shoulders and tried to shake sense into her.

"If they catch us, Stana, we will be killed." Militsa's words were purposefully harsh. "I know where we may find some men who will help us get away, men devoted to the Tsar. We'll go by car as far as possible, but the Red Army is taking over all the roads. At some point we'll only be able to travel by horseback. If we wait too long, we won't even be allowed to leave the city. Thank God we're near Peterhof or we'd have been arrested like so many of the Romanovs. They'll be executed—all of them."

Just then, they heard a pounding on the front door. The sisters stared at each other, fear turning their faces ashen.

The maid didn't move to open it, wringing her hands, and watching Stana for guidance.

Militsa hurried to the window. Lifting the far edge of the heavy drapery covering it, she peered outside. Soldiers had pulled the driver from her car and were in the process of dragging him to a wagon.

"We've got to run," she said. "Come on, Stana, before they go to the back door."

"They might already be there." Stana stood frozen in place, all but petrified.

"If so, it's too late for us, because we can't stay here. They'll take over the house and search every corner of it. We've got to try."

Stana sucked in her breath and nodded, then faced her maid. "Stall them as much as you're able."

Then, holding hands, the princesses took nothing but the clothes on their backs as they ran through the house, stopping only to each grab a butcher knife as they crossed the kitchen.

They were about to reach the back gate of the property when they saw a soldier kick it open. Stana ducked behind a bushy spruce while Militsa hurried to the side of the fence and hid within the thick climbing hydrangea beside it. As the soldier walked through the open gate, Militsa stepped behind him and drew the knife across the front of his neck, severing his artery.

She watched with fascination as blood spurted from the opening.

Stana grabbed her arm and pulled her away. The two ran through the gate into a park situated between her estate and the next. No one else was near ... yet.

CHAPTER 22

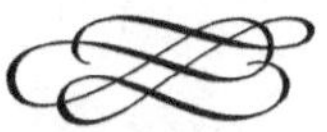

Late one night, Michael heard a knock on the door to his cottage.

It was the young archaeologist, Dmytro. The two had never spoken privately beyond a simple hello and mundane words about archeology.

"I'm sorry to bother you." Dmytro looked nervous. "But I need to talk to you about the dig site."

"Come in," Michael said. Dmytro took a seat on the sofa as Michael offered him a beer. "What's on your mind?"

Dmytro took a long drink of the beer before speaking. "The site troubles me. A lot."

Michael sat facing him. "I'm not surprised. It feels haunted."

Dmytro's eyes widened. "You feel it, too? Thank you. I was afraid you'd think I was crazy. I wonder if we shouldn't abandon it. I feel someone, or something, doesn't want us there."

Michael pondered his words. "I've heard about the volunteers becoming frightened and that there was something strange about the death of the student who had been here. What can you tell me about that?"

Dmytro shook his head. "It was kept quiet. I've heard rumors he was found naked and torn open, but the four team members who saw him won't talk of it. But I can tell you the story they gave to the police was made up." He gave Michael a summary of the "three-students-at-an-orgy-plus-wolf-attack" story.

"That hardly sounds plausible," Michael said. "The police bought it?"

"Or, they were ordered to drop their investigation," Dmytro said. "We'll never know."

"I suspect that's more likely," Michael said.

"But I know something more, something I've never told anyone else." At Michael's nod, Dmytro continued. "I happened to see Wasyl coming back to the inn early one morning on his bicycle. I watched and noticed he left again the next night. And then he was found dead. I kept quiet at the time, and although I thought about checking out the dig site, I was too scared.

"When we came back in the spring, I went up there at night, curious if I could see what might have drawn Wasyl there."

"And did you?"

Dmytro paused, then told Michael about his

night trips up to the dig site and how he would watch strange men chant. But then, every night, he would fall asleep, and when he'd wake up, the men would be gone.

Michael frowned as he heard this story. "That's quite odd. What do these men look like?"

"Like medieval monks, or Knights. Hooded robes, with black pentagrams on the chest."

"Do you think they could be men from town?" Michael asked.

Dmytro shook his head. "I'm sure they aren't. Especially since ... I hope it's not connected, but I used to be a fairly hefty guy. Now I'm losing weight fast. I don't know why."

Michael didn't like the sound of that. "Have you stopped eating?"

Dmytro sucked in his breath. "I eat as much as ever. Maybe more–because I'm hungry. A lot. And, it's hard to admit, but since going there I've had some ... sores ... on my body that refuse to heal."

Michael's concern grew tenfold at this news. He immediately had ideas about what Dmytro might be experiencing, but didn't want to say them. "Have you tried to simply stay away from the site? It sounds like something is attacking you there."

"Those men?" Dmytro paled.

Michael wanted to calm him. "Or a bug of some

kind, or a plant you're allergic to that's causing your skin to react."

Dmytro shook his head. "I'm not talking about a rash. I doubt it's anything so simple. And I've tried to stay away, but as midnight approaches, an over-whelming desire comes over me and it's like I can't stop myself. I get on that damned bicycle and go up there."

"It's got to be connected to the men you see." Michael shook his head. "Do you want me to stay with you, to stop you from going?"

"No. What I want is to find out what's going on, whatever it takes." Dmytro's face was firm, deter-mined. "Maybe we need to go up there together. Or I go, as usual, and you watch."

"That would be best," Michael said, "so their routine isn't interrupted. Something makes you fall asleep, and that's where we start. Tonight, before you go up there, wake me. I'll follow but stay back as far as I can. Do you want to ride up in my car?"

"I'll ride the bicycle as usual." Dmytro rubbed his forehead, then ran both hands through his hair. "I hate going back there, but it's become an obses-sion. And that scares me."

That night, Michael heard a tap on his door about midnight. He opened the door a crack to see Dmytro riding away from the cottage.

Michael waited ten minutes. He drove near the

site, hid his car off the road, and then walked to the camp. The moon shone brightly, and the sky was alive with stars.

When he reached it, he saw Dmytro's flashlight near the top of the trail leading to the dig site. Michael hurried up behind him, keeping an eye on the flashlight. As he reached the top, he saw that Dmytro had settled on the mountain beyond the dig.

And then the young professor turned off the light.

Michael couldn't see into the pit from his vantage point. The pit was too deep. He carefully skirted the site and climbed the mountain as Dmytro had done. There he dropped behind a tree trunk, keeping it between him and the dig, and waited.

About an hour later, a light from a fiery torch arose from the pit. Right behind the first was another, and then another.

The lights bounced slightly.

Michael leaned forward, and soon he could make out the figures before him: nine men in white robes, each carrying a torch. They marched in pairs except for the final one, who walked alone.

It was a march macabre as they walked around the edge of the pit and then split apart so that, rather than with partners, they now walked single file in a big circle. The one creature who had walked alone now moved to the center of the circle.

They began to chant.

The chanting was strangely beautiful, more like singing than actual chanting. He could understand why the soft, melodic but repetitive tune could lull Dmytro to sleep. Then the men began to dance. The one in the center slowly twirled with his arms spread out wide, while the four closest to him moved in a circle in a clockwise direction, and the four farthest moved counterclockwise. Their song sped up and so did their movements. At the same time something about it, the moving, the circles going in the opposite directions, all seemed to induce sleep or perhaps a trance.

Michael was forced to turn his back on the hypnotic dancers and to put his hands over his ears to drown out the chanting as best he could. He knew the danger of sleeping in the presence of demons. For that, he believed, was what they were, even though they might look like men. But men couldn't rise up out of the ground as these creatures had done.

After some thirty minutes, the chanting stopped, and Michael faced the demons again. Six of them left the circle and went to the area where Dmytro had gone. They emerged, three on each side, carrying him as if they were pallbearers.

He seemed to be in a trance, but he was able to stand on his own as they placed a hood over his head, removed his clothing, and then had him lie on the ground on his back. The demon who had stood in the center began to chant as he poured oils over Dmytro's torso from below his chest to his stomach, and over his private parts. Its hands were long and bony, its fingernails so long they looked like eagle's talons, yet they managed to stroke Dmytro gently, almost as a lover might, the sharp points of its talons gliding just above the surface of his skin.

Then, one by one, the lesser demons came closer to watch as the chief demon used a fingernail to slice open the skin beneath the rib cage. The skin looked raw, as if it had barely begun to heal from an earlier cut. The demon dipped its finger deep into the opening and as it withdrew, blood and bile gushed out.

The other demons were approaching a kind of frenzy. The leader who had cut Dmytro stepped back, and the others pounced, using their long tongues and mouth to lick up the fluids until the leader raised his arm and they stopped. The leader then took his fill and when done, poured more of the oil over the wound. The blood stopped flowing which, Michael knew, shouldn't have been possible.

He didn't want to imagine what these demons could do to Dmytro's body if they weren't being somehow restrained. He couldn't help but wonder if he wasn't witnessing a mild version of what had happened to the university student who died here last fall.

The chief demon then caused the others to step back as he used his clawlike fingernail to jab a hole into each of Dmytro's testes. He drew out semen which he licked before stepping aside. The eight creatures moved in and also sucked up drops of semen as if it were dessert. They then began to slowly twirl and spin, round and round until eventually, one by one, they fell to the ground with one another and proceeded to perform strange acts upon each other's bodies. The chief concentrated only on massaging and caressing Dmytro's now turgid member which seemed to be bringing the young professor pleasure.

Watching this made Michael's flesh crawl. He'd spent years dealing with demons, but these were different. They seemed to be a kind of vampire, but had aspects of a succubus—demons, usually in the guise of a female, who had sex with men to steal the strength found in their semen.

Michael wondered if these night singers were, in fact, vampires but they had become so weakened they not only needed blood--and the richest came directly from the liver--but also semen to build nourishment and manly strength.

It was possible that these vampires had been so starved when they found the young student months earlier that they tore him apart in their hunger. Only after that did they realize they needed to keep their host alive. In addition, it seemed they needed to fill his psyche with enough pleasure that he returned to them of his own accord as Dmytro was doing ... perhaps because they could not travel to him, or to anyone else.

But if so, who or what had awakened these night-singing vampires from wherever they had been? What caused them to once again walk the earth?

As Michael watched Dmytro, he realized the young man hadn't told him the whole story. Dmytro had to know his body had been perfumed, and should have seen the good-size cut just beneath his rib cage and the puncture holes on his scrotum. They weren't "strange sores" on his body, but very specific openings. Dmytro was in denial, which was typical of someone possessed.

Demons often lured their prey in this way, giving an extreme almost narcotic-like pleasure until the prey was trapped. At that point the pleasure vanished, and the prey was left with only pain. With that technique they managed to fill Hell with people. Even peaceful and placid Buddhists knew demons lured humans in that fashion. Buddhist

Hell was one of the most terrifying places Michael had ever heard described.

The chief vampire again oiled Dmytro's body, then allowed the others to kiss and fondle him as they dressed him and carried him back to the spot where his flashlight lay. That done, just before the sun began to lighten the eastern horizon, they proceeded back into the pit and vanished into the ground.

Michael sat on the ground, his back against a tree trunk. The night singers had seemed stronger, even somehow thicker and more substantial than they had before their sick ceremony. They had to be stopped.

Michael hurried down the trail to the campsite and waited. He didn't want to wake Dmytro in the state he was in. Better to let the wounds the vampires inflicted heal a bit before he woke him.

Although this type of demon was new to Michael, for the past few years, he'd learned there were more varieties of demons than he'd ever imagined. And that they could take over a good man's body completely, as they had that of his father.

From all he'd heard and remembered from his childhood, William Claude had never been a good man, and had treated Michael's mother, Jane, horribly. But the power-hungry demon that now lived in his father's body was even worse. At times he wondered if there was anything at all left of the intelligent man—genius, some would say—that his father had once been.

But there was no time to think about that now.

He needed a way to stop these strange night singers.

Just then, he saw Dmytro appear on the trail. He watched until Dmytro reached the camp.

Dmytro yawned. "Did anything happen?"

"How do you feel?" Michael asked.

"Sleepy. Why? Did you see something?"

"Any pain, anywhere at all?"

Dmytro looked strangely at him. "Pain? I do feel something sore inside, under my right rib, but it's been that way for a while now. I think I pulled a muscle. Other than that, I actually feel good. Quite good. Why? Did you see something I should know about?"

"Let's put the bike in the car's trunk," Michael said. "I'll drive you back to the inn. There, we'll talk."

After Ceinwen's mad dash from Wales, she found an inexpensive rooming house in Edinburgh. She had to find a way to get on with her life without

Michael or his demonic father. She couldn't put friends or family at risk.

But as time passed and the horror of what had happened to Rhys, who had managed to survive somehow, she realized living in hiding was no life. For all William Claude's talk about lusting after her, she knew it was nothing but talk, and he saw it as a way to get back at Michael.

He should realize by now that she and Michael were through, and that she had no knowledge of the red pearl or anything else about alchemy. And given all that, if he still wanted to come after her, she would be ready.

She took the train to London, and to her surprise and gratitude, she was able to get her old job back at the *UK Daily Mail*. Oh, what stories about the supernatural could she write now!

CHAPTER 23

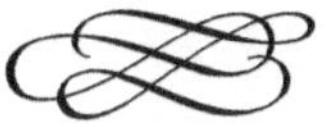

Jianjun had been given the information that helped him locate William Claude Rempart in St. Petersburg by a cousin, Edison Li, who worked at the Canadian embassy in Moscow.

In his own defense, how was he supposed to know the woman seated at the table having coffee with William Claude had been Michael's former fiancée? Or, almost fiancée. From what he'd been told, the engagement hadn't been formally announced, and no ring had been given, although Michael and Irina had "an understanding."

Of course he'd heard about the woman, but he'd never seen a picture of her. He figured she'd long ago found someone else to marry and was probably living the life of a soccer mom instead of sitting around in a café in Russia, of all places.

But still, he felt awful about it because Michael's disastrous trip to St. Petersburg had caused him and Ceinwen to split up.

Jianjun had told Edison all about the situation

and vowed to never again get mixed up in anyone's personal life ever again.

And that was why Jianjun couldn't hide his surprise when Edison phoned to say he had found Irina Petrescu.

"You're sure she's the same woman Michael has been searching for?" Jianjun asked.

"I have an acquaintance working at the Romanian consulate," Edison said. "He needed information from me, and so I asked him for information in return. What's weird is he found that Irina Petrescu is supposedly dead but when he looked under her parents' names, he found that a woman named Solina Motrescu had the same parents and same date of birth. In other words, somehow, her name has been changed but her original birth certificate was still on the records because they'd never gotten around to doing a system cleanup of old records. Pretty clever for my friend to find it."

"Very," Jianjun said, wishing he thought of that.

"Anyway, I felt bad about what happened to your friend but it looks like this time we hit what you Americans call 'pay dirt.'"

"Hey, I'm Canadian, but I get it. I hope they aren't all common Romanian names."

"I doubt it," Edison said. "But it's worth a try."

"Any idea what she's doing now?"

"That, I can't tell you. But I have an address,

and I'm only telling you because I promised I would help you since you helped me set up that identity on the Russian brides site. Just remember, the family doesn't know about it, okay?"

"I know, already!" Jianjun insisted. "And I appreciate the help. In fact, maybe I'll go to St. Petersburg myself to see what the situation is with Irina Petrescu. Who knows what I might find? It might be something that Michael is simply better off not knowing."

"You would do that?" Edison asked.

"Sure. Especially after what happened the last time I sent him there."

"Are you going there to help your boss or to get out of town?" Edison asked. "I heard from my folks that your parents are really steamed that you abandoned your Chinese wife. They said you'd fallen in love with some *gwei-lo*."

Jianjun gritted his teeth hearing the "foreign devil" term used about Kira Holt. "The American woman had nothing to do with it. The problem was that I never loved Linda. And she didn't love me either. We went along to get along. But that's not good enough!"

"Wow, bro, that's plenty brave. I don't think I'd have the balls. That's why I'd like to find some hot Russian woman before my folks go the arranged marriage route, but so far no luck."

"Have you gone out with any of them?" Jianjun asked.

"Sure, but nothing works out. It might have something to do with me being about 165 centimeters tall, and Russian women around here tend to be taller."

"You're 165 in your dreams. You're 160 in your mother's high heels!"

"Very funny," Edison groused. "So that's the thanks I get for the info I got for you."

"Thanks for the help, Tiny Tim. It's appreciated."

"Screw you, cousin."

"Ha! And good luck with your Russian brides."

Jianjun hung up the phone and stared at it. He hated that his cousin had brought up the 'foreign devil'—as his parents called Kira.

He rubbed his temples. He couldn't think about her now. It would do no good and only bring more heartache.

His mission was to get his boss out of his funk and into setting up his own archaeological digs, the fascinating, unbelievable, adventurous kind Michael was known for. The ones Jianjun coordinated from nothing and then became a part of. If Michael didn't go back to finding archeological sites to explore, Jianjun wasn't sure what he was going to do.

But at least Michael was at a dig now instead of alone, brooding in the Canadian Rockies.

Jianjun, too, often thought about the trouble he'd caused two people he cared about. He'd never forget the phone call he had received from Ceinwen right after Michael left her to go to St. Petersburg.

"I can understand if he went to Russia," Ceinwen said, *"met this Irina Petrescu, and it turned out they were still in love with each other—although, frankly, I'd find that pretty hard to believe. But instead, he told me to go back to Wales even before he left. It was as if he'd already made his choice. And it was Irina! I had thought I could compete with her, but I wonder if I was wrong."*

"No, Ceinwen, I'm sure that's not it," Jianjun said. *"He doesn't know what he might encounter in Russia and I believe him when he says he just wants to keep you safe."*

"And I'm sure I'm safe here. He's the one in danger. I don't trust his father or the photo that so conveniently had Irina in it!"

"Then stay at the Idaho house and wait for him to return," Jianjun said. *"I'm sure he'll be back once he gets some answers to questions he's had about his family's history. And I'm sorry this happened. I wish I'd never sent him the photo."*

Given all that, he'd often wondered what had

happened that caused Ceinwen to leave their home on the very day Michael returned to it.

He had tried many times to phone her, and for a long time he couldn't locate her anywhere at all.

But just two days ago he got an alert that she was in London and had taken a job at the *UK Daily Mail*. His heart sank. That made it sound as if she had made a choice—and it didn't include Michael.

It was time for him to do something about the mess he'd created.

His cousin could help speed up the process for him to get a Russian visa.

He picked up the phone to call Edison, then put it back down. Such thoughts were foolish. What could he do once he got to St. Petersburg? He knew no one. Didn't speak the language.

He should forget about going and pretend his cousin's call had never happened.

CHAPTER 24

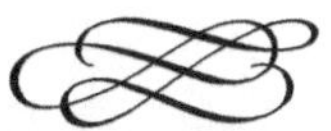

Michael sat out on the front porch of his cottage having a beer and watching the sun go down as his mind filled with Dmytro and the night singers. Somehow, he was going to need to convince Yakiv Koval of the danger. It wasn't going to be easy.

A tiny Ukrainian ZAZ automobile, a sort of marriage of a Fiat and the defunct Yugo, barreled up the road toward the inn.

The ancient ZAZ, once blue but now sun-baked and rusted into mottled shades of purple and teal, stopped where Olena and Andriy stood watching.

A young woman rolled down the window and talked to them.

To Michael's surprise, Olena pointed at his cottage. The young woman thanked her and after a short drive, parked in front of his walkway and got out of the car. Something about her seemed vaguely familiar.

He raked his fingers through his black hair, now past his ears in length, and watched her approach. "Can I help you?" he asked as she reached the bottom step of the porch.

"Only if you're Michael Rempart." She was of medium height, wearing jeans, a sweatshirt, and boots, and carried a large backpack. Her blonde hair was pulled back in a ponytail. She looked about sixteen and very American.

"I am. Who are you?"

"Bethany Gooding. Rachel's sister." She climbed the three steps to stand in front of him and boldly met his eyes. "I'm here so you can tell me where my sister is."

He stared at her, scarcely able to believe her words. He hated thinking about Rachel Gooding, especially since he had seen the corpses of Rachel and Seiji—a horrible, sad sight he would never forget. But he reminded himself he wasn't on this plane of existence when he saw their bodies so maybe, hopefully, somewhere under the sun—or some sun, some place—they were still alive and happy. But he wasn't about to say that to this girl. "I have no idea."

She stepped even closer, her jaw firm. He saw she wasn't as young as he first thought. "I don't believe you. My sister and her roommate went to Japan to look for you last year. Next thing I hear, you and the roommate are back, and no one has heard from Rachel since. That's not like her. I want to know the truth."

"I'm sorry. If you've come all the way out here to ask about Rachel, you've sadly wasted a lot of time and money." Michael stood, about to go into his cabin, but stopped and faced her again. "How did you find me here, anyway?"

"I have my ways," she said, then marched over to stand between him and his front door. "Look, Rempart, if I was able to track you all the way out here in the middle of nowhere, you know I won't take your idiotic response as an answer. And I'm not leaving here without answers." She leaned back against the door and folded her arms. "And now it seems Rachel's roommate has also disappeared."

He didn't like hearing those words and hoped it only meant this young woman couldn't find Ceinwen in Wales. He rested his hands on his hips. "And your point is?"

"Two women have had something to do with you and now they're both missing. You tell me."

His eyes narrowed. "That makes me sound dangerous."

She lifted her chin. "Look, I've come here to face you rather than going to the police with my suspicions. And I have only one question: where are Rachel and Ceinwen?"

He put his hand on the door jamb, causing his much taller, muscular build to loom over her in a way that should have been intimidating. "If you really think I'm some sort of serial killer, shouldn't you turn that little lawnmower you call a car around and leave?"

She stared at him defiantly. "I don't give a rat's ass what you are. I'm not going."

He straightened. "Rat's ass? No way you could be related to Rachel and use an expression like that." Michael noticed the girl's eyes softened at his words. She knew what he meant. Rachel Gooding was one of the kindest, sweetest people he'd ever met and also, she never let the slightest impropriety pass her lips. He had liked Rachel a lot, which was another reason he worried about what might have happened to her.

"Not funny, mister," Bethany announced.

"What's not funny is you coming all the way out here alone."

"I've got ways to protect myself."

"That's good, since these hills are full of bears and wolves. Cars like you've got are better known for breaking down than running. How did you end up with such a thing, anyway?"

She looked unsure about answering, but then said, "No one would rent a car to me for any sensible amount of money. It was cheaper to buy one."

He nodded. "And someone standing around the car rental place just happened to have one for sale?"

She frowned. "Maybe so. But so what? It got me here, and that's all I care about!"

"Beginner's luck," he muttered. "And it's probably hot."

"Forget about the damned car!" she yelled. "Where is Rachel?"

"If I were the serial killer you just accused me of being, would I tell you?" he bellowed back at her.

Her jaw tightened. "I don't think you're a killer, Michael Rempart. But I think you know a lot more than you're saying."

He realized she really was as stubborn as she claimed to be. "Let's go inside. It's turned chilly out here. I've got coffee if you want some."

She followed him, but grimaced as she looked around the small, rustic interior.

"You still haven't said how you found me," he pointed out. The more they spoke, the more aware he'd become of her resemblance to Rachel.

"And I won't."

He reheated the coffee he'd made earlier in the cottage's ancient percolator. She took a seat at the table, and he soon placed the cup in front of her. She put her hands on each side of it, as if needing its warmth against her fingers. Then she took a sip, and nearly gagged. "Oh, my God! If I ever wanted to make a fortune, I'd open a Starbucks franchise around here. This is not coffee!"

"I like it strong. Believe me, it does the job."

She frowned, then took another sip.

He sat across from her and after a moment, spoke. "Listen, I liked your sister a lot. She was—is—a fine, brilliant young lady."

Bethany nodded, but said nothing. He decided to tell her as much as he dared.

"What Ceinwen told your parents when we returned from Japan is the truth. Your sister, Rachel, met a young man there, Seiji Nakamura, and the two fell in love. He was from an old daimyo family, an important family, and things were difficult for him, and for them both. But despite all that, Rachel told me that she had never been as happy, or as much in love, as she was then. They wanted nothing so much as to be together and to have children. That's why the two of them, together—with no one else's input, believe me—decided the best way to live as they wanted was to go off somewhere and not let anyone else know where they'd gone, especially not anyone from Seiji's family."

"But two people can't just disappear," she insisted.

"Oh? People do it all the time. In fact, I thought I'd managed to hide my location pretty well until a few minutes ago."

Bethany folded her arms. "Rachel would never abandon her family. She loves us, and we love her. Everything I ever did was to make myself as good, as smart, and as brave as Rachel. She would never leave me like this without a word. How do you know she's safe?"

"I honestly don't know where she is. And I don't think she went away because she loved your family any less. I think it was because she found someone she loved even more. You have to realize that. Believe that wherever she is, she's where she chose to be, and with a man she came to love very much."

He opened a bottle of water for her and put it down beside her.

She took a long swallow. "So, where is Ceinwen?"

"I believe she's returned home to Wales."

"Why?"

"It's her home." His voice was flat. He didn't want to think about Ceinwen, about how he'd let her walk away without a word. And he definitely didn't see the need to tell Bethany anything more.

He went to the window and looked out at the bleak landscape. After he and Jianjun had watched Ceinwen's plane depart, they had returned to the house near Sandpoint. The house was spotless. She'd left no "Dear John" letter for him, but she had left her clothes, even her suitcase, and a few pur-chases she'd bought for the house. He hoped that meant she would return soon, but she didn't. In time, he realized the only clothes she had left be-hind were ones she had brought to Japan and then to Idaho, just a few things that she'd worn over and over and was probably sick to death of. He expected she had a huge wardrobe back in Wales. As for the home items, she had probably left them for him.

All he knew for certain was that the house felt empty without her—-as if she had never been there with him, had never loved him.

The only thing he found at all out of place was one coffee cup. It was one Ceinwen had never used, and he had never used. But for some reason, it was in front of her favorite cup in the cupboard.

He had stared at it. Why was it there? They never had company, but even if they had, and the company had used that cup, Ceinwen would have kept her own out and used it last before leaving the house.

His thoughts turned to William Claude...

But then he stopped himself. He was over-thinking this, jumping at straws. His father had wanted the red pearl, but he knew Michael would never have endangered Ceinwen by telling her where the pearl was hidden. Whenever he thought about Ceinwen, and he did every day, he always reached the same conclusion—that the best thing for her was to stay away from him. Only then could he be sure she was safe. With him, her life could be in danger.

Also, he believed she was safe now, simply because if she wasn't—if his father was using her to force Michael's cooperation—William Claude would have happily contacted him to tell him so.

Jianjun had been able to track Ceinwen to the airport at Cardiff where she had used a credit card to purchase a bunch of euros. But after that, she fell off the grid. It seemed she was as good as Michael at going underground.

And so he remained in the Sandpoint home for three weeks, then not only left the house but left the country. And the only one who knew his current whereabouts was Jianjun.

But Jianjun would never have told this young woman where he was without his okay. So, how had she found him?

Unless she wasn't at all who—or what—she claimed to be.

Michael went to the small refrigerator and took out some bread, sausage, and cheese. "Can I get you something to eat? A sandwich maybe? I've got some of the local goat cheese and sausage."

"I'm not hungry," she said, but took another sip of coffee.

He noticed how she eyed the food. He made her a sandwich despite her words. He placed it on a plate, cut it in half, and put it in front of her.

"Eat. It'll be quite a while before you come across a restaurant on your way back to whichever airport you used to get here."

She glared at him, at the sandwich, and then picked up a half and bit into it. A big bite, and then she took another, and in no time the sandwich was history. So much for her announcement that she wasn't hungry.

"I can make you an espresso if you'd like," he said.

"Yes, thanks."

He got up and put water in a small steel Italian espresso maker, placed coffee in the top container, then put it on the stove on high heat.

He turned around to ask if she wanted any sugar when he saw her head tilted back against the top wooden rail of the chair, her mouth open. She was sound asleep. It looked so uncomfortable he realized she must have been dead on her feet to fall asleep that way. Her resemblance to Rachel made him take pity on her.

"Bethany," he called.

She barely stirred.

He wasn't sure what to do but then, reminding himself she was Rachel's sister, he picked her up and laid her on his bed. She didn't even wake up as he did that. He took off her boots, covered her with a blanket, turned off the light, and shut the door as he took the espresso for himself and sat on the sofa with it.

He guessed she actually was who she said, and not a demon. He couldn't imagine a demon falling asleep in his presence.

CHAPTER 25

Kira Holt was getting ready for bed. Bedtime had become her favorite, as her back tended to give out after hours of sitting on an office chair listening to her patients talk about their lives and day-to-day difficulties.

In truth, she felt lucky to have been allowed to return to work as a psychiatrist after the FBI fired her from her profiling job. She didn't like having been let go, but at the same time, most of those profiling cases were the stuff of nightmares, and not the sort of thing she should be dealing with at this time in her life. She especially didn't want to take memories of crazed killers home with her.

She had joined an established team of doctors and her business picked up quickly. Also, she was heartened when a number of her former patients came back to her. At times, seeing them was a bit awkward. She had to learn to hold her tongue even more than she normally did as many of them launched into talking about their difficult lives as if she had last seen them only yesterday, rather than more than a year earlier. In more than a few cases she would have loved to say, "let me tell you about real problems." Instead, she did her best to listen with compassion.

Now, she eased herself onto the mattress, turned off the lamp on the bedside table, and shut her eyes.

Her cell phone rang.

She reached for it on the nightstand, then stared. The name on the display was one she had never expected to see again: Jianjun.

Her breath caught. Was it really him? She had told him not to call her, and he'd done just that for five long months. Why now? She shouldn't answer and she put the phone back on the nightstand.

It continued ringing. What if it wasn't him? What if something had happened to him, and someone else was calling to let her know? She struggled to sit up and then answered the call. "Hello."

Silence, and then, "It's good to hear your voice again."

She knew that soft, mellow, slightly accented voice, yet found herself not believing her ears. "Jianjun?"

"Yes."

She bit her bottom lip, unsure what to say or do. She probably should hang up, but she couldn't. She lay back on the pillow in the dark bedroom and let months of loneliness drop away. "You're most likely thinking that I still can't pronounce your name correctly, right?"

She heard his relieved, deep-throated chuckle. "No. I've always liked the way you say it. How are you?"

Her mind raced with a thousand things to say to him—and another thousand that she should never say. In a clipped voice, she asked, "Why are you calling?"

He had a quick intake of breath. "I need advice. Not ... not about me, or my life, or 'us.' I know there is no 'us.' So ... I hope you don't mind that I'm bothering you."

The disappointment she felt irritated her. Of course he wouldn't be calling about his life—or hers. She was surprised at how bitchy she sounded as she asked, "What is it about, then?"

"Kira ... I shouldn't have called. I'm sorry."

He was about to hang up! She half sat. "Wait! It's fine. Whatever your reason, I know it's important. Tell me."

The silence extended, and she understood how awkward he must be feeling. She hated the way she'd snapped at him and without thought added, "I've missed you." She wasn't sure why she said that, but was suddenly glad she had. She lay down again, fighting tears. "I won't deny it. And I've wondered about you and Michael, and how you're both doing. A person doesn't go through all that happened to us and not come away unscathed. Perhaps that got in the way, for just a moment. So," stronger now, she asked, "does this have to do with Michael?"

"I'm always surprised at what a good psychiatrist you are. You know what's in my head before I do." His voice, too, sounded choked. He paused, then his words came fast. "You're right. I'm struggling with a situation involving Michael, and then I realized I know someone who understands him as much or better than me. You. So I thought, hoped, maybe you'd be willing to help me. I know we're not going to meet again, and I know you don't want to see me—"

"Jianjun, stop." She was smiling now, despite the pain his words were causing her. Whenever he was nervous, he talked a mile a minute. Clearly, he was nervous. "What's Michael done now?"

"It's not him. It's the woman he was trying to find."

"Irina Petrescu?"

"Ah, you remember. Good. I expected you would. I have a cousin, well, you know I have many, many cousins, but this one tracked her down. She's in St. Petersburg. He's even found her address."

"She's in Florida?"

"St. Petersburg, Russia."

"Russia? What's she doing there?"

"That, he can't say."

"I see. And you're wondering if you should tell Michael?" Kira asked.

"You know me well. That's exactly it. The last time I got involved, he went to St. Petersburg to talk to her, but when he got there, he couldn't find her or his father. It turned out disastrously, and Ceinwen left him."

"Oh, no! I'm sorry to hear she left. I thought they belonged together," Kira said.

"So did I. It's all my fault. I gave Michael the information that caused them to split up. Now, I don't want to send him on another wild goose chase. I don't know what to do."

"Ah. I see. Taking the blame as usual, Jianjun."

"How could I not?"

"I can give you a number of reasons, but that isn't why you called." Kira pondered the situation. "Actually, if you find out Irina is married or in-volved with someone, maybe has kids, that could be exactly what Michael needs to learn to get over his obsession with the woman. I don't understand why he can't let the past go."

"All I know is, Irina is somehow connected with his childhood and who knows what else. I know he's dealing with more than a young man's infatuation gone bad. But he never told me the whole story. That's why I'm stuck."

"That makes it tough," she murmured. "I wish I knew what to tell you."

"I'm thinking," he added, "that maybe I should go to St. Petersburg and check the situation out for myself."

For most people, the thought of suddenly taking off for Russia would be a major decision, but she knew that Jianjun and Michael had traveled to so many places, a trip there would be practically business as usual. "If you go, would you tell Michael?"

"Maybe after I see what's what, I can decide what to say to him and how to say it."

"It sounds as if you've already made up your mind as to what you should do."

"Am I crazy to go there?" he asked.

"Probably. But it's understandable, too. Given all that's happened in the past, I agree it's probably the best option for you."

"Then I'll do it."

"Promise me"—she questioned the wisdom of what she was about to say but continued—"promise me that you'll let me know when you leave, when you arrive, and what you find out. I don't want you going somewhere that might involve demons and no one knows about it." God, had she really said that out loud? If anyone heard her, they'd want to take away her license to practice psychiatry. But since she had faced demons, she knew they existed, and the thought of her Jianjun out there alone ...

If her situation were different, she'd go with him. But as it was ...

"Promise me, Jianjun," she demanded.

"I will. I'm going to do it, Kira. I'll be leaving as soon as I possibly can."

"Oh?" she was surprised at that. "Your ... home situation allows you to just pick up and go?"

"Yes."

His reply was abrupt and flat. She didn't want to pursue it at all. "Okay. Don't forget to text me."

"Will do. Thank you, Kira. Take care of yourself."

"You, too."

With that, she said goodbye and ended the call.

Not until a few moments passed did she realize that she had thought of him as "her" Jianjun.

CHAPTER 26

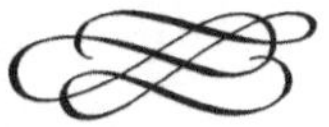

"Oh, my God, did I sleep here all night?" Bethany asked with a groan the next morning as she stumbled from the bedroom. Except for her boots, she was still fully dressed.

"You did," Michael grumbled from the sofa as he sat up. "And you snore. Loudly. The bathroom is right there." He pointed to a corner with a sheet over it.

She looked horrified. "No door?"

"I wasn't expecting I'd need one," he said.

She ducked behind the curtain while he got up and put on water for coffee.

"There's no shower," she said as she sat at the table.

He poured them both some coffee and brought her a cup. "You're lucky there's a tub. You can always wash up, sponge bath style, like in a hospital."

"Great." Her tone indicated it was anything but.

"How soon are you leaving?" he asked, still

standing. "I've got to get up to the dig site. We're close to discovering, we hope, an ancient chapel."

"A chapel?"

"It's complicated." He picked up his keys. "It takes a key to lock the front door, so I'd like you to be on your way before I leave here."

"I'm not leaving." She drank some coffee then put down the cup.

"What do you mean?"

"I'm staying until I find out what I need to know about Rachel."

"You're not staying with me."

"I'll get a room somewhere. Obviously the dig team has rooms. I'm sure I can have one as well."

"The dig team? What do you know about dig teams?"

"I know all about them. Rachel told me. And I've heard college students often volunteer. So, I'm in college and I volunteer."

"I don't believe Rachel was ever on a dig," he said, finishing his coffee.

"Whatever. She knew about them. That's good enough for me. And should be for you."

"I see," he said, his mouth firm. "Let's go to the inn, then. That's where the others are."

"I haven't finished my coffee yet!"

"You have thirty seconds, and then I'm locking

the front door. There are rules for volunteers, like being on time."

"You're such a grump." She drank down several gulps, poured the rest of the coffee down the drain, and grabbed her backpack.

Michael locked the door, and they walked around the corner to the inn. The rest of the team had already left for the dig. As the innkeeper talked about the rooms, Bethany looked more than a little upset by the prices.

"Maybe I can stay with you after all?" she said to Michael in a small voice. "I'll even take the couch."

He faced the innkeeper. "Put her in with Galyna and Olena. I'll cover the overage."

"Who are they?" she asked.

"Two of the team's students. They have room for four, but now there are only two of them. It's not a problem."

"Of course it's not for you! I'm supposed to room with two women I don't know?"

"You can always leave. Or pay your own way."

"I'll stay."

He left her and headed for his car. He somehow wasn't exactly shocked to find her running along behind him. "Can I ride up there with you? My car was making a funny noise on the way here yesterday."

"No," he said.

"All right. I'll drive on my own. I'm sure the car will be fine."

He watched as she got in and cranked it to start. He didn't like the clanging noise it was making. He waved a "come here" gesture at her.

She shut off her car and ran back to his.

"I figure it'll take more time to deal with you if you break down," he muttered. "Come on."

They were up at the campground in a few minutes. Yakiv Koval, his eyebrows high, walked over to greet them as soon as they arrived. "Well, well, I see a friend has come to visit you, Michael," he said with a grin as he eyed Bethany.

"Bethany Gooding," Michael said, "this is the head of the team, Professor Yakiv Koval."

"Good to meet you, Miss Gooding," he said, holding out his hand.

"Professor." They shook hands.

"She wants to volunteer," Michael said. "It looks like you could use some help."

"Certainly. Welcome, Miss Gooding. I'm sure anyone Dr. Rempart suggests we use as a volunteer must be excellent."

"Well --" Michael began.

"I'll try." Bethany said even as she became distracted by the sight of Galyna, Feder, and Dmytro.

"Very nice, Michael." Koval whispered as he ogled Bethany. "I've always heard you were quite the ladies' man. And so young, too."

"It's not what you're thinking, Yakiv," Michael said firmly. "She's the sister of a friend, that's all."

"I'm sure." He smirked. "And do you help pack her little lunch pail before she skips off to school?"

Before Michael could reply, Olena ran toward them shouting, "Come quick! We've broken through. We're at the opening to the chapel."

"Broken through?" Bethany turned back to Michael to find that he, along with everyone else who had been nearby, was running up a narrow trail to what appeared to be a plateau.

"Wait!" She scrambled after them. "Don't leave me here alone!"

***

"Apparently, they've just penetrated the roof of a chapel, one we believe was built by the Knights Templar," Dmytro said to Bethany as they stood at the edge of the pit. She'd noticed him standing alone and had asked for an explanation.

Michael was with Koval lowering lanterns into the opening.

"The Knights Templar?" Bethany repeated.

"Didn't they fight in the Crusades? That's far from here."

"That's why this find is important. We also expect to find tunnels beneath the chapel. Templars often built them. There's a mystique about the Templars, so if we found an important site that they built, we'll all be famous."

"I see," Bethany said, a bit dismayed to learn Dmytro sounded far more interested in making a name for himself than in unearthing history.

"What was the reason for the tunnels?" she asked.

"As a way to escape. The Templars were knights first, in other words, soldiers. They weren't priests. So even though what they built are usually called chapels, many were really fortresses."

"Interesting."

"I'm glad you think so," Dmytro said, and smiled at her.

Michael came over to them. "From what we can see, this find is incredible. The chapel is a good size and the walls and roof are so strong, although they're wood, they've scarcely decayed. It's beyond remarkable. Koval is going to get a few men up here tomorrow who know about construction to brace the area around the opening. We don't want anyone down there and then have the whole ceiling come down because too many of us are walking above it. For now, we'll do what we can without going into the chapel, and finish up early. We're going to have a busy day tomorrow."

CHAPTER 27

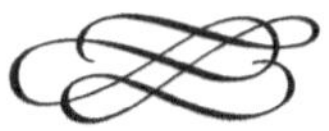

Five days after Jianjun's phone call to Kira, she saw his name on her phone's caller ID. She answered and learned he had managed to locate the elusive Irina Petrescu.

"Her situation doesn't look good, Kira. I've tracked down her address—she had moved from the place my cousin gave me. And I've actually seen her. I've watched her coming and going for a couple of days. It looks like she's with a man and has two kids, a boy and a girl."

"Really? Interesting. Do you think they're married?"

"Could be."

"I suspect she's done a lot of living since Michael last saw her," Kira said. "What was it, fifteen years ago?"

"Nearly seventeen now."

"Are you going to tell Michael?" Kira asked.

"I don't know what to do," Jianjun said. "Do I tell him I found her? How can I *not* give my friend the address of the woman he spent years looking for?"

She pondered his question. "Maybe it's not only your choice. I'm thinking you might talk to her, assess what's going on, and see how she feels about meeting Michael again."

"You're better at that kind of thing that I am," he said. "Can you come here and meet her? I'm staying at a nice place—where Michael usually stays. I mean, I'll get you your own room here, of course, and I'll cover your expenses and—"

"No, I can't." Her voice was firm.

"But—-"

"No. I'm sorry."

"Me, too," he murmured, and then louder said, "I'll talk to her and let you know what she says. Thank you, Kira. You sound good, by the way. It seems all must be going well for you. I'm glad."

"Yes. Everything's fine. Talk to you soon."

With that, she hung up, and felt more conflicted than ever before in her life.

Ceinwen couldn't stand it any longer. She was living in a one-room apartment in London, glad to have a job, but other than that, she felt lost.

After a couple of phone calls to the hospital to

find out that Rhys would survive, she never again inquired how he was doing. She prayed that whoever had attacked him—-which she was all but certain was the demon that was Claude—hadn't also visited others in her family. She once used a burner phone for a call home. Her mother said everyone was fine, but when she asked how Ceinwen was doing and where she was living, Ceinwen replied everything was good, but that she was going to a place with no cell service. Because of her years as a journalist traveling to remote parts of the world investigating other-worldly phenomena, which had become her specialty, her family was used to long stretches of silence. She quickly ended the call.

But now, her gaze went to the new burner phone she had just acquired, and she decided to do what she had vowed she wouldn't.

She phoned Michael.

The call wouldn't go through. She tried a text message, but it was not delivered.

She stared at the phone feeling helpless. Where was he?

One possibility was that he was at some remote dig site, working again. That would be the best thing for him, she told herself. He needed to work. One of the problems they'd had living together was that instead of acting as an archeologist, he stayed home and thought about all that had gone wrong, and that she was in danger as long as she was with him.

It was no way for him—or her—to live.

She called his cell phone time after time over the next two days, always with the same result.

Finally, she phoned Jianjun. If anybody knew what Michael was up to, it was him. But he, too, wasn't answering. At least she had been able to get through to his voicemail, which probably meant he wasn't with Michael. Still, he should know where Michael was.

She texted him.

Two hours later she phoned and texted again. And did the same two hours after that, and the next morning. Several times.

Jianjun didn't answer, and he always answered. And quickly. Something was definitely wrong.

She remembered that his girlfriend, Kira Holt, was a psychiatrist in Los Angeles. She found Kira's office, called it and left a message asking Kira to phone her back, that it was important.

Less than an hour later, Kira did so.

"Thank you for calling," Ceinwen said. "We met last year in Salmon, Idaho."

"Of course I remember you," Kira said. "How is everything?"

"Well, I'm calling because I'm worried. I've been trying to locate Michael and his phone doesn't seem to be working. Then I called Jianjun, but he didn't respond either. He's usually very prompt, and it makes me wonder if the two of them aren't together somewhere doing something dangerous. Do you have any idea?"

"Frankly," Kira said, "I'm getting a bit worried as well. Jianjun should have called me back by now but hasn't. I've tried his number and also received no response. That's not like him."

"Not at all," Ceinwen said, even more concerned.

"As for Michael, he's on a dig in Ukraine. In some mountainous area, probably with no cell service. He's hoping they've found a site that was once built by the Knights Templar."

"In Ukraine? Is that a joke?" Ceinwen asked.

"Hmm," Kira said. "If it was, it was completely lost on me. But Jianjun did sound serious when he told me about it. He said Michael was quite excited to go."

"I see," Ceinwen said, her shoulders suddenly sagging as if she had the weight of the world on them. "Well, I'm glad he's fine. I won't worry now. But I do hope you hear from Jianjun soon. Maybe he decided to meet Michael in Ukraine. Those two travel to some of the strangest places."

"Yes," Kira said, "they do. When he calls, I'll ask him to contact you. Or to somehow let Michael know you're trying to reach him. Those guys always seem to know how to reach each other, even if they leave everyone else in the dark."

"You're right," Ceinwen said with a small chuckle. "So, how are you doing, Kira?"

There was a long pause. "I'm ... fine. Everything is fine. You?"

"I'm back in the UK. Michael and I have sort of called a halt to things."

"I'm sorry to hear it. But if you're trying to reach him, to talk, I think that's a good thing. He's a difficult man. He holds way too much inside, but his heart is true."

"Yes," Ceinwen whispered, "so I've always thought."

But as she said goodbye, she couldn't help but reflect that maybe she'd always thought wrong.

CHAPTER 28

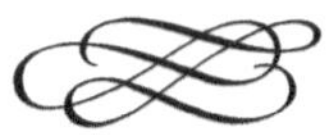

S t. Petersburg, 1919

Militsa and Stana ran through the park behind Stana's home. She remembered the nearby house of an old woman that had an outside door to a cellar that often swung open and shut, as if it no longer had a latch. She guessed the old woman either didn't hear it banging or simply didn't care.

They reached it and pulled the door shut behind them. The cellar was dank, but in it they found pickled foods —cucumbers, apples, eggplant, and cabbage.

They remained hiding in the cellar throughout the day and most of the night. When morning came, the two ate some of the apples and eggplant, and then left.

They walked the three miles to the home of Duke Yussupov who was arranging a way out of St. Petersburg for his family. Militsa explained what had happened at Stana's home the day before. She had sewn many of her jewels into the hem and bodice of the dress she wore, knowing that jewelry, more than rubles, would be useful on their trip and now offered the Duke an emerald ring to allow her and her sister to join his family in their escape.

Petrified to hear that the Red Army was looking for the sisters, the Duke refused to have anything to do with them. He gathered his family, leaving everything but their jewels behind, and fled. The most the Duke would do for the "Black Princesses" was to provide them with an escort to a place where a group of the Tsar's former soldiers were making plans to escape the city.

There, Militsa convinced a young sergeant named Ivan Demidov to allow her and her sister to join the group he planned to lead. In return, she would pay for their provisions as needed. She convinced him that if he would head south, they could make their way over the Carpathian mountains and once there, they would head to Montenegro where the sisters would see that the soldiers were richly rewarded.

Just looking at the jewels on the stately woman before him, the sergeant agreed.

The days quickly turned into a sameness of riding, walking, having too little clothing to keep warm, too little food, and sleeping on hard ground. The soldiers had quickly abandoned vehicles and carriages since too many Bolshevik sympathizers watched the roads. The small procession was forced to travel on horseback into the hills, using back roads and trails. The princesses knew how to ride, but neither had done it for hours on end and ached from head to toe.

Militsa's first action when life settled down to an endless monotony, was to use her occult powers to attack Duke Yussupov and his family for refusing to help her and Stana. She had no idea if her spell would work, but she was so filled with hate for the Duke, she knew if emotion played any role whatso-ever in the occult, the Duke would suffer greatly.

She did manage to help the small band several times by using jewels to buy food and drink for them as well as feed for the horses. She also managed to put a scare into them by having Stana warn the sol-diers of her sister's powers, telling them about her doctorate with the Paris Hermetic Sciences Acad-emy. Few knew what "Hermetic Sciences" were, or even alchemy, but the name alone brought fear to their hearts, and when Stana explained it had to do with the occult, their fright deepened. They weren't sure how much they should believe Stana's words until they witnessed Militsa casting a spell on Yus-supov. A week later, as they passed near a town, two of the soldiers dressed as farmers and went into town to buy bread and learned that a number of aristocrats trying to leave St. Petersburg had been captured and imprisoned. Duke Yussupov was among them.

As time passed, several of the soldiers ran off as the group trekked near their homes, a couple of others tumbled down steep embankments and didn't survive, another drowned, and several simply gave up and refused to go further.

They were down to only nine when they reached the Carpathian mountains, the most difficult part of the journey. Their bodies had grown weak even as their tempers grew increasingly frayed. One evening, as they finished the last of their vodka to calm the men and encourage them to continue on, Militsa and Stana introduced them to the Khlysty ceremony. As the soldiers drank, the two women sang, danced, and then slowly, erotically, began to twirl, soon getting the men to join them as they spun. They soon fell into an orgy.

For the next few weeks, they continued on as food ran out, the horses died, and the men grew too weak even for the Khlysty activities.

"We can't make it," Ivan said. He lay with Militsa on a blanket, his arms around her for warmth and human comfort in the face of death rather than for any sexual reason. "I'm afraid we've failed you."

Militsa stroked the young man's handsome face. "If we can just get over these mountains. We're so close. When we reach Montenegro, we'll see the beautiful blue waters of the Adriatic Sea, and feel the warm sun on our faces. You'll love it there."

"It's a nice thought, but impossible. It's simply too far, and I'm too weak. We all are."

"We've got to keep going," Militsa said. "But we also must stay in the mountains as long as possible. I suspect the Red Army is in the valleys. The Carpathians will save us."

He shook his head. "We have a long way to go."

"We've got to try. Trust me."

He agreed. The group somehow kept going, mostly eating squirrel and fish. Then, each night instead of sleeping, Militsa would sit up praying for help to survive. Years earlier, when she was a student of the occult, she had been taught that there were many planes of existence, and on the plane where she, Stana, and the soldiers were, a number of portals —doorways—to those other planes existed.

She learned that one such portal was in those very mountains, and she prayed for guidance to lead her to it.

But before she found it, she became too weak to go on without Stana's help. She knew that Stana, too, wouldn't last much longer. They had no choice but to act.

In the locket she always wore was poison given to her by Rasputin. He had feared assassination, and said that once he was gone, she and Stana needed to leave the country because all of Russia would turn against them, and their treatment and execution *would be too horrible to imagine. But if they were captured, the poison would be a blessing. She knew he had been right.*

"It's time, Stana," Militsa whispered. "We will take the pills our hero gave us, and with my last breath I will use every scintilla of the alchemical powers I have been taught to assure that the portal to the other plane be opened to greet us. Once there, we will be with him again and we will be able to live to take vengeance on all who have driven us to this terrible end."

"But what if it doesn't work?" Stana asked.

"We won't know, will we? At least our misery will be over. But if it does work, Stana, think of it! Think of the power! We'll come back here first and save these good men—many of whom I've grown fond of. We'll turn them as immortal as we shall be. They'll be under our power whenever we need them, and willing to do whatever we want."

"I don't want it to end like this," Stana whispered. "Not here in this dreadful place."

"We can never know the hour when our appointment with death will come." Militsa put her arms around her and tried to help Stana be strong. "But we must always be ready. And we are. If this works, we'll go back to St. Petersburg, and all will rue the day they turned on us, rich and poor alike. But first, we must send all our hopes, all our prayers,

to the one we love above all others, even more than God himself. Someday, Stana, I pledge to you that we will meet again."

She kissed her sister's cheek, then they each took one of Rasputin's pills, and lay down with his name on their lips, and his visage filling their minds.

CHAPTER 29

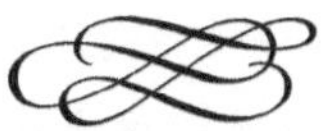

The day after the workers from town built walkways over the opening to the chapel to make it safe from collapse, Yakiv Koval was the first to go down into the opening.

Koval soon called Michael to join him. Michael could see the look of disgust on Veronika's face. The woman clearly didn't like him being there. But he went down the rope ladder they had decided to use.

Michael found himself and Koval in the center of a large circular chamber, typical of those the Knights Templar had built. It was much larger than either of them had expected, with a diameter of about twenty feet.

"I wonder what this room was used for," Koval said. "Chapel? Fortress? Something else?"

Michael took a rag from his pocket. Sometimes the simplest approach was the best. He began to carefully rub a spot on the smooth wall. With the dirt and grime that had caked on the wall for centuries gone, a brilliant blue color appeared. He kept going and Koval joined him. The blue had gold stars in it.

"It is a chapel," Koval said, all but breathless at the magnitude of the discovery.

"We don't know the origin yet," Michael cautioned. "But you've definitely found something of interest here. Congratulations, Yakiv!"

Veronika and Dmytro soon joined them.

Over the next few days, as the dig team worked to carefully clean the walls and ceiling, the four archaeologists learned that the chapel had been built of quite thick pieces of wood in a Gothic style. Slit holes had been placed in the interior walls as if for arrows, a sign that whoever built it had a fortress, rather than a place of worship, in mind.

Most of the team was ecstatic about all they had found, but one night, as Dmytro walked with Michael to his car to go back to the town, he softly said, "That opening means they can get out much easier now."

Michael didn't have to ask who "they" were. He noticed that Dmytro continued to look pale and thin, even though the young professor had claimed that he had given the bicycle to a boy in town and no longer went to the dig site at night.

But, Michael thought, the dig wasn't that long of a walk from the inn.

Three nights later, Michael stayed at the dig's campsite with the other professors to discuss their findings as Bethany and the students returned to the hotel. Before long, Koval got out the *horilka* and the short discussion became a long one filled with anxiety and hope. Finally, when Koval's bottle was empty, they returned to town.

The hour was late when Michael entered his cottage to find Bethany lying on the sofa reading a book. "What are you doing here?" he asked.

"Reading. Enjoying the peace and quiet."

He tipped the book so he could see the cover. "Religious Russian folk tales?"

"It's the only book at the inn that's in English."

He shook his head. "You must be desperate."

She sat up. "I am. Galyna and Olena hate me. They speak Ukrainian, look at me and laugh. I hate them back, so I came here to be alone since you and the other professors don't want me around either."

"I've noticed that Dmytro doesn't seem too bothered by your presence," Michael said.

"I think he's nice. Nothing more."

"Maybe you should have gone to *his* room to wait. Time for you to go back to the inn. Goodnight."

"I'd just like someone to talk to." She put down

the book but remained on the sofa. "I tried talking to Andriy but I guess he's shy or not into women because he all but runs away when I say hello. And Feder thinks talking to me will make Galyna jealous."

"I'm way too tired and drank too much to hear about the love lives of students. You can go back to Idaho, you know."

"And do what? I don't know what to do with myself, Michael. I always thought I wanted to be like Rachel, especially as she went off to see the world. But now, talking to you, I'm not sure what to do. And I know that going back to Idaho isn't going to help."

He looked at her for a while and everything she said made sense to him. He wished he could help, but he couldn't. Finally, he nodded in acknowledgment of her words and then said simply, "You can stay and read if you want, but I'm going to bed."

"Okay, thanks, but just remember that I'm here for you when you'd like to talk about your troubles with *your* love life," she said as she picked up the book once more.

"What was that?" He stopped in his tracks to look back at her.

"I can tell there's something going on that's bothering you a lot. So, when you're ready to talk, just let me know."

He frowned. Was he that obvious? Just then, his phone chimed. They were both shocked at the sound.

"We have cell service now?" Bethany asked.

"It comes and goes. Mostly goes." Michael took the phone from his pocket and was surprised to see Kira Holt's name on the screen.

"Does the call have to do with your love life?" Bethany asked as she took in his expression.

"She's just a friend." He answered as he continued into the bedroom and shut the door.

The connection crackled and cut in and out but he understood her quick hello and question. "Have you heard from Jianjun in the last few days?"

"No," Michael said. "Why? What's wrong?"

"I was hoping you could tell me," she said. "I can't reach him."

"I've been at a dig in Ukraine and we're fairly cut off. The service out here is spotty, although it's best at night, like now." He had to shout over the static. "I thought he was still in Vancouver."

"He's not," she cried.

"What's going on Kira? If Jianjun is in trouble, I need to know."

He waited as the connection again cut out, but then it settled a bit and she quickly explained. "Jianjun got a lead on finding Irina Petrescu in St.

Petersburg. He was worried that it would prove no good and decided to check it out himself."

"What? That's crazy."

"I agree, but you know Jianjun. He felt bad about what happened between you and Ceinwen, and he didn't want to cause you any more trouble."

"He had nothing to do with it," Michael said. "I tried to tell him that. But I know him. If he can take the blame for something, he'll do it."

"I know. And feel guilty, even when he shouldn't."

"*Michael?*" He heard Bethany calling, then a knock on his door before she opened it. "What's going on? You sound like something's wrong."

"Who's that?" Kira asked.

"It's okay. Everything is fine here," he said to Bethany.

"You're sure?" she asked again.

He nodded, and she went back out, shutting the door.

"Kira?" he asked.

There was a pause. Her voice accusing, she said, "I take it that isn't Ceinwen."

"It's Rachel Gooding's sister. She's here hoping to find out more about Rachel."

"Oh, my. I take it you don't want to tell her."

He had never told Jianjun everything that had happened with Rachel, only that it was something that couldn't ever easily be explained. That meant Kira never learned the whole story. "No, I don't."

"What little I heard sounded very strange," Kira said.

"It was. But Jianjun is the one we need to find now. When did you last hear from him?"

"Four days ago. He was in St. Petersburg and phoned to say he'd found Irina, planned to talk to her, and then would call me right back."

"He found her?" Michael was astonished.

"Apparently. But he did say he believed she'd changed a lot since you knew her. He sounded troubled, actually."

"What did he mean that she'd changed?"

"I ... I'm not sure."

The connection suddenly dropped and nearly five tortured minutes passed before he could reach her again.

Michael spoke, "You said it's been four days since you heard from him?"

"Yes. I kept telling myself not to worry, that he must be having a hard time reaching her, must be otherwise busy, and so on. Maybe he was helping her. Maybe convincing her to come to the US to get away from whatever might be troubling her in Russia. Each day, I kept assuring myself he'd phone, that he didn't realize how much I'd worry. But it didn't happen."

"Did he give you any information as to where in St. Petersburg he found her?"

"Not really." Again, he heard the hesitation in her voice and wondered what it was she wasn't telling him.

"He said she's an artist, but I guess isn't doing too well."

"I see," Michael murmured, trying to absorb all this information. "Do you know where Jianjun was staying?"

"He said it's the place you usually stay. He keeps records of such things, you know."

"Ah! I know where that should be."

"Michael, if you're going to go there looking for him, would it help if I came, too?"

"It's not necessary."

"I know that. But I'm so worried."

"It will take time to get a visa. And also my father may still be in St. Petersburg. He may have something—a lot actually—to do with Irina's sudden appearance and possibly with Jianjun missing. I think he's doing all he can to draw me out, along with the red pearl that he wants me to give him."

"But—"

"It's best if you stay where you are. I'll get back to you as soon as I know anything."

"Michael, wait. There's one last thing you need to know. Ceinwen called me. She was trying to reach you by phone but couldn't get through. She'd like to talk to you. I think you should call her. I have her new cell number."

Michael was surprised. "Thanks, Kira. But it's best if I don't try to reach her at all."

———

Michael couldn't sleep that night.

His mind churned with thoughts of Jianjun and Irina and what might have happened to them. And Ceinwen. He missed her and guessed he always would. But she was better off without him.

And always, along with all the worry came the idea that after nearly seventeen years he was close to seeing Irina once more, the real Irina, not some ghostly figure who walked through walls whenever he got too close.

Kira had told him that she had changed, but who knew if Jianjun was telling the truth? For all Michael knew, Jianjun was saying crazy things because he wanted to be sure Kira wouldn't be jealous of him being in St. Petersburg with one of the most beautiful women in the world.

After ending the call with Kira he got in his car and drove to the closest spot with decent cell-service. There, he tried reaching Jianjun by phone, thinking that Jianjun might have decided it was best if he didn't talk to Kira again. He knew how badly Jianjun had suffered when Kira told him she no longer wanted to see him. At the same time, he hoped that Kira's call meant that whatever caused their split had been resolved. But it wasn't his business to ask.

Jianjun didn't answer Michael's call either.

He next tried to find Irina's mother, Magda Petrescu. He had located her a couple of years ago in the US, but shortly after he made contact, she no longer answered her phone or emails from him. He could only hope she was all right. He hated to think that anything might have happened to the woman who had practically raised him after his mother's death. He worried, too, that her absence had to do with him trying to find Irina.

As always, Magda didn't answer.

Desperate, since it was still daytime in the US, he phoned Jianjun's ex-wife, Linda.

"This is Michael Rempart," he said.

"Oh?" She didn't sound happy.

"I'm trying to locate Jianjun—"

"You have your nerve phoning me after all you did!"

"Me? What do you mean? I haven't done—"

"You ruined my life! Don't call me again." Her fast rat-a-tat yelling was like machine-gun fire.

"Wait! Please," Michael said. "No one's heard from Jianjun for days."

"So? You think I have? No way! And guess what?" she shrieked. "I don't care where he is. I don't want to know where he is. And I certainly don't want to hear from you!"

The phone line went dead.

No wonder Jianjun was always trying to find an excuse, any excuse, to leave home.

Michael knew Jianjun had cousins all over the world, but he'd never been given any names or ways to contact any of them. It was ironic, but whenever he wanted to track anyone down, he always asked Jianjun to do it. He was one of the best hackers ever. But what was a person to do when the hacker was the one missing? Michael didn't have a clue.

The only other name and phone number he had was that of Jianjun's father, Li Wong. "I'd like to speak to Mr. Li Wong," Michael said when a woman answered. "One minute." She put down the phone and yelled in Chinese.

A short while later, a man picked up. "This is Li Wong."

"Hello. My name is Michael Rempart. I'm a friend of Jianjun."

"I know who you are." Li spoke slowly, but his words were clipped. He sounded almost as angry as Jianjun's wife.

"I'm trying to track down Jianjun. I haven't heard from him for a few weeks and now, I'm not sure where he is. Do you know?"

"I am no longer speaking to him."

"Oh?"

"He is doing something very wrong. He is getting a divorce. He has a good wife, a fine Chinese wife. But, I'm sorry to say, because of your influence and others, he is no longer satisfied with her. He told her he wants a divorce. It is not good. I do not approve, and told him so."

"I'm sorry."

"I doubt that," Li said, his voice firm. "So, I have no idea where Jianjun is. Perhaps you should contact the woman that caused him to leave his faithful wife. That's all I can tell you."

Michael was taken aback, but murmured, "I understand. I'm sorry your family is troubled in this way."

"Goodbye, Dr. Rempart." With that, for the second time in a matter of minutes, Michael found his call disconnected.

He booked the first available flight the next day from Kyiv to St. Petersburg.

He returned to the cottage to pack whatever was important and to tell Bethany he'd return as soon as he could. He then spent the night driving to the airport.

CHAPTER 30

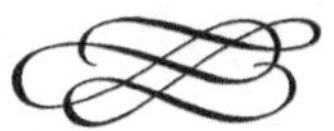

*L*eningrad, 1930

It wasn't supposed to be this way, Militsa
thought. After ingesting Rasputin's poison, she and
Stana awoke to the joyous discovery that they were
no longer trapped in their aging bodies from Tsarist
times, but could live in the bodies of others. They
soon found two youthful and attractive Russian
women. They could eat, drink, love, dance—enjoy all
the best life offered ... which admittedly wasn't much
in Bolshevik Russia. But then one day, those women
found a means to leave Russia and travel to England. Militsa refused to go, and in her outrage, poisoned them both.

Yet, a part of her could understand the women's
wish to leave. All the beauty and elegance that was
once St. Petersburg had been destroyed in the name
of the workers' paradise. The workers were going to
Paradise, all right, but it wasn't one on this earth,
and they were going much sooner than they should

have. Millions had already died in the revolution and its aftermath.

Militsa had known of the attempted assassination of Lenin back in 1918, but she never imagined his revenge. He moved the capital to Moscow and began the Red Terror as the Bolsheviks crushed all dissent against his rule. Thousands were killed, far more imprisoned. And the name, St. Petersburg, was changed to Leningrad.

Militsa watched as a Georgian revolutionary, whose long, tongue-twisting name was shortened to Josef Stalin, gained prominence in the party, and took control of the country. With his Five-Year Plans for agricultural collectivism and rapid industrialization, terrible disruptions in the food production began. Many peasants moved to the cities where there was not enough housing for them.

The two sisters could see that grain shortages and starvation would only get worse as Stalin's plans were pushed harder.

Government programs like the G(lavnoe) U(pravlenie) Lag(erei)—the Gulag—began with about 84 camps, but became forced labor camps that numbered in the hundreds with anywhere from 2000 to 10,000 people in each working under brutal and deadly conditions.

The sisters decided it was time to return to the Carpathian mountains and find their soldiers.

Anything had to be better than living in Leningrad. Militsa could hardly bear to hear that name.

Since Militsa had killed her prior hosts, it was necessary to find new ones. Eventually they found two dewy-eyed revolutionaries from Germany, who hoped to bring a Leninist change to the German government. The women's single session with a Ouija board gave Militsa and Stana access to them both. After easily taking over their bodies, the sisters used their travel documents to head south.

In the Ukraine they found a male guide to take them into the Carpathians, to a place they told him held their parents' graves. He seemed suspicious of their story, but they were paying him well enough that he gladly took them.

Everything looked different in summer, but Militsa had a good sense of the area, and eventually found the spot where she and Stana had died. She was touched to see that the soldiers had put up little grave markers for them, Orthodox crosses with two horizontal bars, one short, one long.

Stana actually shed a tear upon seeing them.

And a respectful distance away, they found eight more crosses upright, and the ninth cross lying on the ground. All but the last man, who had no one to bury him or pray for him, had been interred there. Militsa stood his cross in the ground and hoped that, who-

ever he was, she could wake him as well as others from the dead.

That night, Militsa offered the guide her special homemade liqueur. It rendered him catatonic.

Militsa set out the potions she had worked on perfecting over the years and, with her book of spells, began to work at raising the dead.

Time after time, her spell didn't work, and she was forced to start again.

Her potion supply was down to almost nothing. Frustrated and weary, tears filled her eyes. As a tear fell on the potion, it began to froth and bubble, something it hadn't done earlier. She once more repeated the spell and then fell over as if in a trance.

Stana tried to wake her, but couldn't. She panicked, unsure what to do, where to go. She sat on the ground, holding her sister's hands, and cried.

"Who are you?" a male voice said.

She looked up to see faint, almost transparent men ... ghosts ... standing near and looking at her. She was too frightened to move.

"What has happened to us?" The one who stood in front of the others asked.

"Militsa, wake up, please," Stana cried. "We've got to get away."

"Militsa?" the ghost repeated, sounding confused.

Stana stood and backed away, ready to run off

alone if necessary. But then Militsa opened her eyes. "What happened?" she whispered.

Stana was too afraid to do anything but point. Militsa turned her head and her expression went from fear to exhilaration. She forced herself to sit up as her gaze jumped from one man to the other—all nine--and finally back to the spokesman.

"Can it be?" Militsa said. "Ivan? Is it really you?"

"Princess." The way Ivan sounded the title was almost a sigh, a grateful sigh as his eyes scanned the sky, the sunlight, the greenery around them. "I can't believe this. You said you'd come back for us."

"I did," she said with a smile.

"But you look..."

"Yes, we do look different, but it's us," Militsa said as she held out her hand toward Stana, who took it and helped her stand. And then, side-by-side, the two faced the soldiers. "I do hope you approve of the new us. And I see that all nine of you are here."

"We are, but are we ghosts?" Ivan asked as he and his men looked at their ethereal forms.

"You're the undead," she said. "You'll need nourishment to gain substance, and I brought you that as well." She pointed to a tree where the guide sat staring blankly straight ahead.

Ivan looked at her as if she was mad. "What do you mean? He's human, we can't..."

She smiled. "You've always been such a kind man. If you're careful, you won't need to kill him. Just drink a little from his neck. Or, better yet, from his liver. That's the most nutritious blood, from what I've learned. I've had many, many years to do nothing but study the wonders of this world. It's both more incredible and also more horrible than anything we could have conceived of a mere twelve years ago."

"Twelve years?" Ivan looked at her as if she were lying.

She looked at the other soldiers. "Dine, friends. Our guide won't care. He'll be happy to help you. In fact, Stana and I have developed a taste for blood as well, although we don't require it the way you do. We came up with a regenerating balm—a perfumed oil—which will help his skin quickly heal and be ready for the next feeding."

She had the soldiers move the guide onto his back. She then opened his shirt and showed them where the liver was located. After applying the oil to his skin, she made a slice, only about an inch long, but deep. She dipped her finger into the wound and when she pulled it away, it was covered with blood. She licked her finger and stepped away from the guide.

She didn't need to go further. Instinctively, her vampires, including Ivan, knew what to do.

Her only job was to see they didn't kill their host. Now yet, anyway.

And, since she and Stana had nice young bodies this time, she found herself aroused at the sight of so many strong men. She had read of a means to induce a rapid sexual desire. Once the soldiers had their fill of blood, she would show them the completely masculine "liquid" they next needed to ingest. Once her soldiers had substance to them, she was sure the Khlysty ceremony would bring them joy in being resurrected and under her command once more.

Also, during her last few years in St. Petersburg, or she should say Leningrad, she had looked for information about a portal to other planes of existence hidden somewhere in the Carpathians. She had learned of a spot not too far from where they currently were, with religious sites and tunnels that sounded very much like it could be a portal. She and Stana would lead the nine soldiers there when they were strong enough.

Once there, the men could exist by safely dining on the blood of animals ... along with an occasional human who might be foolish enough to wander far from existing trails.

CHAPTER 31

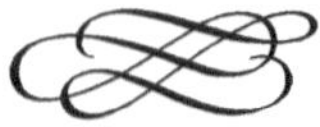

Michael got off the plane from Kyiv at Pulkovo Airport and immediately discovered that, as an American traveling from Ukraine, he was met with suspicion by the customs agent who wanted to know why he was making such a trip, and why he was returning to St. Petersburg for the second time in just a few months.

He explained that he was an archeologist working in Transcarpathia and now was taking a brief vacation, that he had enjoyed the sights and people on his last visit, and was looking forward to spending more time there. He, of course, said nothing about Jianjun. The slightest bit of intrigue or crime and he could end up in police headquarters for hours, if not days.

When he was finally allowed admittance, he caught a cab to the Four Seasons. The suites were remarkably swank, but the hotel was his second choice. The place he most liked to stay in St. Peters burg was filled up. But now, the hour was late, the trip exhausting, and Michael fell asleep immediately.

After a room service breakfast the next morning, he left the hotel and walked to Nevsky Prospect, one of St. Petersburg's most iconic streets. He first heard of Nevsky Prospect many years ago while reading a tale by Nikolai Gogol, a great Russian novelist, who wrote, "... everything breeds deceit. It lies all the time, this Nevsky Prospect ... and the devil himself lights the lamps."

He turned off at the Moika River embankment and followed the waterway to his favorite hotel, the Pushka Inn. It got its name because of its proximity to the apartment of Alexander Pushkin, another of Russia's most famous poets and novelists. Pushkin had died in the apartment after having been stabbed in a duel in 1837 when he was only thirty-seven years old. It now hosted a museum in his honor.

Michael went to the front desk and asked to speak to Viktor Ilyin, the hotel's owner. He had gotten to know Ilyin well over the years. The two would often sit in the office or in Michael's room drinking vodka and talking about the world situation.

Ilyin was in his seventies and once he had

enough vodka in him, he had plenty to say about governments and politicians, not only his own, but those throughout Europe, Asia, and the US. Michael often just nodded and listened politely having learned that in many countries one simply never knew who was listening. But his visit that day had nothing to do with governments or politics.

"Michael, my friend." Viktor gripped him in a bear hug. The man was nearly as broad as he was tall, and he topped six feet. "What are you doing back so soon? Is everything all right? I heard you had called for a room, but we are booked up right now."

"As usual," Michael said with a grin. "It was a last-minute trip, so I didn't expect to be able to stay here. I'm at the Four Seasons."

"Oh, I'm so sorry!" Viktor said with a sly grin.

"I know you are." Michael shook his head, but quickly got down to business. "I came back already because I'm unable to contact a good friend of mine. He knows I've always stayed here, so I was hoping he might be a guest of yours. I know it's a long shot..."

"No problem. What's his name?"

"Family name, Li. Given name, Jianjun."

Viktor called up the guest roster. "He's here. But why all this secrecy? You could have simply phoned and we would have put you through to his room."

"I'm worried about him. I'm sure something is wrong. He's not answering his cell phone. If someone is in there, either with him or waiting for a visitor, it might be bad."

Viktor pursed his lips. "That does not sound good, Michael. I hope you're not mixed up with people you should stay clear of."

Michael nodded. "So do I."

Victor picked up the phone and called house-keeping. "Manya, can you tell me what's happening with room 103? Have you been cleaning it? Is it still occupied?"

He listened, frowning, then thanked his staffer and hung up. "There's been a *Do Not Disturb* sign on the door for days. The head of housekeeping be-came worried about it and yesterday told the man-ager. He went inside. The room still has clothes and a computer. The manager then ran the credit card, putting a hold to cover our bill. The credit card went through with no problem, so the manager thinks the guy may be traveling around Russia. Sightseeing. And he'll be back."

Michael took this in. "I'd like to see the room."

Viktor's face scrunched. "You know I'm not—"

"I know," Michael said.

Viktor stood. "Good. Now, we'll check it out. But first ..." He pulled out a bottle of his personal home-brew vodka and poured them each a shot. It was early, but the last thing Michael wanted to do was to insult his host. He drank it down in one gulp, hitting the glass hard onto the table just seconds after his host did, which brought a huge smile to Viktor's face. "Hah! I think you are Russian at heart," he bellowed, patting Michael on the back.

"Could be," Michael said, trying not to cough as the vodka burned all the way to his stomach. Then he followed the big man up the stairs to Jianjun's room.

The room didn't appear as if anything untoward had happened in it. Michael was glad he didn't see Jianjun's phone. That would have set off all kinds of red flags. The thing was almost physically attached to his friend. But Michael also knew Jianjun would never have left his laptop if he had planned to be away any amount of time. He guessed the departure hadn't been planned.

Michael dug through the clothes and then pulled Jianjun's carryon out of the closet. More than once, he and Jianjun had snuck things out of countries using that carryon. As he pushed one spot on the bottom of the case and pulled on the opposite side, it slid open to reveal a not-very-deep tray. In it were several sheets of paper in Jianjun's handwriting. Some, unfortunately, were in Chinese characters. One set of scribbles included an address.

He took the papers and the laptop, then turned to Viktor. "Now, I have one last favor to ask you."

"You mean something more than entering my guest's room and allowing you to walk off with his valuable computer?"

"That's right. Can you give me the name of a good, reliable, private investigator? One who might not be afraid to get involved with something that could very likely go sideways."

"Sideways?"

"Kaput."

Viktor grinned. "Ah! We use that word in Russian, too. I know such a man. Let's go to my office and I'll phone him and set up a meeting for you."

Michael followed Viktor from the room. "Good. And I know the perfect spot for it—the coffee shop in front of the Kazan Cathedral on Nevsky Prospect." That was the spot where his father sat with Irina Petrescu when the photo of them was taken.

They returned to Viktor's office, and the meeting was set up for four p.m. that afternoon.

Michael then thanked Viktor for all his help, headed back to his hotel room, and phoned Kira Holt.

She picked up on the first ring. He filled her in

on all he'd found out that morning, ending with having Jianjun's computer. "I'm hoping that when you were staying with him in Salmon, you may have gotten some idea of what his password might have been."

"Hmm," she murmured. But then after a moment she said, "He once told me he always thought of me when he started it up, but I can't be sure the comment had anything to do with his password."

"Well, it's a start," Michael said. "Knowing Jianjun, it won't be anything easy like your name or birthday, but it could well be your name plus the date you met, or your name and something otherwise meaningful to the both of you. He's especially numbers-oriented if that helps."

"I guess after a few wrong tries you'll get locked out, right?" She sounded worried.

"I do know some workarounds to extend the number of tries, but eventually, yes, that'll be what happens. Write down the possibilities, text or phone me with them and I'll use a program to feed them into his computer. It'll be interesting to see if I can hack into my hacker's computer."

"If you can, you know he'll be mortified." It was the first bit of mirth he'd heard in her voice.

"I guess we'd better not ever tell him," Michael said, adding, "We'll find him, Kira."

"Thank you for saying that." She sounded

weepy. "I couldn't help but sit here all morning, for several mornings, to tell the truth, plus afternoons, evenings, nights—all the while thinking that if he were still alive, he'd—"

"Don't go there, Kira," Michael ordered. "I don't want to hear that anything might have happened to him because he was trying to protect my feelings. Is that clear?"

There was a long pause. "I understand," she whispered. "Believe me."

Michael bought himself a cup of coffee at the outdoor stand in front of the Kazan cathedral. The area was empty except for a woman struggling with two small children. She sat for a moment as she put a jacket on the youngest child, and then she got up and left.

Michael took his espresso and moved to a counter to add a couple of packets of sugar. When he again turned toward the tables, he saw a stocky, broad-shouldered man seated at one of them.

The fellow stared hard at him.

Michael approached. "Anatoly Kozlovsky?" he asked.

The older fellow nodded. His blond hair was quite thin, and his jowls flowed over his collar, hiding a thick neck. Although the day was warm, he wore a double-breasted overcoat and looked more like a Russian FSB agent than anything else. At the same time, Michael thought, he looked like the right man for the job.

He introduced himself.

"Viktor Ilyin is good friend." Kozlovsky's deep voice boomed. "He say I should take good care of you. That you are very smart fellow."

"I appreciate that," Michael said. "I'm here because I'm looking for two people." He went on to tell him a little about Irina Petrescu and how Jianjun had come here to meet Irina, but now he, too, was missing.

"You think if we find Petrescu, we find your friend?" Kozlovsky asked.

"I'm hoping there's a connection. If not, I have no idea why Jianjun would be missing." He took the papers he'd found in Jianjun's room and handed one to Kozlovsky. "This sheet has an address. I don't know if it's connected to Irina Petrescu, but it may be the place to start."

Kozlovsky studied the paper, then nodded. "I know that street. Many apartments. Some good; some not. It is near Obukhovsky Bridge on Moskovsky Prospect. Five minutes away. We take my car. You want to go now?"

Michael was heartened by the man's willingness to act immediately even as he inwardly quaked at the thought, after so many years, of finding Irina. "Yes," was all he could manage.

Kozlovsky drove an older model Lada Granta, a utilitarian car made to withstand cold Russian winters. True to his word, they arrived in five minutes. A more careful driver, one who obeyed speed laws and stop lights, might have taken longer. Kozlovsky parked, then led Michael down a street lined with shops and restaurants. At what looked like an alley, he turned in and stopped at the first doorway. A flight of stairs brought them to apartments over the storefronts. Kozlovsky pounded on the third door. The whole building seemed to shake. Michael thought he really might have been with the FSB.

A woman opened the door next to the one they stood at and said something in Russian. Kozlovsky answered back, and the two had a short exchange before she went back inside.

Kozlovsky faced Michael. "She say they move out. Maybe owner knows where to find them. He has restaurant downstairs. We talk to him."

Michael nodded and followed the big man back down to the street, and along the Fontanka River a short way before Kozlovsky turned from the sidewalk, taking stairs down to a small basement restaurant. He spoke softly to the waitress, who gave him and Michael unhappy glares as she led them through the restaurant with badly chipped walls, the smell of onions and cabbage heavy, to the door to the kitchen. There, she had them wait.

In a moment, a short man with curly black hair pushed open the door and marched over to them, his hands on his apron-covered hips. He eyed Michael and Kozlovsky, then laid into Kozlovsky with rapid fire speech. Kozlovsky put his hands up as if trying to appease the man, then answered back with equal force. Finally, the man stormed back through the swinging door. Kozlovsky looked at Michael, cocked his head toward the door, and led the way. They walked through the busy kitchen to a room at the very back of the building.

"You look for my tenants," the owner said to Michael.

"Yes, Irina Petrescu."

He turned to Kozlovsky and spoke. Kozlovsky translated. "He say, 'I had to throw her and her worthless boyfriend out. They don't pay rent. I was sorry about the kids, but what can I do? I can't take in every beggar.'"

Michael swallowed hard at the news of a boyfriend and kids. When he saw Irina's mother, she had told him Irina had no children. He guessed she had been lying. He did his best to hide his emotions as he asked, "Does this man know where we can find her?"

The two men talked for a while, then Kozlovsky said, "She works at Hermitage. She fixes paintings, paints on them, you know?"

"Restoration?" Michael asked.

"*Da*. Sounds right. It's a job, but it doesn't pay enough when she has four mouths to feed." He shrugged one shoulder.

Michael's lips tightened.

"We go there now and find her," Kozlovsky said.

"Now? Isn't it too late? The museum should be closed."

Kozlovsky frowned. "That is when the workers do their jobs."

Michael nodded and followed.

When they reached the Winter Palace Square, Kozlovsky led Michael to the spot where employees entered the Hermitage. Just inside the door, they were stopped at a guard station. Kozlovsky gave their names and again did all the talking. The guard got on his phone and in a short while looked at Michael and said, "Okay."

"Wait here," Kozlovsky said. "They send someone to help you. I go now."

"Wait. How shall I pay you? Now, or...?"

"You will need more help. I send you bill when this is over."

Michael was surprised at first, but quickly recognized that even if he found Irina, Jianjun was still missing. Kozlovsky was most likely absolutely correct. Michael nodded, and when he was about to thank the big man for his help, Kozlovsky was already out the door.

One of the museum's docents arrived at the guard's station. The guard pointed at Michael.

"Please," the woman said, gesturing to Michael to go through a heavy door into the back quarters.

They took an elevator to the fourth floor and then he followed her down a long hallway before they reached a workroom with a number of paintings and statuary on easels and tables. Many were covered with sheets or plastic, and an equal number were not. A few people were seen working on the pieces.

The docent hurried to a corner near the back, and there Michael saw the back of a thin woman of medium height studying a painting done in the pointillism style made famous by Georges Seurat. A spotlight to her left was aimed at the painting. But Michael's gaze was fixed on the woman. She had long brown hair pulled back into a single braid, and wore a smock over jeans, with loose black flats on her feet.

Michael could feel the pounding of his heart, it was beating so hard and so fast. She wasn't moving at all but stood stiffly, as if waiting for something terrible to happen.

Of course, they must have already told her he had asked to see her. And she had to have given her consent to get him this far.

So he had to be the terrible thing she was waiting for.

CHAPTER 32

Nothing was going the way it should, Galyna thought, as she reached the dig site all alone. It was early evening. She didn't like being there by herself, but there was no one she wanted with her.

Feder was driving her crazy. He had been a nice diversion at first, but he was jealous of the way she had fawned over Michael Rempart, as if the man even noticed her! Also, Feder wasn't half as intelligent as he thought he was. He might be more of an albatross than a help to her career.

And she definitely wasn't desperate enough to want to be with Yakiv Koval. The professor all but drooled whenever she walked by. She found him too eager and leering.

Andriy was a wimpy little slug, and Dmytro bored her.

So she was on her own in the quest to find something that would make her famous. She might be the first one to, perhaps, find a Templar artifact or, better yet, an opening to another room or a tunnel. That would give her special attention from journals and published papers, even though this dig was otherwise a team effort.

Now that Rempart had gone, everything seemed to have slowed down. And he only left a brief email saying he'd try to return soon. His horrid American friend had said he'd received a call late at night about a missing friend and then dashed off. At first, Galyna had thought Bethany was his girlfriend. But it was clear the two scarcely knew each other and certainly weren't intimate. She wished Bethany would just leave! No one wanted her there.

That afternoon, Galyna had been assigned to work with Veronika. As they were getting close to finishing for the day, she announced she'd developed a migraine and thought the best thing for it was to walk back to town, taking in the fresh air.

Feder had offered to go with her, but she scowled at him, saying that when she had a migraine, she needed to be alone.

He backed off.

A little way onto the dirt road, she went into the brush and hid until the jitney and Koval's car went by. Then she darted back to the camp and up the trail to the top of the dig.

Now that she was here, she checked her equipment, including extra flashlight batteries, and then lowered herself down into the chapel.

Alone, she found it creepy. When others were near, it wasn't scary at all, but was bright with the sun streaming through the opening in the roof. But as evening approached, less and less light entered.

Koval had insisted that she and the other students work on removing dirt, grime, and dust from the chapel's interior walls when they should have been looking for the entrance to the tunnel, or at minimum, a door to another room. Who knew what treasures might be past the main chamber? She wanted to know, and now she was going to find out.

She had a flashlight, but she didn't need it yet. Judging directions, if the Templars had built the chapel, the sanctuary should be on the east side of the building. Often, a door led past the sanctuary to a small room, and possibly there she would also find the entrance to the tunnels. She got down on her hands and knees and used her knife to poke through dust and dirt along the floor, trying to find a spot that felt "different" from the rest of the wall, a spot where she might find a door opening. By staying close to the floor, she would avoid any chance of harming any painting or other artwork that might be there.

As she worked, something brushed the calf of her leg. A light touch. A mouse, she thought, surprised that a mouse might be down here. She kicked out her leg, and the feeling went away.

She kept jabbing her knife along the spot where the wall and floor met, still hoping to come across a doorway. All of a sudden, she felt something on her head. She squealed, reached up to bat it away, but felt nothing. She jumped to her feet and used both hands to run her fingers through her hair, just in case something was still there. The thought that there were mice or lizards or some such thing down here made her decide to turn on her flashlight. The chapel had become fairly dark, but she was determined to find a door out of the circular room that night. She doubted she would get many more chances to be alone here.

She felt stiff from having been on her knees for so long, but used the flashlight to better inspect the area where the wall and floor met. She didn't see anything that might be a doorway and was about to kneel down again when she felt an arm circle her waist.

She jumped. "Feder! You idiot!" She spun around.

Before her stood a tall, broad-shouldered man in a hooded robe, the hood jutting so far forward that in the darkness she couldn't see his face. The front of the robe had a large, black, five-pointed star.

She backed away as she lifted the flashlight to

his face. But before she got very far, he grabbed the light and yanked it from her. His fingernails were so long and sharp they sliced into her hand and wrist where they touched.

Blood began to trickle out from the cuts and she cried out, stepping backward, only to be stopped by the wall.

From the darkness, other similarly hooded men rushed toward her, but the man in front of her raised his arm and the others stopped. Then they began making a strange humming sound.

The leader, or so she assumed, then grabbed her arm, his grasp hard as he lifted her wrist to his mouth and licked away the blood.

Her legs nearly gave out from fear even as she tried to blink away the darkness, tried to see what she faced. But then the man came closer, this time being careful not to cut her as he stroked her hair, then her ear and her cheek.

Her breathing quickened.

This is a joke, she told herself, a costume. Some of the local boys who were interested in her and always watching her. "This isn't funny! Who are you? What are you doing here?"

She tried to run, but he grabbed her and slammed her hard against the wall, momentarily stunning her.

The others moved closer and reached for her.

Her flashlight, still lit, lay on the ground but cast enough light she could see that they all had the same long, sharp fingernails as they poked at her.

She screamed as one of them reached out and grabbed her T-shirt and lifted, its sharp nails jabbing right through the thin material and shredding it.

She tried to break away as other claw-like hands reached for her, their sharp fingernails causing her skin to bleed. But then she heard a deep rumbling, "Stop!"

The attackers let her go and backed away.

The order had come from the leader, and in that gesture she saw some hope. "Help me," she cried, and threw herself at him.

All around her she could hear the other men's raspy, heavy breathing as they inched closer. The leader's hands slid over her even as he kept his talon-like nails from hurting her.

She felt faint and breathed deeper, knowing she had to keep her wits, and had to keep the others away from her. She reached out and touched the chest of the leader. It felt rock hard.

"Protect me from them," she pleaded. "Help me."

Again, only a single wave of his arm caused the others to back away even further. But then he put one hand around her neck as the other slowly slid over her shoulders, over her breasts, and down to her ribs. There, he pushed aside what remained of the fabric of her T-shirt and poked and prodded her skin.

The others began a melodic chant. She didn't understand what was happening.

The leader suddenly picked her up. She clutched his neck, both out of fear of being dropped or tossed, as well as fear of those other men grabbing at her again.

Up close, she could see the man's eyes glowing, but they were an amber color with long black slits instead of irises. Eyes that looked as if he could see in the dark. But eyes that did not look human.

More fear than she had ever known filled her, and she was sure she was looking into the eyes of death. She couldn't hold back her tears. "Let me go, please," she begged. "Please, have mercy."

He lay her down by a wall of the chapel, his body between her and the others, and knelt beside her. But then his forefinger lightly brushed her cheek, allowing it to become wet with her tears. He lifted the finger to his mouth and then sat back, as if studying her in the darkness for a long while.

"Please," she whispered, "please."

"It's been years since I saw a woman's tears," he whispered, his voice dry and gritty, as if he rarely used it. "I won't let them hurt you. But you must trust me."

Then the man bent and licked the blood from the wounds the others had made on her skin, his mouth gentle, almost like kisses. He then poured something cold and liquid on her belly and rubbed it over her skin, over her wounds, almost lovingly. He tore off the last of her clothing and as she quaked with fear, he continued to smooth the liquid over her everywhere, his touch intimate, caressing.

She could scarcely breathe, too scared to even attempt to protect herself. But then a sharp, horrible pain stabbed her right side just below her rib, and she screamed in agony and fear.

"I must do this," he whispered. "I must." Then he held her down and began to drink.

"No! Stop!"

"Hush." His hand covered her mouth, and he pulled her closer, all but crushing her body to his, even as he continued to feed. "Don't worry, you'll be safe."

The others gathered closer, their mouths working as if they wanted to tear her apart with their teeth. Between pain, the fear, the smell of these monsters around her, and the sound of this madman drinking her blood, her mind shut down completely.

CHAPTER 33

Michael's heart pounded as he watched the docent speak to Irina. She hadn't yet turned around, but he knew it was her.

Now, here, he wasn't sure what he should say or do.

He noticed that Irina's hands shook. A thick drop of blue paint fell to the ground from the small brush she held and she placed the brush down on a cloth and took a rag to wipe the floor. When she stood again, she said something to the docent who faced Michael, gave him a brief nod, and left the studio.

Irina kept her back to him as she unbuttoned and removed the paint-stained smock she wore, laid it over the back of a chair, then took a moment to smooth her hair with both hands. He watched as she lifted her chin and squared her shoulders. Then, finally, she turned.

Her expression was somber and her large blue eyes widened as they met his gaze.

He walked toward her and, when just a few feet away, stopped. He could scarcely breathe. As he studied her, the years melted away. Even wearing old clothes, wisps of dark hair askew around her face despite her efforts to smooth it, she was still beautiful. Her eyes were large, sparkling ovals, with light makeup that enhanced them. Her full lips were rigid, and he couldn't help but focus on the small indentation at the bottom of her chin. How had he ever forgotten it? Her face was thinner now, more angular, but he would have known her anywhere.

His mind filled with words that he wanted to say, and yet none of them seemed right. Finally he went with what he knew must sound silly. "Hello, Irina."

Maybe that was why the tension that filled her seemed to ease the slightest bit, and her eyes softened. "You have become famous." Her voice was the same as he remembered, low and velvety, with barely a hint of an accent after having grown up in the United States.

"A dumb TV show; a lucky find on a sunken pirate ship. They're nothing."

"Let's go out on the balcony, Michael. I can use some air." The double doors on one side of the room led to a small roof deck with a couple of tables, chairs, and ashtrays. She sat, and he joined her. She then pulled out a pack of cigarettes and offered him one. He refused. She lit a cigarette and took a long drag, then held the smoke a moment before blowing it away from him. It seemed to relax her.

"How have you been?" he asked. Another stupid question, he thought.

She lifted one eyebrow. "Fine."

He couldn't do this. He wanted her to know he'd heard about the money she'd accepted from his father. He wanted her to know how much it had hurt and disappointed him. His mouth went dry. "Really?"

"Of course."

"And ... I've heard ... rich."

"What?" She sounded surprised.

He sucked in his breath, then the words—seventeen years' worth—exploded from him. "Looking around at how you're living and working here, it makes me wonder how you managed to spend all the money my father gave you."

Her face lost all color. She stood then, her eyes flashing. "Money from your father? Oh, sure. He gives me money all the time." With that she turned to leave him there.

He jumped to his feet and grabbed her arm. It felt strange to touch her again ... unreal. And yet he remembered the many times they had touched and loved years ago. "I'm sorry, Irina. Sit, please. I shouldn't have said that. It's just that I've spent seventeen years wondering why you walked out without a word. Wondering why you took that money. I think I deserve an answer. After that I'll go and I promise if you don't want to see me, I won't bother you again."

She stood close to him, taking in everything about his face, his expression. He had spent so many years wishing he could see her again, and now that she was here, he'd nearly blown it. He let go of the wrist he still held. "Please," he whispered once more.

Slowly her shoulders eased and her demeanor became less angry and rigid. "I suppose you're right. There are clearly some misunderstandings. But this isn't the place for such a talk. And I need to go back to work."

"When can I see you again?"

She studied him. "I can't tonight but come back here tomorrow at midnight. We can meet then."

"The same place where I came in today?"

"Yes."

"You're sure you'll be there?" he asked.

"I promise."

But then, in a childish acknowledgment of the bitterness he still held inside, he added, "And this time, is your promise one I can trust?"

Anger but also hurt flashed across her face, an anger and hurt that, he was sure, mirrored his own.

"Yes," she whispered, then hurried back to the studio.

He desperately wanted to believe her, but for some reason, he could not.

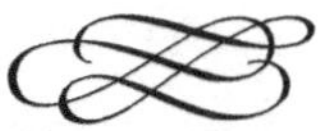

The next morning, no one could find Galyna. Koval demanded to know why. Dmytro did the questioning.

No one had seen the girl when they went back to the inn after working at the dig. It turned out that Feder thought she was in the room with Olena, and Olena had assumed she spent the night with Feder. And Bethany was staying in Michael's cottage while he was out of town.

Andriy knew that Olena and Feder had been looking for Galyna, but he hadn't seen Yakiv Koval. And Galyna had confided in him about Koval. Probably because Andriy was the one man on the team she could in no way use, and since she had nothing but disdain for the other women including her "best" friend Olena, she often talked openly and frankly to Andriy. She had told him that now that Koval had made what looked to be a big discovery, he might be worth something to her after all.

He suggested she wait until she was sure the find was as big as Koval seemed to think.

Also, Galyna knew Koval had returned early to his room to do some reports when she suddenly developed a migraine and also headed back to the inn. Or, in Andriy's mind, to Koval.

He was sick when he learned that she hadn't spent the night with Koval either. Thoughts of what had happened to Wasyl haunted him.

Koval was beside himself that no one had the brains to worry about a missing student.

"How are we going to get funding—ever—if another student has been harmed?" Koval ranted. "This is madness. Veronika and Dmytro, you two were in charge when I left, and you allowed a beautiful young woman to go off walking along the road all by herself? There are all kinds of dangerous animals in these woods, and the most dangerous are the two-legged kind! Are the two of you *trying* to destroy my life? I won't be trusted to oversee latrine duty if anything has happened to that girl!"

"We'll find her," Veronika said. "All the students have walked back and forth on their own. The road is completely isolated and no one else uses it."

"That's the problem, you idiot!" Koval yelled. "I've been sending releases to the press, likening our little group here to *The Magnificent Seven*. But if she's gone, there's only six of us. There is no 'magnificent six!' And the press will, if anything, liken us not to the discoverers of a new Templar chapel, but to the slaughter of the Templars by the Pope's forces on Friday the thirteenth—for which Friday the thirteenth has forever been feared!"

"Calm yourself, Yakiv," Dmytro said, not able to take the man's self-centered bellowing any longer.

He was afraid he might know what had happened. Michael had warned him that having tasted his blood and other fluids after so many years of having none, that the vampires might go in search of more sources of nourishment. He likened them to an addict, who might be fine as long as they had no supply for their addiction, but one slip, and they'll crave it in increasing quantities all over again.

Michael had feared that such a craving might grow to a point of deadly violence, as had happened with Wasyl. The thought of those vampires with Galyna was sickening. He almost hoped they never found her ... or what was left of her.

And if they had enjoyed killing her, would he be safe if he went to them again?

Again ... just as he did every night.

Instead of giving the bicycle to someone in town as he had told Michael, he'd hidden it in the woods. And the gash just below his rib cage never healed. Each day he taped a cloth over it to prevent it from seeping through his clothes. But each morning when he awoke in his bed, he'd find that he was fully dressed, the bandage was gone, and the wound was seeping once more. Even worse, his testes were perpetually swollen and sore, and he was still losing weight. "They're killing me," he thought. Yet, despite Michael's explanation that the creatures were vampires, despite the warning of what might happen as they took possession of him, the pleasure he felt each night had become his personal addiction. He couldn't stop himself from going to them.

Maybe if he had help he could manage to break away.

With that thought, he went to Michael's cottage and found Bethany. "I think it's too dangerous to stay here," he told her. "I'm going to leave. Do you want to go with me?"

Big, blue eyes stared a moment, and then she smiled. "Absolutely."

"Since you have a car, we can go as soon as we're ready. I need only ten minutes."

She nodded. "That works."

It took him less time than that to put everything in his duffel bag and return to the cottage. She was ready only a couple of minutes later.

"Let's go," he said, and they hurried to her car.

They had just reached it when Koval stopped them. "What are you two up to?"

"We're leaving," Dmytro said. "We didn't come here for this."

"You would run off when a student is missing? Don't you know how guilty that makes you look?"

"Guilty of what?" Dmytro cried.

"The girl is beautiful. You figure it out! You need to stay and help with the search. We hope she simply stepped off the road for a moment and fell or somehow got hurt. Feder is organizing a search. You should have done it, but at least he is. You two need to help. If we don't find her, I'll call the police. What will they think if I tell them the two of you ran off immediately after the girl's disappearance was discovered?"

Dmytro heaved a sigh, then faced Bethany. "He may be right. I don't know if we want the Ukrainian police to arrest us or even to question us."

"I think so, too," she whispered.

She returned to Michael's cottage, and Dmytro followed Koval to help with the search.

Veronika told Koval she was going up to the dig site to look for Galyna. Koval argued that it was a waste of time, but Veronika suspected otherwise.

She had been a young girl in Transcarpathia when she first heard her grandparents talking of the vampires that walked the Carpathian Mountains. They told of how, during the Russian Revolution, a group of aristocrats and soldiers loyal to the Tsar fled the Bolsheviks by attempting to cross the mountains in winter.

They didn't make it. A few years later, signs of vampire attacks were seen in nearby villages. The people swore they were those soldiers raised from the dead. The town was careful and eventually, by locking up and not traveling at night, the attacks stopped.

Veronika had been fascinated by the story, and the older she became, the more curious she became about it. Who were those people? Why did they die? Did any of them survive? And if they became vampires, how did it happen, and where did the vampires go?

She began studying history, but it didn't take long before she realized that archeology, focusing on Transcarpathia, would be the key to learning the truth behind the myth. In time, her curiosity turned into an obsession.

"Things are different at night," Veronika told Koval and left the inn, intent on her mission.

He hurried after. "The least I can do is give you a ride," he said. "But I simply can't imagine the girl would go back to the dig unless she was badly hurt and confused. She should know the best thing to do was to head for the town. But you're right. We need to look everywhere before we call the police. I'll even keep you company as you waste your time."

"No need," she said, walking faster. But he wouldn't back off and finally she accepted a ride.

Within minutes they arrived at the camp. He stopped in front of the tent. "Let's look inside."

"Fine, if you want to waste your time," Veronika said. "If she's anywhere around here, it's in that pit and you know it. You know how ambitious she is. She probably decided to do some searching on her own and got herself into trouble."

They climbed up to the pit and Veronika dropped the rope ladder down into the chapel. "I'll go down," she said. Enough sunlight filled the chapel that she didn't need her flashlight. As she climbed down she saw the girl near the chapel wall. "My God! She's here!"

Veronika ran to the girl and stopped. She lay on a straw pallet, atop a soft blue throw that looked like silk, but her face, her body were so white as to look bloodless ... dead. Veronika gasped.

A piece of what appeared to be homespun cotton covered her from the waist down but she wore no shirt and Veronika saw lacerations on her neck and chest, the largest being below her rib cage on the right.

Veronika reached out and placed her fingers to the girl's neck to try to find a pulse when she noticed what appeared to be puncture marks. Her mouth went dry as the word "vampires" filled her mind. She ignored it, placed her fingers over the artery and then looked away to concentrate. She saw something step out of the wall. Something large and wearing a cloak. She froze.

"Is she alive?" Koval called.

The man ... image ... whatever, vanished as quickly as it had appeared. Veronika looked down at the girl, her fingers still on her neck. "Yes! I feel a pulse!"

Koval quickly reached her side and gasped. "What happened to her?"

"I don't know. There's no blood on the ground around her, but she must have bled a lot," Veronika said.

"What's this?" Koval asked, lifting the homespun that covered the girl. It immediately disintegrated in his hand and Veronika couldn't tell if he was more shocked by that or by the sight of a fully naked Galyna.

Veronika took off her jacket and quickly covered the girl. "Galyna," she called. "Can you wake up? Galyna?"

When she remained unconscious, Veronika turned to Koval. "Can you carry her out of this pit? Or should we get others and make a sling of some sort?"

Koval stood quivering. "I don't understand what's happening here."

"We need to get her out, Yakiv," Veronika said, her eyes jumping to where she had seen the man's figure, but nothing was there. Had she imagined it?

"What if she has broken bones?" he whispered.

Veronika ran her hands over the girl's arms, legs, and ribs. "Wasyl didn't have broken bones, and it doesn't look like she suffered any wounds but these cuts."

"Why do you mention Wasyl?" Koval demanded. "This is completely different!"

"Is it? She has cuts and gashes over the area where Wasyl was torn apart. But for some reason, she's been allowed to live."

Koval turned ashen.

"I don't think we'll do any worse harm if we lift her out of here right now," Veronika said.

"I'll get a rope to help," Koval said and climbed out of the chapel. By the time he returned, Galyna had awakened. She was confused and not speaking, but able to walk. The two professors led her out of the chapel to Koval's car.

"We'll tell the others that she fell from the

mountain and we have no idea why she climbed up it. But as she fell through brush and trees, she got all kinds of cuts and bruises and must have hit her head because she's now quite out of it," Koval said.

"No more lies, Yakiv!" Veronika ordered, thinking back on the vision she'd had. "We need to tell the authorities everything and then leave here."

"She's nothing like Wasyl, I said!" Koval shrieked. "No wolves attacked her!"

"No wolves attacked Wasyl either," Veronika spat out the words. "And like her, there was no blood around his body. This isn't safe, Yakiv! You and I know what kind of monster drinks blood, human blood. My whole life I've heard stories about this area, about demons, vampires. I laughed at them, couldn't believe them, but now I think they're true. When will you admit it as well?"

"You're insane. Leave, then. But I'm not going. I'm going to find what I came here for. We're so close, Veronika. And because one stupid student went off on her own and encountered God-only knows what, I'm not about to sink my career! If you want to go, it's your choice."

"Two students, Yakiv. Two of five." Despite her words, she couldn't help but think he was right. She'd given up everything for this career, this life. Should she walk away now when she was on the verge of learning what she had wondered about all these years? If there were such things as vampires, didn't she want to see them and prove to the world, to herself, that they existed? How could she give that up now? "From now on," she said, "we make a rule that we only go up to the dig site in pairs."

"Of course," he murmured.

But even as she said it and he agreed, she couldn't help but wonder if it would make any difference.

CHAPTER 35

Bethany jumped at the sound of footsteps on the front porch of the cottage. It was night, late night and she had been sitting alone, thinking about going to bed, but afraid to, given all that was happening around her.

She hadn't practiced remote viewing since joining Michael in Transcarpathia. But now, with all the strangeness at the dig site, she wondered what he knew about it. She tried hard to remotely view Michael, but nothing worked. She wondered if it was because Merlin wasn't with her. But she hesitated to contact him again. He had become strangely demanding and bossy. Too late she realized he had pushed her to use her life's savings to come to Transcarpathia to meet Michael, even to buy a crappy car. Of course, she wanted to find Rachel, and Michael should have been the key to that, but she now believed he really didn't know her sister's fate.

Also, the sheer power Merlin had over her had become frightening.

She even began to wonder if he was something more than human ... which probably meant that this entire Transcarpathian experience was turning her mad as a hatter.

Footsteps again walked across the porch. Should she open the door, demand to know who was out there? Or grab the longest knife she could find in the house?

Then she heard a knock. No one that was scary would knock, would they?

She opened the door to find Dmytro. "I saw your light," he said. "I was worried about bothering you, but then decided you might be having as much trouble sleeping as I am."

Relief surged through her. "Yes, I am. Come in. Have you heard how Galyna is doing?"

Word had quickly spread that Professors Koval and Masur had found the girl on the dig site and said that she'd fallen down the mountain.

"She's doing surprisingly well. Hypothermia. Nothing broken. Warming her up and giving her water and food helped."

"Do you believe the story about her getting disoriented and climbing the mountain? I mean, why would she do that? Even disoriented, it makes no sense."

"Don't ask me to explain any woman, let alone Galyna," Dmytro said. "Thank God she's safe. They say she can't remember anything from the time she felt a migraine coming on."

He joined her as she went to the cupboard where Michael had put a bottle of the local white wine. She held it up. "Would you like some?"

"Love some."

She sat by him on the sofa. He asked about her home state. Like most of the world, he'd never heard of Idaho. She asked him about Kyiv. She was amazed at its complex and important history, and he was shocked that she didn't know it was once the capital of an area that expanded from what's now Ukraine through Belarus and Russia. His interest in archeology stemmed from the many ancient sites around Kyiv, particularly one said to be 25,000 years old.

He told a good story, and she was thankful for his company as they finished the wine.

"What do you think is going on at the dig?" she asked after a while.

"Nothing I want to think about at this time of night, with such pleasant company and good wine."

"But doesn't it scare you? It does me," she confessed.

"Come closer." He put his arm around her.

"We're together, and we'll stay near each other when we're at the dig, okay? We'll be all right."

She looked up at him and nodded her head. He leaned toward her. She let him kiss her. He was a nice fellow, and the wine had left her feeling warm and friendly. She placed her hand on his shoulder as his arms tightened. She felt his tongue touch her lips. He was getting a little more into this than she wanted and she turned her head away.

But then his kisses continued to her cheek, her ear, and he nuzzled her neck. She felt a little bite as his hand went to her breast. She didn't know which startled her more, but she drew back from him, pushing his hand aside.

To her horror, his face had changed. No longer was he the sweet young professor, but his eyes had turned yellow and the irises were long, black slits staring not at her but at her neck. He grabbed her arms tight.

She cried out and jumped to her feet, shoving him hard as she did.

He looked up at her, startled, and she saw Dmytro again.

"I'm so sorry, Bethany," he said, sitting upright. His fingers gripped the seat of the sofa and confusion swam over his face. "I didn't mean to ... I mean, I didn't hurt you, did I? You looked so sweet, so beautiful. It was the wine. Please, don't say anything to Professor Koval! I mean, I know you aren't a student, but he could think I was acting inappropriately."

She touched her neck. There was no blood, no torn skin. As the shock of what she saw, or thought she saw, wore off, she realized her mind had been playing tricks on her. "It's okay. I'm just jumpy about everything here. And I wasn't expecting ... I'm sorry but I just don't feel that way about you."

He stood up and gave her a quick nod. "I understand. I should go now."

She walked with him to the door. "I did have a very nice evening with you, as a friend," she said. "We'll do it again soon, okay?"

"Sure," he muttered and hurried out the door.

CHAPTER 36

Two nights later as Irina had directed, Michael went to the Hermitage employee entrance a little before midnight. The night was freezing with an icy wind blowing off the Neva. Michael could scarcely imagine how cold St. Petersburg must be in the dead of winter, since even in spring the chance of snow was high.

The door was locked, but the guard opened it for him. "Irina Petrescu?" he asked.

"Yes," Michael said.

The guard nodded, gestured for Michael to step inside the building, and made a call.

He stood in the hall and waited, and soon Irina appeared. She had her coat over her arm. "I was thinking that, since it's freezing outside and many places are closed this time of night, we should stay here in the museum. We can talk without being disturbed."

Michael was surprised, but went along with her. They got into an elevator and she pushed the button for the third floor. When they stepped out of it, he followed and almost immediately found himself in a long hall with magnificent Renaissance paintings on the walls. But even more stunning than a lot of the art pieces were the large coffered ceilings with gold on the peripheries and domed centers with beautiful murals.

"Are you sure—" Michael began.

"Relax. It's all right. I walk around here all the time." She turned down a hall and stopped at a large, beautifully carved door. Removing the key from her pocket, she unlocked it. "This is one of the actual chambers where the Romanovs spent time. The furniture has, of course, been reupholstered many times, but the overall effect is the same."

He followed her into the room. It was probably the most magnificent room he'd ever been in, filled with sumptuous artwork, statuary, and lush, intricately carved furniture and window coverings. She took his hand and pulled him to the back wall, then let him go as she stepped behind a hand-painted screen. She returned with a man's black military jacket with epaulets on the shoulders and rows of metals and gold braid across the chest. "Put this on. It belonged to the last tsar."

"I can't wear this," he said.

She laughed. "Of course you can. Nicholas

won't mind. Besides, I'm going to dress up as well. It'll be fun!"

She put the jacket in his arms and again disappeared behind the screen.

He did as told, curious as to what she was up to, and surprised at how perfectly the jacket fit. Before many minutes passed, she stepped into view. He was speechless.

Her arms were raised as she tried to secure a loose strand of shiny, dark brown hair. "I'm sorry to say they keep the jewels locked up," she said. "This would look far more beautiful with the right necklace."

"You don't need jewelry," he murmured.

She dropped her arms. "Thank you."

Her black dress was floor length and sleeveless with a deeply cut bodice showing off a considerable amount of milky white skin. The material was soft and gauzy, with a silver thread throughout. She had pinned her hair up in a style often seen in photos from Alexandra's time. She was breathtaking.

"I thought you might enjoy this little costume party," she said. "It gives a sense of what it was like when this was the Winter Palace and not merely a museum."

"Was that one of Alexandra's dresses?" he asked.

"No, but it belonged to one of her best friends,

Princess Militsa of Montenegro. I feel a strange affinity for her, and as you can see, her clothes fit me perfectly. It must be because Montenegro isn't all that far from Romania. Or, at least, I'm closer to a Montenegrin than someone from northern Russia. And, she was a fan of Rasputin, as am I."

That shocked him. "Really? The mad monk? The one many people say caused the people to turn on Nicholas and Alexandra?"

"He was misunderstood," she said, her voice firm with a hint of anger.

Michael thought it best to drop the subject. "That could be," he remarked as he walked around what could easily have been the Romanov sitting room, him in a military jacket, and Irina in a gown.

"This feels like magic." Michael faced her, his voice wistful.

"What's wrong with magic?" she asked coyly.

"Nothing, although I trusted you were Irina and not a witch."

She smiled. "And so I am. But that doesn't mean I haven't learned a thing or two from associating with your father all these years."

Shock coursed through him. "You mean he kept in contact with you after you left Wintersgate?"

"Come and sit with me." She took his arm and led him to an elegant settee decorated with needlepoint and gold leaf. They sat side-by-side. He noticed she had put on perfume, its scent heavy, floral, and intoxicating. "He tried to keep contact, but I don't like being beholden to anyone. That includes Claude."

Michael pursed his lips. "Claude" was the name his father preferred close friends to use—particularly female friends. To Michael, he was always William Claude. He feared discussing his father would cause nothing but arguments. "Before we talk about my father, I need to ask about my friend, Li Jianjun. He came here to meet you and now he's disappeared."

"Your friend?"

"He told his girlfriend that he intended to meet you and he'd call her back after you two conversed. But he never called back."

"I assure you, I've never met any friend of yours here."

"Yet you didn't seem particularly surprised when I showed up. I think it's because of Jianjun that you knew I was coming."

Her jaw tightened. "So now you accuse me of lying? You've grown so distrustful, Michael. If you want the truth, ever since you found my mother a couple of years ago, I knew it was just a matter of time before you found me. I expected we'd meet in St. Petersburg. And what better place for us to talk than in the Winter Palace?"

"What do you mean?"

"Well, your whole life has been about finding the past, hasn't it? Finding as much about mankind's past as you can dig up. But even more important for you, I believe, has been finding your own."

His body stiffened. "My past has nothing to do with archeology." He was unable to mask his anger.

"Oh? Why else would you bother to dig up old bones and buildings? It's hardly exciting or meaningful these days."

He frowned. "You never did appreciate my interest in archeology, did you?"

"Frankly, I don't see why you care so much about the distant past when the present is already too difficult to understand."

He shook his head. "You know it doesn't work that way. Often the past has answers for the present, if not the future."

"Perhaps. In any case, I have a friend here who understands more about this place than anyone I've ever met. And what she says definitely affects the future."

"Who is that friend?" Michael asked.

"You may meet her at some point. Or, maybe not. But that's not why we're here." She took in a deep breath before she spoke. "I'm glad to see you looking well, Michael. I've always felt bad about the way we parted."

"Not as bad as I did, it seems."

"Is that what you think?"

"I understand you're with someone, married, perhaps. And you have children, I hear. I wasn't so lucky, but I'm glad for you, Irina. It's everything we talked about except for a house in the suburbs, two cars, and a dog." He smiled, to indicate that the last part was mainly a joke.

But she looked stricken, her voice barely more than a whisper. "At one time, that was all I ever wanted."

Her reaction was troubling. "What happened?" he asked, serious now.

"Your mother's death."

That was the last thing he expected to hear. "How can you say that? You were only a child when she died."

"But I was an adult when I learned the details." Her face was solemn, almost tearful.

Now, he felt stricken. "What details?" he whispered.

She hesitated, then shook her head. "I don't know that--"

"Irina, I came here to find out all that happened back then."

She nodded, but a while passed before she

spoke again. "I learned everything shortly after you went away to Oxford for your last year. You were so busy back then, too busy for me as you worked to finish your dissertation. But it didn't matter because I was sure that soon we would be married, even though I was just the housekeeper's daughter."

"You know your mother was more than a housekeeper to me. Magda raised me after my mother's death. And William Claude certainly was no parent. I loved your mother. And you were my scuzzy little sister until, one day, I noticed that you weren't."

"And I was crazy in love with you since I was about ten," she admitted.

He shook his head at that, remembering what a tomboy she'd seemed to him as a ten-year-old.

"And that," she said, "was what made my discovery so hard."

He felt a chill. "What discovery?"

She spread out the full skirt of her dress so it draped smoothly across the chair to the floor then sat with her back ramrod straight, her head elegantly lifted. "Would you trust me if I said you are better off not knowing?"

"I trust that you believe that, but ... it haunts me."

She nodded. "I imagine it does." She bowed her head, her gaze fixed on the floor. "One day, Claude told me a horrible story about the past, and he showed me passages from your mother's journal to prove that his words were true. Do you know what I'm referring to?"

Michael nodded, heartsick. "I've seen her journal, and I know she had an affair with your father while she was living in Greece."

Irina's face became hard and emotionless as their eyes met. "And so you also know that a short while after my father's death, as my mother desperately looked for any kind of job, she was offered the opportunity to work in the US for a very rich man. She took the offer, believing the wealthy 'Mr. Rempart' had brought my mother and me to this country to work in his home, his mansion, in order to help us 'poor refugees.' Instead, all he really wanted was to make your mother face, every day, the widow and child of the man she had loved."

"Yes." Michael's jaw tightened. "It was cruel of him. Typically cruel, I should say. But also ironic because, if he hadn't done that, I never would have met you or have fallen in love with you. He admitted to me that it was because of your father that he wanted us to split up. He said that was why he bought you off."

"What? Bought me off?" she asked, puzzled.

"That was why he gave you enough money for you to agree to leave me."

Her face paled. "You believe I took money to leave you?"

The same cold hurt that filled him whenever he thought of the way his father had thrust the check at him, to show how Irina had wanted money more than him, swept over him once more. "He kept the endorsed check, Irina. I saw it." He sucked in his breath. "I have to admit, he offered you a helluva sum. But it was nothing compared to all the Rempart money. Nothing compared to what I have. And that's why I don't understand why you listened to him—if, of course, you loved me. If you did, you would have known the past had nothing to do with the two of us. And that I had more than enough money for us to live however you would have wanted."

She stood and glared at him. "*Money? You think all this was about money? You're as sick as your father!*"

"Irina, please." He stood as well. "All I know is you accepted his check. You endorsed and cashed it. *Two million dollars!* It's ironic, but he always told me that, as a Rempart, I would be unlucky in love. He said he wanted to show me your true nature— and the check you took from him was his proof."

She shook her head, her eyes sad. "I can't believe you listened to him."

"I didn't want to. I searched for you, but as time went by, I thought he might be right."

"Of course you did! God, but I'm a fool!"

He put out his hand to her, but she stepped back. "Don't touch me," she demanded. "And don't ever bother me again." She ran from the room.

He dropped his hand, staring after her in shock. What had she meant? Was he wrong, all these years, about Irina and the money his father gave her? But she did take it. What possible reason could she have had?

***

Back in his hotel room, Michael looked at his phone and found a text Bethany had sent telling him about Galyna's disappearance and how she'd been found at the dig the next day.

He texted back, telling her the dig site was dangerous and not to go there. He said the only way to stay safe was to remain in the town, and that he'd return as soon as he could.

Damn, he thought. He had tried to warn Koval about the site, saying they needed to either leave or make sure no one – ever – went up there at night. But Koval wouldn't listen. He kept pushing and finally Koval agreed, but Michael was sure it was only to humor him. And now that he wasn't there, he doubted Koval was following their agreement.

Michael felt torn between returning to the dig and dealing with what he knew was happening there, but also, he needed to find Jianjun. And then there was the problem of Irina. He wrestled constantly with what she could have meant when she said he was as sick as his father and called herself a fool.

He poured himself some vodka from the bar and drank it down in one gulp, all the while thinking of how, years ago, Irina had disappeared when he had planned to formally propose, to give her a ring. And it *was* her endorsement on the two million dollar check from his father. She never denied it.

He drank another, then another, but couldn't make himself stop the memories of how his father had laughed at him, saying Irina loved money far more than him. He hadn't wanted to believe it. He couldn't! But still...

Finally he went to his bedroom and tried to sleep, but was tormented by strange dreams.

One in particular haunted him even after he awoke.

In it, there were four girls and one young boy elegantly dressed. But the children and their mother were horribly frightened. Mama, as the girls called her, had had a vision about a bad man who would find an ancient secret and use its power to kill them. They had to protect themselves. No one else could do it.

Michael recognized the same room he and Irina had sat in. And the children, he guessed, were the children of Nicholas II and Alexandra, the children who had been mercilessly shot to death.

But in his dream, Michael stood before them. They had begged for his help, but as he tried to move forward, an icy hand gripped his shoulder. A figure appeared behind him, its eyes burned, and its face glowed white. Skinny, claw-like fingers reached for his neck.

He grabbed the creature's arms to force it away even as he felt his neck constricting, heard the crunch of bones as his windpipe broke and it became harder and harder to breathe. As he fought the powerful demon, its face turned into Irina's.

He abruptly woke and sat up in the bed, perspiration beading his forehead.

Was this, he wondered, a nightmare brought on by too much drink? Or was it some kind of prophecy?

CHAPTER 37

Early the next morning, Michael heard the vibration of his cell phone indicating he'd gotten a message.

It was from Kira and listed some possible words and dates that Jianjun might have used as his password—ones that might have caused him to think about her. When they first met, first kissed, when she first told him she loved him, first...

He tossed it aside. *Who in the world remembers such things?*

Although he'd only been in bed for three hours, he got up, dressed, and headed out to the sitting room to take a closer look at Jianjun's computer. He opened the laptop, and then his own, side-by-side. He was setting up a program he'd been given a couple of years earlier that should be useful in trying to crack the password on Jianjun's computer. He'd never bothered to test the program or even to try to learn how it worked. All he knew was that Jianjun would never use anything remotely simple.

His phone buzzed and when he saw it was Bethany, he answered.

"Are you all right?" he asked. "Staying put at the inn?"

"I'm so glad I got through. I kept driving south of Potchiv, holding the phone out the car window and when I reached a high spot overlooking a valley, I saw two bars and called. When are you coming back here?"

"I don't know. My friend is still missing. And you need to leave the dig."

"I can't. I've got to wait for gas to be delivered to Potchiv's station. It's empty. And my car is close to empty as well. I've got enough for a couple of trips to find cell service, but that's it."

The phone crackled for a moment. "I hope it gets there soon," he said when the phone worked again.

"Me, too. Things are getting really weird here," Bethany added. "It's scary. Galyna swears she can't remember what happened to her. I've heard she has some weird cuts on her body."

"Did Koval call the police?"

"No. He said there's no reason to, that it must've been a wildcat of some sort. A lynx, maybe."

"That makes no sense," Michael said. "Whatever you do, do *not* go up to the dig. And don't go out, at all, after dark."

"I won't," she said. "So what's happening with your friend? Any news?"

"I've got his computer. If he took a planned trip, he wouldn't have left it behind. That's what worries me. Now, I have to figure out how to break into it, which won't be easy."

"Do you think it'll give you an idea where he might be?"

"It's the only lead I've got. Jianjun usually puts his whole life on his computer. Hopefully, he's continued to do that. But how do you hack into a hacker's computer? That's the problem."

"He's a hacker?" she asked.

"That's someone who knows how to break into—"

"I know what a hacker is. I've done it myself."

Michael stopped fiddling with his computer's software and gripped the phone tighter. "You?"

"To be honest, I had help. Lots of help. I met one fellow, in particular, who seems to really know a lot. In a chat room he helped me get onto the dark web."

"Oh great, sounds like a real gem."

"He is."

"Was he good enough to help you find me in Ukraine?" Michael asked.

"Well," he heard her hesitation before she admitted, "that was someone else."

Michael hated the idea of allowing a stranger into Jianjun's computer, but he needed to find out if it had any useful information. "At this point, I'll take any help I can get."

"I'll try to reach my guy right away. Text me everything you can about your friend's online presence."

Michael hesitated, but if it meant finding Jianjun ... "I will."

"One last thing," Bethany said.

"Yes?"

"On second thought, forget it."

"What?" he asked. "Something about the dig site?"

"It was ... when I was with Dmytro."

"What happened?"

"I'm sure it was my imagination."

"Did he do something? Did he scare you?"

"I thought I saw something kind of weird. Very weird. But like I said, I'm sure I just imagined it."

"You need to keep away from Dmytro. He's into things that could become dangerous," Michael said.

"Are you kidding me? What kind of things?"

"Nothing I can explain now. Just don't be alone with him. I'll be back as soon as I can, but if you can safely get away from there and go home, I suggest you do that."

"Maybe," she murmured, then ended the call.

Michael was troubled by Bethany's questions, and her statement about Dmytro made him wonder if the vampires weren't taking over Dmytro's body. For them to "turn" their prey, those they didn't kill, was common practice. Bethany was about as practical and down-to-earth as he could imagine, and if she saw something, it was real. He could only hope she took his advice.

He didn't bother with more sleep but spent the rest of the morning gathering Jianjun's online information to send to Bethany.

That done, he filed a missing person's report with the St. Petersburg police. He knew that would be the best way to find out if Jianjun had been in an accident and was in the hospital or, God forbid, worse. He had no sooner returned to his room when he got a call from Bethany.

"I got hold of Neptune and although we couldn't get into any serious stuff yet, we did hack into Facebook. Neptune's a whiz at it. He can see who goes where and what anybody does on that site. And he found out that Jianjun visited a Theosophical site in St. Petersburg. I thought you'd want to know that right away."

Michael was stunned. "Are you kidding me?"

"Not at all. Here it is." She gave Michael the information. He logged onto Facebook, a platform he generally avoided, and found the page Bethany mentioned. "I don't get it. Jianjun is the last person who would be interested in the Theosophists."

"What are Theosophists?" Bethany asked.

"*Theos* is the Greek word for God, and *sophia* is Greek for wisdom, so the Theosophists study the wisdom of God, according to Helena Blavatsky. She was a Russian woman born around 1830 or so, to a family somewhat connected to Russian society. They weren't high up, but they did have money.

"She lived a rather normal life until she abandoned Mr. Blavatsky, her husband, early in their marriage. It was a scandalous action for a woman of her time. She spent the rest of her life traveling through Europe, India, and America trying to find out the nature of life and the reason humans exist."

"That's amazing," Bethany said, her voice filled with awe.

"I'm sure it was, not to mention difficult. In the U.S., to make money, Madam Blavatsky claimed to be a medium and charged wealthy customers to contact the dead. She used levitation and all kinds of tricks and techniques to convince her customers she was legitimate. There, she learned about a Civil War veteran, Colonel Henry Olcott, who had also been part of a commission that looked into Lincoln's assassination. So he was no lightweight. He happened to be investigating a medium in Vermont at that time and writing newspapers articles about his findings."

"So he was a soldier and then got into séances?" Bethany's voice sounded incredulous.

"Or, spiritualism, as they called it," Michael replied. "Helena Blavatsky decided to prove to him that she was a true medium, knowing a positive report from such a reputable man would establish her. She got him to believe her, which—to my way of thinking—means he had to be one of the most gullible military men I've ever come across."

"Wow," Bethany said.

"Madame Blavatsky gained quite a following. She also wrote books and was a popular speaker. Not long after the two met they began the Theosophist Society, their attempt at connecting Eastern spiritualism with Western thought. A few years later, they became fascinated with Hindu gurus and swamis much like a lot of the rock stars of the 1960s and '70s did with Maharishi Mahesh Yogi and others. They went to India. During that time, the Theosophist Society grew quite a bit."

"A success story," Bethany said.

"More like a fad. And like any fad, it died out. Soon, Blavatsky and the Colonel hardly made enough money to live. Blavatsky's books became less and less popular, and she died in poverty. But the Theosophists continue to this day, so I guess they do have something people like. Last I heard, they're especially popular in England. I didn't know they existed here in Russia."

"I wonder if your friend went to a meeting."

"I can't imagine Jianjun at such a place." Michael shook his head. "But it's worth looking into. More than ever, we need to get into his computer to find out what caused his interest in the group."

"I think Neptune will be able to do it," Bethany said, "if anyone can, that is."

CHAPTER 38

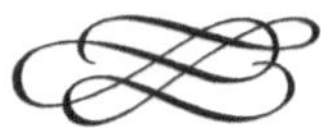

Michael had to walk up and down Bol'shaya Morskaya Street several times before he found the place he was looking for. He knew it had to be nearby because the directions to the St. Petersburg Theosophist Society headquarters stated it was near the Vladimir Nabokov museum, located in the house where the novelist had been born and raised. Nabokov's family had fled Russia when Lenin and the Bolsheviks took over the government. Nabokov always referred to his childhood home as "the only house in the world," although he never did return to the city since it remained under Communist rule throughout his life.

Finally, Michael found the Theosophist Society's location. It was three stories up in an old building a half-block from Nevsky Prospect. Michael climbed the stairs and matched the Cyrillic letters shown on the Facebook site with that of a paper taped to the wall beside the door. It looked more like a private residence than an office.

He guessed that made sense. The group probably didn't bring in enough dues to cover a full-time office or even a staff. He knocked.

"*Voyti,*" came the response.

He opened the door to see a small living room so thick with tobacco smoke everything had a brownish-yellow haze. Behind a wooden desk laden with stacks of papers and an old computer sat an even older woman. "Is this the Theosophist Society?" he asked.

"Yes, welcome," she said with a heavy accent. "You are English?"

"American."

She stood and gathered some brochures. As she did, he looked over the posters, paintings, and sketches that covered the walls. There were several poses of Madam Blavatsky, of course, but what most caught his eye were a number of alchemical symbols as well as drawings of Pushkin. He knew the poet and novelist had dabbled in the occult. A wave of spiritualism had swept Russia and Europe around the time of Pushkin's death. Some of its followers included alchemy in their studies, Pushkin among them.

He remembered reading that in one of Pushkin's unfinished works, his character, an alchemist, proclaimed, *"I do not need gold; I am in search of truth."*

"Excuse me," the woman said, breaking into Michael's thoughts. "I can give you these. They are all in Russian, but I can help you with questions."

"Do you have meetings?" he asked.

"We are having one tomorrow night at eight o'clock. Here."

"Good. A friend of mine suggested I come here," Michael began. "His name is Jianjun. I think he went to your last meeting."

"Jianjun?"

"Li Jianjun, or Jianjun Li," Michael explained. "Originally from China. Did you meet him? He spoke well of the group."

"No. I don't remember anyone from China." Her eyes narrowed with suspicion.

"I see. Well, thank you for the information. I'll try to attend tomorrow night's meeting if I'm free," Michael said.

"Yes. Please do." All signs of friendliness were gone now as cold eyes stared at him.

He knew by the woman's glare he wouldn't get a second chance to talk to her and so he asked, "I see that your group has an interest in alchemy."

"We are interested in many things."

"I know some great alchemists," he added. "Do any come to your meetings?"

"Of course not." She raised her chin. "Everyone knows alchemy is a hoax."

He smiled. "Of course it is." He then said goodbye.

It was a strange place and once outside he felt able to breathe again. He didn't know if his difficulty had been from the smoke or the apartment's stifling atmosphere.

He had just stepped onto the sidewalk when an older man who had been leaning against a building put his cellphone into his pocket and stepped directly in front of Michael.

Michael stopped and stared. The two were of equal heights and equal builds. "Keep away from Theosophist group," the stranger said, his accent thick. "We don't like strangers."

"Oh?" Michael said. "Why would that be?"

"Very dangerous. People get hurt if they are not invited. You are not invited."

Michael nodded. "Point taken."

The stranger stepped aside, and Michael continued toward his hotel. He was definitely interested in the Theosophists now.

That night, Bethany phoned back.

"I've got Neptune on the line as well," she said. "He's got some information for you."

The two men greeted each other, and then

Neptune said, "I suspect his password is a lot of numbers. Eighteen of them. They've got to mean something, or he'd never memorize eighteen at random. Hackers keep passwords in their heads."

"Eighteen is crazy," Bethany said. "Are you sure it's not words?"

"Probably not words. Something hard to imagine," Neptune said. "Eighteen is like ... a dozen and a half? Does that mean anything?"

"It's also two times nine, three times six," Bethany added.

"Six ... wait. That's a hexagram," Michael said. "Jianjun really likes the *I Ching*. It's all about hexagrams. I wonder if that's a connection."

"Hey, man, that might be it," Neptune said. "I've seen charts that show hexagrams being put into binary numbers—which are what computers use. Maybe he's combining the two things he loves into his password."

"What are you talking about?" Bethany asked.

"It's easier to show you than try to explain. What do you think are the most important numbers on the dude's possible passwords?"

"If we're talking about things he loves," Michael said, pulling out the list of potential dates Kira sent him, "then, knowing Jianjun, corny as it sounds—he's a corny guy – I'd say it's the date Kira first said she loves him. And since she knows it as well, it had to be significant for them both."

"You're kidding me," Bethany cried. "I've never heard of a guy who remembers something like that. It's so mushy!"

"Or romantic," Michael suggested.

"No way," Bethany insisted.

"I agree with her," Neptune said. "But what is the date? I'm trying to find one of those charts on-line right now. We can see if using the *I Ching* hexagrams makes sense."

"August 27," Michael said, reading Kira's text.

"Okay, give me a minute." There was a pause, then Neptune came back on the phone. "Oh, man, this is crazy. It's a system—a binary system—that was set up by some philosopher named Shao Yong, who lived around the eleventh century. Man, that was hundreds of years before the West started playing around with binary notations, as far as I've ever heard. Anyway, it's complicated, so I'll give you guys the links so you two can also play with all these numbers and crazy little hexagrams."

Michael opened the link Aiden sent and discovered there were several ways to change a hexagram into binary code, but the Shao Yong was the most common system. He hoped that's what Jianjun used. "Taking the date, we need 8 - 2 - 7. Let's see what we've got."

Going through the chart, he found the hexagram for 8 was 100000, 2 was 000000, and 7 was 000010. He typed them all into the password slot and held his breath, then hit "enter."

It didn't work.

"Darn," Bethany said. "Maybe he isn't quite the romantic you thought he was."

"It should have worked," Michael said, rechecking the binary code he used. "Why didn't it?"

He picked up the list Kira gave him and looked for something equally romantic. "Oh ... wait, before we try a different date. I'm looking at the dates Kira gave me. She wrote them the American way, but Jianjun grew up in China and now lives in Canada, so he'd follow what most of the world does and use day then month. I'll try that."

He keyed in the binary numbers for 2, 7, and 8. The icon spun, and then they were in. "Hah! That was too easy!" he said with a smile. "Jianjun will never live this down."

"Congrats, guys," Neptune said. "I hate to do this, but I'm dying from lack of sleep, so I'm going to bed."

"Thanks for all your help," Bethany said.

"It's okay, kid. Glad it worked. I'll get some shuteye and then check back later to see if you need anything else."

"Thanks, Neptune," Michael said.

"No problem." Neptune then hung up.

For Michael and Bethany, getting into the computer was as good as a shot of adrenaline. Bethany stayed on the phone, talking with Michael as the two went through the computer's history to see what Jianjun was looking at before he went missing.

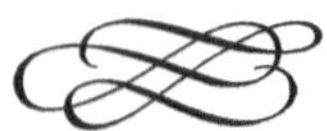

CHAPTER 39

Michael didn't find out much from Jianjun's computer that he didn't already know, especially since more than half of what was there was in Chinese. He already had Irina's former address and information about her job at the Hermitage. And it offered no hint as to Jianjun's interest in the Theosophists.

He rented a small, inconspicuous Russian car, a Lada, so he could get around town more easily as he checked out hospitals, and even the Canadian consulate. He had heard nothing from the police since filing the missing person's report.

That night, he decided to go to the Theosophist meeting—not inside, but to simply watch who went in or out. He was especially curious if the fellow who warned him to stay away would go to a meeting.

He parked across the street from the Theosophist building, making sure he wasn't near a street lamp, but still close enough to watch the foot traffic.

He was astonished to see Irina enter the building. In all, only seven others went inside around the eight o'clock meeting time. The pushy Russian wasn't among them.

About two hours passed before Irina appeared on the sidewalk. She started walking in the opposite direction from Nevsky Prospect, toward a more residential area. He got out of his rental, quietly shut the door and followed her, staying close to the buildings and in the shadows.

After a few blocks she turned into an apartment building. He ran to it, catching the main door before it shut. He heard her walking up the stairs and followed, finally reaching her on the fourth floor as she pulled out a key to the apartment door. She jumped and spun around at the sound of his footsteps.

"Michael! What are you doing here?"

"I know you're hiding something from me. You need to tell me where Jianjun is."

She frowned. "Come inside."

She walked into the small apartment. It was dingy, and Michael could hear the sound of a man's snoring. Irina shut the bedroom door but not before Michael noticed that the bed was a double, and the fellow was on one side of it. She said nothing about him.

"Would you like some cognac?" she asked. "It can be a nice change from vodka."

"That would be fine," he said as she got out two snifters. "I know Jianjun went to the Theosophist Society headquarters, and you were at their meeting tonight. I suspect you met him there."

"No. As I told you, I don't know him." She handed Michael a glass. "*Noroc,*" she murmured.

Hearing the word suddenly brought him back to his childhood. Irina's mother, Magda, would pour the kids grape juice, red wine for herself, and they'd toast each other, Romanian style. How he had loved it. "*Noroc,*" he repeated softly.

She moved to the sofa and sat, Michael joined her.

"If your friend went to the Theosophists," she began, "it might have been for the same reason as you did. To find me and follow me. But he failed. I never met him."

"If he's hurt or ... or worse because he came here looking for you, I can never forgive myself."

"Why?" She frowned at him. "Your words make no sense."

"He knew finding you was important to me."

She finished her brandy. "I'm sure he'll turn up. People get into trouble easily in Petersburg, and end up detained by the police for days. That could be what's going on. I don't think they have the 'one phone call' rule in Russia like they do when you're arrested in the States."

"I hope you're right," he whispered.

"I'm sure I am. But, since you're here, I have something important to show you. Come."

She opened a door to a second, tiny bedroom. A night light illuminated the room slightly. There were two beds. In one, a girl with long, dark hair slept, and in the other was a very young boy with blond hair.

"My daughter and Tavas' son," Irina whispered.

Michael inched a tiny bit closer to better see the girl who lay on her side sleeping peacefully, then backed out of the room as Irina shut the door. "She's lovely," he whispered, then turned his head, not bearing to look any longer at her. Thoughts he'd once had of marrying Irina, being a father to her children, rushed over him.

"How old is she?" he asked.

"Twelve."

Quick math told him that only four years after leaving him she'd conceived a child with another man. He dropped his gaze. "I see."

She placed her fingers on his hand. When he lifted his eyes, she gave him a tender smile then tilted her head in a long, meaningful look.

"I loved you as a romantic young girl," she whispered, "and memories of it still warm me. We would have made beautiful children, Michael."

"I think so." He took a deep breath. "I'm surprised you and Tavas aren't married. Thinking about it?"

She walked back to the sofa and sat, as he did. She lit a cigarette and drew deeply on it. "Not at all. Men mean nothing to me anymore. My daughter is my world, and I thank God for her."

"What about her father?"

She shrugged. "Love dies, Michael. It always dies."

"Not always," he whispered.

She didn't argue, but stared at the apartment's one small window into the night. Then she took another drag from the cigarette, carefully knocked off the tip, and placed the cigarette against the edge of the ashtray to save it for another time—a testimony to how little money she must have. "I need to ask you something. Something difficult," she whispered.

"Go on," he urged.

She pressed her lips tight, then met his eyes. "If anything happens to me, would you take care of my daughter?"

He was shocked. "Me? I don't know anything

about children. I have no wife. Not even a home any longer."

"And I have no one else that I trust with my most, my only, precious possession. I know you would always protect her and be good to her."

"Of course, but there must be—"

"*I don't trust anyone else with her.*" She didn't shout, but he'd never seen anyone more intense.

Still, he simply couldn't believe what she was asking. "Irina, it's just by chance that I'm here. Surely, if I hadn't found you, you would have asked someone else to care for her if tragedy struck."

"Maybe you being here isn't as much by chance as you think," she said. "Maybe there was some purpose that brought you here, to me, now. And I can only hope that the purpose is for you to take care of my child if I can't."

He winced at her words. "Is there something wrong, Irina? Are you sick? Why all this talk?"

"No, not sick, but I fear for her if I'm not here."

"Nothing will happen to you," he insisted.

Her face looked drawn, pinched, as she stared at the floor, as if seeing things only she could see. "I feel I'm nearing the end of the trials I've put up with for so many years."

He took her arm, forcing her to face him again. "That's silly. It's not for us to know when we will face our Maker."

"True, but we also have intuition. And mine is telling me I've fought longer than I ever expected, and that I'm tired. I'm so tired, Michael. I want to be done with this."

He took her shoulders. "No. You're still young. Come with me. Get away from here."

She broke free and stood, walking to the window. "I can't, and I won't."

He remained seated, not wanting to push her further. "What about Magda?" He spoke softly, gently. "Where is she?"

"She's dead. She couldn't take it any longer. And neither can I."

"Magda is dead? No, I can't believe it. What happened?"

Irina's face was emotionless. "Her heart."

Magda was the kindest person he'd ever met. It hurt to think she was no longer in this world. "I'm so sorry, Irina."

"I'm not. And I'm sure she's not."

He stared, unable to comprehend such bitterness toward a good woman.

Irina then faced him. "My daughter's name is Zoe."

"Zoe?"

She smiled. "It's surprisingly international, which is what I wanted for her—French, Greek,

Italian, although you Americans often add a 'y' at the end."

"I like it." He studied the contour of her face then said, "Soon, she'll be a teenager."

"Yes," Irina whispered with a slight smile.

"That's an age when a girl needs her mother."

"It's a difficult age, true. She'll need someone strong to help her get through it. She's very smart and willful. If she's with you, she will try your patience."

"I said I know nothing about children, and teenage girls, even less. But you'll be here. I know you will!"

She shook her head. "I have a strange feeling, Michael. You know us, Romanians. We always feel things and worry about death, evil spirits, vampires, demons, and the like." She tried to smile at those words, even to laugh about them, but it didn't really work. "Why do you think Dracula is from my country?"

He couldn't just sit there and listen to her a moment longer. He went to her and took her hands. "You're going to be fine. You're going to live a long, long time. But if ever Zoe needs me—for any reason—I'll do whatever I can for her."

"Thank you. I'm going to put that in my papers so that, if something were to happen, you could bring her to America. It's a better place for her to grow up. She's a smart girl. Brilliant, in fact. Sometimes she scares me. "

"Irina, don't talk that way!"

"I'm sorry. I don't mean to be morbid." She dropped his hands, stepped back, and folded her arms.

"You'll be fine. As soon as I find Jianjun, I'll go away and you should be able to stop thinking about the past. We saw a lot of sadness, Irina, but happiness, too. I remember a lot of happy times when we were kids, then teenagers, and later, when we realized we weren't kids any more and fell in love. I was never so happy. The future, I thought, was bright."

"Me, too." She smiled with her lips, but her eyes refused to obey. "I know you've always loved Pushkin, and when I found a poem of his that reminded me so much of us, I put it to memory. This is how it ended:

I loved you without hope, a mute offender;
What jealous pangs, what shy despairs I knew!
A love as deep as this, as true, as tender,
God grant another may yet offer you."

He knew the poem well, and his eyes burned with

unshed tears at the words of a once great love that had somehow died.

"And now, Michael, I have all this." She opened her hands to take in the apartment. "But this isn't living."

"Let me help you."

She shook her head. "There's no help for me. Go. Please. And thank you for saying if, God-forbid, it ever became necessary, you would watch over my daughter. That's a relief. A definite relief."

He nodded, and with a last look at the door that led to the sleeping Zoe, he left the sad apartment.

CHAPTER 40

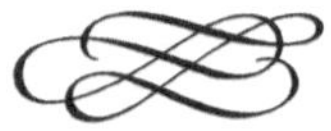

Michael was awakened by a loud banging on his door. It was six in the morning.

A woman wearing a policeman's uniform, a round fur cap on her head, glared at him. "I am Sergeant Zhuk of the St. Petersburg police. You are Michael Rempart."

A chill went through him. "I am."

With her was a uniformed officer who looked imposing but said nothing.

"You have an acquaintance named Jianjun Li," she announced.

He felt as if his heart had stopped beating. Bracing himself for the bad news he snapped, "You know I do. I told the police that I was looking for him. What's happened to him?"

She lifted her chin, her tone harsh. "May we come inside?"

He realized they stood in the hall, him in a T-shirt and pajama bottoms. "Yes, please. But … tell me."

She walked into the hotel room, her compatriot with her as she slowly marched around the perimeter of the room eying everything including the two laptops side-by-side on a table. She had dark blond hair and narrowly set hazel eyes. Her shoulders were broad, and she looked strong. The officer with her was male, a little shorter and seemed like the jumpy, tense sort who would shoot at the first sign of danger.

Michael was beside himself wanting to shout at her to tell him what they knew about Jianjun. Finally she faced him. "You did not tell us your friend is a murderer."

His mouth dropped. Was this a joke? But she didn't look as if she ever joked. He was expecting bad news, but this was crazy. "What are you talking about?"

"He is in our prison. There were some difficulties with the transliteration of his name which caused us to temporarily overlook him in our system."

"I don't care about that," Michael said firmly. "I want to know why you called him a murderer. Jianjun would never hurt anyone. Was it an accident?"

"Our officers found him at the crime scene with traces of the victim's blood under his fingernails."

Michael was aghast. "Jianjun doesn't even

know anyone here! Who was he supposed to have killed?"

"An American woman. Her name was Patience Hewson."

The shock Michael felt skyrocketed. That was the name of the older woman who had been his father's housekeeper back in Wintersgate. "What do you know about her?" he demanded.

Zhuk's eyes narrowed. "We ask the questions."

He nodded, but waited for her answer.

"The woman was here on a tourist visa, but we have been unable to locate where she was staying or where she was touring. It seems she arrived in St. Petersburg, and almost immediately vanished from view until her body was discovered."

"And where was that? And where was Jianjun?"

He could see her growing irritation at his questions, but she answered. "He was picked up drunk and lying in a gutter near the body. His clothes were stained with her blood. The murder weapon, a knife, lay by his side. The blood was that of the Hewson woman."

"I know of a Patience Hewson." He spoke cautiously. "She worked for my father in the United States. I last heard he was here, in St. Petersburg. Have you spoken to him?"

"Are you suggesting this Li Jianjun killed him as well?"

He gritted his teeth. "No! Jianjun didn't kill anyone! I'm suggesting you talk to my father. If this is the Patience that worked for him, he might know something about what happened to her."

"Do you have his address?"

"No, I don't."

Her eyebrows rose, and she smirked as she caught her fellow officer's eye for a quick moment. "But you do know he is your father?"

He tried to hold in his temper. "All I'm suggesting is that William Claude Rempart might know something about what happened to Patience Hewson, and might know who is framing Jianjun for her murder."

"That, Mr. Rempart, is a lot of 'suggesting.'" She took a photo from her pocket. "Is this the woman you knew?"

It looked like a blowup of a passport photo. Why, he wondered, had Patience come to St. Petersburg? When Wintersgate burned down, Michael had set her up with a pension so she could enjoy retirement. He wondered what had happened. "Yes," he said. "That's her."

"We'll wait here as you dress. You need to come with us. If you must use the bathroom, you will leave the door open."

"There's no window," he said. "I'm not going anywhere, and I have no reason to."

She frowned. "Then, I will allow you to shut the door. Get ready quickly. I don't like to waste my time."

She sat in a chair and seemed quite comfortable to sit and watch him get ready to go with them.

As the other officer drove them to the police station, Sergeant Zhuk asked Michael a lot of questions about him and his father. Questions he was loath to answer, so he gave the shortest, simplest answers he could.

Once at the station, she put in requests for William Claude Rempart's passport number, and then for the place he was staying.

"Why is it you do not know your father's location?" she asked.

"We aren't close. He's watched over by his assistant, Mr. Stedman, who has been with him many years."

"I see. And what is the assistant's first name?"

"I don't know. I've always just called him Stedman."

Her eyebrows went up, her lips a hard line, and he could almost hear her thinking "bourgeoisie" as her eyes hardened. She was about to ask more questions when a clerk came in and handed Zhuk a piece of paper.

"Ah." She looked at Michael. "Now we, at least, know your father's address. Unfortunately, an officer went there to bring him to the station for questioning, but received no answer. We will go and check the location. Perhaps the housekeeper isn't the only one deceased."

The two officers put on heavy black jackets with fur collars and rounded fur-edged black hats. Michael wasn't sure what he should do, so he simply remained seated and watched them. But the sergeant soon faced him and ordered, "Come!"

The two officers marched out the door. Michael rolled his eyes and followed.

Sergeant Zhuk used the large brass knocker on the door of the dacha, a country estate. It overlooked the Gulf of Finland and was quite close to the Peterhof Palace.

Michael should have known his father wouldn't be living in some boring apartment. In the time of the Tsars, several aristocratic families had built their homes near Peterhof, and somehow William Claude had managed to secure one of those as his residence. It was massive, with an ornately decorated façade of angels, gargoyles, roses and vines, along with marble and onyx tiles and massive windows.

Zhuk pounded again and then waited. Her colleague stood back with Michael. She seemed about to order the officer to break open the door when they heard a rattling of the doorknob. An older man dressed all in black pulled it open.

"May I help you?" he asked.

"Stedman!" Michael started forward but the police officer's arm stopped him.

"Quiet!" Zhuk ordered, then faced Stedman and pulled out her badge. "I am Sergeant Zhuk."

Ignoring the woman, Stedman's gaze went to Michael. "Master Michael! What a surprise! Oh, my! Are you in trouble with the law?"

Sergeant Zhuk glared from one man to the other, then addressed Stedman. "You know this man?"

"He's the son of Mr. William Claude Rempart, who has leased this estate."

"And is that man here?"

"Yes. Certainly."

"I would like to speak to him."

Stedman raised his chin and squared his shoulders. "I'm afraid Mr. Rempart is elderly and tires easily. He is lying down in his chamber."

"Lying down? So, you were not out earlier this morning?"

"Oh my, no. Of course not. We don't go any-where much."

She glanced at Michael with a frown, then turned back to Stedman. "A police officer was here earlier. He came to take you to the station, but received no answer to his constant knocking."

"I'm sorry. I may have been dozing or in the back somewhere. At my age, the ears don't work as well as they used to. And this is a very large estate."

"So it is." Her constant frown deepened. "But I must speak to this William Claude Rempart. I do not care if he is lying down or sitting up. I do not care if he is sleeping. I will see him."

Stedman nodded. "Right this way, please." He gestured for them to enter the home and then led them to a beautifully ornate living room with a view of the Gulf of Finland.

Stedman offered refreshments, but all refused, then he went off to get William Claude.

Michael wasn't sure what to expect when he saw his father for the first time since the horrifying encounter during which William Claude nearly killed him and Ceinwen trying to get the red pearl.

But Michael never expected to see him looking old and frail. He used a cane and when he turned to look at the police sergeant, Michael saw that his jaw and neck appeared to have been badly burned. The uneven pattern made it look as if he'd been scalded by a hot liquid. Michael wondered if it had happened during the fire at Wintersgate.

William Claude cast his dark eyes on Michael and smiled—a cross between a skeletal grin and one filled with a strange mirth. "Well, Michael, whatever are you doing in this city? And with the police, no less. Are you here for me to bail you out, as usual, son?"

Michael stood. "Father," he said, with a slight bow of the head. "It's nice to see you, too. And looking so well."

William Claude's eyes blazed.

Sergeant Zhuk stepped forward and introduced herself, then said, "I'm here because of an investigation. Do you know where your housekeeper is, Mr. Rempart?"

The old man grinned. "I should hope she's out in the kitchen preparing my lunch. She slept in at breakfast, it seems. Again. Right, Stedman?"

Stedman straightened. "I'm afraid Cook has taken a little vacation, sir. I've been cooking for you."

"You? I was wondering why her cooking had gone to hell. You should've told me."

"Yes, sir," Stedman said.

Zhuk looked confused. "Is her name Patience Hewson?" The older men assured her it was. "And is this her picture?" Again both men nodded.

"Why did she leave her job without her employer's approval?" Zhuk asked tersely.

Stedman faced her. "Well, you see, our housekeeper did complain a bit. She said she didn't leave retired life and come all this way to do nothing but work. She wanted to see the area whether 'his lordship liked it or not,' to use her expression. I believe that's where she is."

"Oh? She just went off on her own?" Zhuk asked.

"She is a bit headstrong," Stedman said. He rushed across the room to help Claude sit down in a tall wingback chair.

"Did you check her room to see if she took her suitcase or packed any clothes?" Zhuk asked.

"Oh, my gracious, no," Stedman said. "I would never presume to go through her belongings."

"What about you, Mr. Rempart?" Zhuk said. "Weren't you at all worried about your housekeeper?"

"What? Worried?" He looked at Stedman. "What's she talking about? Wasn't Cook here yesterday?"

"No, sir. It's been a few days."

"Oh." William Claude's gaze slowly moved from Stedman to Zhuk.

It was all Michael could do not to call a halt to this charade. His father wasn't addled, and he certainly didn't need a cane. But he also knew it would do no good for anyone to have Zhuk go into full investigation mode. Besides, he didn't believe his father or Stedman had hurt Patience. And they just might know something about Jianjun.

"Jianjun has been accused of murdering Patience," Michael blurted.

"Murder?" William Claude said. "Are you saying Cook is dead? She can't be. She just cooked my dinner last night."

Zhuk looked from one to the other. "Mr. Stedman, would you show me to Patience Hewson's room?"

"Of course."

She looked at the uniformed officer and gave him a nod. He would remain with the Rempart men.

They sat quietly for a while, then William Claude said, "So Michael, what brings you to Russia?"

"I found Irina."

"Ah, I see." His lips formed a severe, straight line. "Did she happen to tell you she has a daughter now?"

"Yes, she did."

"Irina has changed," William Claude said.

"Maybe not so much," Michael countered.

"Oh, yes. She's changed a lot. Be careful of her,

Michael. That's the only 'fatherly' advice I'll give you about the woman. She's not at all the girl you once knew."

"I don't believe that."

Claude looked at him, and slowly, his grin grew into a hearty laugh.

They then continued to sit in silence until Zhuk returned.

"We are done here," she announced to no one in particular, then turned to Michael. "We will take you back to your hotel. And you are not to leave Petersburg."

CHAPTER 41

Sergeant Zhuk refused to answer any of Michael's questions or even say whether or not she'd found anything of note in Patience's room. But she also failed to forbid him to ask questions of others or investigate on his own.

He immediately went to see Viktor at the Pushka Inn. They sat in Viktor's office, with its view of the canal and Moika River. Viktor took one look at Michael and immediately poured them each a shot of vodka.

"Michael, take this." He handed him the drink. "Good to see you again, but I can tell by your expression you aren't here to see this lovely face of mine."

"I need the name of a good criminal attorney. The charge is murder." Michael downed the shot.

Viktor stared at him. "At least I know you're not the one charged since you're walking the streets." But then his voice dropped, "Or, are the police after you?"

"It's for my friend, the one who was missing. The police have had him locked up, not letting him make a phone call or anything as they questioned him."

"Michael, Michael! What have you gotten yourself into?" Viktor spread his arms wide. "Just knowing a man like that, let alone going to visit him in prison, is enough to make sure the police will watch you. You can't do it. You've got to get out of the country while you are free to travel. You could end up being stuck here as a material witness, or who knows what? Don't get any more involved than you have already."

"I'm already involved and I can't leave. I need the name?"

Victor hesitated, then sat and opened a small desk drawer, took out a stack of business cards and shuffled through them, finally pulling one out. "I suggest you talk to Vladimir Stepanov." He gave Michael the card with Roman script on one side and Cyrillic on the other. "God be with you, friend."

"Thank you, Viktor. And thanks for the vodka. I hope not to bother you again." He took the equivalent of several hundred US dollars from his wallet. "For your private investigator friend, in case I'm not here when he sends his bill."

He found a taxi outside the Pushka and showed

the driver the Cyrillic side of the card. "Okay," the driver said in what was an almost universal word of acknowledgment.

The driver stopped on the southern side of the city near some famous cemeteries and then pointed to the building Michael needed to go to. Michael paid him and hurried inside.

The receptionist knew enough English to take down Michael's name, although she pronounced it Mikhail. She gestured for him to sit.

Before long, she showed him into the office. He and Vladimir Stepanov introduced themselves. Stepanov was not what he was expecting. He was quite young—early thirties at best, tall, blond, and appeared to be no stranger to the gym.

Michael explained Jianjun's predicament. The young attorney frowned with worry about the case. He said the first thing they needed to do was to talk to Jianjun.

Stepanov drove Michael to the prison, and he was impressed that it didn't take the attorney long to get them admitted to see Jianjun, but only for ten minutes.

They were let into a small room that may have once been white but its paint was yellowed and peeling. The room was empty except for a metal table and two metal chairs, one on each side of the table. The lawyer took a chair and Michael stood behind him.

Soon, a guard entered with Jianjun in handcuffs.

"Michael, thank God!" Jianjun cried at the sight of his friend. Michael saw tears in his eyes, a testament to how frightened he was.

Michael had already been warned he was not to touch Jianjun, not even to move when the prisoner entered the room. "I've brought you an attorney, Vladimir Stepanov. We'll get you out of here."

"How did you find me?" Jianjun asked.

"I filed a missing person report."

"But how did you know I was missing?"

"Kira phoned me."

"She did?" For the first time Michael saw a hint of life in Jianjun's eyes.

"What happened?" Stepanov asked. "And what is your connection to the deceased?"

"I don't have any at all," Jianjun said.

Stepanov frowned. "The police report said you were drunk and covered with the dead woman's blood."

"I wasn't drunk," Jianjun insisted. His lips were firm as he stated, "I rarely drink alcohol. Michael can tell you. But my clothes reeked of vodka, they were sticky with blood, and I'm sorry to say, I seemed to have thrown up and pissed myself as I lay there all that time." He dropped his gaze a moment, then added, "I can understand the police reaction to the way they found me. But their conclusion is completely wrong."

"It was her blood on your clothes and under your fingernails."

"And I was out cold," Jianjun insisted.

Stepanov continued. "You were found near Peterhof. How did you get there?"

"Same question, same answer," Jianjun said. "I've never even heard of Peterhof."

"Okay, then, what's the last thing you remember before the police found you?"

Jianjun stiffened, his gaze darting between Michael and the attorney. Finally he said, "I met an attractive woman. We talked, I asked her if she'd like to get a drink, she said yes. She said she knew a secluded spot, and I agreed to go with her. When she turned into an alley, I followed. The next thing I knew, I was awakened on a street, told I was under arrest, and I'd lost an entire day in the process."

"Were you robbed?"

"I don't know. The police took everything—wallet, passport, and phone."

"What was the woman's name?"

"I didn't know her long enough to ask."

"Did the police do any tests on you?" Stepanov asked.

"Blood and urine."

"Okay. I'll get those results. What else can you tell me? Why are you in St. Petersburg?"

"I came here for vacation," Jianjun said. "I've always wanted to see it."

Stepanov frowned at that answer and was about to ask more when the guard stepped forward and pointed to the clock.

"Time's up," Stepanov said, then faced Michael. "I'll start with the toxicology tests. They could make or break his story."

Jianjun stood and the two men told him not to worry, they'd get him out of there, but he looked fearful as the guard roughly led him away.

As Stepanov and Michael left the prison, Stepanov looked at his paperwork. "It looks like the detective investigating this case is Sergeant Zhuk. I've dealt with her. Fair but formidable. We need to have a talk with her."

Michael nodded and followed the attorney without saying a word, as all his thoughts were with the story Jianjun had told Stepanov. He wondered what the real story was.

Stepanov drove straight to the police station to see Zhuk. Fortunately, she was in the office. Her usual scowl deepened as Stepanov spoke to her in Russian. Michael heard Stepanov say "Li Jianjun" and guessed Stepanov was explaining he was the attorney for her prisoner. They soon switched over to English for Michael's benefit.

"I'd like to see the toxicology work done on my client," Stepanov announced. "You did do blood tests when he was booked, did you not?"

"Of course," she said stiffly. "It offered no surprises. His blood alcohol level was extremely high, but not so high he could not function. No drugs in his system. And the third-party blood we found on him exactly matches that of Patience Hewson."

"Thank you for the succinct summary," Stepanov said. "Now, I'd like to see the numbers for myself."

"Fine." She pulled open a file drawer in her desk, flipped through a few folders, then pulled one out and gave it to him.

He opened it and began to read. Michael peered over his shoulder, but everything was in Cyrillic lettering.

Stepanov looked confused, glanced up at Zhuk, then down at the folder she gave him again. "Are you sure this is the report you saw on Mr. Li?"

"Of course. Why?"

"Look at it. What does it say?" He spun the folder around so the words were facing her.

She read it over and stiffened. "Impossible." She flipped through the pages, one after the other, then went back to the beginning and flipped through them again. "This is not the report I was given."

"What's going on?" Michael asked.

Stepanov lifted a finger to silence him. "Why are you holding my client?"

"This is not the initial report!" She took the folder and in a fire-storm of Russian berated the nearby clerk, who kept shaking his head. She then marched into her superior's office and slammed the report on his desk.

Stepanov was completely focused on the detective, and Michael simply waited. Whatever the report said, it was enough to outrage Zhuk and to put a smile on Stepanov's face.

Zhuk's superior was standing now and talking into the telephone. Before long, a couple of men entered the office, carrying blue folders—folders that looked a lot like the one Stepanov had been looking at.

Zhuk and her boss flipped through the new folders, then looked at each other and shook their heads. The two newcomers hurried out of the office. Zhuk's boss waved his hand dismissively, and Zhuk, rather meekly for her, left his office.

She walked to the desk where Michael and Stepanov waited. When she looked up, her eyes were more like a whipped puppy than the tough cop Michael had faced up to this point. She swallowed. "Apparently, there was some sort of mix-up in the laboratory reports initially," she said. "The report I saw was not Mr. Li's. I'm sorry to say I was not informed when the error was caught. Based on the new evidence, we will not be holding Mr. Li. But I will caution you that he is still involved in this case, potentially as a suspect, but definitely as a person of interest. If he did not kill Mrs. Hewson, then who did and why did that person try to frame Mr. Li? We request that Mr. Li not leave St. Petersburg, and we will continue to hold his passport."

Michael was shocked and relieved by her admission.

Stepanov turned to Michael. "This new report shows that Jianjun had no alcohol in his system, but did have on his skin a chemical nerve agent, what we call Novichok, an acetylcholinesterase inhibitor. In other words, he was poisoned by a substance that takes very little of it applied to the skin—or nose or mouth—to quickly incapacitate. In only a slightly larger dose, it may well have led to his death. Your friend is lucky he didn't die."

"My God!"

Stepanov turned to Sergeant Zhuk. "Mr. Li is clearly a victim. I will drive to the prison to pick him up. I'm sure you will be releasing him immediately. Also I will be looking into getting his passport released so he can move to safety. I will need his personal belongings as well. But I do understand your need to question him, and I'm sure you will have his full cooperation."

Zhuk nodded. "*Spasiba.*"

Michael was surprised to hear her give such a polite sounding "thank you." With that, he followed Stepanov from the office.

Stepanov returned Michael and Jianjun to the Four Seasons. Michael called ahead and asked to be moved to a two-bedroom suite. He didn't want Jianjun alone in the Pushka Inn or anywhere else. When Michael arrived at the Four Seasons, the suite was ready.

Jianjun was simultaneously exhausted and wired. Michael got him up to his suite without having him check-in as a guest, which caused a couple of raised eyebrows at the front desk, but they knew better than to question the actions of a man who paid for such expensive lodgings.

Jianjun had all but sleep-walked into the hotel room but suddenly, he smiled. "My laptop! Hallelujah."

Michael laughed, and it was all Jianjun could

do not to take it into the shower with him—but he knew he had to wash the stink of the prison off his body before he did anything else.

He took a long shower and came out wrapped in one of the hotel's thick white bathrobes.

While he was showering, Michael ordered room service, and the meal was quickly delivered—another benefit of staying in the pricey suite.

He let Jianjun sit and relax awhile, glad to hear his friend slowly starting to act and sound a bit like himself as the terror of being in prison and charged with murder slowly seeped from his bones. He also began to eat. "I knew you'd come," he said to Michael more than once as they enjoyed pelmeni, ravioli-like dumplings in a broth with sour cream.

Jianjun had been especially overjoyed to hear that Kira was the one who worried about him enough to call Michael. "Despite everything, she still cares about me," he said with a huge smile as he poured himself a second cup of tea.

That was when Michael knew he was enough on the mend to be asked about Irina. "I understand you found Irina," Michael said.

"The address I'd been given was wrong, but I managed to track down where she worked. I went there and waited until I saw her leave, around midnight. I followed and found out where she lived. I watched for a couple of days, trying to learn her situation. She's living with some fellow and they have a couple of children. Given all that, I decided I should talk to her and ask her if she was willing to see you. I was going to tell you I'd found her, but if she didn't want to see you, if she didn't want her happy life disturbed by a visit from you, I would tell you that and urge you to walk away and not look back any longer."

"Makes sense," Michael murmured.

"I suspected, though, from all I saw, that wouldn't be the case. She doesn't look happy. In fact, the way she's living looks miserable, and the fellow she's with seems to just sit around the apartment drinking. I never saw much of him. I guess he at least watches the kids at night, since she works until midnight.

"Did you ever see William Claude meet with her?" Michael asked.

"No. I saw no sign of him at all. My cousin's information gave an address, but it was a house that had been abandoned years ago."

"Strange. What happened next?"

"It's a long story," Jianjun said.

"We've got all night," Michael told him.

CHAPTER 42

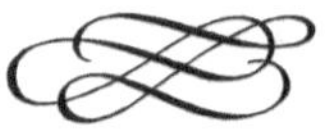

Jianjun explained to Michael how, after finally locating Irina, he had been so nervous about actually talking to her, he'd spent three days just watching her—observing her comings and goings and any interactions she might have.

Eventually, he got up the nerve to face to her. He thought it best to approach her in front of the Hermitage. There would be a lot of people around, so she shouldn't feel scared.

He got there an hour early. But her usual report-to-work time came and went and he never saw her. He continued to wait, thinking she might just be running late.

To his surprise, a young woman approached him. She was quite pretty with full cheeks, curly black hair, and eyes the color of chestnuts. Her dress was eye-catching and colorful. She wore several beaded necklaces, dangling earrings, and bracelets, and a ring on every finger.

"You don't give up, do you?" she said with a smile.

Jianjun was startled, but she seemed pleasant. "What do you mean?"

"I saw you yesterday and the day before watching my sister. What do you want with her?"

"I'm afraid you're mistaken," he said, turning his back to her.

The woman was persistent and moved in front of him again. "She's not coming today. It's her day off. But I know where she'll be tonight, if that interests you. My name is Stana, by the way." She stared at him, a curious expression on her face.

"Why would you help a stranger meet your sister? Although you're wrong about me. The woman I'm waiting for doesn't have a sister."

"Irina Petrescu, right?" she said.

"Yes, but— "

"Don't worry about it. As I said, she's off today. But you can buy me some coffee and we can talk. So, what's your name?"

In the coffee shop, she explained that she used to work in the Hermitage with Irina—although she preferred to use what she said was her sister's pet name, Militsa. She insisted the two really were sisters. Jianjun thought it best not to push her, but to listen. Like Militsa—or Irina—she did art restoration, but now that summer was coming she was creating original paintings of famous sites in the city to sell to tourists, explaining she made a lot more money that way than doing restorations.

As they talked, she realized Jianjun hadn't seen any of the sites she painted, and she insisted on giving him a tour.

They walked all over the heart of St. Petersburg and she told him about its history, the crazy tsars, the assassinations, the revolutions. And she knew a lot about Rasputin. Jianjun had never heard much about the man besides him being called a "mad monk" and that he had great influence over the Tsar and Tsarina. But Stana had a way of talking that sounded as if she actually had known him. She made history come alive, and Jianjun had to admit he enjoyed their afternoon tremendously.

He hadn't laughed much in recent times, but Stana knew how to make jokes and got him to laugh along with her. It felt good, really good. Jianjun found her delightful.

But many of her stories were also quite sad. She told him how the Tsarevitch, Alexei, had been born a hemophiliac which meant every time he got a simple bruise it could be a death sentence. Jianjun had had no idea that hemophilia was quite painful, especially around the joints as they swelled with blood from nearly unstoppable internal bleeding, and Alexei would scream in agony at such times.

Alexandra would be nearly mad with worry that he might die. It was a time when few hemophiliacs made it past childhood. But then she met Rasputin. More than once, when Alexei was in pain and his life in danger, Rasputin would throw the doctors and their medicines, some of which were blood thinners, out of the boy's room. Also, he had the ability to calm Alexandra's fears. When Alexei would see his mother more at ease, the child would also relax, which helped his blood to clot.

Because of this, Alexandra opened the family's private residence to Rasputin, causing many to suggest the two were having an affair.

Actually, Stana said, Rasputin probably had no time for the Tsarina because he was so busy with all the other women in Petersburg society who would go to him for "private spiritual counseling." It was an open secret that many women were part of his "cult," to the fury of their husbands. Word spread that he had an incredibly large and magical "member" that could cure all sorts of ills.

That story was so pervasive that after Rasputin's assassination, it was said his special body part had been cut off by the assassins who were jealous of his prowess. Before long a number of places opened up throughout the city claiming to possess the "true" Rasputin member and, for a small

fee, patrons could view the incredible object preserved in formaldehyde.

That went on for years. One such protuberance
was later found to be that of a horse and another
was from a bull.

Jianjun found this to be an especially funny
vignette and laughed out loud ... until he noticed
Stana wasn't laughing.

"The people of the time were such fools," she
said fiercely. "They never did understand him."

As the hour grew late, Stana said if Jianjun still
wanted to meet Irina she had an idea how to make it
happen. Irina would be going to a Theosophist Society meeting that night and asked if he'd like to
attend as Stana's guest. He agreed.

He then hurried back to his room to find out
what in the world a Theosophist Society was before
going to their meeting. He'd never heard of it.

He soon learned quite a bit about the Society
and its strange founder, Madame Blavatsky. It
turned out he needn't have bothered.

At a large building on Bol'shaya Morskaya,
Stana led him past the elevator to a stairwell that
brought them down to a basement. They went
through a maze of doors and hallways until Jianjun
felt as if he'd entered a different world.

The room was dark, lit only with votive candles,
as if in a church. A fair number of people seemed to

be in it but he could only see their silhouettes and hear the hum of their voices. The air was heavy with weed or hashish and many other sweet-smelling smokes. Jianjun's eyes immediately began to burn and soon were watering so much, he doubted he could have seen much even if the room were well lit.

Someone handed him a glass with a clear liquid. Someone else offered him a pipe. Even in the dark, he could see how filthy it was. He refused it, but Stana took it and sucked in a lot of smoke, slowly exhaling. She stared at Jianjun the whole time, making him so uncomfortable, he took a small sip of the drink. It burned his throat and tasted as if it might be rubbing alcohol. As soon as he could find a spot, he put down the glass.

Stana put her arm around his waist and pulled him into the room where she introduced him to a couple of her friends, a man and two women, saying they were the ones who spoke the best English in the group and were happy to tell him all about their society. Despite this being a Theosophist Society meeting, Stana and her friends scarcely mentioned Madame Blavatsky's name.

They explained that this chapter of the Society went back to a time when Rasputin himself was a member. They saw him as the group's guru.

"He was very holy," Stana said. Not only was

there no hint of sarcasm, she sounded almost reverent. "He opened his home—he had a wife and children—in Siberia to the elites of St. Petersburg, but only to women. He didn't like the idea of strange men in the house with his wife. But women were welcome. He had room for eight, and often all the beds were taken. He'd walk through his little town with them, and he would openly hug and kiss his favorites, showing one and all how blessed they were. It must have been wonderful to be there with him."

Jianjun swallowed hard. "I see."

Another woman took hold of his arm and walked him away from Stana. "I thought I'd rescue you," she said. "Stana can go on all night about Rasputin."

"So I've gathered," Jianjun agreed. "It seems he still fascinates people."

"And so much of it isn't at all true. For example, even though some horrible gossips claim he was the real father of the Tsarevitch Alexei, he wasn't. Stana and Militsa hadn't yet introduced him to Alexandra when Alexei was conceived."

"Stana and Militsa?" What, he wondered, was she talking about? He remembered that Stana had said her pet name for Irina was Militsa. What was going on here?

The stranger suddenly wrapped her arms around his shoulders and pressed against him as she whispered in his ear, "They may be devoted to him, but I find other men a lot more interesting."

Jianjun froze, so shocked by the woman's closeness as well as her words that he was sure his ears had turned so red they glowed brighter than the votive candles. The whole place quickly moved from weird to scary.

As he tried to disengage himself from her, she was telling him how interesting she found him. And shy. Then she added that before the night was over, he wouldn't feel that way any longer.

Somehow, he managed to pull himself free and headed deeper into the room, desperate to find Irina, say what he needed to, and get out of there.

He also wanted to find out more about the "Stana and Militsa" business, but decided that could wait.

And then some music started.

Stana caught his arm. "You can't wander off and miss out on the fun, Jianjun-ka."

Jianjun-ka? He blinked hard because the smoke had nearly blinded him and now his head was throbbing. "Fun?" he murmured.

"Don't you know about us Khlysts? Rasputin was investigated several times as being a possible a leader of the Khlysty. He denied it because no one understands us. Our philosophy is simple. We seek eternal salvation by total repentance of our sins. And we know that true repentance can only come about when the sin is a big one. I mean, can you repent for telling a white lie? Not really. And since repentance is easiest for those who sin big, we do that."

He had to replay her words in his mind, so appalled was he by what she said. "You purposefully sin big? You are joking, right?"

"I never joke. Christ died for our sins." She then patted his behind, making him jump. "We wouldn't want his death to have been in vain, would we?"

He backed away, now wanting to leave as quickly as possible. "I'd better look for Irina."

But she hooked her arm in his, holding him tight. "You'll see her. She loves this part. We start with a song that forms a ladder to God."

The music had been growing louder as they spoke. As if on cue, the group began to sing. Stana included, as she wrapped his hand with both of hers, holding him tight, even as she smiled up at him.

The song sounded strange, low, almost chant-like. The people nearest him—the only ones he could see—all had intense gleams in their eyes as they sang.

Soon the singing stopped and everyone moved to the center of the room. Stana pulled Jianjun along with her.

They formed two circles, the men in the center, the women on the outside. Stana gave Jianjun over to a friend, a massive friend. Everyone in each circle held hands as the circles moved in time to the music, the men clockwise, the women counterclockwise. The music sped up and so did the people until they were going very fast at which point, they let go of each other and began spinning alone. Some brought out small whips, *khlysts,* Jianjun heard them called, and began to beat themselves.

Jianjun rushed to a wall and leaned against it as he looked at the dancers or twirlers or whatever they were. Over time, the movements grew more sexual, as the music and dance seemed to be driving everyone into some sort of frenzy—although he suspected the narcotics and alcohol had even more to do with it. He tried to spot Irina as women's faces came into view, but the room was too hazy and dark, and his eyes still watered.

The English speakers he had met earlier somehow found him and encouraged him to "give it a whirl," so to speak. He said no, but they grabbed his arms and pulled him into the crowd, turning him around faster and faster in the darkened room. It reminded him of how he had felt as a kid wearing a blindfold and playing pin the tail on the donkey. As soon as they let him go, he nearly fell over. His heart raced, his eyes could scarcely focus, and he was dizzy.

The English speakers twirled away. He saw Stana spin by, but never Irina. It was all quite hypnotic. Even the candles developed a strange scent. His head was now throbbing so badly the entire room seemed to pulsate. Many of the candles had gone out, and the scene grew more eerie as bodies floated by, some with whips, others simply enjoying pleasures of the flesh of whoever happened to be near—male, female, or both.

He finally felt steady enough to try to walk away when two women grabbed him. One pulled at his shirt while the other dropped to her knees and tried to unfasten his belt buckle. He shoved her hands away, but she slid them up and down his legs.

Between the music, the drink, the smoke, the sweaty bodies, the smell of sex, and these strangers pawing at him, he suddenly felt nauseous. Breaking free, he stumbled, fell to the ground, and half-crawled from the room.

He wasn't sure how he made it out of the building, but once outside, he threw up in the street. Several passers-by frowned at him with the expression of someone watching a person too drunk to hold his liquor.

He didn't care. He was never so relieved to breathe fresh air.

The next morning, he was still in bed when Stana waltzed into his room. He thought he'd locked the door, but when he got back to his hotel the night before, he was still feeling sick and dizzy.

Stana crossed the room and sat on his bed. "I'm sorry you didn't get to meet Militsa, I mean, Irina, last night," she said.

He pulled the blanket up to his neck, glad he was wearing pajamas. "I don't know that would have been the best place to meet her." He couldn't imagine suddenly meeting Michael's former fiancée in the state she might have been in.

"She's sorry and told me she'll gladly meet you tonight at one of our favorite pubs. Of course, tonight she has to work, so it'll be after midnight, if that's okay." She crossed her legs and her skirt slid back to reveal much of her thigh and shapely calf.

He swallowed hard. "It is."

"Great. Two blocks down the street, heading away from the Hermitage, is a Georgian restaurant. Do you know it?"

"Yes, I've seen it."

"We'll meet at the corner just past the restaurant at midnight."

"Okay."

"But that's hours away, so why don't I join you?" She patted his bed and leaned closer.

He jumped out on the opposite side from where she sat. "I'm, uh, busy," he muttered, now standing in the middle of his room and feeling like an idiot.

"Don't you want to be saved?" she asked, surprisingly innocent-sounding.

"Not at the moment."

"Your loss." She got up to leave. "Don't be late, Jianjun-ka." She walked up to him, gave him a kiss that made him wonder if he wasn't an idiot for not taking her up on her offer, and then sauntered from the room.

Before midnight he went up to the Georgian restaurant and stood against the embankment along the canal watching for Stana. He hated to admit it, but he'd thought about her all day... her taste, her scent, the lushness of her body. It was almost as if she'd cast some sort of spell on him.

It was exactly midnight when he saw her on the corner across from him gesturing for him to join her. He crossed the street only to see that she had continued down the block to an alley. She again waved at him to follow and then stepped inside it. He knew a lot of local bars had back entrances, especially for after hours, so he wasn't wary of doing as she bid.

He turned the corner into the alley, and then all went black.

He didn't wake up until the police stood over him.

CHAPTER 43

After hearing Jianjun's story, Michael realized Irina had lied to him. Even if she didn't know Jianjun's name, she knew enough to trap him. And who was this mysterious Stana? And why did she call Irina Militsa? He wondered if they were working with William Claude, despite all Irina's denials.

The next day Michael bought some oil paint supplies at an art store. He took the bag with the shop logo prominently displayed with him as he went to the employee entrance to the Hermitage. Fortunately, the guard wasn't one he'd seen before, so he said Irina's name. The guard checked the employee roster and the bag Michael carried, then waved him in.

Michael took the elevator up to the room where he'd first seen Irina. She was there.

A woman came up to him speaking in Russian. He handed her the bag of paints and pointed at Irina.

The woman brought the paints to Irina, who turned around to see who had sent them to her. Surprise filled her face, and she approached Michael. "Why are you here?"

"Jianjun is free," he said. "Why did you set him up?"

She looked exasperated. "Come. We'll talk."

She led him to a room that seemed to be a storage area for pottery, sculptures, statues, furniture and clothing that he guessed was either being rotated through the museum or simply had been replaced.

The clothes were on hangers, mannequins or dress-makers' dummies. One such headless mannequin wore a monk's gown of the type Rasputin often wore in photographs.

Irina stopped at that one, her hand on the mannequin's shoulder. "So tell me what happened to your friend."

"He didn't die, if that's what you mean. The police realize he'd been drugged, and I know your friend who calls herself Stana led him to be captured. Why did you do it, Irina?"

"The police?" She looked frightened.

"That's right. And who is this Stana?"

"I don't know!"

"You're lying. I've had enough lies from you." He glared at her. "Stana told him she'd take him to meet you. Instead, it was a trap, and he was arrested for a murder he didn't commit."

Her hands balled into fists as she shouted at him. "Why do you think I had anything to do with such a scheme? I didn't!"

"Stana referred to you as Militsa. What's that all about? Wasn't that the name of the woman whose dress you put on? A friend of Tsarina Alexandra? Why would she call you that?"

Irina paled. "I don't know any Stana! So how should I know what she calls me?"

"You were at the Theosophical Society meeting. So was Stana, and so was Jianjun. You keep lying to me, and I'm sick of it. Tell me what's going on here!"

She looked trapped but then blurted, "Your father made me!"

Usually, he would love to blame all ills of the world on William Claude. But not this time. "Why would he do that?"

"To get you here, of course. He knew, if your friend was missing, that you'd come looking for him."

She said the words too quickly, almost as if she'd planned them. Claude hadn't looked or acted as if he'd been expecting Michael. "I saw my father two nights ago. He was surprised I'd returned. So what's really going on, Irina? Why do you keep lying to me?"

"I'm not!" she cried. "And Claude is the only one who would want you here, unless you have other enemies in Petersburg."

He shook his head. He still didn't believe her. "I know one thing, the police will be asking you these same questions. I hope you have better answers for them than you do for me."

"I can't fight Claude. I thought – hoped – that you could. But now, I'm not so sure." She turned and put her arms around the monk's robe as if she were hugging him, her forehead against the headless mannequin's shoulder in a bizarre embrace. "And now, you say the police will be after me. That's the last thing I need."

"Is it?"

She caught his eyes for a second, then dropped her gaze. "They'll put me in prison and I didn't do anything, but I'll never be able to explain. They'll take my daughter. I need you to help me."

"Help you? How? You won't tell me anything. None of what you say makes sense. And you're lying about Jianjun."

"Don't you see?" She all but shouted. "I'm as much of a victim as you are."

Michael shook his head. He didn't know how to get through to her.

"You could help me, Michael, if you wanted to. When you do, come and find me. Not before."

"Irina –"

"Not before, I said!" She stormed from the room.

He thought about chasing after her, but to what end? Nothing she said made sense, and he had no idea who to trust. There were only two people in the world that he did trust. He nearly lost one of them to Irina's trickery, and the other he had ignored and caused to leave him just so he could search for the past.

How was he supposed to help Irina when he couldn't even help himself?

The one person who could answer a lot of Michael's questions was, unfortunately, William Claude.

As much as Michael suspected it was a fool's mission to attempt to get his father to divulge anything, he drove out to the coastal area near Peterhof. He somewhat remembered the route Sergeant Zhuk had taken, and soon, he managed to find the address where his father had been staying.

But when he reached the home, instead of the beautiful palatial country estate he had seen previously—the kind of place William Claude would choose and that looked like something right out of tsarist Russia—the home before him had been neglected for years. It was decaying and bits of fancy plaster masonry had fallen from the façade to lie on the ground.

He would have thought he'd made a wrong turn except that he remembered the carved front door with its large brass knocker. They were the same, only the door's black paint was peeling, and the brass was green and mottled instead of shiny. He tried the front door, then other doors and windows, but the place was locked up tight.

He went around to the back of the estate. The garden was overrun with weeds and filled with dead twigs and bushes. It abutted an equally weed-filled plot of land, and the back gate lay open with only one hinge stopping it from falling to the ground. The back door rattled loose in its jamb and it took little shoulder effort to cause it to spring open.

The home's inside was in even worse shape than its exterior. It looked and smelled as if squatters may have lived there for a while using it as sleeping as well as bathroom facilities. There was no sign that anyone had lived there for many years.

He hurried from the house. What the hell was going on?

CHAPTER 44

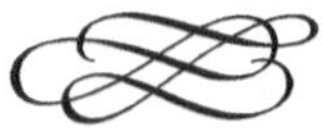

"I went to the location of the house my father had been renting, and it's all changed," Michael said to Jianjun when he returned to the Four Seasons. "It's as if the house I'd been in was a mirage. But now he's gone and I have no idea where. I tried to talk to Irina, but she won't tell me anything I don't already know and everything else she says is a lie. I'm afraid I've been chasing a fantasy. It's time I give up and concentrate on what's real. I need to get Bethany away from that dig and, most of all, to find Ceinwen. I've been an idiot and I need her to forgive me."

"That's probably for the best, boss," Jianjun admitted.

"At least having seen Irina helped me to put aside the idealistic fantasies of my youth. I still have a lot of questions about what happened when we were young. But I don't think I'll ever learn the answers. At least I tried." He poured himself a vodka. "We'll talk to Stepanov. As soon as he gets you your passport, you should leave the country. Go back home."

"Where are you going?" Jianjun asked.

"Back to the dig. Bethany wants answers about Rachel, answers I can't give her. Just as I have to accept that there aren't always good answers, so does she. Plus, I'm worried about her." He swallowed a healthy swig of the Zyr vodka. "I've seen demons-- vampires—at work there."

Jianjun's mouth dropped open, then he shut it and shook his head. "Of course there are. Just another day at the office, right, boss?"

"Not funny," Michael grumbled.

"You never told me how Bethany found you in such a remote place," Jianjun said.

"She says she hacked her way there."

Jianjun looked skeptical. "Using what?"

"She wouldn't say."

"Listen, because of your father, I've got you behind so many firewalls, I don't know if I'd be able to hack my way into your stuff. I can't imagine how she broke through it unless she's a better hacker than me, which I find hard to believe."

"She had help. And her helper, along with some suggestions from Kira, got me into your computer. You might want to change your password."

Jianjun blushed so fiercely his face looked ready to ignite. "Kira gave you some dates?"

Michael smiled. "She did."

"Oh, man. But how did you figure out the rest?"

"Only because I know you quite well."

Jianjun grimaced. "Too well, obviously. But anyway, about this hacker, did you put stuff about the dig on your computer?"

Michael thought about it. "Not really. I sent an actual letter in reply to the first one I received from Professor Koval, thinking they probably had no cell service at the site. And they sent a letter by express mail in return. All I did online was book a plane ticket to Budapest. Going through Hungary wasn't the closest route, but in many ways the easiest."

Jianjun looked worried. "That's what I thought. So how did this girl find you if your computer had nothing to hack? Are you sure she's who you think she is?"

"Fairly sure, yes." But then Michael pondered the question further. "That seems all the more reason for me to hurry back there."

"And for me to go with you."

They were arguing about that when the front desk buzzed. Michael answered and was told he had a call.

"Michael, I'm sorry for the way I left you yesterday," Irina said. "I'll be in the lobby at midnight tonight. It's time I tell you the truth. All of it."

It was nearly midnight, but Professor Veronika Masur couldn't sleep.

She got out of bed, opened the door to her room at the inn and peered down the hall to Galyna's room. She noticed that the girl hadn't been spending time with Feder since they'd found her with cuts all over her torso in the chapel. Veronika couldn't help but wonder why.

She also couldn't rid herself of the vision of the man—demon—whatever it was, who seemed to step through the wall when she found Galyna. Stories of the vampires said to dwell in those mountains filled her mind, and a dark tunnel, closed off from the rest of the world for centuries, would have been the perfect spot for them to hide.

But also for them to starve … not to death, however. They were immortal. They couldn't die, but they could suffer.

Veronika had loved the stories she'd heard about them when she was a child. And she'd been half in love with the vampires ever since, always feeling sad about their lonely existence. What good was it to live forever if you were alone, without love? She particularly adored the stories about vampires who found someone to love them, even to join them as mates, and how they would hunt together for fresh, new blood.

Ever since seeing that "figure" she wondered if they weren't just stories. Could the vision she saw have actually been a vampire?

There had been a lot of cuts on Galyna's body. Could there have been more than one vampire?

She swallowed hard at the thought.

She wondered how Galyna felt having them use her that way. Did it make her feel powerful, knowing how much they needed her blood? Clearly, they kept her alive for a reason, and hadn't killed her the way they had Wasyl. Could it simply have been because she's a woman? Did that make her more interesting to them?

Just the thought made her heart beat a little faster. Vampires had always struck her as the sexiest, most erotic, of the demons. Was that why she'd never found a human male who interested her? They simply couldn't compete with the tragic and romantic image that had filled her head since she was a girl.

The more she thought about it, the more she knew she'd be willing to give a few drops of her blood to help one of them survive.

She wondered if she should approach Galyna. Talk to her frankly about what had happened to her? No, she could imagine the girl laughing at her —and worse, telling the others what she had asked.

Instead, she would watch Galyna, see if the vampire or vampires that had taken and used her, doing heaven-only-knew what, would come to the inn seeking her, or if the girl liked being with them enough to go back to the dig on her own.

She opened the door to her room just slightly—enough so she could hear other doors if they opened and hear any footsteps. It was an old, creaky inn. Not a place anyone could easily sneak around in.

She didn't have long to wait. She heard doors open and shut, and footsteps. She peeked from behind her open door to see Dmytro in the hallway. Soon, Galyna joined him, and then the two hurried out of the inn.

Veronika put a heavy coat on over her nightgown, donned heavy socks and shoes, then rushed out to follow the two. The thought crossed her mind that they might be lovers on a tryst—if so, they'd certainly kept it quiet from everyone.

The moon was full that night, making it easy for her to see the student and young professor ahead of her, even as she stayed far back. They turned in the direction of the dig and soon reached it.

Veronika hid on the steep footpath up to the excavation, still able to see them, but not daring to move closer for fear they'd turn around and spot her.

Dmytro and Galyna walked to the edge of the deep pit, but didn't go down it. Instead, they lay down. They didn't move.

It was all Veronika could do to stay awake. But then she saw lights coming from the pit along with a soft hum. And then a procession of ... what? Beings wearing long robes and monk hoods that hid their features came out of the pit carrying fire-lit torches. Oh, my, she thought, as she counted nine of them. This was the most fascinating, exciting thing she'd ever seen.

One of them went straight to Galyna.

Veronika could scarcely breathe when she saw the girl stand up as he approached. He was still a few steps away when she ran to him, throwing her arms around the being's neck. He held her a moment, then scooped her up and walked off with her. Veronika wanted to see what they did next, but they went into an area free of moonlight.

Her heart all but fluttered; she had never seen anything in real life as romantic as that embrace.

She was tempted to try to find them, but then she saw the others pick up Dmytro and carry him down into the pit and out of her sight. Danger be damned, she thought, as she crawled to the edge of the pit and peered into it.

The beings began to sing a low, haunting tune as they removed Dmytro's clothes and oiled his body. They all seemed to be enjoying themselves, including Dmytro who had begun to writhe with pleasure at what they were doing to him. She had never watched a pornographic film, but she couldn't imagine it showed more than what she was seeing.

One of them sliced open a spot on Dmytro's torso and she watched blood trickle out of it. The creatures began pushing and shoving each other as they all tried to take their share of the rich nutrient while Dmytro cried out in what sounded like a mixture of pain and pleasure.

Yes! They were vampires! She'd known it. All along, in her heart, she'd known what they were.

She could bear it no longer. She wanted, needed them ... much as they would need her.

Filled with joy, she pulled off her coat and ran down into the pit. "Take me," she said. "I can help you. I know who and what you are, and all you've been through. I don't blame you. I cry for you, and I cry with you!"

The vampires watched her and when she joined their group, they left Dmytro and surrounded her. They jabbed at her, their sharp nails cutting through her nightdress and her skin. The cuts were stinging and painful and soon blood marred her clothing.

"Easy now! That hurts!" she said as she peeled off her gown. "I want your oils, your gentle touch on me. I can give you what you need."

But then they lifted her and carried her near the torches and for the first time she had enough light to see their faces under the hoods—their snakelike eyes.

"What are you?" she cried. Finally, she was afraid. "Stop! You aren't the vampires of my dreams. Get away! Leave me! You're ... you're hideous!"

Instead of answering, the vampires bared their teeth in a gruesome smile, then tore her open to enjoy a rich, juicy feast.

CHAPTER 45

At midnight, as Michael got off the elevator he caught Irina's eye. She said nothing to him, but walked out of the lobby. He followed. Outside she waited for him to catch up to her and they walked in brisk silence, side by side, through the Alexander Gardens. They passed the Bronze Horseman, one of the city's most famous landmarks, built by Catherine the Great to honor Peter the Great. Whenever Michael passed it, he thought of the legend that the city would survive as long as the Bronze Horseman stood to protect it. In 1941 when the German army circled the city and cut off all rail and other food supply lines, the people fought back, fortified the city, covered the Bronze Horseman with sandbags and a wooden shelter, and somehow managed to hold the Germans at bay. The city survived what came to be known as "The Siege of Leningrad." The assault had lasted nearly 900 days and in the process, nearly three-quarters of a million people died from starvation as well as shelling from the German artillery.

The people of the city, Michael thought, had withstood more death and hardship than anyone should have to endure, yet they continued on. He admired them for that.

Irina reached a small pub and then turned and went inside. Cautiously, he followed. She found a table in a quiet corner, and ordered vodka and *za-kuski*, a platter of foods that supposedly helped prevent drunkenness.

They sat in silence and the waitress immediately brought their shots. They drank them down quickly, and she poured seconds, as was the custom, and then brought them a platter with a mixture of pickles, herring, bread, caviar, salted cucumbers, onions, and potatoes.

Michael ignored the food and waited for Irina to speak.

"I'm leaving St. Petersburg," she said.

"Why?"

"It's time. Too much is happening. Your father. His housekeeper's death. Your friend, Li Jianjun. Too many pieces will lead the police to me and I can't have that."

"So you are involved with all of them," Michael said. "That's the only way you could have known the dead woman was his housekeeper."

"Yes, but not by choice, believe me, Michael. But before I go, I thought it was time for you to hear the whole, ugly story. I know that's why you've come here. Why you walked away from a comfortable life. But if you want to know the story, be warned, it will change you forever."

"How can you say that?" he asked.

"I've learned many things I never dreamed were possible, but they are. The truth sometimes hurts more than you can ever imagine."

"You're right. But I've always known there was more to the story."

"It's a long tale," she said. "And it will make the most sense if I begin early on, and that goes all the way back to the time when my mother was Claude's housekeeper, you were away at Oxford, and I was a young, surprisingly innocent twenty-one-year-old, helping my mother and living at Wintersgate."

He nodded and remained silent.

As Irina began her story, her mind filled with the images and emotions of days long past.

She especially remembered the afternoon that changed life completely. It seemed only yesterday, not seventeen years earlier.

She had peeked into Wintersgate's morning

room to see if any cakes from the afternoon tea still sat on the buffet. The morning room had been the favorite of William Claude's late wife, Jane, and she had managed, with comfortable, lightly colored furnishings, to give it a warm and cozy feeling—or as warm and cozy as a dark, Gothic-style mansion could be.

The room appeared to be empty, and the scones on a plate beside the tea service looked delicious. Irina headed for them.

"You are fooling yourself, my dear."

She nearly jumped out of her skin as Mr. Rempart stepped into the sunlight from a dark corner of the room.

His words confused her. "I didn't mean to disturb you, sir."

"Come in, come in. Did you not hear what I said to you?"

She wasn't sure what to say. "I did, but I didn't understand, sir. Do you mean something about the scones?"

He barked a laugh. "Take one of the blasted scones, would you, and the cup of tea that you so obviously want, and then come and sit with me. I've been meaning to talk to you for some time, but it isn't an easy topic, so I've put it off."

As he settled in one of the easy chairs in front of the large bay windows looking out at the Atlantic, she did as he requested. He had always scared her, although he was a distinguished man, tall, svelte, and always well-dressed. She imagined he must have been good-looking when he was young, with high cheekbones, a patrician nose, and piercing black eyes. His thick hair, she suspected, was prematurely white, and he wore it somewhat long and flowing straight back from his forehead, almost like a lion's mane.

As she joined him, she put the cup on the round table between them and balanced the plate with a scone on her lap.

"Eat," he commanded. "I don't fancy talking to you with your mouth full."

The scone could have been sawdust as she quickly ate and washed it down with tea, all the while wondering what the disagreeable topic might be. She didn't think Mr. Rempart found anything "not easy."

When she finished, she wiped away the crumbs from her mouth with her napkin, and then squeezed it between her fingers, unsure what she should do next. She remained stiffly seated, her gaze darting from the view of the ocean to the floor, but never at Mr. Rempart.

The silence lengthened.

Finally, he held up a green book. "Do you know what this is?"

She had never seen it before. "No. I'm sorry, sir," she murmured.

"It's my late wife's journal. Did you know she wrote a journal?"

It was a very strange question. How could she know such a thing? "No, sir."

"You should know it. You know why?"

She shook her head. He opened the journal to the middle and put his finger about half-way down the page. "Come over here, girl, and read what this says, right where my finger is."

Irina stood and looked down at the page, then gasped. "Constantin Petrescu," she whispered. Mr. Rempart snapped the journal shut, and she sat back down again, perched on the edge of the chair, her heart pounding.

"Do you know who that is?"

"That was my father's name."

"Exactly. Your father and my late wife were lovers." She must have looked as stricken as she felt because he suddenly chuckled. "I see the shock on your face. You think *you* were shocked! You should have seen me when I found out. The thought of her with anyone else made me sick! And a poor Romanian fisherman working the waters off Greece no less, far from his home, his wife, from *you*." He shook his head. "But she was a sick woman. I knew that for years, Irina. For years, I protected her, or tried to. I allowed her to spend time on a small Greek island to calm her nerves. I suspect your father took advantage of her."

"No!" Irina said. "I can't believe any of this…"

He smirked. "She thought she loved him. Look, here." He flipped through the journal, found a page and then handed it to her. "She even wrote poetry about him."

Irina quickly read the passages Mr. Rempart had pointed out to her. She read of Jane Rempart's love for her father, and still couldn't believe the words. She looked over the journal—a fairly thick book of handwritten pages that covered many years. It all looked legitimate.

"Michael doesn't know any of this," Mr. Rempart said. "He doesn't know how your father treated his beloved mother. He was only ten when she died, you know. And he worshipped her."

Irina might have been afraid of Mr. Rempart, but when he brought up her relationship with Michael, she steeled herself. "What happened between our parents has nothing to do with us," she said firmly. "It's a shock, yes. It is to me, and I know it will be to him. But it happened many years ago. They are both long dead now. Somehow, we will get past it."

"You think?" He smirked.

"Of course! I think, perhaps, they were two unhappy people who found each other." She bowed her head, all but overwhelmed by this news and what it might mean when Michael found out. "It's all over now."

"Is it?" Mr. Rempart asked. His eyes were like steel spears while his mouth twisted into an ugly smile. His demeanor chilled her to the bone. "If you think you felt shocked when you learned about their affair, how do you think your mother felt?"

Irina felt chilled. "What do you mean?"

"Your mother was an attractive woman when I first brought the two of you to work in this house," he said. "Where do you think you got your looks? A young widow and her daughter from Romania—refugees, one might say, wishing to come to America to get away from their sad memories. And —miracle of miracles—I saw to it that the two of you came here."

"What are you saying?" Irina asked, horrified at the cold gleam in Rempart's eyes. She had always thought she and her mother had ended up at Wintersgate due to good fortune. It was like a palace to her, and Michael was her Prince Charming.

"That surprises you, does it? You'll be even more surprised to learn my wife knew exactly who you two were." He chuckled. "Oh, how Jane hated me for bringing you both here—the widow and child of the man she loved! For a while, I thought I'd have to get a food taster!"

Irina shrank back from him. She remembered Jane Rempart, even though she was only five when she died. But Mrs. Rempart had always been nice to her, and looked at her with a smile even though she had the saddest eyes Irina had ever seen on a woman.

"Over time," Mr. Rempart said, "I came to appreciate your mother more and more. My so-called wife had moved out of our room some time earlier, and I've always enjoyed having someone to warm my bed. But Magda wouldn't hear of it. No, she was too in love with the memory of her sainted husband. I got sick of it and showed her how wrong she was. She couldn't read much English, but she could read your father's name over and over in Jane's journal. And she could read the word 'love,' and it was easy to point out words like 'my heart aches for him,' and on and on."

Irina pressed her fingers to her mouth, trying not to think of how her mother must have felt.

Mr. Rempart leaned back against the chair, his gaze on the sea. The water seemed to have grown colder, rougher than it had been just a short while earlier, and it turned progressively turbulent as he continued his dreadful tale. "Magda was furious. She grabbed the journal and ran upstairs. Jane was in the turret room—three flights up. I could hear Magda yelling at her, Jane shouting back... but then, all went silent. I had no idea what happened. And then I heard Michael's heart-wrenching screams outside.

"I ran out. The boy had been somewhere on the land and came back to the house to find his mother lying on the stone patio, blood pouring from her head. Magda had pushed her over the railing."

Irina jumped to her feet. She had been only five when Jane died, but she still remembered the commotion, the tears, and how she'd been sent to stay with a neighbor for a few days. When she returned, the house was sadder and quieter than ever. "No! Never! My mother would never have done that. If anything, it was an accident."

He pressed his fingertips together. "That's what we told the police, of course. I said it was an accident, that Jane was alone up in the turret room, and must have gotten one of her dizzy spells and fell. And Jane was light as a feather at that point, and sickly. It wouldn't have taken much to push her anywhere. But I also let it be known she suffered from depression. Many people in the area knew that was true. They had seen her walking around like a zombie when she returned to Wintersgate after her beloved Constantin had been killed."

A horrible thought came to Irina. "How was my

father killed?" she whispered. She'd been told it had been in a street fight with some ruffians.

Although Mr. Rempart didn't smile this time, she thought she saw the typical ugliness in his eyes as he muttered, "How should I know?"

She shuddered.

"I told Magda not to worry," he continued. "I said I would protect her and you. And I did. Very well, in fact, for a number of years until she let herself go. She put on way too much weight, and let her hair become scraggly. No matter, I'd grown tired of her by then."

"My God, you ruined her life," Irina shrieked. "You destroyed her!"

"No, no! I saved her. Of course, she also knew that I had the journal which proved she had a motive to kill my poor Jane. And I also kept the dress Jane was wearing the day Magda pushed her. I don't think there's an expiration date for fingerprints. Were I to give the dress and journal to the police, along with telling them that Magda finally had confessed to me that she'd killed Jane out of jealousy ... well, she would be looking at spending the rest of her life in prison."

"Stop!" Michael said. "Just stop." He never expected ...

Not Magda. He had loved her like the mother who was lost to him. She had raised him, hugged him when he needed comforting. Sat with him when he felt scared or lonely.

He shut his eyes. Irina's story had too vividly brought back the day his mother died. He was only ten. It was the worst day of his life.

He had seen his mother out on the balcony off the turret room. It had been her sanctuary in the massive house. She had looked down at him and waved. He was afraid he'd be told to go back inside and do his schoolwork and since he wanted to stay outdoors, instead of acknowledging her, he ran around to the far side of the house.

Over the years he often wondered if he had waved back, told her he was going up to the turret room to join her—if he had done *anything at all*—might it have prevented her from jumping? Because that was what he had always believed had happened. He knew she hadn't 'accidentally' fallen over that railing. It was too high for that. But he also thought that—if his father wasn't with her—she must have been alone, which meant she had to have jumped.

But now to learn that Magda was there, that she might have pushed Jane over the railing, or gave her a shove which in Jane's weakened state caused her to lose her balance and fall...

A shudder went through him and he covered his face with his hands.

"Do you want me to leave?" Irina asked.

He lowered his hands. "No. I just need a minute. I never dreamed ... God, I can't imagine how Magda ..." The news had felt like a physical blow. He did his best to gather strength and then raised his chin as he faced Irina once more. "I came here to find out everything. Please, go on."

CHAPTER 46

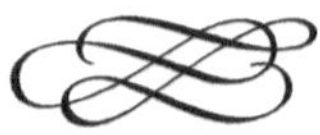

Irina didn't want to continue, knowing the loathing Michael would feel for her once he'd heard everything. But he deserved to know ... didn't he?

She drew in her breath and, as her mind wandered to the past, she continued.

She knew that Mr. Rempart's threats against her mother weren't idle. Of course, Magda could claim Jane's death was an accident, but how would she prove it? It would be her conjecture versus Rempart's power.

With his 'proofs' and his money he could easily influence the police to arrest Magda, prosecute her, and see to it she was imprisoned for many years.

Irina faced William Claude, her chin high. "Why have you told me this now?"

"I've decided to give you a choice," he said. "But first, sit down instead of stomping around like a petulant child!"

Her heart pounded as she sat. Mr. Rempart never gave 'choices.' "What kind of choice?"

"It's very easy, my dear. Your relationship with Michael, who may or may not want to have anything more to do with you after he learns about all this, or your mother's freedom."

Her heart twisted. "I don't understand."

"I believe you do." He stared at the sea, then faced her. "The thing is, I'm tired of living here. I want to do some traveling, but I don't like doing it alone. I want some companionship. You and Magda are still Romanian citizens, which means you can easily buy property there. I have my eye on a beautiful estate on the Black Sea. I'll give you the money, and you can even put the home in your name so if I were to die of natural causes, it would become yours." His lips tightened. "Of course, if I were to die of unnatural causes, I would have certain people release to the police the proof that Magda murdered Jane. And I'll include in it that any property you were given by me needs to be transferred elsewhere. You could try to fight that in court, but without money, good luck."

His gaze raked over her, letting his words sink in. "So, my dear, what is your choice?"

Her mouth was dry. "I need to speak to my mother," she whispered.

"You are such a child!" He got up and stood

before her, then placed his hand on her shoulder. "Are you sure you want to do that?"

She pushed his hand off of her and glared at him, but her eyes were questioning.

He paced in front of her as he continued. "For one, your mother already feels guilty, extremely guilty, about Jane. So how do you think she'll react if you tell her you have a choice of sparing *her* life if you give up the love of *your* life? Just what do you think her answer will be?" His eyebrows lifted. "In case you don't know, I'll tell you. She'll say, 'Go with Michael. Don't worry about me.' Will you be able to dash off to happily screw with your boyfriend while your mother rots in prison? Or, who knows? She might not be able to bear the thought of prison and take the coward's way out. Suicide."

"No!" Irina stood.

He pushed her back into the chair, then with his hands on the armrests he loomed over her. Power and strength all but radiated off him. "And just what will Michael think of you when he learns about your 'choice'? Nothing like learning that his wife sent her mother off to prison so she could frolic with him."

She couldn't believe what she was hearing, what he was ready to do to destroy her life, just as he had her mother's, his wife's ... and, she now realized, her father's. The man was a monster.

And what would Michael's reaction be when he learned about all this? She believed he would want to help her and go after his father, but he was just starting out. He had gotten his doctorate after years of work, he had his whole life, a brilliant career ahead of him. And he couldn't fight Mr. Rempart. No one could. And Michael, she feared, would lose everything trying.

"Don't look at me that way," he said, standing upright once more. "I'm the victim here. My wife was an adulterer. I gave her everything. I would have given her the world had she asked. But instead she turned her back on me."

"You caused it!" Irina screamed. "The woman I remember didn't have a cruel bone in her body."

"Not a cruel bone, but not a loyal one either." He reached down and stroked her cheek as his voice turned soft. "She fell out of love with me. Maybe I was too old for her, too set in my ways. Just not exciting enough. I tried to win her back, but she ... she was tired of me. It happens. And now it's time for you to give up your childish love for my son."

Irina couldn't bear his touch. She stood and walked away from him, her arms folded tight against her stomach. "I can't. I just can't."

"You're strong, Irina. Stronger than Magda. Stronger than Michael, and much, much stronger than Jane. Here's what we'll do. I'll give you a check for two million dollars which you will deposit into a bank account that I'll help you set up. Then, you, Magda, Stedman and I will go to the Black Sea where you will purchase the estate I want. You'll have more than enough money left to buy newer, better furniture, and pay servants to run it. And once we're settled, we can all start over. Magda won't have to work, while you and I can travel, enjoy life. I'd love to show you Paris, Irina. You would love it. And maybe we can get you those painting lessons I know you've always wanted. I've seen some of your paintings. They show real talent. What do you say, my dear?"

Tears filled her eyes. "But Michael—"

"Has his archeology! You know how much he loves it. Hasn't he been in Oxford all these years instead of here, with you? What does that tell you? He doesn't really know you, Irina. Not like I do. But he's my son, and once he hears the real story, he'll leave you. Believe me, he'll be out of here and back at Oxford faster than you can say 'Irina Petrescu is a love-sick fool' because that's what you'll be if you rely on him. As I said, I know him well."

She couldn't bear it and screamed at him. "I know him, too. We love each other!"

"Then, why does he gladly leave you each

year?" he bellowed. "Have I ever left you? I've been here, taking care of you and your mother *despite what she did*, year after year after year!"

She knew Michael loved her, but when she thought of what Mr. Rempart could do to her mother...

How could she do anything other than protect her mother, just as her mother had always protected her, raised her, loved her beyond everything else all these years? She couldn't live with herself if she did anything else.

She had no choice. "You win," she whispered.

He smiled. "Now, I want you to call me Claude."

With those words it seemed her body turned to stone and she knew she would never again be the girl she once was.

That same evening, Claude told Magda about his decision to buy a home in Romania. She was stunned, especially when Claude told her Irina would go as well, and that her daughter had a sudden change of heart about Michael.

When Magda questioned Irina about it, Irina merely stared at her mother, her face impassive. "It's none of your business."

Claude soon moved them all to the estate he'd selected. He had overseen Irina's purchase of it with the money he'd given her—a check for two million dollars; a check she'd had to endorse to put it into her account.

Soon after, he moved the house from Irina's name into a trust. The remainder of the money was moved out of her bank account and put into a safe on the estate. Finally, he got her the best fake passport money could buy. It showed "Sorina Motrescu," and he had "Irina Petrescu" marked as deceased. He made sure Irina's name no longer appeared anywhere at all that might offer a clue as to her whereabouts if anyone were to search for her ... which he knew would happen.

Once he had settled along the Black Sea, Claude set up a laboratory. He spent hours in it working on alchemy. In time, he invited Irina to come and watch, and maybe to learn. She found herself intrigued, and it gave her something to do. Living as she did, she was afraid to go to the village near the home, and afraid to associate with people her own age because of the questions they might ask. And Claude insisted the maid and gardeners only talked to Magda, never Irina.

She could scarcely look at Magda. Whenever she tried, everything Claude had told her, and the way she had been forced to walk away from Michael, from her life, rose to the surface. She couldn't let her mother know about "her choice" and so, although she knew it wasn't fair, the easiest thing for her was to ignore her mother altogether. The result was that the only person she associated with was Claude.

She was young, and so very lonely. In time, even his company was preferable to total isolation.

In his laboratory, they would work on his concoctions together. He explained about his quest for immortality, and one day he admitted he was doing it all for her, so he would always be there to protect her from the cruelness of the world. He tested the gold-enhanced alchemical concoctions on himself. Since he found them to be invigorating and in no way harmful, he urged Irina to take some as well.

She always refused.

During this time, Claude had told Irina to keep up the pretext of being in love with Michael and to use her US cell phone for texts and calls so he would think she was still in Wintersgate. She found that easy to do and filled her messages with love for him. He responded in kind.

And then the day came when Michael would be returning home from Oxford with his new doctorate degree. Two days prior to Claude leaving Romania to be in the US when Michael arrived, he told Irina he would explain to Michael that his engagement to her would never happen.

Irina couldn't bear what was to come and couldn't stop her tears and despair. Claude finally convinced her to take just a little of his gold-laced potion to settle her nerves. "Magda will wonder what's wrong with you if you keep this up! Do you really want her to know?"

The potion was strong and hit her hard, leaving her mind in a fog, a blissful, pain-free fog.

Then, for the first time, Claude took her to his bed. She was still there when he left in the morning for his trip back to Wintersgate.

The whole two weeks Claude was gone, she stayed in his room and each day Stedman would bring her food and more and more of Claude's "magic elixir" to help her forget all that had transpired.

When Claude returned, he cut back on the amount of his potion she was given, leaving her craving it. Each day she went to his laboratory where he would administer a tablespoon of the pain-numbing medicine. And just as she went to his laboratory, in her zombie-like state, she went to his bedroom whenever he wanted her there.

Magda knew what was going on, and she tried to reason with Irina to stop the madness, to fight him. Claude was the devil, her mother said. He had tempted and used her and he would eventually toss her aside. "Don't ever believe anything he says. He's doing this to get back at our family. He hates all of us because his wife cuckolded him. He'll never forget that, and will destroy us all. He broke his son's heart with lies about you. You know he did! Do you really think he cares about you at all?"

"Broke Michael's heart?" Irina spat out the words, even as she couldn't bear to think of him. "Where is he? I don't see him here, pleading for me to go back to him! Do you?"

Nothing Magda said mattered to Irina. Claude grew weary of the older woman's evil looks and sent her back to the US, to live in a small house he'd bought in North Carolina, under threat of death if she ever said anything about him or Irina or their life in Romania.

Month after month he and Irina continued to work in the laboratory as he chased his desire for immortality. As "the world's greatest living al-chemist" he was sure that if anyone could develop a formula for it, it would be him.

At the same time, the concoctions Claude devised grew increasingly tempting, and she gladly tested them for him. Even more than her daily gold-laced potion, these made her feel, if not immortal, powerful. She loved the feeling. "We'll both become immortal if these work!" she proclaimed one day.

His gaze turned cold, colder than she had ever seen it. "Or at least, one of us will."

As time passed, Claude began spending more

and more time away from the Black Sea estate. Despite his promises, he never brought Irina anywhere with him. At the same time, he grew better at alchemy as he grew adept at connecting with other planes of existence—particularly demonic planes. Demons were always ready to latch on to humans who were curious about them.

He began to conjure up demons at will and showed his skill to Irina. At first she was frightened, but soon thrilled at the power she saw. To control demons was more than she had ever imagined possible.

"Teach me how to do it," she had asked.

"You can't. Few people can. You have to have it in your blood. Rempart men do. Not many others."

"That seems wrong. There must be some way for me to have such power."

He studied her with interest. "I can think of one way that might work, in a sense."

"What?"

"If you bore my son. You and I, together, could train him. Although his powers would come from his genetic makeup from me, it would be as if you were the one conjuring demons." Then his eyes darkened. "In fact, you may have come up with a great idea! If my new son possesses anywhere near the ability that Michael has—although the fool won't use it—I suspect he and I, together, could achieve immortality!"

"Yes," she said excitedly. "Let's do it."

But it wasn't easy for Irina to become pregnant, and she often wondered if the fault lay with Claude's age. He felt her disappointment and stayed away more often than ever, but finally, after more than a year of trying, she was with child.

Claude insisted she immediately stop taking his potion. Withdrawal was terrifying and difficult but eventually she realized how badly it had affected her way of seeing the world ... and Claude.

During that time, as Irina's body changed shape and grew heavy, Claude stayed away for increasingly long periods. Irina was sure he had found other women more to his taste. If so, she was thankful.

When she went into labor, she had Stedman call him, assuming he would want to be there for the birth of his son.

Claude waited. After a few hours, Stedman phoned to tell him he had a daughter.

He didn't bother to return home for another two months.

When he showed up, Irina was furious. "I thought we were going to have a son, Claude. For all your great alchemical abilities, it seems you can't control everything!"

"It's you," he roared. "You're too weak-willed! At least Jane knew how to produce boys!" He turned and stormed from the house.

Things grew worse between them. He had no love for Zoe, no interest in her at all. To him, it was as if she had never been born.

But Irina threw herself into working in his laboratory. Whenever he was away, she would practice everything she had seen him do. For her, immortality be damned. She wanted to conjure and control demons—demons to protect her and Zoe from the monster that was Claude.

Time went by slowly, but one day in the laboratory, when Zoe was only two, Irina picked up her fussing child and, holding her close, made the little girl smile by showing her one of Claude's sparkling philosopher's stones. Zoe grinned and patted the stone as her mother recited a demon-summoning chant she'd often heard Claude utter.

To her amazement, it worked.

A small demon seemed to come from out of nowhere and appeared before her in the lab. It had so frightened her and the now screaming Zoe, she commanded it to go away. It did. She soon realized it was only when she held Zoe that she could summon the demon. Without the child, she could not. So it wasn't only male children that inherited the Rempart abilities with alchemy!

When Zoe was age five, Irina's life took another turn. Claude had Stedman inform her he wanted her out of his life. He had found someone younger, prettier, and smarter than she could ever be.

Irina was glad to hear it. She had hoped to stay at the estate, but soon discovered the money he had given her to run it had dwindled down to almost nothing. Unable to pay for its upkeep, she had to sell. But when she tried, she'd learned that it was owned by Claude's trust, not her.

Penniless except for some jewelry for which she'd got pennies on the dollar, she had few choices left and fled to Paris, taking with her the only thing of real value in her life ... Zoe.

CHAPTER 47

Michael was all but numb with both outrage and sorrow at the revelations Irina had, one by one, divulged. He had trouble even finding words to say to her. "My God, Irina, I never dreamed ... I know my father is no good, but I had no idea how completely evil he's been all these years. Much as I don't want to believe this is true, I know it is. I'm so sorry he put you through all this. And I'm sorry for Zoe, that the girl should have such a cruel, heartless father."

Irina sat stiffly, her face a mask. "I made mistakes," she said. "I did. And I allowed many things to happen that I now hate myself for. But I got Zoe away from him, and I've tried to be a good mother to her."

"I'm sure you are," he said.

She gave him a wry smile. "In Paris, I even tried marriage, hoping to find happiness, a normal life. That was a joke. Eventually I met a Russian, Tavas. I never loved him but I saw he was good with his son, and knew I could trust him with Zoe, so I stayed with him. We ended up here. When I took my job at the Hermitage, I felt as if I had found a home. I'm not sure why, but I began to use alchemy once more—setting up a small lab in my kitchen. With Zoe's help I used the skills Claude had taught me and we created our own philosopher's stones. More than one. I used them to try to turn cheap metals into gold, but I couldn't. Not even Zoe could perform that trick.

"Anyway, one day, I brought Zoe with me to work. We hid in the Hermitage until everyone else went home, and then we went to a room still furnished as it had been when it was the Winter Palace and dressed up in clothes we found there. It was such fun! We kept going back and then one day, Zoe pulled a philosopher's stone from her pocket. She wanted to use it to hold a tea party and call up other people—ones who had lived there a century before. I never in my wildest dreams imagined it would work, but soon I found myself in a world filled with people who, amazingly, understood me. I felt as if I were one of them."

"And Zoe?" Michael asked. "What about her?"

Irina laughed. "She found them boring. They were all adults from the early 1900s, so she stopped coming to the Hermitage with me—a typical twelve-year-old. But I found that once the door between that world and this was opened, I didn't need Zoe to open it again. I went there after work, as often as I could."

"What brought on this feeling of kinship?" Michael asked.

"A Montenegrin princess named Militsa."

"Oh?" Michael's breath caught as the first inkling of who – and what – the mysterious "Militsa" was, struck him.

"We immediately bonded," Irina added. "Her sister, too, became a friend. Her name is Stana. So you can see why, when you asked me about Stana, I couldn't exactly explain. The two sisters watch over me. I don't know what I would do without them."

"But you must have realized the dangers behind what you brought forward using Claude's black magic. From what I've learned, those two women are hardly guardian angels."

"They are to me! And what did it matter as long as I was happy and Zoe was safe? I could have gone on like that forever. But then, one day last fall, Claude contacted me here in St. Petersburg and again my life changed. I should have known he was always aware of where I was living. He told me to meet him at a coffee shop. It's never good to refuse him, so I went. We sat a while, not speaking about anything much, and then he left. I realize now, it was to get a picture of us together, to draw you here. I suppose he expected you to bring your philosopher's stone, the red pearl, that he wants so badly. He would have stolen it, but you didn't bring it, so his clever plans amounted to nothing. Good for you, Michael! I didn't know you had it in you."

He cringed. "I was wondering why you'd let yourself be a part of that."

"Why indeed," she said. "Frankly, you were the last person I wanted to see."

"But I saw you around the city and at the Peter and Paul Cathedral, and then you'd disappear. Weren't you doing that because William Claude told you to?"

"I've never been to that Cathedral. I never saw you before the day you came to my work site looking for me."

"I can't believe it," he said.

"It wasn't me. It must have been Militsa. The more we work together, the more she looks like me. It's strange, but unless I allow her to borrow my body, which I'm happy to do at times, she isn't 'substantial'. In any case, she's always planning, always five or more steps ahead of everyone else. And she does it for me. She's a friend. My only friend."

Her words about Militsa "borrowing" her body were beyond troubling. Accounts of demons inhabiting people's bodies were found in all cultures throughout history, including the Bible. "So why did this insubstantial Militsa want to see me?"

"To check you over, I'm sure," Irina said firmly. "In fact, I suspect she may be the reason you've returned."

"She what?"

"She believes you'll help me and she likes the idea of having you here. She is quite fond of men, you see. I've let her use my body many times to attend Khlysty meetings where things get a little ... raunchy. But it's the least I can do for her. She deserves some fun in her life."

Michael's skin crawled at her words. "How did Militsa get me to return here?"

"Militsa and Stana dropped breadcrumbs for you to follow. They knew a place in Ukraine that would interest an archaeologist. Something about the Knights Templar."

"They set up the dig?"

"They've had connections with the site for many years and realized archeologists would find it fascinating."

He couldn't believe what he was hearing, or what she was implying. "The place has vampires, Irina. And they've already killed one student and, I believe, are on the path to corrupting and possibly killing more."

Irina shrugged. "If true, the students must have provoked them. My friends aren't killers."

"Are you sure? Your friend Stana lured Jianjun to a spot where he was given a drug that could easily have killed him, and then he was brought to a place where he could be framed for a murder. And I suspect she and her friends killed Patience Hewson, a sweet old lady."

"What do you mean, sweet?" Irina was angry now. "She worked for Claude, didn't she? And the sisters were only trying to help me out. They knew you'd come to St. Petersburg if Jianjun was missing. Actually, Stana could have killed him outright, hidden his body, and you'd never be the wiser. You and your friend are lucky she took the path she did. Besides, who are you to talk, when you nearly killed your own father?"

"What are you talking about?"

"I saw the scars on his face and neck after he returned from seeing you in Idaho."

"But I never ..." He stopped. Ceinwen! Was that why she fled from their home? Why she went into hiding?

Michael felt physically ill as he realized the confrontation that must have taken place. And if Ceinwen had scarred William Claude, what had he done to her? Michael's world began to spin even as he reminded himself that she could drive, fly, went home to Wales. But still ...

"All I care about is Zoe. If you won't protect her, I'd rather see her dead." Irina's words hurled him back to the present. She couldn't be threatening her own child, could she?

"I don't believe that." Michael struggled to hold himself together in the face of all this. He wanted to rage, to hit something, or someone ... like William Claude.

"Don't test me," she said.

Michael's blood chilled at the harshness in her. "I won't, Irina. Zoe's too important and I won't take any chances. But you've got to get your friends to stop the attacks on the dig team."

"Militsa wants me to go the dig site. She died near there, you know. Her and Stana. It's only fitting that I visit their graves."

He shook his head. "The place is too dangerous."

"We'll be fine, Zoe and me."

The vampires ... the connection between the dig, Militsa, Stana, Irina, even William Claude and Ceinwen ... suddenly it all came together. "You can't take Zoe there, Irina!"

"Of course I can, and I will. You can come along to keep us safe if you want. I really don't care."

He could scarcely believe how cold she sounded, as if Militsa were already more a part of her then she knew. "Whoever thought it would be like this between us?"

She looked taken aback by his comment. Then she leaned forward, elbows on the table, head bowed, and seemed lost in thought. "The sad part is," she said, somberly looking up," I never wanted you to know about any of this. No one in this macabre tale is innocent, Michael, and equally, no one is completely guilty. So much of this happened because, just as your father told you, Rempart men are unlucky in love. He was – with Jane. And she broke his heart."

Michael shook his head. "No. He never had a heart to be broken."

Just then, the pub owner came over and told them it was closing time.

CHAPTER 48

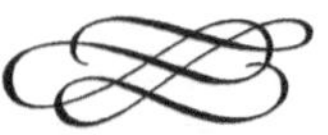

"Where have you been?" Andriy asked when Stana opened the door to her cottage that night. His face was tight, his voice loud. "I've come here night after night. Why didn't you tell me you were leaving?"

"Andriy, relax." She gave him a quick peck on the cheek. "Come inside. I've missed you."

"No, I don't think you have." His tone was petulant as he walked into the little room. "I doubt you even thought of me."

"Where is all this coming from?" she asked as she removed his jacket then poured him a glass of wine. "Here, this will make you less angry."

"I doubt it," he mumbled although he took a sip.

"Sit with me," she said as she crossed to the small sofa, and then patted the seat beside her.

"I've been through hell here," he said, joining her. "People are dying. Dr. Masur. Dr. Koval is missing. We can't stay. It's way too dangerous.

You've got to come away with me. Let's go back to Kyiv together."

She smiled. "I don't think so."

"Why not? If you cared about me half as much as you say, you'd want to come with me. You'd want us to leave this dangerous place. There's something in these mountains. I don't know what, but I don't like it."

"You really don't know what it is?" she asked. "Do you really have no idea?"

He looked at her questioningly. "Of course not. Why should I?"

She wrapped her arms around his neck. "Tell me, have you ever been happier than you are here, with me?"

His arms circled her waist, and he tried to kiss her, but she turned her head. "Answer me, Andriy."

"You know I never have. I love you, Stana. I've told you that."

She ran her hand over his cheek then slowly down to his neck and rested it there. "I know. I can feel, here, how your heart beats for me. That's why I think you don't want to leave here, because if you did, that would mean leaving me behind."

"What do you mean? I said you need to come with me. Back to school. Finish your dissertation. Get your doctorate."

"No, sweet one. I belong here. This land, this

mountain, is where I get my strength. Instead of me going with you, I want you to stay with me. Would you do that?"

He was stunned at such a suggestion. "Well..."

"Do you really have to think about it?" she asked with a fetching smile.

He smiled back. "Not really. If you want me to stay with you, how can I refuse, but –"

"No matter what?" she interrupted.

He studied her. "No matter what ... if it means you care about me."

"Of course. As the others leave the dig, there'll only be the two of us left here. You'll be everything to me, Andriy. My life's blood. How would that be?"

He could scarcely believe what he was hearing. She had never spoken to him before with such passion. "It would be wonderful."

"I'm glad." She pushed him so that he sat on the battered sofa. She slowly removed her outer garments—T-shirt and jeans. Left with only a short, thin chemise and panties, she straddled his lap, her knees on each side of his hips. He had scarcely known such joy, his hands going to her breasts, and then, as she bent forward to kiss his lips, his hands found her knees and slowly slid up along her thighs while she trailed her kisses down his face to his neck. "Andriy," she whispered, "you are much too bold."

"What?" He murmured, not quite understanding. All he knew was he could scarcely breathe for wanting her, it had been so long, too long. But then he felt a sudden pain as she bit down hard enough to puncture the skin of his neck. She then held the skin between her teeth and pulled on it, ripping it open, and splitting his artery in two.

She sat back smiling as his blood shot out. She filled her hands with it and then spreading it over her neck, her heavy breasts, her stomach, between her legs. He watched as she continued to smile until his heart no longer pumped, and he saw nothing more.

Although it was the middle of the night and Olena was nowhere around, it didn't matter to Galyna. She was glad of it. Olena didn't know her secrets.

Feder lay comatose on her bed. She had needed his blood, but she'd fed too much this time. He'd come to eventually, and when she wanted him again, he'd be ready. She simply needed to learn not to be so greedy. She couldn't kill him. She needed him to live. It was the only way she could help keep Ivan, her vampire hero, alive. He'd saved her. He'd protected her from the others and vowed to protect her forever. She liked that ... a lot.

Their first night together, after he'd found her in the chapel and fed off her, he'd actually apologized for the pain he'd caused. But he had needed to be strong in case the others attacked. They wanted her, and they would have killed her.

She could smile about it now. She had felt both pity and gratitude toward him—something she'd never experienced before. And once she got used to his strange looks, she even found him oddly handsome.

He told her his story of leading a group of soldiers and two aristocratic women away from sure death at the hands of the Bolsheviks. "One of the women, one of the aristocrats," he'd said, "was a sorcerer and after my men and I died, she brought us back as the undead."

But then he confessed he didn't want this life. "I'd rather have died and stayed dead," he'd said, "because now, I'm evil."

"But you're not. You could have killed me or let the others do it, but you saved me. You're good, not evil." She kissed him, gently at first, but then realized to her amazement and with some horror, that she actually desired him. With that, she took charge, possessing him in a very human way. But pleasant as that was, when he drank her blood, the feeling was beyond orgasmic.

She began sneaking up to the chapel ruins every night, wanting him both as a man and a vampire, despite his warning of what she would become. She didn't care. With him, absorbing his essence, she felt she had more strength, more power, than she'd ever dreamed of. She loved him using her--how could she not, when he was the best lover she'd ever experienced? Even his snakelike eyes were a turn-on. But the constant loss of blood also made her weak.

Feder refilled her supply. Poor, lovesick Feder.

Her reverie was interrupted when Dmytro walked into the room and stretched out on Olena's bed. "I want Bethany," he announced, his arms beneath his head. He paid no mind at all to Feder, as if seeing the man with blood on his neck was customary.

"Why Bethany?" Galyna asked. "Olena would go with you in a heartbeat ... so to speak."

"Olena doesn't interest me. And Bethany rejected my attention a while back. She really should have been nicer to me."

"You can't keep Bethany," Galyna said. "Have your fun, but then we should give her to our friends, to help all of them grow even stronger."

"Another death?" Dmytro asked angrily. "That

would be hard to explain—especially once Veronika Masur's body is discovered. What your friends did to her was disgusting!"

"They aren't my friends," she said. "Anyway, Koval will come up with an excuse for her death. He needs this dig to succeed more than ever."

"I don't give a damn. I only want Bethany! I'll turn her into one of us, make her worship me."

Galyna frowned, putting a finger to her lips. "Quiet."

"Why? Are you jealous?"

She shushed him then went to the door. "Someone was out there," she whispered "Someone was listening. And I don't think it's the first time"

Dmytro frowned. "Olena?"

"Probably." She quietly opened the door, and crept into the hallway, Dmytro behind her.

They saw the innkeeper and his wife at the front door, each carrying a small suitcase. The innkeeper paused only long enough to tape a piece of paper to the window next to the door, and then they rushed outside.

"Why are they sneaking out that way?" Galyna said as she and Dmytro hurried down the hall after them. As Galyna stepped out onto the front porch, she turned so she could read what the innkeeper had posted on his window.

Vampires! Stay away!

"Stop them!" she cried out loud.

The innkeeper was trying desperately to put a key in the lock of an old station wagon. He looked up just long enough to see Galyna and Dmytro running toward him. Stricken, his hands shook even more.

"Hurry! Hurry!" His wife screamed.

Galyna reached the old woman and swung her away from the car. The wife stumbled, then fell, begging for help from her husband, for mercy from Galyna.

The elderly innkeeper got the key into the lock as Dmytro barreled into him, knocking him to the ground. Dmytro pounded the man's head against the hard, rocky earth.

Wasting no time, Galyna and Dmytro tossed the unconscious innkeeper and his terrified wife into the back seat of the station wagon. Galyna ripped off the woman's headscarf and despite her struggling, tied her hands behind her back. The innkeeper needed no restraints.

The two got in the car, Dmytro at the wheel.

"That was unexpected, yet satisfying," Galyna said, as Dmytro drove away from the inn. "Nosy innkeepers!" She laughed and Dmytro grinned back, as they headed for the dig site.

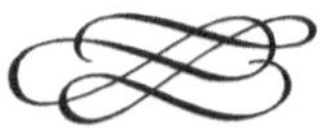

CHAPTER 49

Michael drove Irina to her apartment and parked while she went inside.

As soon as he was alone, he tried to phone Ceinwen. Her phone had been disconnected. It didn't surprise him. Somehow, he had to find her, but knowing her, she could be anywhere in the world at this point.

Frustrated that there was nothing he could do at the moment, he watched for Irina in the rearview mirror and soon saw her and Zoe step from the apartment building, each with a suitcase, and followed by Tavas. The man was clearly enraged, waving his arms and speaking angrily, then jumped in front of Irina, stopping her. She paused, listening, but then grabbed Zoe's arm and hurried around him.

Michael got out of the car and helped her put the bags in the trunk as Tavas paced angrily in the distance.

Michael was curious about Zoe. This was the first time he could see what she—his sister—looked like. But she stood apart, in shadows, and then quickly got into the back seat. When Michael slammed the trunk closed, Tavas turned away, his back stiff, his fists clenched.

"Give me the keys," Irina said to Michael "I know a shortcut to your hotel."

They settled into the car. Zoe hunched in the darkness, everything about her seemed angry and bewildered by all that was happening. Michael felt for her. God, what a mess William Claude had wrought on everyone.

"Your fellow looked unhappy," Michael said, as Irina whipped up one street and down another. "You sure you don't want him with you?"

"He's not anything to me. He was useful. Nothing more."

Michael refused to respond. This was not the Irina he'd once known and loved.

Instead, he turned to face the girl in the back seat. He still couldn't see her that well unless Irina drove beneath bright lights. At such times, he'd see a serious child with dark brown hair--the same color as her mother's--tousled from sleep. And, every so often, she regarded him with questioning, somewhat hostile, eyes. Dark brown Rempart eyes, so like his own it was unnerving. "Are you all right?" he asked her softly. She huddled in her heavy gray coat, looking cold and sleepy. She nodded yes, even as she pulled her coat tighter.

"Good," he said.

She turned her head toward the window. Something about way she held herself, the angle of her head and chin in profile, reminded him of her mother. He wished he knew what to say to comfort her, but as he'd tried to explain to Irina, he had no experience with children. Feeling inadequate, he turned forward to watch the streets go by. He could only hope that getting Irina to the dig might in some way end the dangers there. Once that was done, he needed to track down Ceinwen. He needed to talk to her. Needed to explain all that had happened. He felt sick having learned, too late, that William Claude may well have confronted her in Idaho.

Irina whipped down an alleyway, going too fast for comfort. He hoped she knew what she was doing.

"*Mami*," Zoe said, leaning close to her mother and uttering words in Romanian.

"Speak English, Zoe. Show Michael you know his language," Irina ordered, then glanced quickly at Michael. "She knows Romanian, French, English, and Russian. She asked me why you're here."

She then gave Zoe her answer. "We're going on a long trip to someplace new and exciting. It'll be fun."

It was all Michael could do to remain silent as she used the word "fun" in connection with the dig site, with its vampire night singers. It was strange to learn that the demons she had called forth, Militsa and Stana, had apparently learned all they could about her and those around her so they could work their evil, to bring terror and death to innocent people.

Michael worried about her and Zoe going to the place those demons had set up, but at the same time, it made sense. So much in alchemy was like the infinity symbol that resembled a sideways eight: circle round and round and end up the same place that you left. Irina had begun this by bringing forth demons with her philosopher's stone and somehow, she needed to end it the same way.

They all remained quiet for a while until Irina said, "Did the police tell you not to leave Petersburg because of your friend's troubles?"

"Yes, although I think they've dropped the charges."

"It's better not to take chances. The government carefully watches the airports, but the train from St. Petersburg to Helsinki is less scrutinized. It's a four-hour trip. I'll get our tickets. They'll check our passports and visas on the train and in Helsinki, but for Americans and those of us in the EU, it's no problem to enter Finland."

He had no choice but to trust her as she dropped him off at the Four Seasons and circled the block, waiting for him to return.

Jianjun sat on the couch hunched over his laptop. Only his eyes looked up when Michael walked toward him. "About time you got back, boss."

Michael went straight for his carry-on and as he packed, he quickly explained. "I'm going back to the dig site—with Irina and her daughter. You should head home as soon as you get your passport back."

Jianjun didn't bother to ask any other questions. He knew his boss far too well. "I'm leaving here as fast as I can," Jianjun said. "But don't you think I should come with you?"

"You've gone above and beyond already. More than enough," Michael said, his hand on the doorknob, ready to head off. "Stay safe, and if you run into any problems, call me."

"I will. Since the police told you to stay in town, you might want to shut off your phone, or even take out the SIM card so they can't track you. If you need a phone in Russia, get a burner."

"You think of everything, don't you?"

"I try, boss."

Jianjun was the best right-hand man a guy could have, but there was no time for banter. He had to get going. Fast.

Irina drove straight to the train station. She pulled into a parking spot and handed Michael a shopping bag she'd put in the backseat next to Zoe. "Put these on before you go inside," she said. "Tavas is close to your size, only a little heavier. Thankfully he didn't balk too much when I told him I needed a jacket, pants, shoes, and a cap. You'll need to wear these so you won't stand out so much in the station. Once we board the train, you have to show your passport but it's better not to attract the attention of the local police. To them, we should look like a family going for a day trip."

The word 'family' reverberated in his head as he thought of how, as a young man, he had wanted the kind of family that would enjoy holidays and or simple outings. The idea of ever having such a family seemed hopeless now.

"Zoe and I will go inside to hopefully get tickets

for the first train. Bring the luggage," she said, handing him the car keys, "and we'll meet you in the lobby."

As he changed clothes inside the cramped car, he racked his brain for a way to help Irina get free of the demons, William Claude, and everything else ruining her life, but he came up with nothing.

With his own clothes in his carry-on, Michael joined Zoe and Irina in the waiting room, and cozied up to them as if they were, indeed, a happy family. They only had a few hours to wait for the express train, just three-and-a-half hours, from St. Petersburg to Helsinki, but those hours would seem like an eternity.

Zoe sat between Irina and Michael when two young policemen walked by, eying the threesome. Irina and Zoe joked back and forth with each other in Romanian, at least Michael thought they were joking. Michael smiled as well, although he had no idea what they were saying. Clearly, neither did the police, but it was enough for them to continue on their way.

When they were gone, Irina and Michael gave each other a look of relief.

"No one in St. Petersburg speaks Romanian," Irina said. "This will work. Trust me. And if it doesn't, I'll tell them in Russian that you don't understand. Just say nothing."

"I know the Russian word for no is *nyet*," Michael added with a grin.

"Only use it if you can't avoid it because your accent is pure American."

Michael nodded. "Point taken."

As the time came to board the train, they nervously waited in line. The ticket taker studied them as they showed their tickets. When they found their seats, Irina whispered to Michael, "Only one more time to worry about. When the conductor walks through, he'll look at our passports, take our tickets, and feed them into his little computer. Something could, potentially, show up there."

He nodded. They had second-class seats, he and Irina together, Zoe in front of them with an older woman traveling alone beside her. Again, as they sat, Irina warned Zoe that she would need to be quiet the whole time they were on the train. The girl nodded, looking irritated, but then she put in ear pods and leaned back in the seat.

They were about a half-hour into the trip when the conductor demanded Zoe's passport and ticket. He took it, then frowned, eyeing the girl as he input the number, then tore off the stub he needed to keep, gave back the remainder, and moved to Irina and Michael.

Michael pretended to be asleep, but Irina nudged his arm when the conductor stood next to them. Waving her passport and ticket in front of his face, she told him, in Romanian to get his out, too. Pretending to be tired and grumpy, he handed everything over, and then shut his eyes again, head against the window, Tavas' grimy cap covering his hair. The conductor frowned, apparently not expecting to see Michael with a US passport. He looked carefully from Michael to it, then tore off the ticket stubs and returned everything else before moving to the passengers behind them.

Michael allowed himself to breathe again.

As they passed through customs into Finland, they again showed their passports. But once past security, they were free.

In Helsinki, Michael hailed a taxi to the airport. He bought three tickets to Budapest. For the first time he saw the EU passports were for "Solina and Zoe Motrescu." He remembered Irina's story of how William Claude had changed all her papers.

"You've had to use this name all these years?" he asked, as they settled in for the long wait before their flight.

"For all official situations." She shrugged. "It was easiest. Claude is very efficient."

His father was not only efficient, but devious. No wonder it had been impossible for Michael and Jianjun to find Irina for so many years.

But William Claude was far more than devious.

He was pure evil. Michael had fought against that evil most all of his life, and as he settled into the secure area of the airport to wait for their morning flight, he couldn't help but wonder how much more malevolence he'd have to battle when they arrived back at the dig.

CHAPTER 50

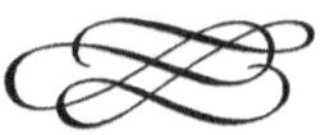

Bethany was shoving clothes into her backpack when she heard the knock at the door of Michael's cottage. She didn't have time to talk with anyone. She just wanted to find a way to leave all this madness, but still, she opened the door. She was surprised to see Olena. She thought everyone had already gone up to the dig site. "Something happened," Olena said. "Come."

"What happened? Where are we going?" Bethany asked.

"To inn. Dmytro say he want to talk to all of us."

"But I'm not part of the team any longer. I quit it. I'll be leaving soon."

"You come hear Dmytro now."

Friendly as ever, Bethany thought, as she put on a jacket and followed.

Dmytro, Galyna, and Feder were there, but Andriy, and Professors Koval and Masur weren't. A chill went through Bethany at the looks on their faces. She also noticed that the inn itself seemed dead-- no coffee, no smell of breakfast, no bustling in the kitchen. Fear filled her over what had happened.

"I have bad news," Dmytro said. "When neither Doctor Masur or Doctor Koval showed up for our morning meeting, I went to the dig to see if they were there. I found Doctor Masur. She looked as if she must have fallen climbing down into the chapel and died of a broken neck. Dr. Koval is missing. Andriy might be with him, or wandering around here somewhere. But before we worry about the others, we will honor Veronika by burying her at the site."

That made no sense to Bethany. "Bury her? What about the police? Medical examiners? Her family? Don't you need to call someone?"

Galyna glared at her. "People die all the time in Ukraine. We aren't as squeamish about death as you are in America. Here, we deal with death ourselves. We don't go running to authorities for every little thing. And it's too late for a doctor. The woman is dead."

It was on the tip of Bethany's tongue to say that she didn't think a woman, a professor, dying was exactly a "little thing," but considering the way both Galyna and Dmytro were glaring at her, she hesitated to say more. "Tell us about Doctor Koval," she said instead. "Why would he be missing?"

"He might have found Veronika's death was too much for him. Or he might be a victim himself."

"Isn't that more reason to call the police?" Bethany couldn't help but ask. "And what about Andriy and the innkeeper and his wife? They can't all just vanish."

"They haven't," Dmytro stated. "I've heard they're searching for Dr. Koval."

"When the police came here after Wasyl died," Galyna interrupted, "all they did was cost us time. And now, we are close to finding the reason we're here, and why we've put up with all of this."

Dmytro lifted his chin. "We will carry on. It is what Doctor Masur would have wanted. And I'm sure Doctor Koval will turn up as soon as he is himself again. We know the man must be deeply shocked. For now, Olena, Feder, and Bethany, stay here in case Professor Koval and the others show up. Galyna and I will handle everything at the dig. We don't need to work today. It's a time for prayer."

Bethany returned to the cottage to finish packing. She'd been surprised to see Dmytro taking charge and speaking firmly. He was so different from when she first arrived here--sweet, a little lost, a tad pudgy. Now, he was bony, his skin almost pure white, and he seemed to think he was God's gift to everyone. It made no sense.

Something about him made her skin crawl.

A knock sounded on the cottage door.

She knew exactly who it was.

"I'm not feeling well," she called out, not opening the door. "I'm staying here."

He hit the door, and it sprung open. And in that moment, standing in the doorway, she saw a monster—a demon. But then Dmytro stepped into the cottage and the monster was gone. She was seeing things ... but how could Dmytro be strong enough to knock open a wooden door? "What's wrong, Bethany?"

She shrank away from him. "I don't know. The flu, maybe. I'm sick to my stomach."

"Let me see." He followed, put his hand on her forehead, then felt her lymph nodes along her jaw as if he were some sort of medical doctor. She noticed his fingernails were growing quite long and sharp. She remained still, afraid to make a fuss. "I don't feel any swollen glands, and you aren't feverish."

"It doesn't matter. I'm sick. I need to lie down."

He put his hands on her shoulders, his nails digging into her skin. "For a while there, I thought we were going to become great friends. I'm sorry you've changed your mind about me." He brushed a lock of hair off her face and tucked it behind her ear. "You should stay at the inn with the others while I'm away."

"I'm fine here," she whispered.

He dropped his hands. "Rest up for now. Tonight I'll fetch you and you *will* come with me." Then he walked over to her newly filled backpack and took her car keys from its pocket. "Since you're ill, we wouldn't want to take the chance that you'll try to drive. I'll be here later for you."

Then, with a skeletal smile, he walked out the door.

She shut and locked it, then slowly slid to the floor, leaning back against the door. What she saw—imagined—had looked like ancient drawings of the devil and his demons as horned, lizard-like monsters, some with wings, but all had tails and long claws.

Clearly, it had nothing to do with Dmytro, and was all from her own fevered imagination because of this horrible place. But then she remembered at church one day an elder had said, "The Bible tells us that many times Christ cast out demons. Why should anyone think they've all gone away now?"

———

Ceinwen paced back and forth across her studio apartment. She had used her newsroom search capabilities to hunt for archaeological digs in Ukraine and what she found made her nervous. She came across several press releases from the University of Kyiv team telling about the possibility of a Knights Templar chapel being located near a tiny town called Potchiv. But she also learned a student had been killed there by a pack of wolves.

The police had been called in to investigate and, for some reason, the investigation had dragged on, which made Ceinwen suspicious that a lot wasn't being reported. And then the story disappeared, as if the death and the possible find had ceased to be of interest.

A press release announced that after a hiatus in winter, the team was back at work and had reached the chapel. University bulletins said studies were ongoing to determine the origin of the site and that the team expected to soon locate any tunnels that might exist.

The last report was dated a week earlier.

Michael must be there, she thought, which might explain why she hadn't been able to reach him.

She phoned Kira with the news.

"I've spoken several times to Michael," Kira said.

"You have?" Ceinwen was surprised.

"He went to St. Petersburg and found Jianjun," Kira explained. "He'd been arrested for murder, of all things. Jianjun is not a killer. Michael hired an attorney who discovered it was all a mistake. Other than that, all I know is that they're both all right."

"Great news!" Ceinwen said, although she sensed there was something more lurking beyond the story of Jianjun's arrest. "Are they still in St. Petersburgh?"

"Yes, last I heard." Kira hesitated, but then with words tinged with regret, she added, "I've decided to cut Jianjun out of my life. Michael, too. I still . . . well, I don't believe Jianjun and I can ever make a relationship work. So it's easier this way."

"I understand completely," Ceinwen said. She'd felt the same way about what she had with Michael, but still... "I tell myself the smartest thing is to stay away from Michael, from everything he's involved in. And yet..."

"It's hard, I know," Kira murmured. "And, one more thing." Kira sounded as if she had something important to say, but didn't really want to. "I'm so sorry, Ceinwen, I did offer Michael your new phone number. But... he didn't take it."

"I see." Ceinwen had steeled herself for news like this, but to actually hear it was heart wrenching. "Thank you for telling me."

"I think he wants to protect you," Kira quickly added, "from him and those around him."

Ceinwen's throat felt tight as she whispered, "That could be."

But as they finished the call, she wondered if he really wanted to protect her, or move on to someone else—Irina.

She tried to put Irina, the dig, and Michael out of her mind. But it didn't work. The whole thing about an archeological team suddenly inviting Michael to Ukraine, on the border with Russia, had bothered her from the first time she heard about it.

Claude was in St. Petersburg, as was Irina, and that was where Michael had gone to find Jianjun. None of this was a coincidence.

She needed to look for answers—Rempart family demonic, alchemical answers.

Oxford's Bodleian Library was filled with rare and esoteric books about Russian demonology. There, she researched Russian alchemy and found, to her surprise, that there was no tradition of it in Russia. In the Western half of the country, it was considered a European and Near Eastern interest, and in the Eastern half, they thought alchemy stemmed from China.

In Russian literature, almost all alchemists were from Europe. Despite this, she couldn't help but think that everything Michael and those around him were going through was because of alchemy, particularly due to William Claude.

She kept researching, preferring to bury herself

in the study of Russian alchemy rather than to think of Michael in St. Petersburg with Irina Petrescu.

Alchemy, she found, hadn't been mentioned in serious Russian literature until the nineteenth century. Pushkin was interested in both alchemy and the occult, which caused Ceinwen to remember that Michael liked staying at an inn near the Pushkin museum. In one of Chekov's works, he had a woman call her brother an alchemist when she found him doing useless, idle work, and Tolstoy called an alchemist he wrote about "a romantic wayfarer."

She paused at that. In a sense, it described Michael.

But as interesting as Ceinwen found this study, none of the information helped her decide what to do. She couldn't help but feel the dig was a good place to start.

She told her boss at the *UK Daily Mail* about a strange archaeological dig taking place in Ukraine and that it had stories of supernatural happenings connected to it. She wanted to learn the truth and expose the myths. Since that had always been her forte as a reporter, her editor gave the okay as well as funds. In no time at all, she was jetting off to the Ukraine ... and hopefully not into danger.

As soon as morning arrived, Jianjun phoned his attorney for advice on leaving St. Petersburg. Stepanov suggested he go to the station, request his passport, then immediately head to the airport. If the police didn't cooperate, he needed to have the attorney's number on speed dial, particularly if it looked as if he might be arrested again.

At the station, Sergeant Zhuk turned over the passport, but again asked that Jianjun remain in the city. He said he'd consider it, which he highly doubted she believed, and caught a cab to the airport.

Standing at the airline counter to buy a ticket, he was so nervous he feared he'd get stopped for excessive fidgeting and perspiring. He stared at his phone the whole time.

Over and over he thought about what his attorney had told him. The police still had no leads on what had happened to Patience Hewson. A video from a bank near the spot where Jianjun told them he was following an attractive young woman, showed Jianjun but no one else. Jianjun had been alone. Period. As such, they had been unable to locate or identify the woman he said he was with.

So far, since the American embassy was silent about Patience Hewson's death, the police were inclined to chalk this up to a bizarre, random attack. Arresting a Canadian citizen based on no actual or even circumstantial evidence in addition to the strange way the laboratory reports had been tampered with, made pursuing the case against Jianjun all but impossible. And then, of course, there was the fact that medically, he would have been unconscious at the time he became covered with the deceased's blood.

All of it was good news. Still, Jianjun finally breathed a sigh of relief once the plane took off and he was out of Russian airspace.

In Zurich, he booked himself a direct flight to Los Angeles. He did it before allowing himself time to second-guess his action. Actually, he'd quadruple-guessed it, but bought the ticket anyway.

As he got on board, he debated with himself whether he should phone Kira to let her know he was on his way to see her, or to simply show up at her townhouse.

If he phoned, and she made it clear she didn't want to see him, that would be that. He'd get on the next plane to Canada. But that would mean he wouldn't get to see her, and maybe, he'd never see her again in his life.

He hated that possibility.

The thought of not seeing her was too hard to bear.

It had been five months since he'd last seen her.

That was a long time. Lots and lots could have changed for her.

But if he just showed up at her apartment, how might that turn out?

For all he knew, she had a new boyfriend. She was beautiful and smart, a career woman. She knew a lot of important people. Men—important, rich men—should be willing to crawl through shattered glass for a date with her. Through hot coals. Through a shark tank. Hell, he would!

In fact, when he thought about it, he had no idea why a woman like her had ever paid any attention to a nobody like him. But she had.

Maybe that was why he needed to see her again. Just to remind himself of how far beyond his reach she was, so that he'd stop thinking about her and stop telling himself "someday," or "if only." Because for him, someday would never come. And if-only's had passed him by long ago.

One glimpse. That was all. Hell, she'd probably tell him she'd gotten married, and gaze upon him with pity. As the plane soared over the Alps, he couldn't shake the thought.

CHAPTER 51

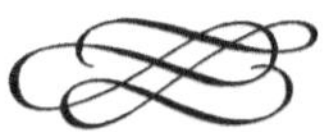

Once in Budapest, Irina found a driver willing to transport them into Ukraine for a substantial fee. They'd fed the driver a complete story, that Michael was a famous archeologist, as proven by his papers, on his way back to his dig team, that he was bringing along his partner and their daughter to show them a bit of Ukraine's beauty, starting with the town of Mukachevo with its castle and gothic cathedral. The driver had fallen for every word.

Going across the border was always slow and the line of cars was long, but they eventually made it to the guard station. The driver told them he had a very important person in his car, then embellished the story. As Irina translated for him, Michael worried that the man was saying too much, but the guards were caught up in the tale, and before long, they crossed into Ukraine.

In Mukachevo, they tried to find a car rental company, but nothing was available for them without having to give way too much information about who they were. They didn't want to do any of that. Instead, they found a Ukrainian driver who was willing, for a price, to take them to the town of Potchiv.

It was night as they entered the town, and Michael was surprised to see it empty. He asked the driver to wait and went into the inn where the dig team had been staying. A sign was taped to the window, but he didn't know the language. Inside, he rang the bell at the front desk but when no one answered, he headed back to the kitchen. It was empty and looked as if it hadn't been used for days.

When he went back outside, Irina and Zoe stood on the porch with the luggage. "The driver was afraid to stay," Irina said. "He pointed to a sign in the window and hollered 'Vampires! Stay away!' It was all I could do to get him to wait long enough for us to take our bags. I took down the sign and threw it away. It's all nonsense!"

"Is it?" Michael muttered. "No wonder the town looks abandoned."

Grabbing the luggage, he led Irina and Zoe to the cottage he'd stayed at. Bethany's old ZAZ was parked out front. He'd told her to leave, to get away from this evil place, but it looked as if she hadn't. Now, with the inn empty, he hoped she was inside the cottage.

He was glad to find that the key he'd hung on to

still worked. He ushered Irina and Zoe inside, turned on the light, but felt the emptiness of the place. There were dishes in the sink and the un-made bed made it clear Bethany—or someone--had been living there. If it was Bethany, where was she now? His heart sank at the realization that she and the entire dig team might be dead.

He could only pray he was wrong.

He desperately wanted to go up to the dig site to look for Bethany, for anyone, but given what he knew was up there, and considering the sign on the inn's window, he didn't dare leave Irina and Zoe alone. In truth, he feared for all of them.

"I'm hungry," Zoe said, tugging on her mother's hand.

"We all are," Irina said, giving her daughter a quick hug.

Michael decided the best thing for now was to stay put, eat whatever they could find in the cottage and let Zoe and Irina sleep. He himself would keep watch, hoping Bethany would return.

Alive.

Yakiv Koval had been hiding high on the mountain overlooking the excavation site when he saw automobile headlights off in the distance, near the town of Potchiv. Could it be that someone—the police, hopefully—were coming to inspect the dig site? Someone should be wondering why there had been no dispatches from him for a couple of days.

He began to cry with the hope that this long nightmare would finally be over. That he would be rescued. He needed to get down the mountain, but fear crippled him and he stayed in his hiding place. Tears of fright and desperation rolled from his eyes.

He felt as if he'd been hiding there forever, but it was only two mornings ago that he'd risen early at the inn to find no brewed coffee and no one preparing breakfast. The innkeeper and his wife were nowhere around, so he went to find Veronika to complain about the poor service. But she, too, was missing. What in the world, he'd wondered, was going on?

He knew she'd been bizarrely curious about chapel after finding Galyna up there. He hurried up to the dig, sure he'd find her there, to inform her she would need to prepare breakfast for the team.

When he didn't see her above ground, he climbed into the unearthed chapel. The morning sun streaked through the opening, and ...

The thing on the ground was Veronika, or what was left of her. And to his horror, the innkeeper and his wife lay there as well, their bodies butchered.

The bile rose quickly from his stomach to his throat. He bent over and violently vomited.

More fear than he had ever experienced in his life came over him. Why were the innkeeper and his wife there? Had someone, *something*, grabbed them from the town and brought them up here? That meant the town was no longer safe. Or was it ever? A town with no residents and only an inn and gas station for travelers ...

He didn't even wipe his mouth but ran like a madman away from the dig, from the town, and from his students. The only thing he could think of was to go over the mountain and pray that another valley, another town, was on the other side and that there he could find good people to help him.

The climb was difficult and slow. After climbing for hours, the summit seemed farther off than ever. Finally, he had no strength to continue and lay on the ground, shaking and in tears. The mountain was too steep, too rocky. He didn't have the skill to go on.

After resting, he started back down. He didn't want to go anywhere near the excavation, but he had to get back to his car so he could get away. He stopped when it grew too dark to clearly see safe footing. He had no choice but to spend the night on the mountain.

His mouth was dry and his stomach ached with

hunger. He found an area by a rock face that was concave and sat, hoping to shelter himself. He grabbed some nearby stones as weapons—not that they would do much good. Fear and hunger kept him awake as the night deepened.

The moon was high when a glow of lights shone from the direction of the dig and he heard a strange yet mesmerizing sound--singing but without words, more like a hum, or a chant.

He carefully crept about until he could see the dig site through some brush. He saw a bonfire surrounded by men in hooded robes. He stared hard and then spotted his beautiful Galyna. He felt his heart would stop at the sight of her. But ... what was she doing?

Toward the bonfire she danced, twirling and spinning round and round, and wearing a thin, almost sheer floor-length dress. He didn't understand, but she looked like a goddess among those ... those what?

His blood turned to ice.

Who were those people?

The men crept closer to her, but then one of them thrust an arm in the air and the others obediently backed off. The leader strode to Galyna as the others now chanted the eeriest song Koval had ever heard. The two danced slowly, erotically, performing a bizarre pantomime of a vampire drinking blood from the neck of a beautiful maiden. They then ran from the firelight and out of view.

The other men took their place near the fire, their singing and dancing much faster now, and in the firelight he saw them pull Olena into their midst. But this was no pantomime. They were actually drinking her blood as they handed her off from one to the other. Her head lolled back, giving them full access to her neck, and she seemed dazed, more like a rag doll than a person.

Vampires! Koval's breathing quickened at all he was seeing. As frightening as it was, he couldn't take his eyes off what was going on. They continued to dance, to hum their eerie chant, and once sated, the creatures' interest in Olena turned sexual. But while Galyna had appeared happy, Olena could have been dead.

Did she have any idea what was going on, how she was being used?

And then he saw Dmytro. How could it be that he was involved in this, too? Koval's curiosity turned to shock when he saw that Dmytro was trying to pull Bethany into the dance. She struggled, kicking out at him, but Koval realized it was all in vain when he saw that her wrists had been tied behind her back. There was little she could do.

Dmytro soon picked her up and carried her away from the bonfire and the dancing.

Olena now lay on the ground, alone, ignored by the throng of robed creatures. He gave a momentary thought to rescuing her, but quickly decided self-preservation was more important.

Quite a bit of time passed before Dmytro again joined the group. But now he was alone. Where, Koval wondered, was Bethany?

Dmytro walked right past Olena and joined the vampires, dancing and spinning with them before they all dissolved into what Koval could only term an orgy.

For the first time, Koval forgot about his hunger, his thirst, and his aching body, and wished he was a photographer as well as an archeologist. What pictures he could take! This, more than mere Templar ruins, would make his fortune. To think, he had proof of vampires in our midst, killing some people, turning others—so it seemed--into demons just like themselves, all the while performing a strange, erotic, singing and chanting ceremony.

But he didn't have a camera. Later, he thought, after he got off this damned mountain, he'd come back another time and record it.

For now, all he could do was watch.

Strangely, some part of him found himself wishing he could have joined in. But he suspected that way lay death.

As the first light filled the sky, the vampires and

the others left. Koval had no idea where they went. All he knew was that he feared going anywhere near the dig site. He tried to find a path around it down the mountain, but no matter how many trails he followed, he always ended up right back where he started, which made no logical sense to him whatsoever. Finally, bewildered and exhausted after having been awake for more than twenty-four hours, he couldn't stop himself from falling asleep.

When he awoke, the sun was again low; night was falling. He sat up, weaker and more parched than ever. But then he saw the car's headlights approach the campgrounds.

He would be rescued! Finally!

He was about to force his aching body to hurry down the mountain, but something made him hesitate.

Having stayed up here now, a second day, observing what was going on, he realized the only safe time to move was midday. No vampires were around in bright sunlight ... he hoped. But now, with the sun going down, dare he risk going back down there?

He should wait for the next day, just to be safe.

On the other hand, he was so hungry and thirsty. He'd heard that drinking one's own urine helped. So far, he wasn't desperate enough to try it. And he feared he might be too parched to form any.

Maybe, if he hurried, he could make it safely to the car.

He abandoned his thoughts about the past two days and allowed himself to think only of the present. He had to get back into town. Back to safety. To sanity.

He tried, slipping and sliding his way down the steep incline as the sun dropped behind the mountains much faster than he thought it might.

The moon lit the sky before he reached the dig site. He was running across it to the trail down to the campsite—and from there, freedom!—when he saw Galyna up ahead.

"Professor," she said, a wide smile on her beautiful face.

He stopped, staring as she slowly approached. He swallowed hard at how revealing her dress was. Where had she found such a thing?

"Where are you going so quickly?" she asked. "Did you come up here to find me?"

"No. I was just leaving. I'm heading back to the inn," he muttered.

"Yakiv, don't be silly." She stopped in front of him, then smiled as her hands drifted over his shoulders. "My! Look at how wide your shoulders are! You're so strong. I've always admired that about you."

"Oh? Well..."

"Don't be shy." She let her arms slip around his neck.

He placed his hands on her hips and couldn't help the feeling of desire at her nearness, particularly as memories of the dancing, singing ... the orgy he'd witnessed played in his head. He forced such thoughts aside. "Of course. But ... but I've got to go now."

"Do you?" She stood on tiptoe and whispered in his ear. "Really?" His hands slid lower cupping her backside as his heart pounded. Was she really offering...?

But then, sanity prevailed, and he took a step back.

"Don't leave me, Yakiv," she murmured as she unbuttoned the top button of his shirt. "You can spare me five minutes, can't you?"

"Well—"

She yanked hard on his shirt, sending buttons flying off, baring his chest. He couldn't protest as her hands kneaded his heated flesh, then slid downward to his stomach, the waistband of his trousers, and, at last, slid inside. He'd wanted this for so long, and suddenly all resistance vanished. He somehow managed to place his mouth over hers. Tasting her warmth. He pressed her hard against him as his hand slid under her low neckline, trembling and desperate to touch the soft curve of her breast ...

What was happening?

Powerful arms grabbed him. Long, sharp finger-nails pierced his flesh and ripped him away from her.

"Stop! What?" he cried. He couldn't break away from his captor, couldn't tear his eyes off Galyna. He ached for her and he knew she wanted him, but ... but now he saw disgust written on her face. She ran the back of her hand over her mouth as if to wipe away his kisses, his touch.

He couldn't bear that any more than he could bear the agony of the claws that held him.

"Please, Galyna," he begged. But before he could ask for her help, an excruciating pain just below his rib cage stopped his breathing. It would have brought him to his knees but his captor held him upright while Galyna stepped close. She had a smile on her face as she plunged her hand into the opening. Her smile widened as her fingers twisted and turned inside him.

"Thank you," she whispered, then laughed as she pulled out his wet, blood-and-bile-soaked liver and took a bite.

CHAPTER 52

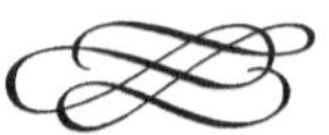

Jianjun left the LAX terminal and rented a car for the slow, tedious ride through Los Angeles traffic to Kira's townhouse in Santa Monica. By the time he reached the building and found a parking spot, it was eight at night. He sat in the car, wondering if he should get out. He was almost afraid to ring the bell. What if no one was home? He guessed he could get a room somewhere and try again in the morning.

Maybe it would be better to come back then. Who goes around ringing doorbells at eight o'clock at night? Actually, a lot of people. It was hardly late.

But if she was home, and she was living with a man, or married, or whatever, this was the time of night he would find that out. And he really needed to know.

There were lights on in her townhouse. They could be for security, to fool burglars into thinking someone was home when no one was.

He was coming up with excuses. Lots of them.

Taking a deep breath, he climbed out of the car, went to her door, and rang the bell.

He waited, and as he'd feared, there was no answer.

He debated with himself, then pushed the bell one more time and immediately wished he hadn't. That was being pushy. If she was there and didn't want to answer the door, he shouldn't stand out here ringing the bell like some crazed Quasimodo. He should leave.

Oddly relieved at that decision, he turned to go back to his car when he heard the deadbolt click. He spun around as the door swung open.

Kira gawked at him in complete shock.

He took in everything about her: her lovely face with its nearly translucent skin and the light freckles across her nose, her sky-blue eyes, her fiery red hair. Then his gaze drifted down her body ...

His mouth dropped open as he stared.

"Come inside," she said.

"Kira, I ..." He followed her into the living room.

She slowly eased herself onto an armchair. He remained standing, feeling awkward and unsure, and then all but dropped onto the sofa.

They eyed each other a long time before, finally, he spoke, "Is—"

"Don't you dare ask if this child is yours!"

He frowned, unsure how to react to her words. "I shouldn't?"

She struggled to her feet, walked over to him and socked his arm hard, before sitting heavily on the sofa beside him. He had forgotten how quick she was to get physical—in good and bad ways.

"How's that for my answer?"

"Kira," he whispered. He couldn't help but smile at the thought that he was going to be a father. "Why didn't you tell me?"

"You're smiling?"

"Of course! This is so ... I can't believe it."

She frowned. "I meant to tell you when the time was right."

"Right? How about as soon as you found out? That seems right to me." He was breathless.

She intertwined her fingers, her hands clasped tight. "But babies sometimes miscarry. And given that I'm 'older' and all I'd been through—I didn't expect to stay pregnant, frankly. To be honest, I thought maybe the doctor had made a mistake."

"So what? I'd have been here to help you go through whatever happened."

She fumed. "Right. Or maybe I should have just showed up at your house! I remember what it was like the one time I did that. Your wife didn't know me and I hadn't even met you yet, but she surely jumped to conclusions and yelled at you about 'all your women.' I should have listened to her!"

He took her hands, hoping to calm her down. "Kira, I don't get it. I mean, we were always so careful."

She pulled her hands away, then walked ... waddled ... over to the refrigerator where she got out two bottles of water. "We were. But sometimes things fail. Who knows why? Besides, I know you don't want kids. You've told me that often enough and said it had been a point of contention with your wife. And I certainly had no plans for unwed motherhood. But here I am."

"I didn't want kids with Linda because we had such an unhappy marriage I felt it would've been wrong."

She nodded but the eyes she fixed on him were worried. "There was another issue I had to face. The creatures around us ... my father and what happened to him. I mean, he was possessed through most of his life, including when I was conceived. Do I carry some weird genes from him? I don't think I show signs, but what if I pass some of my dad's difficulties on to this child? I've had nightmares of having my own version of Rosemary's baby!"

"Who?"

"It's an old horror movie. Don't worry about it."

She took a deep breath, then put the water on the counter. "What I'm saying is, I worried about this baby—about what it might be." She lightly touched her stomach. "I decided to abort it. But as I was driving to the clinic, I couldn't do it."

He walked up to her and gripped her upper arms. "I'm glad you didn't. Just as you're fine, our baby will be as well."

She stepped back, and his hands dropped. "You don't know that for sure! Anyway, I went to the doctor, and he did ultrasounds and amniocentesis and every test I could think of. All the time, he's been assuring me the baby is fine, and that every test shows him to be quite normal. I realized I do want him, and I will protect him."

His voice was choked as he murmured, "We're having a son?"

She nodded. "I kept thinking about telling you," she admitted. "But, believe me, it's not exactly an easy thing to contemplate doing by phone. Especially given your situation. And I didn't want you to think I was calling because I wanted anything from you. And then, I thought, what if the baby wasn't healthy? Or died? Should I disturb your life with Linda more than I already have? And for a reason that might not even be necessary?"

He shook his head, a smile on his lips. "You always did have a knack for having the most pessimistic take on everything."

"That's me, the happy warrior." She sat back down on the arm chair.

"When is he due?"

"Two more months."

"So you're seven months ..." He stared at her. "You mean you knew, or at least suspected, that you were pregnant when we separated? When you told me to go back to my wife and never see you again?"

"I learned I was expecting when we were together in Salmon." She looked away. "As I mentioned, I didn't want you to feel stuck with me. I mean, you're married, a very traditional, very strong Chinese marriage. I understand that, and I always have. That was why I had to leave, had to never see you again. I wanted to tell you but, because of your parents and the way you were raised, I was afraid you would feel obligated to reject us both. I could handle it for myself, but not for our child."

He sucked in his breath. "It's funny, I always thought we were so close, that we could tell each other anything, and now I learn the most important things, we don't say. I've also kept something from you."

She gave him a curious look.

"I'm getting a divorce. I, too, didn't want you to think you'd be stuck with me because I was now free, so I didn't tell you. But the truth is, after we parted and you said I should go back home, I tried to do it. I really did. But once I was in Vancouver, in what will soon be Linda's house, I knew I couldn't stay there and live a lie. So I filed for a divorce and left. It'll become final next month."

She stared at him as his words sunk in. "I'm sorry."

He stiffened. Sorry? Was that all she could say, that she was sorry for him? All the joy he'd felt learning about their baby suddenly disintegrated. "I see." He found himself fighting back tears and walked away from her so she wouldn't see his weakness. He slid his fingers in his back pockets and stared out the window at the bright city lights as he spoke. "I get it. I really do. You're so good at everything you do, you don't need me. Probably don't even want me in your life. I offer you nothing." Then he faced her once more and raised his chin, no longer caring if she thought he was weak. "But damn it, Kira," his voice broke, "a baby needs a father. I can't just walk away and pretend my child doesn't exist. I won't do that!"

Seeing his reaction, Kira could no longer hold back the tears she'd been fighting. "God, of all the men in the world that I could have fallen in love with, why did I have to pick one who's so darn unsure of himself? I meant I'm sorry that you had to go through a divorce. It's a difficult thing, even if the marriage is bad. It's a loss of hope, of innocence, if nothing else. But I wasn't rejecting you. Not at all."

"You weren't?"

She walked up to him. "Of course not! And I'm glad to hear how you feel about our baby."

He placed his hands on her face, his thumbs wiping the tears he found there. Then he placed his hands on her belly. "I don't know the words to express how happy I feel at this moment."

She couldn't help but give a slight laugh as she pulled Kleenex from her pocket and handed the tissues to him. "I don't know what to do with you."

He laughed with her as he wiped his eyes, and then gently kissed her.

She put her arms around his neck. "Can you stay with me a while? Or do you have a flight to catch?"

"I'm not going anywhere, Kira. The only place I've ever wanted to be is with you."

CHAPTER 53

Michael left Irina and Zoe as soon as the sun appeared in the morning, and headed up to the dig site.

He reached the campground and when he went into the tent, it was empty. Could they all have gone into the chapel and tunnels at the same time? That made no sense, and it wasn't safe. They needed someone to watch the instruments when underground to make sure there was no sudden shifting of the earth.

He guessed he had no choice but to climb down there himself. He was about to step onto the rope ladder when he saw movement up on the mountain along with something the color of Bethany's blonde hair.

Hope filled him.

It didn't take long to climb up to where he thought he'd seen the young woman. In a hushed voice he called her name. No answer.

He found her in a thicket, curled in a ball as if

trying to make herself small. Her hair was loose and wild, her clothes torn, and she was barefoot. He inched closer, then knelt.

"Bethany."

She blinked, her eyes glassy and unfocused and then tried to run.

"No." He caught her wrist. "It's me, Michael."

She froze and studied him. Then, without speaking, she reached up and gently touched the side of his face. He helped her to her feet, and pulled her jacket shut, but not before he saw the raw, open skin on her neck. He knew what created a wound like that and the thought sickened him. It had stopped bleeding, but she was frighteningly pale.

Holding her to his side, he hurried her down to the camp, fearful of who or what might be watching them. Before he could do anything else, he needed to get her back to the cottage, to tend to her wound and help her to feel safe.

She kept stumbling and nearly falling until he picked her up and carried her.

"Is that the girl who's been staying here with you?" Irina asked as Michael entered the cottage and placed Bethany on the sofa.

"Yes. She's weak and anemic and ... and I'm sure she's been attacked by--" He didn't utter the word vampires, wanting to keep that horror from

Zoe, but he knew Irina would understand. "We need to get food into her."

"There's no more in this cottage," Irina told him, staring at Bethany. "I've already looked."

"Give her water. I'll go to the inn and see what I can find."

"Of course," Irina said as Zoe quietly took in everything, including the wound on Bethany's neck. The girl looked frightened as her gaze jumped from Bethany to Michael and then to her mother. Michael hated that a child--his sister—had to be subjected to this, but it couldn't be helped. Someday Irina, or he, would have to explain it all to her. But not now.

Leaving Bethany to be cared for by Irina, he went to the inn. Michael couldn't help but wonder if the innkeeper and his wife had abandoned it. Who could blame them if they'd realized vampires were nearby?

He made his way through the cold, empty rooms to the kitchen. In the refrigerator he found some blood sausage. While it was a popular food throughout much of this part of Europe, it had a different connotation for him now. But he knew it would be filled with nourishment for Bethany. For Irina and Zoe, as well.

He heated it using the inn's stove, and as it cooked, he checked the bedrooms. They still had computers, tools, and equipment, not to mention clothes. The team hadn't packed up and left. They were here, somewhere.

As soon as the sausage was ready, he put a lid on the sizzling pan, tucked a loaf of somewhat stale bread under his arm, and hurried back to the cottage.

But when he arrived, it was empty except for Bethany looking like death as she lay on the sofa. Blood seeped from her neck. He dropped the food on the table and rushed to her. She was still breathing, but he could barely feel her pulse and her skin was cold.

"Irina! Zoe!" he called as fear gripped him. Where were they? He needed to search, but first he had to stop Bethany's blood loss. His mind raced with awful thoughts of what might have happened here.

He grabbed a pillow case and tore it into rags to dab at the blood oozing from her. The wound was raw, as if ...

Good God, he didn't want to think about it. He applied a light pressure, trying to staunch the flow.

Bethany opened her eyes and stared at him, then slowly, her vision seemed to focus. "No," she whispered and tried to get away from him.

"Stop, you'll cause the bleeding to get worse."

"Don't touch me!"

"I won't hurt you, I promise."

"You brought me to them," she cried, then turned her head from him.

A chill went down his spine.

"Did this start to bleed by itself?" he asked, afraid to hear the worst.

"Why, Michael?" she whispered, her voice shaky.

"Hold this," he told her, pressing her hand against the cloth-covered wound. He rummaged through drawers until he found some tape and gauze. "Did someone break in?" he asked, leaning over her, almost hoping she'd say "yes."

But she remained silent as he bandaged the wound, then helped her sit up.

"Here, drink," he said, tilting a bottle of water to her mouth. She drank it down quickly then tried to speak, but was too weak.

"Are you hungry?" he asked.

She nodded.

He scooped sausage onto a plate and sat on the sofa next to Bethany. "This should help." He cut a bite-sized piece, speared it with a fork and held it to her mouth. After some hesitation, she took a bite, then another and another, eating as fast as he could feed her. Color slowly returned to her cheeks, and her eyes seemed clearer.

"Can you tell me where Irina and Zoe are?" he asked.

She shook her head and stared at the food. Frustrated that she couldn't or wouldn't answer him, he continued to feed her. Finally, she stopped eating.

"Please, Bethany," he said. "Tell me what happened here. Where are Irina and Zoe? Did they run? Were they taken? I've got to go out and find them."

"No," Bethany whispered, grabbing his arm. "She'll kill you."

He winced at the fear and desperation on this once brave girl's face. "Can you tell me what happened?"

"So many deaths," she murmured. "Veronika. Maybe Dr. Koval. And Andriy--he was found dead on the road, his throat torn out."

He'd feared the worst, and now he was hearing more than he'd been afraid of.

"And the others?" he asked. "Dmytro?"

Her eyes went wide, full of terror.

"Where are they?" he asked.

"Dmytro." She touched her neck. "I fought him. Last night I tried, but..." She blinked away tears. "You'll think I'm crazy but ... he's turned into a vampire. I couldn't stop him. He drank my blood, and then ..." She shut her eyes, unable to say the words.

"I'm so sorry," Michael whispered.

She started to reach for him, but then turned her head away. "I should have left when you told me to, I tried, but then... it was too late." Her eyes closed for a moment, as if trying to block out the horror she'd experienced. She breathed deeply, then looked again at Michael. "I pretended to pass out and eventually he must have grown tired of me and walked away. That was when I ran and hid. I planned to wait until daylight and get as far as I could get from this place. But I was so weak, so scared." She swallowed hard. "I don't know what I'd have done if you hadn't found me."

"I should have told you everything I suspected before I left," Michael whispered. "Or, I should have taken you with me. I feared for Dmytro's possession. I should have realized, seeing his interest in you, that you'd be in danger. This is my fault."

"No, of course it isn't," she murmured, and then placed her hand atop his for just a moment as she offered a tiny smile. "Besides, I thought vampires were only in books and movies. Not real."

His heart went out to the brave young woman. "That's said to be the devil's greatest trick. But to pretend such demons don't exist makes them no less real when they enter our world. They're from a realm of existence that isn't here, but they're all the devil's minions. And they're real. I'm so very sorry you had to face that."

"My God," she whispered.

"God." He nodded. "I'll admit I was once a Doubting Thomas, but no more. And asking for God's help is definitely a good place to start."

She looked surprised to hear him say that, but then she nodded with understanding. "That sounds like something my father would say. Thank you. And there's something more I have to tell you ... something about the woman you brought here."

Michael was afraid to hear her words. He steeled himself.

"She sent her daughter outside to wait for you and then . . . then she attacked me. She wanted blood. She's a vampire."

The words shook him, and yet he couldn't help but think about some of their conversations where she was the woman he once knew one minute and the next she'd say something so harsh it took him aback, as if she was a different person. And she did talk about her special affinity for the demon Militsa, even admitting that Militsa used her body to take part in the Khlyst ceremonies. "I didn't know, believe me. Although, on some level ... God, I'm a fool." He couldn't go on.

"I was afraid you'd turned as well."

"No," he whispered. "Never. I won't let that happen."

"They have too much power, Michael." she said. "What can you possibly do to stop them?"

"I'm not sure, but I do know we're going to find you a good hiding place," he said as he helped her put on warm clothes, shoes and socks. "And then I need to find Irina and Zoe."

They went to the inn and found a storage room in the cellar where he prayed she wouldn't be found by anyone... or anything. It was already stocked with bottles of water, non-perishable food items, blankets, sheets and pillows, everything, he hoped, that she would need while he was gone.

"Where are your car keys?" he asked.

"Dmytro took them."

"Of course he did," he muttered. "I'm going to the dig. Somehow I've got to put a stop to this."

"I know you have to go, but—"

"The moment I'm gone, move anything and everything against the door and don't open it unless you're sure it's safe. Trust your gut."

She dragged in a trembling breath. "Be careful, Michael."

He hated leaving her when she looked so scared, so vulnerable, hated closing the door behind him, but he had couldn't stay any longer.

CHAPTER 54

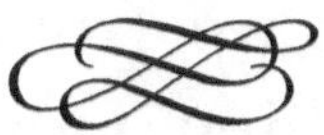

Once outside, Michael checked Bethany's car just to make sure the keys weren't in it. They weren't, so he had no choice but to head up to the campsite on foot. It took long minutes, more than he had to waste, and when he reached the camp, it looked abandoned. He climbed the trail up to the dig, and when he reached the top, he saw Irina and Zoe on the edge of the pit. "What are you doing here, Irina?"

Irina jerked her head toward him as he approached. Her smile was bright, as if she were happy to see him. "We were looking for you! Your friend Bethany is quite sick. She started bleeding again and when I tried to help her, she thought I was attacking her, that I was one of … them." A true look of worry settled on her face. "We need to get her to a hospital."

He couldn't help but notice the blood on her clothes. "I've just come from her," Michael said. "I bandaged her, gave her food and water, and I'm sure she'll be okay. But I don't understand why the bleeding started."

"She tried to get up from the sofa," Irina explained. "She kept calling out your name, and it was all I could do to make her lie back down again."

He studied her face. Her story sounded truthful. And hadn't Bethany feared him as well? But Bethany's words had also rung true. Trust your gut, he'd told Bethany. He had to do the same. "You said you came here looking for me. But I told you I was going to the inn."

She grimaced. "You were gone so long I guessed you might have come here knowing you'd find first-aid kits, maybe even antibiotics. I just needed to find you, and it seemed like coming here was my best bet."

"Maybe," he said. Something about her, the way she spoke, even her eyes, seemed off. "We need to get back to her—"

"Is the girl okay, all things considered?"

"She's mending."

"She isn't saying crazy things, is she? That's a sure sign of delirium."

"Not really," he lied. He couldn't possibly tell Irina what Bethany had said. "She didn't say much of anything," he lied again.

"That's good." Was that a look of relief he saw on Irina's face?

"She was asleep when I left. I was worried something might have happened to you and Zoe. Right now, I need to look for the others. After that, we've all got to get away from this place."

"You sound afraid, Michael."

"I am afraid. For you. For Zoe. For Bethany."

"And you believe you can take care of yourself?"

"I have for a very long time."

He looked around the excavation, at the pit they stood next to. Everything appeared normal, like most every other archaeological site he'd worked at.

But then a question struck him. "How did you know how to find the dig?"

Irina laughed. "How quickly you forget. You pointed it out to me when we arrived."

He had pointed out it was 'up that road.' That might have been sufficient for her to find it. And she did have a logical explanation for why she was here. God, but he wanted to believe her!

"You're tired, Michael. I can tell, especially when you start asking foolish questions."

He was tired. He wished he could get the hell out of this place, but he had to look for the students, for Dr. Koval—if any of them were still alive. He wished he could tell Irina and Zoe to go back to the cottage and to watch over Bethany. But, much as he wanted to trust Irina, he just didn't know if he could.

"Tired or not," he said, "I—we—can't leave until we find the dig team. This doesn't make sense. I want to look in the chapel. You and Zoe wait here."

"Nonsense. We'll go with you. Zoe is full of questions about archeology that I can't answer."

"Oh?" Pleasantly surprised, Michael turned to the girl.

She nodded shyly and stayed near her mother. But then he reminded himself never to forget that, despite her youthfulness, she was William Claude's daughter. And he had no idea, really, how much she understood and possibly liked about the demons her mother had conjured.

"I can teach you most anything you want to know," he said. "But we'll have to do that later. Okay?"

She frowned. "No, please, let come with you."

Michael caught Irina's eye and shook his head.

"It could be too dangerous down there for you," Irina told her daughter.

"But I want to learn all about archeology!" The girl wailed. "It's important!"

"It is not," Irina said. "You're curious, nothing more. You stay here with me."

"I won't!" Zoe spun toward Michael. "You'll let me come along, won't you? You'll watch me so I don't get lost, right?"

He glanced at Irina, then said, "You need to listen to your mother."

"I do, when she's being reasonable. I just want to see it!"

"I believe she said no."

Zoe turned again to Irina. "Please, *mami*!"

"Stop!" Irina said, finally. "I can't abide your whining!"

"It could be bad down there," Michael warned Irina.

"I understand that," Irina said. Then she shook her head and smiled at him. "Ignore her, Michael. You do what you need to. I'll watch my daughter."

Just then, he heard a scream. Zoe! He spun around to see her scrambling up and off the ladder. He glanced at Irina, who also looked stunned.

As they'd talked, Zoe must have gone off on her own. But now, she ran into her mother's arms. Irina held her close.

"What happened?" Michael asked.

Zoe merely pointed toward the dig and then buried her face against her mother's shoulder again.

"Stay put," Michael ordered, before latching onto the ladder. As he began his descent, the stench gave a warning of what he might find. He climbed down and turned on his flashlight. His stomach convulsed at the sight before him.

On the floor of the chapel Veronika's remains were rotting and putrid, while what was left of Yakiv Koval's body looked relatively fresh. Then he saw the innkeeper and his wife, what was left of them.

Apparently, the vampires no longer feared killing their hosts and were gorging themselves.

He tore his gaze away from the ghastly sight and saw an opening in the far wall of the chapel. Stairs carved out of granite went down to an area lit with battery-operated lanterns. The team had apparently found tunnels after all, for all the good it had done them.

He climbed out of the pit and went to Irina and Zoe. "Let's get out of here. We can use Bethany's car once I figure out how to start it without a key. We need to get the police out here."

"No, Michael," Irina said. "No police."

"I don't know what you had hoped to accomplish here," Michael said, "but things have gone too far. Two professors plus the innkeeper and his wife are down there—their bodies mutilated. This is beyond us."

"You're wrong," she said. "It isn't." She raised her hands and six men—night singers, vampires—

wearing hooded robes seemed to walk out of the ground itself and surrounded them. But as these six moved closer, Michael remembered that there had been nine such beings. Where were the other three?

"What is this?" Michael said, searching the area for a means of escape.

"Come," Irina ordered, holding Zoe's hand. They climbed down the ladder. Michael had no choice but to follow as the night singers pushed him to the very edge of the pit.

Once on the chapel floor, hurrying past the decaying bodies, Irina led the macabre procession into the tunnel. They descended the stairs and a little way past them were two steel cages, the type a large dog might be placed in. Curled up and lying on the floor of one was Feder, and in a similar position in the other was Olena. Both were awake, but looked at the procession with eyes that appeared not to comprehend, eyes that seemed no longer human. Both were shirtless despite the cold and had puncture marks and gashes on their bodies, particularly on their abdomens and necks. As he passed Olena, she bared her teeth, emitting a low growl as she stared at his neck. Michael turned his head, unable to look at what had been done to these once bright students.

Irina never faltered, but continued to pull Zoe along with her. The girl looked terrified by all she was seeing.

The procession continued deep into the tunnel, the passage lit by lanterns the night singers carried.

Michael wasn't about to go quietly but searched for a way to break free. As the walk continued, he couldn't help but reflect on the change in Irina. She had been the love of his youth. But so many deeds had been done that could never be undone, so many wrongs that could never be made right. He was filled with regrets about her life, about his, and for all that might have been but never was, through no fault of their own. His heart ached for her. She hadn't deserved any of it.

And what about Zoe? The poor child. Couldn't Irina see the harm she was inflicting on her daughter?

Up ahead, he saw a glow from a fire. What could that mean?

As they neared, he saw a fiery opening in the ground, a molten, bubbling cauldron, like the mouth of a volcano about to spew lava. The glow was all but blinding. Michael stopped, unable to see beyond the smoke and fire.

The night singers shoved him closer to the cauldron.

Irina walked toward him, but it wasn't Irina as she had looked when they entered the tunnel. This Irina wore the dress she had put on the night they'd been in the Winter Palace, the black dress of Princess Militsa.

"You now see my true form, Michael," she said. At her side was a beautiful young woman with thick, curly black hair, lots of jewelry, and similarly dressed. Princess Stana, he guessed. On Irina's other side stood Zoe, Irina's hand—or Militsa's--clamped the girl's wrist tight. But Zoe's eyes met Michael's and held as if she understood more than a child of twelve should.

And then he found out where the other three night singers were. They pulled William Claude to the edge of the cauldron. A thick gold rope was wrapped tightly around him, pinning his arms to his sides. Another gold rope was around his neck like a dog collar ... or a noose. "So she got you, too, did she, boy?" William Claude said with a chuckle. "This makes me feel not quite so foolish."

"What's going on?" Michael stared at William Claude. How could this happen to his powerful father? Something was wrong, very wrong. He faced Irina. "How did he get here?"

"He's very good at mind reading as you know,"

Irina said. "But not as good at discerning what's a lie and what isn't. So I simply thought about us going to the place where you'd hidden the red pearl —these tunnels. I also thought, for his benefit, about how wonderful it was that you found me after so many years and how, together, you and I would be able to do so much with our pearl. We'd have immortality and power. I thought about the back entrance to the tunnel, how we'd take the pearl and go out that way to avoid seeing any people. The foolish man believed my every thought, my every emotion."

Michael could hardly look at her. She had every right to be vengeful, but now she seemed as evil as his father.

"He flew to Kyiv and then paid a lot of money to be escorted up here. My friends"—she waved her hand toward the demons around her—"met him, killing his driver and Stedman. But a quick death was too easy for Claude. It was all so simple, I'm almost shocked."

"Why are you doing all this?" Michael asked.

She looked at him with such disgust, it was all but a physical blow. When she spoke again, her voice was no longer her own, it sounded deep and reverberating, and he realized Irina was completely lost. Militsa had taken over. "Your family destroyed mine. Your father had mine killed, I'm sure of it! And what he did to my mother ...

"When we were in Romania, my mother was warm and loving, even after my father's death. She believed we were both 'fortunate' to have been chosen from so many to be given a job at your father's beautiful estate. But then, all that changed, and she was never the same. She did love you, Michael, and she felt terrible for your sake over all that had happened. That was why she stayed with Claude, so that she could make sure you were all right. In time, I think, she even came to understand what had made your mother so lonely and unhappy that she turned away from her husband to seek love where she could find it.

"Magda did all she could to make up to you for the horrible thing she'd done. I'm certain, as you should be, that she never meant to cause your mother to fall from that height. She may have wanted to push her against the stone, to hurt her, but not to kill her. So... she was filled with guilt but at the same time, I'm sure a part of her was also glad she didn't have to look at the woman who stole her husband's heart. And that dichotomy tore at her. In a sense, the day your mother died, mine did as well."

"Don't listen to her, Michael!" William Claude shouted. "It's all lies. She's trying to win your sympathy. I'll tell you the true story someday but right now we've got to get out of here. You can save us both Michael, and Zoe as well. Use the red pearl."

Michael frowned at his father's words. Believable, perhaps. But he'd learned long ago to never believe William Claude. He focused on Irina.

"That was a terrible tragedy, Irina," Michael said. "But it happened years ago. You don't want to do this now."

"You still don't get it," she said, slowly shaking her head as she regarded him. "I hate both of you!"

Michael winced at her words.

William Claude shouted, "Use the pearl, boy!"

Irina looked from one to the other and grinned. Then with her gaze fixed on Michael, she said, "I've seen how vile mankind can be. It doesn't deserve to go on. The Remparts don't deserve to go on. And even my sweet Zoe can't exist in this horrible world. It will destroy her, just as it did me."

"You can't mean that, Irina," Michael said. "She's innocent."

"And this way, she'll remain so." She glanced at the night singers. "First, the old man!"

"Dammit, boy!" William Claude raged at Michael.

"Irina!" Michael yelled. "Don't do this!"

The night singers holding William Claude's ropes dragged him closer to the cauldron.

"Stop, Irina," Michael called out again.

"Wait! Irina!" Claude cried. "You don't—"

"Scream, Claude!" she demanded. "Scream and beg for your worthless life."

"I did everything out of love," he cried.

"Liar!" She nodded at the demons.

"Please, Irina! Michael, stop them!"

Claude's screams echoed through the tunnel as the demons pushed him into the fire.

"No!" Michael couldn't move, shocked that the man he once saw as completely powerful could have been killed so easily.

He faced Irina, but instead of the woman he once loved, he now saw the demon she had become—the horrible twisted thing that her hatred for Claude, for his family ... for him ... had made her. And he saw that she still held Zoe. Her hate for Rempart blood couldn't really extend to her own child, could it? Zoe had been born out of hate, but through no fault of her own.

And then, with a shudder, he realized Zoe was in the hands of a demon, a woman who was not her mother.

"Stop this madness," Michael cried, hoping to somehow reach the woman he once knew. "Let Zoe go. I'll protect her just as you asked me to."

"You don't fool me, Michael. I know you're as happy as I am to see that vile old man dead! Admit it." But then she looked down at Zoe and gently ran her hand over the girl's long, dark hair.

"Please, you know you don't want to hurt her," Michael said even as he struggled to free himself.

Suddenly, Stana stepped forward and grabbed Zoe, trying to pull her out of Irina's hands, perhaps realizing that enough of Irina existed to stop Militsa from hurting her child.

"*Mami!*" Zoe screamed, holding her mother tight. But Irina stood as if frozen, while Stana tried to pull the girl away.

"Zoe, use your power!" Michael yelled, still unable to break free from the demons holding him. "It's your stone, Zoe. Use it!"

Zoe reached up and took hold of the long, thin gold chain her mother wore around her neck, its end tucked into the bodice of her dress. She held on as Stana dragged her, causing Irina to stumble and almost fall. The chain broke and the small round locket attached to it fell to the ground.

"No!" Stana yelled as the locket rolled toward the cauldron. She lunged for it, as did Zoe. And Zoe got there first.

Stana remained on her hands and knees as she glared at Zoe. "Give it to me! *Now!*"

Zoe backed away.

"My stone is in this locket," Zoe said. "I made it,

I command it. Only because of me are any of you here."

"Zoe," Stana said, her voice firm, "You don't know what you're saying, what you're doing. Give me the stone!"

The night singers eased away from the cauldron as if they feared for their very existence. Finding himself suddenly free, Michael hurried to Zoe's side. She might be an alchemist, but she was still a young girl. He took her hand.

When his hand met hers, a power surged through him stronger than he'd ever felt. She glanced at him, her eyes wide, and then they turned red and fiery.

Even the pouch she held began to glow.

"Let's get out of here," Michael said, unsure of how long the shock of Zoe as creator of the stone would keep the night singers in check. Stana fumed, but seemed aware of Zoe's power. And he feared what was happening to Irina. He guessed she was unable to move because her need to save Zoe was warring with Militsa's desire to kill the girl. But if Militsa won ...

"They all need to understand my power," Zoe said. "Everyone does." The child's glare went from Michael, to the vampires, to the demonic Stana and to her mother, or the woman who'd taken over her mother's body and mind. "I want them all to be nothing but the rats that they are!" She held her hand high and the vampires, Stana, and even the Militsa/Irina creature suddenly turned into ugly, long-tailed rodents.

Michael tightened his grip on Zoe's hand and pulled her from the fiery opening. Having learned there was a way out of the tunnel other than back to the dig site, he went that way, hoping to find a village and people there to help them.

CHAPTER 55

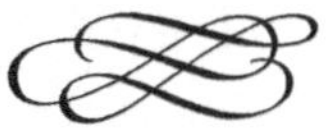

Time seemed to drag on forever as Michael hurried Zoe through the tunnel until, finally, they reached its mouth and stepped out of it to find themselves high on the mountain.

Michael had no idea how they had climbed that high. The sun was sinking, so he knew which direction was west. At least they were on the mountain's north side, rather than facing south toward Potchiv.

Around them, the terrain was rocky and steep. He held Zoe's hand as they carefully began the long descent.

Michael had never seen anything like what he had witnessed with Zoe and the vampires. He guessed they had been created by alchemy raising them from the dead. And somehow that put them under the power of a philosopher's stone. Only that would explain how Zoe's stone could have caused those demons to change form.

That she chose to turn them into rats reminded him of how young she really was.

He wondered if the rats could change back to the way they had been and come after him and Zoe again. It wouldn't surprise him. Despite her stone, they were still demons and as such were clever and evil.

And then his thoughts went to the death of his father. It made no sense. William Claude had all kinds of powers. He never went anywhere without at least one philosopher's stone, if not more. And then there was the demon inside him. How did that demon not come forward to save him?

Clearly, he had expected Michael to pull out the red pearl. He never did believe that Michael would go anywhere without it. Could all this have been a ruse just for William Claude to get his hands on the pearl? Michael really didn't think so. He couldn't see Irina or even Militsa going along with such a scheme.

Maybe, for once, William Claude had out-smarted even himself.

But now, he and Zoe needed to get off this mountain. He realized he'd never seen the night singers anywhere but on the mountain. Could this mountain be the portal between this world and theirs?

He'd learned that some demons were "stuck" in one particular area of this world, usually at or near their place of death. Others, a higher form of demon like Militsa and Stana, as well as the one that had lived in William Claude's body, were able to take over human bodies and travel by many means, human as well as ethereal.

But now, he had a much more earthly worry.

During daylight, the Carpathians were known to be dangerous to climbers, and at night, the dangers more than doubled. Transylvania, home of Dracula, was in the Carpathian Mountains of Romania, not all that different from where they now were.

But the biggest danger was that they might become lost and unable to find their way to a small town. They needed to somehow find some sign of life. These mountains contained a number of old world forests because they were so lightly inhabited.

As night fell, he found a sheltered area where he built a small fire both for warmth and to keep away snakes, bears, or other dangerous wildlife.

He suggested Zoe lie down and sleep.

Michael also dozed, and when he opened his eyes, dawn was just beginning to brighten the sky.

Zoe was sitting up and staring at him.

"Did my mother want to kill me?" she asked, sounding once more like the little girl she was. For that, he was grateful. The other Zoe, the youthful alchemist wielding a frightening amount of power, worried him.

He rubbed his eyes and sat up. Of course, she would be upset and wondering about that. "I believe she was afraid for you and that caused her not to think straight. But remember," he said, trying to soothe his sister's fears, "always remember she wasn't herself. If you mess around with demons and vampires, bad things almost always happen. Never forget that, Zoe."

"My mother knows that," Zoe said, her expression tense, almost pleading. "She warned me many times."

"Unfortunately, grown-ups aren't known for taking their own advice. They sometimes do pretty stupid things, especially when they get scared."

She looked away. "I guess."

God, but she sounded like a teenager already, questioning everything he said. The problem was, he had no idea how to tell her what was really going on. "If we find your mother, let's hope she's her old self again," he said, standing. "We should move on. We've got to try to find our way back to the village."

She stood, not saying anything more. He didn't know if he'd ever met such a quiet, serious child. But her next words surprised him. "Are you my father?"

His breath caught, and he had to think a moment about how much to explain to her. "Why do you ask?"

"Maybe because I've never felt close to anyone except my mother. You're different. Like, maybe you understand me. But I don't know why I think that."

"It's nice that you do," he said. "But I'm not your father."

"Are you sure? You and my mom knew each other long ago, and she acts different with you. Like she likes you."

"We were friends from the time we were little kids," he said with a smile.

"Do you have any children?" she asked.

"No children. No wife. I'm just a loner."

She said nothing for a while, then spoke. "I shouldn't have said I feel close to you. My mother wouldn't like it."

"I don't mind. I don't have many people who feel that way."

She stared at him a moment, then said, "Me, neither."

He waited for her to say more if she wished.

"Back when we were in danger," she began, "when you took my hand, it felt like two magnets coming together. Do you know what I mean? Was that weird? Did I imagine it?"

"No, you didn't," he murmured. "I felt it, too. I believe it made us stronger than either of us alone. I think that's why the philosopher's stone suddenly had so much power."

Again, she took a while to thoughtfully ponder his words. "Why did it happen?" she asked.

He realized he should tell her. Despite her years, she was smart and needed to know the truth. "As I said, I'm not your father, but we are related. We have the same father—different mothers. I'm your half brother."

"My brother?" She studied him. "My mother always told me to say Stas was my brother because we lived with him. But he isn't, and I didn't like pretending."

"Well," Michael said, "now you don't have to pretend anymore."

She took a second to think, then asked. "So where is he? Our father?"

Michael's shoulders sagged. He couldn't tell her everything. Not yet. "I'm afraid he's dead."

She nodded then said nothing for a long while. "What about your mother? Is she alive?"

"No," he whispered.

"Do you have other brothers or sisters?"

"No."

"So you're all alone?"

"That's right."

She nodded, and after a long while said, "I guess it's good then that I'm here."

He looked at her, stunned at her words. "Yes," he said, once the sudden lump in his throat let him speak again. "I'd say it's very good."

Ceinwen reached the town of Potchiv in a small rental Toyota. But when she arrived in the town, she found it wasn't a town—at least, not any longer. The few cottages appeared empty. A small petrol station was next to an inn, but there were no people, no signs of life.

Where, she wondered, were the archeologists and their team?

She stopped at the inn and was surprised to find the door unlocked. The inside was quiet as a tomb. No one answered when she hit the bell at the registration desk.

Back outside, she took out her cell phone and saw that it had no bars at all which was no surprise.

She walked around a bit and saw a single car, an old, small vehicle that looked as if it were on its last leg parked in front of a nearby cottage. It was fairly clean, so someone might have recently used it.

She went to the cottage and knocked on the door.

When she received no answer, she knocked again. She waited a few moments longer and then tried twisting the door knob. It was locked.

Finally, she returned to the inn. Someone had to show up there soon. It might be empty, but it didn't look abandoned.

She walked through the building, calling out as she did, but no one answered. She knocked on bedroom doors. No response. Half the doors were unlocked, so she peeked inside. Clothes and toiletries, even a few computers, were there. She rubbed her arms to ward off a sudden chill.

The only place she hadn't tried was the cellar. She found the stairs going down, but she saw a door at the bottom of the stairs. It looked dark and creepy. She had seen enough horror movies not to go down there alone.

"Hello!" she called out, deciding to give it one last shot and hoping if anyone was around they'd realize that anyone who spoke nothing but English, with a Welsh accent no less, was hardly a threat. "Is anybody there?"

No answer. She gave up and headed for the parlor. Hands on hips, she looked around the room as she pondered what to do next. Wait? Head back to some other town with a sign of life?

But then to her shock and fright she heard a noise coming from the cellar.

She looked around for something heavy to grab, something to defend herself with. She could run, but if whoever had been in the cellar was coming because she had called out, maybe they had information that could help her. She backed up near the inn's front door and waited.

"Who's there?" a woman's voice called.

Ceinwen was stunned to hear an American accent. She spoke quickly. "I'm a friend of Dr. Michael Rempart. I was told he was in this town at an archeological dig. Do you know him, or know where I can find him?"

"I know him," the voice called. "But I don't know that you do."

Ceinwen wasn't sure how to answer that, so decided on a bold approach. "What do you want to know about him? I used to live with the man. I can tell you things that would make your hair curl."

She heard what may have been a door opening, footsteps on the stairs, and suddenly a disheveled, sickly looking young woman with a thick bandage on her neck stood before her.

"My God!" the woman said. "You're Rachel's old roommate!"

Ceinwen studied her. How could this stranger...? But then she realized the girl looked a lot like Rachel. "You're Rachel's sister."

The young woman suddenly burst into tears.

Ceinwen's head was spinning, but she approached and put her hand on Bethany's arm to steady her. "What happened to you? What's going on here?"

The girl looked straight at Ceinwen, her gaze penetrating and full of fear. "Vampires."

CHAPTER 56

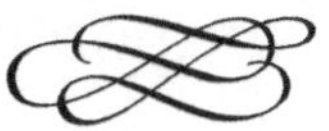

Michael stopped when Zoe's steps grew sluggish. They had no food or water and would need to find some soon.

They sat on boulders. They couldn't stay here long, only a few moments, but Zoe needed whatever rest he could allow her.

He would have used his phone in an attempt to locate where he was, but if it didn't show, the effort could waste what little power he had left. He was more interested in saving his battery to use the phone as a flashlight if they needed to travel at night.

Zoe had been quiet since learning Michael was her half brother. He guessed she needed time to absorb the information.

Just as, he had to admit, he did. Irina's story about living with William Claude had been crazy. He didn't want to believe it, despite being certain Irina wouldn't lie about it. And Zoe was proof of its truth. Still, to suddenly learn that so much had happened to Irina and her daughter ... and that her daughter, this little person, was actually related to him ... was beyond jarring. It was mind-blowing.

And what was he supposed to do with her now? He knew nothing about children. Nothing.

Yet he couldn't help but wonder what her life had been like, moving around Europe with her mother, not knowing anything about her father, yet understanding she possessed a bizarre ability. He'd been lucky that way. Although he knew, theoretically, about his power as an alchemist, the first time he'd had to use it in a serious way was only a few years ago in Idaho. Even at his age, it was frightening, daunting, and made him question everything he ever thought he knew about the world.

But Irina had said she discovered the girl's ability to help conjure demons when Zoe was only two. No wonder Zoe felt alone.

"I think it's time to move on," he said, standing and stretching his neck and back.

"They still want to hurt us." Her words were soft when she looked into his eyes. "I should have done more than turn them into rats. They've shrugged off that change. I can feel them looking for us."

"It's okay," he said, holding a hand out to help her to her feet.

As they started walking along a deer path, she asked, "How did you and my mother meet?"

He wasn't particularly surprised at her question. "Your grandmother worked for my father. She was his housekeeper, and after my mother died, she helped raise me. We were kids together."

"My mother told me about growing up in a big house. She said that it was the happiest time of her life. That's why she made sure I learned English. She always said she'd like to go back to America, and she thought it would be a good place for me to live. She also said it was expensive just to get there, and she needed to save money. But she never did."

"I'm glad she taught you English so well since my French is terrible and I know no Romanian at all."

She grinned. "I speak four languages."

"So I've heard. That's pretty impressive."

She shrugged, as if it wasn't all that uncommon, at least for her.

"Was my mother ever your girlfriend?" she asked, as they trudged along.

The question took him aback, but he quickly realized it was the sort of thing a nearly teenage girl would wonder about. "For a while. But then I went away to university, and that kind of ended things."

"Ah." She pondered his words. "My mother

never told me why she left America. Do you know why?"

How to answer that, he wondered. "What little I know is confusing." That, at least, was the truth.

She was quiet for a while but then asked, "How do you and I have the same father? Did she meet him in Europe or America? And"—she gave him an odd look—"he must have been quite old."

He nodded. "So it seems. But I guess he was charming."

She frowned. "And now he's dead."

"That's right."

"The way the old man who was thrown into the fire spoke to you ... the things my mother said ... it made me think *he* was your father." Her gaze bore into him, waiting for the truth.

Michael looked away. "We'd known each other for many years. Come on, let's hurry. We don't want to chance those vampires catching up to us."

A long while later, as they stopped for another quick rest, Zoe asked, "You seem to understand about the philosopher's stone. No one else does, not even my mother, but she said my ability makes me an alchemist like my father. I tried to talk about it to my friends, but they said I was making stuff up. Are you an alchemist like me?"

"I don't practice it. And you need to be very careful with it. When you open yourself up to letting strange beings in, they're often ones you don't want in your life—like those vampires. It's simply too dangerous."

"But my mother said my abilities were good!"

"I'm sure they are. But think of it this way. You're good, but it doesn't mean every person you come in contact with in this world is also good, right? It's the same with any plane of existence. There are some good creatures—often people refer to them as angels—but there are at least as many bad ones. They're often called demons. You just never know which you'll meet."

"Do you know how to make a philosopher's stone?" Zoe asked.

"I've never tried."

"Why not?"

"I have no interest in using one."

"I like using them. Without me, my mother wouldn't have been able to make any. She doesn't have the ability. I've made one other, even bigger than the one she used. Let me show you." She dug deep into her jeans pocket and pulled out a tiny red rock, no bigger than a kernel of corn. "It's small but I know, or I should say, I feel, it's a lot stronger than the one I made for my mother."

She placed it in the palm of his hand and it immediately began to glow red. "See what I mean?"

That she could do such a thing jarred him. "That's incredible."

"Keep it, Michael. I think you need to keep it close."

He stuffed it deep in his pocket. "Why did you make the stone?" he asked.

"So no one could push me around. Some kids in school are jerks. Teachers, too. This way, I'm the boss."

Michael worried about that answer. He was, he thought, going to have quite a bit of work cut out for him if this girl were to stay with him. But, feeling as she did about her alchemical abilities, he couldn't imagine trusting anyone else to raise her.

They had climbed down a bit more when Zoe stopped dead. "My mother is near."

He faced her, puzzled. "Why do you say that?"

"The stone knows."

He had never heard of a philosopher's stone doing that unless--and the thought chilled him--it had some sort of demon trapped inside it.

"Where is the stone?" he asked.

She gave him a suspicious look. "I have it."

"I won't take it," he assured her. "But if there's danger, take it and hold it tight in your hand. We might need it."

She nodded.

"Has a philosopher's stone ever done that for

you before? Let you know when someone was approaching?"

"No. But my mother was always with me. She's closer now."

Michael frowned. "Let's go."

They were hurrying as much as they could on the slick granite slope when Zoe cried out. "They're here. Just below us. Hidden behind the trees."

Michael followed her gaze. He couldn't see a thing, but sensed that Zoe was right. "This way," he said, leading her off to the side. They crept along, soon off the granite and onto an area with mountain pines. But the needles that covered the ground were so thick they couldn't see how steep the land had become. Two steps in, they both lost their footing and slid, unable to stop.

***

"Kira, this is Ceinwen. I've been told Jianjun is alright, and—"

"Yes. He's here with me. Everything is fine," Kira said. "Thank you for calling."

"Great, because I'm hoping he can help me."

"Sure. Let me give him the phone."

Bethany had directed Ceinwen in her rental car to the hilltop where there was some cell service.

Jianjun soon got on the line. "Ceinwen, how can I help?"

"I'm calling about Michael. I'm at the dig site and there's been a lot of trouble here. Demons and vampires. And it sounds as if most of the dig team is dead or has been turned." That all sounded twisted and strange, but the weird and unimaginable had become par for the course for Michael and Jianjun over the years. "I'm here with Bethany Gooding, Rachel's sister. She came here to find Michael and—"

"Yes, he told me. He was worried about her being there. So, where is he?"

"That's what I need you to try to find out. He came here with Irina and her daughter. At one point Irina was alone with Bethany. She attacked Bethany just as the vampires had done. Bethany tried to tell Michael about it, but she isn't sure he believed her. He then went off to find Irina and her daughter and hasn't returned."

"Good God, I warned him that there was something weird about Irina."

"Bethany and I drove up to the campsite, but there's no sign of them anywhere. Michael said in no uncertain terms that Bethany shouldn't go near the dig itself—that it's dangerous. I can't help but think that might be where the vampires nest. I don't want to go there just exploring, but if they have

Michael, I'll do it. I'd like police help, but once the police get involved, if there are deaths, we couldn't explain them and could all end up in a Ukrainian prison."

"I get the picture," Jianjun said. "But to stay there, it's dangerous for you and the girl."

"No way I'm leaving here without him."

"Got it. Okay, so, you'd like me to try to track Michael?"

"That's right. As far as we know, he still has his phone with him. Cell service is all but impossible here, but maybe you can detect something."

"Maybe. In the past I've downloaded GPS tracking software to his phone," Jianjun said, "to find him if he got himself lost on one of his digs. I should be able to track the signals and text you his coordinates. If you don't get a text within the hour, phone me back."

She agreed, hating to wait, but she had no choice. All they could do was go back to the inn and hope Michael would return. And that demons wouldn't show up first.

CHAPTER 57

Michael and Zoe's slide seemed to go on forever before it finally stopped. To Michael's surprise, the sky had turned dark. Somehow, it was night. He sat up, brushing the dirt and pine needles from his hair and clothes.

Zoe stood, doing the same. "I'm afraid you need a bath," she said with a laugh as she reached up and picked some needles from his hair.

"I'm not the only one," he joined her with a smile, all the while hoping that whatever or whoever was following them was still high on the mountain.

"Where did the day go?" she murmured as they both stood. They were on a well-worn footpath. With a start, Michael realized that even in moonlight, it looked far too familiar. They were on the path up from the camp to the dig site and were just steps from the top.

"No, no, no!" he murmured.

"She's closer," Zoe whispered. He grabbed her

hand. It had crossed his mind that the tunnel, or perhaps the entire mountain, might not be in the real world dimension, that the mountain could be a portal between this world and another. It seemed, now, that was the case, which meant that even running in a straight line could cause a person to end up right back where he started–an impossible feat in the real world. Michael had seen this phenomenon in the past.

"You didn't really think you could escape us, did you?"

Irina stood at the top of the footpath looking down at him. Four of the night singers were with her, as well as Dmytro. Soon, four more approached from behind. One of them held Galyna's hand. They poked and prodded Michael and Zoe up the trail.

Michael put an arm around Zoe's shoulders keeping her close while his other hand reached into his pocket and grabbed the philosopher's stone she'd given him. As soon as he touched both the stone and Zoe at the same time, a surge of power filled him. The way Zoe glanced at him, he knew she felt it too.

"Come here, Zoe," Irina said when they'd reached the top.

Zoe shook her head.

"I'm sorry I scared you earlier, *sufletul meu*. But

I was angry." She held out her hand. "The stone wants you with me. That's why it brought you back here. You feel it, and so do I. That's how we knew where to find you."

"You can't use it," Zoe cried. "It's mine."

"You can't turn on us this way, child. We belong together! You and me, and with this stone, we can do whatever we want. We can travel away from here, Zoe. Finally free of him and his father. They're both worthless."

"What do you mean, his father?" Zoe asked.

Irina looked at her own daughter with such disgust, it chilled Michael. "Don't, Irina," he begged.

But she smiled. "His father was the ugly old man you saw earlier," she said bitterly. "The one I gladly killed."

Zoe turned to Michael, her eyes accusing. And then she stepped away from him. "You lied."

"No," he whispered. "I simply didn't answer."

But she only shook her head.

As soon as Zoe moved away from him, the power emanating from the philosopher stone seemed to diminish. Two night singers stepped closer, their dagger-like talons stretched wide, ready to attack. At the same time, Zoe looked from him to Irina. Her eyes turned cold, chillingly cold. "But if Michael is like his father, then, so am I."

"What?" Irina glared at Michael with shock. "You told her?"

"Only that we're related. She needed to know."

Irina faced Zoe. "There's no way I'd ever allow you to be like your father. That's why we're going away from here."

"Zoe," Michael said, "a demon named Militsa created all this using a philosopher's stone, but I'm sure yours is stronger."

Irina stepped closer to them both. "What stone, Zoe? Give it to me. He doesn't know what he's talking about. You're my child. *Inima mea*—my heart. I've always protected you, put you above everyone and everything else in my life. You know I'd never hurt you."

"*Mami*," Zoe whispered. Michael heard how forlorn she sounded, how young she was, and it broke his heart that she had to face such evil.

"She's not your mother now," he said softly. "She's Militsa. She wants to kill us both. Your mother would never put you in danger. You've got to believe that. Don't listen to her."

"No. I'm your mother, *fata mea*," Irina said. "You know it. Our stone—the one we made together —knows it too. Now, give it to me."

Just then, they saw the glow of fire coming out of the excavation pit. Irina smiled. "They're destroying the chapel, burning it down," she said.

"The dig team members, except for Galyna and Dmytro who have joined us, will burn and the chapel will finally do what it should have done centuries before! It will collapse with no trace that it ever existed."

She then faced Michael. "Those Templars did know how to build a strong fortress, Michael, for that was what it was originally. They helped the Knights of St. John and others as they fought Genghis Khan's warriors. But, as happened with most of the world, they lost and fled. Now the fire will cleanse the land of them."

"It would have been good if the world could have seen the Templar fortress," Michael whispered.

"Why? Those people were nothing. All of this is nothing. It's only value was as a way to bring you here, to rid the world of all Remparts and your powers."

"But I'm a Rempart, too, *mami*," Zoe said.

"So you are," Irina said, her voice frightening to hear.

"Zoe, you must remember that she's not your mother," Michael said. "She's a demon."

"Don't listen to him, child. Remparts lie and destroy," Irina shouted. But almost immediately, she changed. Tears filled her eyes as her expression turned sad and she spread her arms wide. "Come to me, child. Bring me the stone. You know you're my reason for living. How many times have I told you that?" She got down on her knees. "Come here, please. I can't bear it if you don't."

The girl ran to Irina and put her arms around her mother. "*Mami*," she whispered.

Irina stood then kissed her forehead. "My sweet girl."

But then Zoe looked up at her, confused, and slowly backed away. "You're not her," she whispered, then louder, "Where is she? Where's my mother?"

"Maybe you can find her in there." Irina grabbed Zoe's arm and began to pull her toward the opening to the burning chapel.

"No!" Zoe screamed and dropped to the ground as Irina dragged her closer.

The night singers held their claws against Michael's neck, ready to slice it open at the slightest word from Irina. He forced all his concentration on Zoe's philosopher's stone still in his hand. "Reach for it, Zoe" he called.

She glanced at him, immediately understanding and thrust out her hand. Although the two couldn't touch, a crackling current, like an electrical charge, flowed from her fingers to the stone he held.

He could feel the stone react to her power as well as his own. "Irina!" he called, "Help your daughter! Don't let Militsa do this to her. Irina, you can do it. I know you're still here and you want to protect your child. Everything you've done has been to protect her. Don't let Militsa, or Claude, win now. Please, Irina. Help Zoe."

Suddenly Zoe was flung far from the fiery opening. She scrambled to her feet, but then looked back to face the woman who had tried to kill her.

"Run, Zoe!" Michael shouted.

But the girl didn't. And Michael turned to face the demonic Irina, but instead he saw the woman he once loved.

"I'm so sorry, Zoe," she said. "I won't let Militsa harm you." And then she turned and threw herself into the fire.

"No!" Zoe screamed.

"Irina, no!" Michael cried, falling to his knees as the flames shot from the pit high into the air. But their pleas were useless. Irina was dead.

The night singers, too, stared without moving at the loss of the one who had resurrected them.

"Kill him!" Galyna cried, pointing at Michael.

Her words shook Michael from his stupor and he ran to Zoe and pulled her away from the pit and all that was burning inside. They hurried toward the trail to the campsite.

But running only got them so far before Galyna

and the night singers stood before them, blocking their way to the trail.

The earth beneath them shook, but then stopped.

Michael held Zoe close as the vampires slowly approached them. He lifted the hand that held Zoe's philosopher's stone. He had no idea about its power or how much harm it might do. But he knew it was strong, and he had nothing else. "Let us go," Michael said, "or you will all be destroyed."

"Stop!" The vampire who had stood beside Galyna shouted. "This has gone far enough. Too far. I want no more killing."

"Ivan, they've killed Militsa," Galyna shouted at him. "They must pay."

He stepped back, away from Michael and Zoe. "Come, Galyna. Fire doesn't kill demons. Someday she'll return to us. Maybe in another hundred years. In the meantime, we will sleep and await her call."

"No!" Galyna held her ground. "I won't do that."

"Me, neither," Dmytro stepped to Galyna's side. "We want to go on, to live just as we do now. We're the ones in charge here. We don't need you. It's you who need us!"

"I'm sorry, Ivan," Galyna said. "But I won't go with you."

Ivan's snakelike eyes displayed no emotion, but

he shook his head and raised his hand. With that, he and the other eight soldiers walked into the earth.

The ground trembled once more, worse than the last time. Zoe clutched Michael tight as he kept his eyes on Galyna and Dmytro, ready to fight. But then he watched as they turned a dark, ashy gray, as if drained of blood. Their skin shriveled before his eyes, and soon the two sank to the ground, bony, desiccated, and lifeless.

Only one figure, at the very back of the dig, was left. Stana walked toward them. "You may think you've won, but you haven't. I'll never forgive the loss of my sister. Not even your stone will help you now. The fire will destroy the chapel walls, ceiling, and supports for the tunnels. They'll collapse and set off a chain reaction that will bring down this entire side of the mountain, crushing you both."

And then, Michael heard the roar of the earth as fire reached high from the opening of the pit, to light the night sky.

He picked up Zoe, holding her tight as the girl stared at the fire, a look of complete horror and sadness on her face. Michael could feel the heat under his feet as the wooden ceiling of the chapel burned.

They had only reached the beginning of the footpath that led down to the campsite when the shaking earth all but knocked Michael off his feet.

He knew the wooden chapel walls were collapsing, bit by bit, just as Stana had said they would.

The ground beneath them began to crumble, but Michael kept running, holding Zoe tight, trying to get to safety before the entire hillside collapsed, burying them within it.

Soon, rock and dirt filled the air. It bounced off the ground around them. Zoe screamed as he desperately tried to outrun the landslide.

But he couldn't, and soon, just as Stana had predicted, the earth swept over them both.

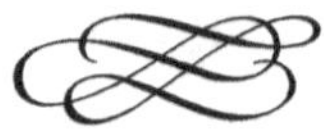

"Give me your hand, Michael. Come on! You've got to try!"

Michael heard a voice that sounded like Ceinwen's, but that was impossible, no more than his imagination, a hope-filled dream, as he knew he neared death. He wanted to move, but the debris was too heavy, and the little air around him was all but gone.

And Zoe, his sister...

He, like her mother and her father, had failed her.

"Michael, you've got to help me."

Ceinwen's voice again, and then he felt dirt being brushed from his face, a cool hand touching his forehead before his head was forcibly lifted and turned so the air could reach him. His mouth was forced open. Fingers pulled dirt from inside it, from inside his nostrils. Air, cool, cleansing air, rushed into his lungs.

"Michael, darn you, don't you dare die on me!"

Ceinwen demanded. "I'm going to get you out of here, somehow, but you're a heavy brute, you know. So wake up and help, why don't you?"

It's her! He had to live. He tried to inhale, but coughed, nearly choking, his nose and mouth still filled with too much dust.

His eyes didn't want to open yet, but the amount of dirt weighing down his back lessened, and somehow he began to breathe again. As the dirt felt lighter, he was able to lift himself a little.

"That's it," she cried. "You're doing it! Keep moving!"

Finally his eyes opened, and even as he had to rapidly blink trying to clear the dirt and dust from his eyelids and lashes, he saw Ceinwen, his beautiful Ceinwen, working to push the dirt off his back and legs. He couldn't believe this was really happening, but then he coughed again, and the pain from his dust-filled lungs told him it was.

He coughed harder, struggling to get the gunk out of his mouth, nose, throat, and lungs so he could breathe the sweet air around him. He slowly lifted himself.

Zoe lay beneath him, face down, and absolutely still.

Seeing her there, he felt as if his heart had been torn from his chest. He had covered her, trying to save her from the rocks, even trying to form a little air pocket around her head. Her eyes were shut, her skin gray and lifeless.

"God, no!" he whispered as he worked even harder to sit up and get his weight off her.

Ceinwen grabbed his arms at the shoulders and pulled him up.

"What's this?" Ceinwen asked as she saw the child.

"Zoe," he whispered, brushing her hair back from her face. It was cold. "Please, Zoe, wake up." His heart pounded with the fear and guilt that his weight, coupled with the dirt that fell on him, had crushed her. "Help me," he said to Ceinwen as they pulled her free of the debris still on her and turned her over. She was limp and pale as death.

He touched her neck and felt a light pulse. "She's still alive!" He opened her mouth, making sure it was free of dirt, then rolled her to her side and hit her back. She gasped. He hit it again and somehow she began to breathe, and cough, all the while struggling for air.

"Breath, Zoe," he urged. She coughed again and again, the dust coming out like puffs of smoke from a pipe.

Finally, he helped her to sit up and bend a bit forward, patting her back to help her clear her lungs.

"Are you okay? Any pain on your arms or legs?

Anywhere?" he asked when she seemed to finally get her breath back.

She faced him, her expression stricken, unbelieving, and then threw her arms around his neck, buried her face in his chest, and sobbed.

"It'll be all right," he whispered, kissing the top of her head and rocking her. To his surprise, tears fell from his eyes. "You're safe now," he told her, his arms tightening. "You're safe."

"We'd better get out of here," Ceinwen said. "I don't know what caused the mountain to slide the way it did, but it might start again. Can you walk, Michael? I've got a car here."

He slowly managed to get to his feet, then quickly wiped his eyes. Every bone in his body ached, but he didn't think anything was broken. He then helped Zoe to stand.

"I can carry you if you can't walk," he said.

"I can walk," she said, but leaned heavily against him.

Ceinwen looked from Zoe to Michael, saying nothing, as they hurried to her rental car.

Zoe lay down on the back seat while Michael got in front next to Ceinwen.

"I can't believe you're here," he said. "How did you find me?"

"It wasn't easy." She started the car.

"I thought I was a goner back there. I thought we both were," he said, glancing back at Zoe.

"Jianjun traced your phone to the mountain, but then it vanished," Ceinwen said. "I remembered when we were in Japan and ended up in another dimension we were always close to the place we had been in 'this' world. From what I'd heard from Bethany, it seemed that another dimension might be around the dig site, so I went there hoping to find the portal. Believe me, I never imagined that, whatever you were doing up there, it would bring down half a mountain!"

He shook his head. "Neither did I."

She gave a small shudder. "I was almost to the campsite when I saw you and the girl running. Then the landslide hit. You made it off the mountain, but then the last bit of earth fell and... and you were both gone. It was horrifying. I drove as close as I could and, thank God, I saw where you fell and could reach you."

"Thank you," he murmured. "I don't know if anyone else could have figured out where we were, and I know I couldn't have gotten out of there without help." He glanced at the back seat, at the sad, scared child huddled there. "I hate to think..."

Ceinwen glanced at him. "With all we've been through, I don't think I ever saw you shed tears over anyone before."

He looked embarrassed. "There was a lot of dust in the air..."

"Sure." She smiled. "She looks just like you, you know."

"Even I see a similarity," he admitted. "Around the eyes, I think."

"Right. Bethany told me Irina and her daughter were here with you," Ceinwen added. Then, with her voice low, asked, "Did Irina..."

"She's gone," he whispered.

"I'm sorry," she said, and after a moment added, "At least you've found your daughter. She's a surprise, I take it."

Daughter? Michael gazed at her. "Zoe isn't my daughter, Ceinwen. She's my sister, my half-sister."

Ceinwen stared at him with shock as she realized who the girl's father had to be.

CHAPTER 59

They drove past the town of Potchiv to the high point on the hill so that Michael could phone the local police and tell them there was a disaster at the dig site involving the students and professors. He gave his location so they could talk to him when they got there.

They then rushed back to the cottage where Bethany nervously waited. Bethany ran straight to Michael and hugged him. "I was so worried about you."

"If Ceinwen hadn't found us, we wouldn't have made it," he said.

She stared at Ceinwen. "Really?"

Ceinwen shrugged. "That one has more lives than a cat, so I doubt a mere landslide could stop him, but I'll take the compliment."

Michael got water for him and Zoe, then sat with her on the sofa, keeping her close, sensing she didn't want to be alone. He offered Bethany and Ceinwen a short version of what had happened in the chapel and tunnels. He'd save the long version for later when Zoe was asleep.

"We've got to be careful what we tell the police," he said, "about the students, the professors, the innkeepers, and all the other craziness. We need to be sure we tell them the same thing, and we can't mention demons or vampires or anything like that."

Zoe was old enough and wise enough to understand what he was saying. She asked what they should say instead, and he came up with a plan.

A burly police sergeant and a female officer soon arrived at the cottage and immediately began asking questions.

Michael explained that the entire dig team had gone up into the tunnels except Bethany who'd been sick. Even the innkeepers went to bring them food. When he, his partner Irina, and Irina's daughter Zoe arrived, they found Bethany worried because no one had returned. When they went up to the dig, they smelled something burning, and realized it was coming from the chapel or the tunnels. He was about to go down the rope ladder to see if the dig team was there when he heard a loud crack and the ground began to shake.

He picked up Zoe and ran. At first Irina was right behind them ... but then the landslide hit and she was gone.

"The fire must have destroyed the old timber

used to erect the chapel, causing the ceiling to collapse," Michael said. "Everything in an excavation of this sort is precarious, it can be quite dangerous, and deadly."

He added that the centuries had taken a toll on the structure. "It had to be weak, and when it collapsed, the ground above it sank, creating a landslide. It's like a mine collapsing, trapping everyone inside. Sadly, the professors and students working to uncover what they felt would be one of the biggest finds of the century, were trapped. Helpless. We can only hope," he said solemnly, "that they didn't suffer."

The sergeant and officer eyed each other.

"We'll never know exactly what happened," Michael quickly added. "It's very likely that as the team went deeper into the tunnel, they encountered pockets of methane or carbon monoxide—odorless killers." He took a drink of water, his throat still parched from the dirt. "Deadly gases in mines are a common hazard, which I'm sure you know," he said. "As for why they were all down there at once, I can't explain it. That's not how archaeologists normally operate."

The female officer took Zoe off alone and asked some questions of her, but his sister was as smart as Michael had believed and when her story corroborated Michael's, she soon returned.

Michael guessed it all sounded plausible, because the police officers eventually looked satisfied as they jotted down notes. "You will go with us to oversee the excavation of the bodies, if such an excavation can be performed," the sergeant said to Michael.

"I'm afraid I can't," Michael said. "I must return my girlfriend's daughter to her family in Romania. When they learn what happened, I know they will want the girl with them as soon as possible."

"We want you to stay," the sergeant demanded. "This dig has had many strange occurrences. We need to investigate much further."

"I'm sure you do." Michael showed him papers that gave his credentials as an archeologist so he could enter Ukraine to work on this excavation. "You can contact me at any time and I'll tell you what I know about the situation, which isn't much. As you can see from my visa stamps, I wasn't here when the tunnel was opened. I had gone to St. Petersburg and just yesterday returned. I, too, lost many friends from this dig. But I need to take care of the child before anything else. It's a sad situation."

The sergeant's lips tightened. "One last question. Your passport shows you went from St. Petersburg to Finland, to Hungary, to here. Why didn't you just fly into Kyiv or Lviv?"

"My girlfriend had some difficulties in Russia. She felt it would be easier for her to simply use the train into Helsinki." Michael paused, then added, "I didn't ask her for details."

"And you arrived in Ukraine two days ago, what were you doing before you came here?"

"We stayed in Mukachevo with a friend of Irina. Her name is Katya. I don't know her last name."

"Where did you stay?"

"She drove us to her house. I don't know the address."

"Could you find it?"

"I doubt it."

The sergeant's eyes narrowed. But then he stood. "Fine. Go. And I suggest you leave the country quickly. Some others might not be as easygoing as I am. After all, the team was fine, you returned, and now they're all dead. It looks suspicious, but ..." He shrugged and walked away.

As soon as the police left, Michael went in search of Zoe.

He found her sitting on the steps outside the cottage's back door, a lonely, dismal spot. He sat down beside her. "You haven't said anything about what happened to your mother. Do you want to talk about it?"

She bowed her head. "She was never happy, but I didn't think she was that sad. It makes me feel bad that a part of her, the bad part, wanted to ... to take me with her."

He patted her hand. "But in the end, she realized she didn't want to hurt you, and it was her action that saved us both. You have to always remember that. It was the craziness around her, the vampires and monsters, some who were all too human, that made her do and say things she didn't really mean."

"Maybe," Zoe said. "Or she had turned evil."

"Evil?" He was surprised to hear a word like that from someone so young.

"There's evil in the world, Michael," she said, her little face serious. "I've seen it. I think you're right—it took over my mom. But I can fight it. And I will."

He frowned, thinking she probably didn't really understand all she was saying. "I'm sure you will. You're quite strong."

"I am. And I also have lots of opinions."

"Oh? Such as?"

"For one, you need to go and talk to Ceinwen. Alone. I see the way she looks at you. You can leave me. I'll be fine now."

"Are you sure?"

"I am. Don't worry."

He left Zoe on the porch and went inside. He found Ceinwen sitting on the sofa.

Bethany saw him enter the room and stood. "I think I'll go find Zoe and see how she's doing."

Michael nodded. "She's just outside the back door."

Bethany hurried away.

He walked over to Ceinwen and stopped short of sitting next to her. She looked up at him, her expression unreadable.

"Michael," she said flatly.

"I've so much to tell you," he said, feeling awkward. "Starting with I'm sorry"

"No need. You did what you had to."

"I don't know why you came here but—"

"I'm sure you don't," she interrupted, then stood and faced him. "At least my timing was right. I'll head back to London soon. I have my old job back at the newspaper."

"You do?" He was surprised to hear that.

"It's almost as if I'd never left."

"Are you happy to be back?" he asked.

She shrugged. "It's a good job."

"That's not what I asked."

"I guess it suits me. And I'm good at what I do."

"I know you are," he said, then paused a moment before asking, "do you have a flat and all?"

"A small one."

"In London?"

"That's right. What's with all these questions?"

He paused, then said, "I'm wondering how your life is now, and if there's any hope of things going back the way they once were between us."

She stiffened, her eyes sad as she studied him. "I don't know."

He took her hands. "I've missed you so much, Ceinwen Davies. And now, with my father gone, I don't have to worry that I'm putting your life in danger by being around me."

She pulled back her hands and clasped them together. "I see."

He had been hoping to hear more. But then he had an idea as to why she was remaining so quiet. "There is Zoe." He drew in his breath. "I promised Irina I would take care of her. I have to do it. And, I want to."

Her eyes searched his, her gaze intense. "Of course you need to take care of your sister. I would expect no less of you."

"That's good, but you also need to know that Zoe is an alchemist."

Ceinwen frowned. "Please tell me you're joking."

"And she's a very powerful one."

Ceinwen gawked at him. "Then let's hope she takes after her brother, and isn't her father's daughter."

He had hoped for some clue from her, some softening, but he wasn't seeing it. "Do you think you might ever see yourself putting up with a teenage girl and a nearly middle-aged man who's one of the world's biggest jerks?"

She bit her bottom lip, her hands clasped even tighter. "I'm sorry, Michael, but I have to ask you something, even though I know I might hate your answer."

He nodded.

She took a deep breath and then said, "If Irina had lived, would you have stayed with her? Maybe married her?... Loved her the way you once did?"

Finally, he understood. His voice was soft as he tried to explain. "I'm glad I found her, glad we talked ... a lot. I learned all about the life, the sad life, she led. I love my memories of her, I love how I once felt around her, and I'll never forget her. But she and I both knew the love we once had was gone —just as our younger selves were no more. She wasn't the woman I want to be with now. You are." He paused, but knew he couldn't stop there. "I love you, Ceinwen. Only you."

She smiled, finally. "That's what I needed to know because ...I love you, Michael. So very much."

He drew her up from the sofa and into his arms. He kissed her tenderly, then held her close, taking in the scent of her, the warmth, the joy he always felt when she was near, and the realization he wanted her near, always.

Just then, they heard the back door rattling and a couple of coughs. They pulled apart slowly as Zoe and Bethany entered the cottage.

"It's, uh, getting cold out there," Bethany explained somewhat sheepishly as she and Zoe studied them both.

Michael smiled at Ceinwen, and then he faced the girls. "It's okay," he said. "You two did good."

CHAPTER 60

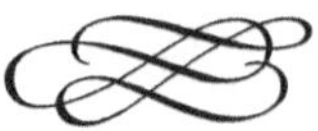

Michael, Ceinwen, Zoe, and Bethany arrived in Boston two days later, exhausted from their long journey and all that had happened.

Bethany was flying on to Salt Lake City. She had already contacted her father with her flight information, and it sounded as if the whole family would be there to meet her and welcome her home. She could hardly wait to see them, to see the farm, and all the wonderful things she hadn't bothered to appreciate in the past.

Someday, she was sure she'd want to travel again, but not for a while. She had seen and learned things she could never explain—and didn't want to. And the more she learned about this and other worlds, she couldn't help but reflect on what was truly important in her life. For her, it came down to family, community, God, and love.

And, she couldn't help but smile as the thought came to her that she just might drive up to Salmon one of these days.

At one point, when she and Michael were alone, she asked if all the strangeness she had witnessed--the other dimensions, the demons, creatures, and places they'd encountered--was a clue to the reason she couldn't find Rachel. He admitted that was so. She asked if there was any reason for her to continue to search.

"Not in this world," was his reply. Such words should have sounded cryptic, but they didn't. It hurt her heart that she would never see her sister again, but she understood, and that was what most mattered.

During the long trip home, Michael made time to phone Jianjun to see how he was doing and to fill him in on all that had happened. He then received the amazing news that Jianjun was not only back with Kira, but was about to become a father. After congratulations were given, the two talked about how new responsibilities meant their lives were about to change forever.

And they were both good with that. Even Michael, who always saw himself as the ultimate loner, suddenly liked the idea of having Ceinwen and Zoe with him. A sister ... and maybe, in time, a wife ... children. He shook his head. He never would have believed it. Maybe it was because for the first time, he felt free of his past, of the people and the unanswered questions that had weighed on him for most of his life.

He knew he would never look back with anything but sadness over all that had happened to Irina, and how her life had turned out. But at least he could do the one thing she'd asked of him—look after her daughter and try his best to keep her safe.

Zoe, he could already tell, was strong-willed and would challenge him. But whenever he looked at her, he couldn't help but feel a quiet joy that they'd found each other.

After tearful goodbyes with Bethany, he, Zoe and Ceinwen left the Boston airport in a rental car to bring them to Wintersgate.

Michael had called ahead for a suite at a resort in Hyannis, but Zoe wanted to see the Rempart family home--her family's home—and the house where her mother had once lived.

Upon reaching Wintersgate, Michael was surprised to find the tall iron gates open. As he approached the once elaborate mansion, it pained him to see the charred destruction of its upper floors.

He'd expected to show Zoe the exterior of the house, have her view the Atlantic, maybe even walk along the beach, and then leave. He never expected the estate to be buzzing with construction workers —a lot of them.

As they got out of the car, Zoe gaped at the enormous home, even at the frieze of malevolent-looking winged griffins over the entry door. Michael had always detested them so, of course, they had survived the fire. In fact, the bottom floor and foundation appeared little harmed. The fire had begun in William Claude's second floor laboratory and traveled upward from there.

"All that was our father's house?" Zoe asked.

"It was," Michael said. "It was where your mom and I became friends. And now, it's half yours."

"I like it! And look at the ocean! Can I go see it?"

"Be careful. Don't get too close to the edge of the cliff."

"I won't!" she called as she ran off.

He and Ceinwen smiled at each other and he took her hand.

"Who would have thought we'd ever come back here," she murmured.

"Not me," he said as a man with a hard hat headed his way. "Looks like we're about to find out what all these workers are doing here."

"Michael Rempart?" the man called.

"Yes. What's going on?"

He handed Michael his card. "I'm a general

contractor. Your father said you'd be showing up one of these days, and we needed to do everything we could, as fast as we could, to get the house ready for you and his daughter."

"I'm surprised," Michael said. "But I guess I shouldn't be. He'd always loved this place, so I should have expected he would want it repaired."

The contractor added, "It'll be ready in no more than six weeks. I hope that'll be satisfactory to you."

"Sounds good. How long have you been working on it?"

The contractor's eyebrows rose. "Long? Try this morning."

"This morning?" Michael repeated.

"Well, your father only called me early yesterday. But with the bonus he's paying to get it done fast, believe me, I put a huge crew on the job."

Michael's skin went cold at the words. "I see. Thanks."

As the contractor walked back to his men, Michael glanced at Ceinwen. Her shocked expression, he was sure, matched his own.

And then it all became clear.

They had spoken a bit about William Claude's visit to her in Idaho. Michael suspected she'd told him barely half of what had gone on, but she did tell him about scalding Claude with bacon grease. He remembered seeing the scars, and it suddenly dawned on him what had seemed wrong when he saw his father—or what he had presumed was his father—in the tunnel before the man was thrown into the cauldron. He had seen no scars.

Michael glanced over at Zoe and waved his arm for her to come back to them, then he protectively drew Ceinwen to his side.

"What now?" she whispered, concern and fear filling her voice.

Michael just shook his head, his shoulders heavy and his lips a thin, firm line. "To tell the truth," he said, "my father setting all this up, somehow doesn't surprise me at all."

AUTHOR'S NOTES

Some of the lesser known figures of Russian history during the last days of the Romanov dynasty are presented in this book, and I found researching them to be fascinating. I've attempted to portray most of the history of the last days of Tsar Nicholas II and his family in an accurate, albeit truncated, manner.

As for the "Black Princesses," their lives after the revolution were quite different from the soldier/vampire drama presented in the book, although Princess Militsa actually was a student of the Black Arts, particularly hermeticism, which is basically alchemy surrounded by mysticism. She remained with her husband, who was a Russian Grand Duke, until his death in 1931. Her sister, Princess Stana, however, had an unhappy marriage. Somehow, despite her and her husband having had two children, she managed to get a divorce. As if that wasn't scandalous enough, she began having an affair with the brother of Militsa's husband, who was also a Grand Duke. Under Russian Orthodoxy, it is forbidden for two sisters to marry two brothers, but after several years, when Stana was 39 years old, the two were allowed to marry. Sometimes it pays to be friends with a Tsarina.

Both sisters did, in fact, play an important role in introducing Rasputin to the royal family, and were heavily involved in imperial intrigue and gossip.

After the Bolsheviks gained power, in 1919, Militsa and her husband managed to escape Russia by way of Crimea on a British battleship, the Marlborough, with some of the surviving Romanovs, including Youssupov, who was Rasputin's assassin. Stana and her husband also escaped via Crimea. Another sister, Elena, was married King Victor Emmanuel III of Italy. She helped Stana and Militsa find shelter in Italy and at times in France, until the Fascists took over power in Italy and forced Victor Emmanuel III to abdicate. Stana died in 1935, and Militsa went to Egypt where she lived until her death in 1951.

An interesting side note is that a few years after the Bolsheviks assassinated Nicholas and Alexandra and their five children, an almost never-ending line of adults began to come forward claiming to be one of the children and saying they had somehow escaped the slaughter that took place in a remote area in Siberia. Especially popular was the claim to be Maria, Anastasia or even Alexei. All pretenders have been proven to be fakes. However, for an unknown reason, the Bolsheviks didn't bury the bones of two of the children (Alexei and one of his sisters, either Maria or Anastasia) with the other family members. Their alleged remains were not found until 2007 by amateur archeologists. Although DNA tests showed a kinship to the Romanovs, to date, the Russian Orthodox Church has not agreed to bury them in St. Peter and Paul's Cathedral with the rest of the family and has ordered further investigation.

Meanwhile there were also people claiming to be descendants of Rasputin, who was rumored to have fathered many illegitimate children. Only three of his legitimate children, a son and two daughters, survived to adulthood. They were sheltered by the Imperial Family after Rasputin's murder. Of course, such protection vanished after Nicholas abdicated.

Rasputin's son died of dysentery in 1933, and one daughter died of typhus in 1925, but the third child, Maria, had a long and rather strange life. After becoming a young widow with two children to support, she left Russia around age 26 and became a cabaret dancer—more because of her name than her dancing ability. After that, she became an animal trainer and caught the attention of either the Barnum and Bailey or Ringling Brothers circus (she mentions both). The circus brought her to the United States, but she soon left it after being mauled by a bear. She told a variety of stories about her life, often contradictory, but apparently she re-married at least once and held a number of odd jobs. She gave interviews about her father for money, and collaborated on a book about him right before her death.

Maria Rasputin died in 1977 in Los Angeles. At one point, she told the Associated Press, "My father was a very kind, very holy man. Always he thinks of others—never himself, only others. Many people were jealous of him."

WHAT'S NEXT?

Dear Reader,

I hope you enjoyed this journey to Russia and Ukraine with archeologist Michael Rempart. Thank you for following Michael's journey to this point. With his life now completely upended caring for his half-sister, and learning his father has survived, in **Ancient Passages**, *you'll find that Michael's attempt to deal with all this leads him to heart of Sicily. It may be part of Italy now, but its Greek heritage is very much a part of the island, as it continues to have ghosts of Greek gods and goddesses roam through the ruins of time-worn temples.*

For you enjoyment, below, is the opening of **Ancient Passages.** *Also, if you're interested in the history behind Ancient Deceptions, be sure to check out my website, JMPence [dot] com, and you'll find information and photos under* The History Behind the Ancient Secrets Novels.

Chapter 1

1200 B.C. Sicily

Kronos had long feared his children. And now he knew his fears had been justified.

His mother, Gaia, goddess of the earth, had once warned him a son would overthrow him one day, just as he had overthrown his father, Ouranos.

Ouranos, god of the sky, had disliked and distrusted his Titan children and cast them down to Tartarus, deep within the earth. Gaia hated him for his treatment of her children and asked her sons to rid her of him. She made a sickle for them to use.

Only Kronos was willing to do as she wished. One night, he attacked his father, castrated him, and threw his severed testicles into the sea.

Kronos then declared himself ruler of the world. With the assistance of his Titan brothers and sisters, his reign came to be known as a "Golden Age" where everyone prospered. But Gaia's warning about his children never left his mind. When his wife, Rhea, bore a child, he would take it from her and swallow it.

Rhea deceived him with one child, however. When Zeus was born, Rhea sent him to Crete to be raised, and she gave Kronos a large stone wrapped in a blanket to swallow. Years later, a young man Kronos didn't know brought him food and a cup of mead. He drank it down, not knowing it was lightly poisoned. It caused him to regurgitate his children, now adults.

The young man was his son, Zeus. He and his siblings, with their base on Mount Olympus, created a fighting force that challenged Kronos and all the Titans. For ten years they fought, and now, the Titans had been defeated, and Kronos was overthrown by his son, just as his mother had warned..

Zeus sent them deep into the Underworld, Tartarus, for all eternity.

But Kronos wanted to leave some sign on earth that he had once been a great ruler. He took the sickle his mother had made for him to use against his father and buried it deep beneath a town just beginning to form, a town called Satigiano, in the mountains of Sicily...

Chapter 2

Cape Cod, Massachusetts
Michael Rempart stood at the entrance to his family estate, Wintersgate. He had electronically opened the front gate for the taxi to bring his best friend up to the door of the mansion. Li Jianjun had also been his assistant when he was actively involved in archeology.

Michael would be glad to see Jianjun again. It had been five months since they last saw each other in St. Petersburg, Russia, but a lot had changed in both their lives.

Four months ago, Michael took over raising his half-sister, Zoe, after her mother's death. Before that, he was simply a wealthy, unmarried professor of archeology. At age forty-three, tall and lean, he had already made a name for himself in the archeological world with some rare and magnificent findings. Plus, his wavy black hair, dark eyes, and a somber but intellectual visage didn't hurt when he hosted a show about famous sites in archeology on a popular streaming channel. Television audiences soon called him the "real life Indiana Jones."

But now, his old life had all but vanished in the wink of an eye.

ABOUT THE AUTHOR

J.M. Pence has spent a lifetime immersed in the hidden currents of history—with a particular emphasis on the enigmatic worlds of East Asia. Pence lived in Japan for a year, absorbing its history beyond textbooks and temples. That fascination with what lies beneath the surface—what history remembers and what it forgets—fuels the *Ancient Secrets* novels.

Now, based in Idaho, J.M. Pence weaves carefully researched historical realities with haunting supernatural elements, creating stories where ancient knowledge refuses to stay buried. The *Ancient Secrets* series is available in ebook, print, large print, and audiobook editions.

To learn more and stay up to date on upcoming releases, visit JMPence.com and join the mailing list.

Supernatural Suspense

Ancient Echoes

Top Idaho Fiction Book Award Winner

Over two hundred years ago, a covert expedition shadowing Lewis and Clark disappeared in the wilderness of Central Idaho. Now, seven anthropology students and their professor vanish in the same area. The key to finding them lies in an ancient secret, one that men throughout history have sought to unveil.

Michael Rempart is a brilliant archeologist with a colorful and controversial career, but he is plagued by a sense of the supernatural and a spiritual intuitiveness. Joining Michael are a CIA consultant on paranormal phenomena, a washed-up local sheriff, and a former scholar of Egyptology. All must overcome their personal demons as they attempt to save the students and learn the expedition's terrible secret....

Ancient Shadows

One by one, a horror film director, a judge, and a newspaper publisher meet brutal deaths. A link exists between them, and the deaths have only begun
....

Archeologist Michael Rempart finds himself pitted against ancient demons and modern conspirators when a dying priest gives him a powerful artifact—a pearl said to have granted Genghis Khan the power, eight centuries ago, to lead his Mongol warriors across the steppes to the gates of Vienna.

The artifact has set off centuries of war and destruction as it conjures demons to play upon men's strongest ambitions and cruelest desires. Michael realizes the so-called pearl is a philosopher's stone, the prime agent of alchemy. As much as he would like to ignore the artifact, when he sees horrific deaths and experiences, first-hand, diabolical possession and affliction, he has no choice but to act, to follow a path along the Old Silk Road to a land that time forgot, and to somehow find a place that may no longer exist in the world as he knows it.

Ancient Illusions

A long-lost diary, a rare book of ghost stories, and unrelenting nightmares combine to send archeologist Michael Rempart on a forbidden journey into the occult and his own past.

When Michael returns to his family home after more than a decade-long absence, he is rocked by the emotion and intensity of the memories it awakens. His father is reclusive, secretive, and obsessed with alchemy and its secrets—secrets that Michael possesses. He believes the way to end this sudden onslaught of nightmares is to confront his disturbing past.

But he soon learns he isn't the only one under

attack. Others in his life are also being tormented by demonic nightmares that turn into a deadly reality. Forces from this world and other realms promise madness and death unless they obtain the powerful, ancient secrets in Michael's possession. Their violence creates an urgency Michael cannot ignore. The key to defeating them seems to lie in a land of dreams inhabited by ghosts ... and demons.

From the windswept shores of Cape Cod to a mystical land where samurai and daimyo once walked, Michael must find a way to stop not only the demons, but his own father. Yet, doing so, he fears may unleash an ancient evil upon the world that he will be powerless to contain.

Ancient Deceptions

A dig in a remote site uncovers demonic killings & buried secrets that shatter archeologist Michael Rempart's world in this sweeping supernatural thriller that crosses time and space from the present to the last days of the Russian Tsars.

When Michael unexpectedly receives a recent picture of a long-lost love, a woman he thought was dead, he gives up everything to search for her and to find answers to questions that have plagued him through the years. Instead, he uncovers more mysteries as he's drawn deeper into the occult and the ancient power of alchemy.

Ancient Passages

The heart of Sicily, where ancient myths echo through crumbling ruins and long-forgotten gods lurk in the shadows ...

Michael Rempart, renowned archaeologist, finds himself in a new role as guardian and protector to his increasingly troubled half-sister, Zoe. Seeking refuge, they retreat to a secluded dig site in the remote Sicilian countryside—the place where legend has it the goddess Persephone was abducted by the Hades, god of the Underworld.